HAUNTED LOVE

Sheridan Anne
Haunted Love

First Published in 2024

Anne, Sheridan
Love, Haunted

Cover Design: Artscandare
Editing: Heather Fox
Interior Formatting: Sheridan Anne

Get ready, Little Birdy.
This one is going to be thick and hard.
But be careful, because it'll also keep you up all night,
begging for more!

Haunted Love is a Dark Brother's Best Friend Standalone Romance

It includes a slight age-gap, forbidden romance,
and a heroine exploring her sexual boundaries.

Haunted Love contains:
Explicit sexual content
Coarse language
Graphic violence
Sexual predators
On-page BDSM themes
Attempted sexual assault
Group sex scenes

1

ASPEN

If you looked up the definition of pathetic, you'd get a picture of me. Actually, scrap that. You wouldn't just get a picture, you'd get a flashing alert in big red letters saying, *WARNING. LOSER. THIS BITCH AIN'T WORTH YOUR TIME. BACK AWAY WHILE YOU STILL CAN!*

Okay, so maybe I'm a little harsh on myself, but how else would you describe a twenty-two-year-old college senior who's sitting alone in her apartment on a Friday night eating ice cream right from the carton? Did I mention this particular college senior just happens to still be a virgin because she's too hung up on a guy who doesn't even know she exists?

Pathetic sums it up pretty damn well. Right?

College was supposed to be my wild years. I was supposed to live it up, sleep around, and make all the horrifying memories that I'll laugh about in the years to come. But graduation is only a handful of months away, and so far, the most daring thing I've done is get drunk at a house party, throw up in a garden of rose bushes, and demand my best friend, Becs, take me home. Did I mention this was all before 8 p.m.?

Surely there's another word for pathetic. How about pitiful? Deplorable? Hell, miserable seems like a good substitute. No wonder I'm practically invisible to the opposite sex. But to that one specific guy, Izaac Banks, I've been especially invisible since I was a kid.

A knock sounds at my door, and I groan, grabbing my comforter and yanking it up over my head. "Go away," I call through my small studio apartment, knowing exactly who stands on the other side. Though the bigger question is, how the hell did she get through the main entrance downstairs? I sure as hell didn't buzz her in. I bet it was Nathan on the third floor. He'd let just about any woman into the building if she smiled at him.

"Open the damn door, Aspen," Becs hollers from the hallway. "There's no way in hell I'm about to let you spend your Friday night eating a pint of ice cream in your ugly-as-fuck, stained Grinch pajamas."

My gaze drops down my body, taking in my old pajamas. How the hell did she know? Am I that predictable? But more importantly, how does she know they're stained? My accidental ice cream spillage only happened twenty minutes ago. You know, after I made my way through the first pint of ice cream. Though, admitting that I've made it to the halfway mark of my second pint isn't going to help my case.

"First off, don't be an ass about my Grinch pajamas. They're cute," I call back. "And second, I'm not your project tonight. Find some other unsuspecting loser to corrupt."

"I won't hesitate to kick this door down," Becs warns. "I'll need you to loosen the hinges from inside first, but mark my words, Aspen Ryder, I'll do it."

Ahh shit.

I groan again, rolling my ass off the couch and trying to balance my feet on the hardwood floor. Carrying my second pint of ice cream with me, I make my way to my front door and reach for the deadbolt. My unruly bun flops to the side of my head as I hold the ice cream spoon in my mouth.

Twisting the key that permanently lives in the back of the door, the last of my cheap security obstacles are out of the way, and I pull the door open, finding Becs looking like every man's wet dream. Her thick blonde hair is out and free while her makeup is flawless, but her body though . . . shit. She's outdone herself this time. Becs is undoubtedly gorgeous, but tonight, she looks like a Victoria's Secret model, gift-wrapped to perfection in the smallest black dress I've ever seen. Her thigh-high boots add an extra six inches to her already towering height.

Then before I even get a chance to tell Becs that whatever grand plan she's worked up for the night isn't going to happen, I'm blinded by a bright flash coming from the back of her phone.

"Say cheese," Becs grins, flipping her phone around and glancing at the screen. A booming laugh tears out of her as my brows furrow, having absolutely no idea what the hell is going on. But where Becs is concerned, I can guarantee that I'm not going to like it. "Oooh, that's a good one."

She barges past me into my small apartment, and I kick the door closed behind her. "What the hell are you talking about?"

Becs quickly scans my living room, and I can feel the disapproval dripping off her as her lips twist in disgust. Her gaze comes back to mine before she turns her phone and shows me the horrendous image of me plastered across the screen.

My stained Grinch pajamas stare back at me, but that's not even the worst part. My hair is a mess, there's a spoon hanging from my mouth, and I'm clutching the half-eaten pint of ice cream like a weapon. I might have felt pathetic before, but this picture sure as hell confirms it.

I'm a fucking mess. No wonder my virginity has stuck around so long. I might as well Google the local nunnery to join. My dad is going to be so pleased, but unfortunately for Mom, she'll have to wait until Austin undoubtedly knocks someone up to get the grandbabies she's desperate for.

There are no wild oats being sewn over here. The only wild oats I have are the ones stashed in my cupboard, and to be completely honest, I wouldn't touch them with a ten-foot pole. I'm pretty sure they went out of date at least two years ago.

"See this picture?" Becs says, a clear warning in her tone, reminding me that I'm supposed to be focused on the horrifying reality staring back at me. "Either you come out with me to this new club I found, or I'm uploading this to a sugar daddy website with your number and the caption *Help me, Daddy. This dirty girl needs a spanking.*"

I fix her with a hard stare. "I really fucking hate you right now. You know that, right?"

"Trust me, when you find out where I'm taking you, you're going to love me," she says, stepping into me and taking the pint of ice cream out of my hand. "Besides, you were only telling me yesterday that you're ready to start living. Don't tell me I sat on your filthy-ass couch and listened to that hour-long sob story and it was all bullshit."

Damn it. I hate it when my words come back to bite me on the ass.

"My couch isn't filthy," I say, personally offended. "It's just got character."

"Aspen," she says, fixing me with a hard stare. "I pulled a whole Pop-Tart from between the cushions last night. Your couch is a treasure hunter's wet dream. Now, tell me that you meant everything you said. That you're finally ready to pull the Izaac-shaped thorn out of your asshole and start living life like a normal twenty-two-year-old college student."

I let out a heavy sigh, rolling my eyes. "It wasn't bullshit," I groan, regretting my decision to be an open book last night. It must have been the tequila. "I meant every word. I want to start enjoying myself, but I didn't mean that I needed to start right this very minute. Ease me into it."

"Ease you into it?" she scoffs.

I nod enthusiastically. "Yeah, ease me," I suggest. "Because we all know the dangers of going too hard too soon."

Becs' face scrunches. "What the hell are you talking about?"

A wide grin stretches across my face. "Remember when you tried anal for the first time? You sure as hell didn't ease into that," I laugh. "You went in blind and unprepared, forgot the lube, and nearly tore your ass in half. So, from one friend to another, I'm asking you not to allow history to repeat itself. *Ease me into it.* Take it slow. Don't ass fuck me without lube."

"You are not seriously comparing my ass stitches and a night in the hospital to you going to a club with me."

"I thought it was a great comparison," I admit with a shrug and a dorky grin, secretly hoping that the club she plans to take me to isn't one of Izaac's. He owns three of them—Pulse, Cherry, and Scandal being his newest—but Becs knows better than to take me to any of those, even if they are the best clubs in town.

Becs rolls her eyes and strides into the kitchen with the ice cream, making her way to my freezer when she stops, spying the other empty container on the counter. "Wait," she says, glancing back at me, her eyes widening with pure disgust. "You're already on to your second tub?"

I press my lips into a hard line, not willing to admit what she can already clearly see. I'm also not willing to admit the way my stomach seems to be screaming at me for the afternoon of abuse. "Ummmm . . . no."

"Aspen! Gross. My lactose intolerance could never," she says, and the hint of fear flashing in her honey-brown eyes immediately forces an unwanted image into my brain. "This much ice cream would have me redecorating the bathroom for days."

"Thanks for that visual," I murmur under my breath, secretly proud of my iron-clad stomach that hasn't managed to let me down yet, not even with the questionable food truck tacos near campus.

"Any time. Now, go and put your ass through a shower. You're gonna need it where we're going. And don't forget to wash your fanny. And while you're at it, maybe break out the old razor. You're gonna want to shave everything from the chin down," she all but sings, offering me a smug grin. "Make it quick. I'm dying to get out of here."

"Why are you so eager?" I ask, peeling off my Grinch pajamas on the way to the bathroom. Becs is undoubtedly going to pick my outfit for the night, and I can guarantee nearly every inch of my skin will be exposed. But I can't lie, Becs has incredible taste when it comes to fashion. If her business degree doesn't work out, I'm sure she could have an incredible career as a stylist if she ever chose to go down that road.

Becs follows me into the bathroom, hovering at the mirror as I step into the shower. "Just trust me," she says as I turn on the taps and wait for the water to warm. "I don't want to give anything away, otherwise, I'll never get you out of here. All I'm saying is that it's a new club and super exclusive. This guy I know works the bar every Friday night and was able to get an invite with a plus one, so we're checking it out."

"Shit? Really?" I ask, stepping into the water and letting it cascade over my head like a waterfall. The idea of attending an exclusive club fills me with deep curiosity. "What kind of club is it?"

"That's the part I can't tell you," she says, meeting my gaze through the mirror, her honey-brown eyes darkening with excitement.

Ahh crap. That's not good.

"Then what can you tell me?" I say, lathering shampoo through my thick chestnut hair while hoping like fuck I remembered to buy new razors.

"Just that you're going to have an incredible night. And for your sake, I really hope you take advantage of what's on offer. Push your limits, maybe even try something you've never done before."

The fuck?

"I—wait," I grunt, my face scrunching up. "What the hell is that supposed to mean?" I question, trying to make sense of what she just said. It's not like I've never been to a club before. How many different experiences could I possibly be having tonight?

Becs laughs and makes her way out of the bathroom. "My lips are sealed," she sings, her eyes sparkling with silent laughter. "And hurry up. I'll pick you something cute to wear, and I promise you, by the time the night is over, Izaac Banks will be a distant memory."

And with that, she's gone.

Izaac Banks.

God, just his name makes my stomach roil with butterflies.

He's been my brother's best friend since before I can remember. My brother, Austin, is six years older than me, and for as long as I can remember, he and Izaac have been tied at the hip, causing havoc everywhere they go. Every childhood memory I have of Austin also includes Izaac. He's part of the furniture, practically family. Only, that's the problem. To Izaac, I'm just a kid, a little sister he's always looked out for, but to me, that's never been the case.

I've been mesmerized by him since I was ten years old. I was a little girl with one hell of a crush. He's always been the whole damn sky to me. The perfect chiseled abs, with the most delicious devilish grin. The only problem is, he's also the perfect definition of a walking red flag.

Ha. *The only problem.* Who am I kidding? There's a shitload more problems than just that. There's a whole list of problems that come along with why Izaac will never want me. Hell, the fact that he's Austin's best friend is a big one. Every other reason doesn't even matter when that big one sits at the very top of the list.

The women Izaac dates are gorgeous, freaking supermodels, and when he looks at me . . . I see it. Pity. Despite being twenty-two, he still sees me as his best friend's pathetic little sister who has drooled over him for most of her life.

Everything about him should have me running for the hills, yet every time that dark, wicked stare lands on me, my knees go weak. There's not a damn thing he can do that's ever sent me running in the opposite direction, not even walking in on him screwing some random woman two Christmases ago. I just keep holding on to the hope that maybe one day, something might change.

Like I said—pathetic.

I'd give anything to have him think of me in the way that I think of him. But after sitting on the sideline for twelve years, I've realized that's never going to happen.

Being the world to Izaac Banks is nothing but a stupid, unrealistic dream—one I need to hurry up and burn, preferably without leaving any scars.

Ten minutes later, I stand in my cramped bathroom, my clean-shaven body wrapped in a towel as I furiously try to dry my hair, but that's the problem with thick hair, it takes a whole damn village to tame.

"Check it out," Becs says, standing in the open doorway, juggling my black leather mini-skirt and thigh-high boots with a sequin triangle top looped over her finger.

I gape at the outfit.

It's a great outfit. But that sequin top is barely enough to cover my tits. Did I mention it's backless? It has two tiny shoestring straps that hold it together in the back—one hooked around the neck and the other around the back of the ribs. As for titty support . . . none!

Becs bought it for me as a joke last year, and now I guess the joke is on me.

I cringe as I take in her offering, but the look in her eyes suggests I better not fight her on this. I grab the skirt and sparkly top before noticing the tiny black thong in her other hand. Great. Guess we're going all out tonight. Time to retire the granny panties.

Trudging into my living room, I get dressed there since the bathroom is too small for two people. My parents wanted to buy me something bigger, something grand that would be transferred into my name after graduation as a congratulatory gift, but I refused. The college experience I wanted didn't involve living in some posh house my parents paid for, even if it meant I had to bruise their egos. That didn't keep them from splurging on an incredible car for my twenty-first birthday—a beautiful white Corvette. I almost died when I realized what they'd gotten me. It's been my dream car for as long as I can remember, but I never thought they would get it for me. Honestly, I'd always hoped that I'd be able to purchase it for myself one day. Either way, I appreciate their generosity. They've always been so good to me and my brother.

As I pull my outfit into place, Becs dives through my bathroom drawers to find my blow dryer and a brush. As she works on taming my hair, I get started on my makeup, and with each passing second, my excitement levels up. I'm actually doing this!

Within thirty minutes, I'm ready for the night of my life.

Becs pulled my hair up into a high pony, and in this outfit, I was bold enough to go hard on the eyeliner. My mascara is on point, and with my boots adding an extra few inches, I feel invincible.

After grabbing my purse and locking up, we fly out of the building to meet our Uber driver downstairs, and before I know it, we're on our way in the back of a black sedan.

We shoot the shit for the whole drive, and when the Uber driver pulls to a stop in a deserted street, my back stiffens. "Come on," Becs says, grabbing my hand and scooching out of the car.

My brows furrow, but I go with her, trusting she knows where we're going, but honestly, I'm having doubts. Just because I don't have a lot of experience with clubs doesn't mean I don't know what to look for, and this isn't it. The street should be littered with people, and even if I can't see the main entrance, I should still be able to hear the distant sound of music and feel its rumble through the ground . . . but there's nothing.

"Are you sure we're in the right place?" I ask, getting to my feet beside her and closing the car door. The Uber driver takes off immediately, and my stomach sinks. Even that guy knows we're not in the right place, but now that we're out of his car, we're no longer his problem.

"Just trust me." Becs beams, looping her arm through mine and dragging me a little down the street.

My gaze swings from left to right. The street is filled with stores and cafés, and I'm sure during the daylight hours, it would be swarming with people, but now that the moon is overhead, it's a ghost town.

"I'd hate to break it to you," I say with a slight grunt, my cheery excitement quickly dwindling to a dull fear that we could get killed out here. "But there's nothing out here. Are you sure you got the right address?"

"Would you stop freaking out and let me lead you into the biggest corruption of your life?" she says, her eyes sparkling with excitement as she turns and drags me toward a dark alley. My heart races the closer we get to the narrow opening between buildings. "We're almost there."

I groan and allow her to keep dragging me along. "If I end up in a body bag, I'm coming back and haunting your ass for the rest of your damn life."

"Oooh, I like it," she teases. "Sounds kinky."

I roll my eyes when Becs comes to a stop in the middle of the dark alley, her gaze locked on a single black door, perfectly framed into the brickwork of the building. It's big and imposing—the kind of door two college girls shouldn't be knocking on.

One word lingers above the door, giving people the only clue about what lies within—VIXEN.

The letters are carved out of metal in a simple, elegant font, and they stand out from the brickwork, illuminated from behind. The X is much bigger than the other letters, and I find myself gazing at it a moment longer than necessary. It's just a single letter, but for some reason, up on that brick wall, it holds so much power—as if it's a final warning to innocent passersby that what lingers behind this door is not for the faint of heart.

Becs reaches for the handle before glancing back at me. "You ready?"

I shake my head. "Not even a little bit."

She grins wider. "Perfect."

And with that, she pushes the door open, and I prepare for whatever secrets lie within.

2

ASPEN

We step through the door of Vixen into a dark hallway with nothing but dim downlights leading the way. The heavy metal door closes behind us with a loud thud, and I jump as I clutch Becs' hand tighter.

Not wanting to turn back, we follow the dimly lit hallway, and with each step I take, I can't help but feel the exclusivity, that this is a hallway only walked by those who mean something. Socialites. CEO billionaires. Famous athletes and rockstars.

Becs mentioned that this was an exclusive club, and despite barely making it through the entrance hallway, it's clear to see she was right. Only it's more than that. There's an air of elegance to it, and it's clear that this isn't going to be like any kind of club I've been to before.

"Holy shit. This is so exciting," Becs says as we reach a staircase.

We pause at the top, peering down into the darkness below, but with the way the stairs curve, it's impossible to see what awaits below.

The dim lighting is barely enough to make out the steps, and as I put one foot in front of the other, my heart races. It's like a descent into the darkest pits of hell, but instead of the devil waiting at the bottom, I'm promised a night I'll never forget.

As we approach the bottom of the stairs, we're met with a small room that mimics the same dark walls and floors from the hallway upstairs, only the lighting, while still dim, is a lot clearer.

There's a luxury reception desk with the same VIXEN logo I'd seen outside welded to the entrance. A blonde sits behind the desk, her gaze slowly lifting to ours. There's judgment there, but I can't figure out why or what she's seeing. "Welcome to Vixen," she says with a purr. "How may I help you?"

"My name is Bexley Grant," Becs says. "I was extended an invitation for tonight, with my plus one."

The blonde nods, her gaze shifting to her computer screen as if searching for her name. "Ah, yes. Here you are," she says, a polite smile lingering on her lips. "Is this your first time visiting our establishment?"

"Yes," Becs says.

She nods before marking something on her computer and swinging her crystal blue gaze to me. "And you?"

"First time," I confirm.

"Wonderful. And your name?"

"Aspen Ryder," I tell her, listening as she quickly adds it into her computer.

"Excellent," she says, finishing up with the computer and pushing up out of her chair. "I'd like to formally welcome you to Vixen. My name is Casey and I will be your host for the night. Now, as it is your first time visiting us here, there are a few formalities we need to get out of the way."

My brows furrow, watching as she dives through some paperwork on her desk before pulling out a form for each of us. She slides them toward us over the massive desk with two pens. "Please take a quick read through these NDAs and fill out your details, and while you do that, could I please grab a copy of both of your IDs?"

We hand over our IDs and Casey gets back to work, taking copies and entering all our details into her system. While she does that, I drop my gaze to the NDA, wondering why the fuck I would need to fill this out for a club, but I suppose if it's as exclusive as it appears, then an NDA would make sense. Who knows who could be inside. Celebrities behaving badly and wanting to let loose. Maybe Vixen is somewhere they can go to be themselves away from the limelight. Either way, no matter what I see in there, I'm not the kind to spread rumors.

Content with the paperwork, I sign my life away, and after Casey hands us our IDs back, she pulls out a slip of paper. "I'll just need you to fill out these quick questionnaires," she says. "This pertains to your physical health and ensures that you both receive regular health screens and are not carrying any sexually transmitted diseases that can spread throughout our club. Once you have answered all the questions, please sign the declaration at the bottom."

What in the ever-loving fuck? Why the hell would she require this kind of information from me?

"Just fill it out," Becs mutters beside me, insisting that I have blind faith in her, and as my curiosity gets the best of me, I go ahead and start scanning through the document, marking anything that applies to me, and after declaring myself as clean as possible, I sign my life away for the second time in as many minutes.

"Thank you," Casey says, taking both of our forms and quickly scanning through them before filing them away, clearly satisfied with what we've marked. She then plucks one more piece of paper from her desk, only this time as she hands it to us, there's a beaming smile across her face. "Now, assuming you both understand how things work here, this is a guideline. Take a look through the options, and I'll get you the appropriate wristband."

Wristband? What the hell? Why would I need a wristband in a club?

My brows furrow as I scan over the paper, and what I find makes my jaw drop to the black marble floor.

This isn't a fucking nightclub. It's an exclusive underground sex club!

My gaze snaps to Becs, finding her already watching me with a smug grin. "Surprise," she says, looking way too fucking thrilled about this.

"Where the hell have you brought me?"

Becs just laughs. "Just trust me," she says. "A place like this isn't going to allow random assholes to run around getting their rocks off.

It's safe."

"It really is," Casey agrees, clearly able to see the nervousness flashing in my eyes. "My first time here, I was unsure and hesitant, but there really isn't anything to worry about. You can participate as little or as much as you like, or not at all. If sitting at the bar and having a drink is more your style, then so be it."

Oh geez.

"I umm . . . I'm sorry. I must sound like such a prude, but I really have no experience with any of this. Like at all. I'm still a . . . you know. A virgin," I squeak out.

"That's totally fine," she says, pointing toward the paper in my hand. "We have every level of experience covered."

My gaze drops again, scanning over the list and noticing that it's kind of like a menu at a restaurant, but instead of food items, it's a color-coded list of sexual preferences.

I gape at it. Reading over every single one and committing it to memory.

White. Virgin.
Yellow. Intrigued. Willing to be approached.
Orange. Willing to be touched.
Pink. Oral Sex.
Red. Vaginal Intercourse. Private.
Purple. Vaginal Intercourse. Public.
Violet. Bisexual/Gay. Open for same-sex experiences.
Light Blue. Anal sex.
Dark Blue. Multiple partners. Private.
Green. Multiple partners. Public.
Brown. BDSM. Submissive.
Black. BDSM. Dominant.

"Holy fucking shit," I say under my breath.

"I think I'm going for green," Becs tells me. "Maybe violet."

My eyes widen with surprise, gaping at my best friend. "Really?"

"Uh-huh," she says, eagerly nodding her head. "I've always wanted to push my boundaries. You know, I've had a few threesomes, and they're great, but what if there were more guys, and all of their attention was solely on me? Or . . . I don't know. Don't you think it would be hot to experience being with a woman as well? While in front of other people where I'll be put on display . . ."

She lets her thoughts trail off, but I see the thrill in her eyes, and shit. I'm jealous. I wish I had that kind of confidence to explore and push my boundaries, but being so new to all of this, I somehow doubt I'll be taking the kinds of leaps and bounds that Becs is.

"What about you? What color do you want?" she questions, glancing over the paper again. "Are you ready to really do this? Or do you want to just watch and ease into it?"

"I umm . . . I'm not sure actually. Maybe I should go for pink. But then, because I'm still a virgin, aren't I supposed to have the white one?"

"Yes," Casey says. "So, in your case, you will select the white wristband to signify to our other patrons your level of experience, and then you will select another color, to determine what you're willing to be involved with."

"Oh, umm . . . in that case. Pink. No, wait. Red. No, pink. Shit. I uhh . . . red."

"You sure?" Becs asks, more than amused by my indecision.

"Yes. I think so. Definitely red," I say with a nod before swiveling my gaze back to Casey's. "But like . . . what happens if I get in there and change my mind? Just because I have a red wristband, that doesn't mean I have to go through with having sex, does it? I'm allowed to chicken out, right?"

Casey gives me a fond smile as if knowing exactly how to deal with nervous women like me. "Here at Vixen, all our guests are in control of their own sexual experiences," Casey explains. "The wristband is only a guideline so that our patrons are aware of what you are comfortable with. At any time, consent can be given or taken away. It is your choice in what you participate in, whether that be publicly, or in a private room. And if you choose to explore further than what your wristband suggests, that is at your discretion. This is nobody's experience but your own."

"Oh," I say, able to get on board with that, a thrill shooting through my veins and easing the nervousness. "And the private rooms?"

Casey smiles. "Our private rooms are scattered throughout the club. If the door is closed, it's in use. Do not enter unless you've been specifically invited by the participants within the room. If the door is open, you have free rein to enter," she explains. "Each room is themed. We have a few dark rooms, and being new to this lifestyle, I recommend starting there. You might be more comfortable. Our patrons' safety is our top priority. You will be in good hands. The men who like to frequent our private rooms are quite skilled when it comes to understanding a woman's . . . needs, and they will take care of your every desire."

Woah. Can she see my cheeks flush in this dim lighting?

A pulse of electricity shoots down my spine, and before I know it, I feel that pulse deep in my core, and my thighs clench with anticipation.

Am I really going to do this?

Holy crap. This is insane, and yet, I can't wait.

Casey ducks behind her desk, and a moment later, she hands me two wristbands. One white, signifying my virginity, and one red, a clear signal to any man inside this club that I'm willing to have sex . . . in private, of course.

As for Becs, she's handed both a green and violet wristband, and she quickly snaps them into place, proud and excited for what the night will hold.

"You ready?" she asks, taking my wrist and helping me with my bands.

"Yeah," I say with a slow smile.

This isn't exactly how I'd always planned to lose my virginity, but let's face it, I came to terms with the fact that my wild night with Izaac Banks was never going to happen. It's time for me to let go. To explore the limitations of my body and enjoy life the way I should have always been doing.

"One last thing before you go," Casey says, reaching for my wrist. She grabs a stamper and presses the cool ink to the inside of my wrist, and when she pulls it away, I find a dazzling gold moth, the wings shimmering in the low lights. "This stamp will gain you access into the VIP rooms downstairs, and from one woman to another, that's exactly where you want to be. Now, you're both on contraceptives?"

"Yes," we say in unison as Casey re-inks the stamper and presses it to the inside of Becs' wrist.

"Wonderful. All of our members are clean and take regular tests, so you may use a condom at your own discretion. If you want them to wear protection, all you need to do is say the word, and they'll suit up. If someone refuses, do not consent and report them. Like I said, we take the safety of our guests seriously."

I nod, and not a moment later, Casey steps out from behind her desk and leads us deeper into the room to another solid black door.

"Enjoy yourselves," Casey smiles as she pulls the door open. "Welcome to the best night of your lives." As we step forward, the smell of sex and alcohol beckons us to step over the threshold and dive headfirst into a night of wild passion.

Becs takes my hand, and as the sultry music assaults my eardrums, we step into the madness, and the second we do, I feel the hungry stares of the vultures. They rake up and down my body, lingering on the white wristband, and I can't help but feel like a challenge, but I push it aside, trying to remember what Casey said—*I have control. I have the power to say no to anybody. I can participate as little or as much as I want.*

"Why don't we take a look around first?" Becs offers, looping her arm through mine as if knowing that I need a little nudge.

I nod, and as we start walking, I let my gaze sail across the luxurious club. Everything is dark. Floors. Walls. Booths. Furniture. Even the bar follows the same theme. There's a stage for dancers and even an inground heated pool that has steam floating across the top of the water. Not gonna lie, it looks incredible, but considering the woman currently in a world of ecstasy with a man on either side of her, I don't even want to begin to know what kind of DNA is in that water.

Sheer curtains hang throughout the club to separate sections. Some small booth-like areas seem intimate, meant for two people, and some are much larger for hosting bigger . . . parties. Nearly all of them are occupied. Some couples are just having a drink while others are in the wild throws of passion, riding each other, getting off on the attention they draw.

As for Becs, her attention is on the orgy in the corner section. Though, what actually defines an orgy? Equal number of men and women? I don't know. The ones I may or may not have seen on forbidden sites are generally wild and filled with couples frantically fucking like a race to see who can get off first.

But this isn't that. This seems more . . . erotic.

There's one woman surrounded by five men. They're not rough or forceful or thinking about fucking her blindly. This is different. They're gentle. Their fingers brush across her skin and make her shiver. She sits on one man's lap, her thighs spread wide and hooked over his, and his arms tangle around her body, one flicking over her pert nipple and the other rubbing lazy circles over her clit. He kisses the base of her throat, and she leans back against him, arching her back with pleasure, and while it's hard to see from this angle, I'm pretty sure his cock is buried deep in her ass.

This is all about her. The way they touch her, the way they move. It's not about getting off for these men, it's about making her feel. It's about pure erotic pleasure, and I'm so here for it.

There's something so sensual about it, and I don't doubt that this woman will be in a world of ecstasy for hours into the night. She works two of the men with her hands as another drops to his knees and starts working his tongue up her inner thigh, and the moment he closes his mouth over her pussy, I have to look away. It feels like I'm intruding somehow. But am I really? If she didn't welcome the eyes of others, she would have closed this off to a private room.

"Holy shit," Becs drawls beside me, her gaze still locked on the woman. "That's what I want. If I could change positions with her and have exactly that . . ."

Hunger booms through her gaze, and a grin tears across my face. I think tonight is going to be one hell of a night to remember. "Come on," I tell her, pulling her toward the bar. "Let's get a drink and finish checking out the club, then you can decide where you want to spend your time."

Becs nods eagerly. "Good plan. If this is what we've already seen in the first few minutes, then I can't wait to see what else this place can offer. Plus the VIP area. We're definitely checking that out."

I almost dread the idea of what's happening down there, but there's no denying that I'm intrigued. Even if I don't end up participating in anything, this is still the craziest night I've ever had.

We make our way over to the bar, and I'm a little more comfortable here. People are just chilling, sipping on their drinks, and getting to know each other. It almost seems normal, but I know if I were to listen in on some of the conversations around me, all I'd hear is talk of boundaries, kinks, and limits they're willing to push in the bedroom.

The club's music is almost hypnotic, and even before I can order a drink, my hips start swaying to the beat.

Becs orders two cosmopolitans, and as the bartender arrives with our drinks in crystal glasses, a man settles in beside me. I don't think much of it as he steals the bartender's attention and orders himself a whiskey, but the second the bartender slinks away to prepare his drink, the man's attention falls on me.

His fingers brush over my inner wrist, lingering on the white wristband. "Hi, baby doll. Are you having a good time?"

I discreetly pull my arm away, putting a little space between us. If we were in a normal club, Becs would already have this guy in a chokehold, but considering where we are and that the point is to approach new people, I turn to face him, my gaze sailing over his face. He's handsome. Tall. Maybe six foot three. And judging by his expensive suit, he must be somewhat successful.

"I am. And yourself?"

His sultry gaze trails over my face. "I hope to be."

There's a sexy ruggedness to him. He looks as though he's had a long day in the office and is ready to spend his night indulging in a beautiful woman, sinking into her over and over and getting lost in the pure satisfaction her body can offer. But despite the way he's looking at me through a hooded gaze with a promise of one hell of a good night, I know in my gut that this isn't the man who'll be scratching that particular itch.

I offer polite conversation, and when the bartender returns with his drink, he excuses himself, clearly able to see that I won't be falling for his charm tonight. And honestly, I respect a man who just gets it and has the self-respect to walk away before things turn sour.

Becs and I sit for a few minutes, taking everything in as we sip our drinks. She points out the BDSM couple across the room, while I point out the scene playing out through the open door of one of the private rooms. We finish our drinks, and by the time I'm halfway through the second, I'm finally beginning to loosen up. We chat with a few people. One couple invites us to join them in a private room while another puts on a show, loving the attention. And I realize, even if I don't do anything, if I leave tonight with my virginity still intact, tonight is still shaping up to be a great experience.

We must have been here for an hour when Becs takes my hand and pulls me toward the entrance to the VIP area. "Come on, I'm dying to check this out," she tells me, and I have to agree, I am too. A few of the people we've met have offered stories about their crazy nights down in the VIP lounge, and it's left me more than intrigued.

We move across the club, weaving through the couples and parties who have become even bolder as the night wears on. As we reach the top of the stairs and show our gold, shimmering moth stamps to the security guard, we're waved through, and I know without a doubt that whatever I'm about to walk into is going to blow my world into a million tiny pieces.

Vixen has been unreal, like a crazy, wild adventure, but as we descend the stairs into the VIP lounge, a feeling of euphoria takes over and suddenly everything is so damn real. The music upstairs was sultry and hypnotic, but down here, it's electrifying and makes my blood buzz with a hungry energy.

The lighting is different, deeper somehow, and unlike upstairs, people aren't just chilling at the bar. There aren't as many people, but the sexual energy in the room far outweighs that of the main floor, plus the nudity down here is eye-opening. There are more private rooms scattered here, many of their doors already closed. The lounges and booths are filled with people, women draped over the couches as men ravage their bodies.

I see a man with his face plunged between a woman's legs while another man thrusts into his ass. While his body drags slowly in and out, each thrust is powerful, and I find myself wondering if I'm suddenly into watching men like this. The woman is in ecstasy as another man kneels by her head and she takes his thick cock in her mouth. And while this isn't anything we didn't see upstairs, there's a rawness to it, a hunger that simply didn't exist before.

"Okay, this is definitely where I want to be," Becs says, looking around.

"Then go and join them," a voice says from behind us.

We turn to find a man in a suit who's clearly just come down the stairs behind us. He's bold and immediately gets Becs' attention, and I can't blame her. He's hot as hell, and the way his eyes shimmer with desire as he takes her in has a ferocious need flashing in her eyes. He steps into her back, his arm immediately curling around her waist and slipping between her legs.

Whatever he does to her has her grinding against his hand, and when she gasps and groans, it's clear he's pushing his fingers inside her. He drops his lips to the base of her throat. "Such a tight little cunt," he purrs. "Let me show you off to my friends."

Becs rolls her tongue over her bottom lip before quickly sparing me a glance.

"Don't let me stop you," I tell her, seeing the question in her eyes.

She grins back at me before looking up at this bold stranger who's clearly making her knees weak with his skilled fingers. "Okay."

He nods and leads her over to the group she was watching before, leaning in and whispering something in her ear. She quickly responds, and with that, they change direction, moving to a different section of the room that's a little more private. The man nods to a few of the guys at the bar, and they get up and slink toward her. I can only assume these are the friends he wanted to show her off to.

Curiosity gets the best of me, and as I make my way to the bar, I watch Becs for a minute, making sure she's alright.

The bold man steps into her back again, just as he was by the stairs and his hands roam over her body. He's gentle with her, not forceful in the least, but still taking control. He slips his hand back between her thighs as his lips drop to the base of her neck, kissing her there. He murmurs things in her ear, hopefully asking what her limits are, and when one of his other friends steps into her front and gently takes the hem of her black dress, it's clear that Becs is about to get everything she came here for.

They kiss her, touch her, and make her body weak, and as they strip her down and begin sending her into a world of blissful pleasure, a blast of jealousy rumbles through my veins. I wish I had the courage to put myself out there and take what I really want like that.

Becs doesn't even know these guys and is trusting her body to them, and judging by the look on her face, she's never felt so alive in her life.

I need that. I'm ready to shed this good girl image and step into the dark side. I want to feel alive. I want the rush that comes along with being with someone. I want to know what it's like to ride a man and come with his cock buried deep inside me.

I'm sick of waiting for a man that's never going to love me. It's time that I take the leap and allow myself the freedom to discover the limits of my body.

As the men shower Becs in sensual touches and her knees fall open, I have to look away. I know she wanted an audience tonight, but there are just some things I can't watch her do, despite how comfortable she is with her body.

I sip on another cosmopolitan, a deep throb pounding between my thighs as I look around the lounge in a new light. I'm not just looking to take in the sights anymore. I'm searching for the man who'll take my virginity and finally open me up to a world I've always wanted to explore.

I catch the eyes of a few men, each of them delicious in their own right, but nothing about them has me wanting to hold their attention. A bearded man moves in behind me, and when his hand lingers on my waist, I don't make a move to push him away.

His hand roams over my hip and down between my thighs, and as his lips dance across my neck, I close my eyes, giving in to the pleasure. I grind against him, and before I know it, I'm on my feet. Just as I'm ready to ask for more, a flash of something across the VIP lounge catches my eye—A tall man, shirtless and walking away.

I don't see his face, just the wide set of his shoulders as he disappears into one of the private rooms, and when something clenches deep in my stomach, I realize he's the one I'll be losing my virginity to tonight.

3

ASPEN

The door of the private room remains open, and before I can even stop myself, I step out of the bearded man's arms and move across the lounge, that deep throbbing in my core getting hungrier by the second. I can't help but wonder if this is one of those trusted men Casey was talking about—the trusted men who are skilled and able to fulfill a woman's every desire.

God, I hope so.

I step into the doorway of the private room, finding it to be one of the dark rooms the club offers. Dark walls and floors, just like the rest of the club, only instead of the dim lighting the other spaces offer, this has none. All I see is a slight silhouette of the muscled man in the center of the room and a shiver trails down my spine. His back is to me, but I've never been so intrigued.

I'm really going to do this.

"Shut the door," he rumbles, his voice thick with desire, and even though I can barely hear him over the electrifying music, I do exactly as he asks, stepping over the threshold and closing the door behind me.

Any light from the main floor is shut out, and the room falls into a blinding darkness. The music is still just as loud, only now that I'm closed in with this mysterious man, I can feel the music vibrating right through my chest.

My hands shake, and I quickly finish off what's left of my Cosmo before putting the glass aside. He doesn't say another word, but I sense him beckoning me toward him, and I do exactly what he wants, desperate to feel his hands all over my body.

Barely able to see his silhouette anymore, I move across the room until I feel the flutter of his touch brushing down the length of my arm. I shiver, coming to a stop before him, and despite the nerves pounding through my body, I've never wanted anything more. I want this strange man to do wicked things to me, to take my virginity and make me feel alive.

His touch is like a summer breeze right down to my wrist where he collects my wristbands between his fingers, clearly feeling that there are two. A single question lingers between us, and I swallow hard, letting him know exactly why I'm here. "White," I breathe, trembling with nerves. "And red."

Despite not being able to see him, I can sense his understanding, and I can't help but wonder if it has something to do with the darkness that surrounds us. After taking my sight away, I have to rely on my other senses. The music drowns out my ability to hear, so all that's left for me to do is feel.

Feel his touch on my body.

Feel the warmth he emanates.

Feel the way his breath brushes over my skin.

I want it all.

The mysterious stranger takes my hips and turns me in his arms until my back is pressed against his bare chest, and a soft moan falls from my lips just being this close to him. He towers over me. He must be at least six-foot-four compared to my tiny five-foot-four. The top of my head barely reaches his shoulder, but I like that about a man. I like broad shoulders and a wide chest to go along with a muscled frame.

I'm intoxicated by his scent, his cologne being the same one that Izaac uses, but I put it to the back of my mind. I'm not willing to imagine the hands of a man who'll never want me tonight.

His fingers continue brushing over my skin, and I become putty in his hands. My hip. My wrist. My ribs. Every touch leaves me aching for more. And then finally, his hand dives deep between my legs and cups my pussy, and I let out a shallow groan.

He leans into me, his lips skimming over my shoulder. "If at any time you want me to stop, you tell me."

His words are a demand, not leaving room for negotiation, and I nod, knowing nothing this man could do to me right now would have me needing him to stop. And then as if sensing that drive within me, his hand starts working over my pussy.

He cups and grinds the heel of his palm against my clit, and I tremble. He works me through the sheer fabric of my thong as his other hand skims over my bare waist before trailing up to the slim shoestring strap that holds my sequined top together. He gives it a gentle pull and the small knot at my back comes free, and as I grind against his hand, he releases the second string, letting my top fall to the ground.

He doesn't hesitate, curving his big hand around my ribs and up to my full tits. His fingers roam over the curve of my breast as if testing how it feels in his hand, and as his fingers brush over my nipple and send a fierce electric shot straight to my core, my knees buckle.

He holds me up in his strong grasp, teasing every inch of my body before reaching for the small zipper that holds my miniskirt around my hips. He pulls the metal tab with ease, and my skirt falls away, dropping to the ground with my top and leaving me in nothing but my black thong and thigh-high boots.

A growl rumbles through his chest, and I feel the vibration on my back, but it's gone a moment later when he takes my hips and turns me. I gasp, my chest heaving with anticipation, never having felt such a deep sexual need in my life. Don't get me wrong, just because I haven't had sex, doesn't mean I'm not starved for it. I've done everything else and have an array of toys in my bedside drawer that are definitely overused, but I've never felt anything like this.

He pushes into me, his strong hands effortlessly forcing me back a step, and I keep going until my back is pressed against the wall of the dark room. He crowds me, his big body keeping me pinned to the wall as his thumbs hook into the thin waistband of my thong, then as he drags it down my thighs, he drops to his knees.

I suck in a gasp. I didn't anticipate this. I thought it would be straight to sex, but hell, I'm not about to tell him no if he wants to taste me.

He pulls my thong down my legs and over the boots until I'm able to step out of it. Then I feel his hand on my thigh, slowly trailing over every slight curve as if committing my body to memory. His fingers wrap around the inside of my knee, guiding my leg up and over his shoulder, opening me up to him and exposing me in the most vulnerable way, and considering his incredible height, I'm stretched wide.

He leans into me, and I can't resist threading my fingers into his hair. His sharp inhalation sends butterflies soaring through the pit of my stomach. The anticipation is almost too much to bear when he finally closes the gap and his tongue swipes through my slit, trailing from my entrance, right to my clit. My knees tremble, and I'm forced to lean all of my weight against the wall, barely able to keep myself upright.

Reaching up, his warm hand presses to my stomach to hold me still, and when his skilled tongue swipes through my wetness again, I become paralyzed—the perfect captive to his wicked pleasure.

His mouth closes over my clit, his tongue flicking back and forth as he sucks and teases. I groan as I clutch my tit with one hand, teasing my nipple and knotting my other into his hair, refusing to let go. He works me with the kind of skill that can't be human, and just when I think it couldn't possibly get better, he reaches up and pushes two thick, long fingers deep inside of me.

I throw my head back in pure ecstasy, barely able to catch my breath, but he doesn't ease up, determined to set my world on fire. His fingers curl inside me, massaging my walls as they tremble around him, contracting as my hips wildly jolt with satisfaction.

"Oh, God," I groan, inching closer and closer to the edge.

His tongue works me, rolling over my clit, and as his fingers push deeper inside, I can't hold on to it a second longer. I detonate, coming hard on his fingers, my walls shattering around him as I cry out. My high rocks through my body, blasting through my veins and pulsing right to the tips of my fingers and toes.

Everything clenches inside me, but he doesn't dare stop sucking and nipping at my sensitive clit, and with every swipe of his tongue or thrust of his skilled fingers, my orgasm intensifies.

He holds me up as my body trembles with desperation, and as my orgasm eases, this relentless, beautiful stranger pulls back. I gasp, my weight heavy against the wall of the dark room as he gets back to his feet. I'm forced to clutch his wide shoulders to remain upright, but when he steps into me and curls his big hands around my waist, my grip loosens.

I feel his erection through the front of his pants, pressing against my stomach, causing sheer panic to pulse through me. He's huge—a fucking monster, bigger than most of the toys hidden in my bedside drawer.

Surely he won't fit.

Perhaps this isn't a good idea. Maybe I should start with someone a little more . . . proportionate.

His big hand curls around my throat, his thumb stretching to my chin and forcing it up, and despite not being able to see any of his features in the darkness, I feel the exact moment his eyes meet mine. "Stop," he growls in a deep tone that rumbles through his chest. "You're overthinking it. You can take me."

"I . . . you're so big," I whisper, unsure if he can even hear me over the electrifying music.

"Yes. Now touch me."

Oh, God. I'm hit with a wave of nerves as my hands tremble against his shoulders, but the thought of pulling away and not getting to feel his huge cock in the palm of my hand tears at something deep within me.

I need this. I need him.

Pushing aside my nervousness, I go for it, letting my hunger drive me on.

I dig my thumbs into the waistband of his pants and shimmy them down his hips, sucking in a gasp as his heavy cock springs free, landing against my stomach. There's a distinct feel of a piercing brushing against my skin, and it only excites me further. He pushes his pants down until they drop to the ground, and as he steps out of them and kicks them away, I waste no time curling my fingers around his thickness.

I gasp at the feeling of him against my palm. He's velvety smooth with thick, prominent veins leading up to his bulbous, pierced tip, and as I curl my thumb over the top, he shudders against me. "Just like that, Little Birdy. Again."

His words are like a demand, and I find myself eager to please him, immediately rolling my thumb over his tip again. A deep growl rumbles through his chest, and I tighten my hold before starting to pump my fist up and down, truly getting a feel for his impressive size.

His head tilts forward, coming undone from my touch, and it spurs me on. I need to feel him crumble against me, need to hear his ragged breath hitch over the sound of the throbbing bass filling the room, so I work him with everything I've got until his hands are at my ass, lifting me effortlessly into his arms.

My legs lock around his waist, and he buries his lips against my neck—kissing, licking, and nipping at the sensitive skin below my ears until I'm a squirming mess in his strong arms. He pins me with his big body against the wall, and as his tongue roams over my skin, I have a flash of Izaac, imagining his eyes, his touch, his tongue, and cock in my hand. A shiver trails down my skin, the hunger intensifying at just the thought of Izaac ever working my body like this.

I immediately scold myself for going there, but the moment he flashed in my mind, he was here to stay.

He grinds that thick cock against my core, and I start to shudder, the need becoming too much for me to handle. "Do you fuck yourself, Little Birdy?" he questions, his hot breath against my skin sending a wave of goosebumps sailing across me. "Have you ever pushed a big silicone cock up into this sweet cunt?"

His crass tone makes me quiver, but I love it. I've had men with their faces buried between my legs questioning me like this, and it was nothing more than a disgusting turnoff, but with him . . . God. I want to tell him every fucking dirty detail of my life. "Yes," I pant, my chest heaving against his.

"Good," he rumbles, finally reaching between us and taking the head of his delicious cock. "I'm going to fuck you, Little Birdy. If you want me to stop, tell me now. I'm going to take you inch by inch. Deep and fucking raw. It's going to be hard and fast, but I will not hurt you."

Oh, God. My body trembles, but I need this more than my next breath.

My pussy clenches, already shuddering with anticipation, and I nod, panting heavily. "Please," I groan, my fingers digging into his strong shoulder. "I need you inside of me."

He doesn't hesitate, swiping his thick tip through my wetness, spreading it between us, and then finally, I feel him at my entrance. His hand shifts from my ass to my waist, holding me tight, and when he pushes his tip inside, I tilt my head against the wall, the undeniable pleasure already rocking through me.

His fingers dig into my skin, and as I let out a gasp, he takes me another inch, slowly pushing further inside me. "Oh, God," I groan as my walls begin to stretch. He's barely inside of me, but he's already stretching me further than anything found in my bedside table. I'm not sure I can take it.

Another inch. Another gasp.

My nails dig into his skin, and my eyes roll into the back of my head. I never knew it could feel this way, feel so whole and full, and he's not even all the way in yet.

He takes me further, and I will myself to relax around him, determined to take everything he's got, knowing that if I hadn't been working myself up to this in the privacy of my own bedroom for all of these years, I would never have been able to do this.

"Good girl," he says as if feeling the way I relax around him, feeling how I welcome him inside me.

My walls have never been stretched so far, and with one more thrust, he bottoms out, taking me so fucking deep my hips jolt with surprise. "Fuuuuck," I groan, my whole body trembling with need. He pauses, allowing me a moment to get used to his delicious intrusion, and when his lips drop back to my neck, working up to that sensitive spot below my ear, the hunger intensifies.

I need him to move. Now.

As if sensing that wild desperation coursing through my veins, he pulls back, and I feel his piercing teasing me from within. He thrusts again and I gasp loudly, my nails digging in even further. "Holy fuck," I pant, my walls shattering around his thick cock.

"You like how I fuck you, Little Birdy?" he growls, and the more he talks, the easier it becomes to picture Izaac being the one driving into me, filling me like I've always so desperately craved.

"Oh, God. Yes! Again."

He doesn't disappoint, working me again and again, and despite the epic orgasm he just gave me with his mouth, I already feel that familiar tightening in my core. I've never come more than once, but something tells me this second time isn't going to be the last of the night.

He keeps me pinned against the wall but arches his body back and puts space between us. Then just when I'm about to pull him back in, he uses that space to reach between us and press his thumb to my clit. My hips jolt, and heat floods my entire body. "Reach up, Little Birdy. Grip the bar."

My brows furrow with confusion, but I do as I'm asked, reaching up and finding a metal bar bolted to the wall. I curl my fingers around it, holding on for dear life, and the second he inches his hips back, I suddenly understand why. While he was holding me, carrying my weight, his hips were doing all the work. But now, as he pushes into me with longer, deeper thrusts, I need to keep myself up.

He rolls his thumb over my clit and my hips don't stop jolting, the sensitive bundle of nerves working overtime. *It's too much.* I don't want this to end, but I can't hold on to it any longer. "Fuck, I'm—"

"I know, Birdy. Come for me. Let me feel that tight cunt squeeze my cock."

Oh, God. I love his filthy mouth.

He thrusts into me one more time, deep and forceful, and I explode like a coil reaching its limits. I cry out, my body spasming with intense satisfaction as my walls desperately squeeze his thick cock. He lets out a strained breath, his body shuddering with mine, but he doesn't stop moving or rolling his thumb over my clit, and with every second of his touch, every new thrust, my orgasm takes me higher.

My eyes close as the high rockets through my body, pulsing

through me with undeniable pleasure, and I throw my head back, gasping for sweet breath. "Oh, God," I cry, my body turning into a mess of spasms. I've never come like this in my life, never felt this kind of high, this kind of intensity.

"I . . . I—It's too much."

"Ride it out," he rumbles, continuing to rock his hips as the pressure on my clit intensifies, demanding every ounce of pleasure from my body.

I focus on his touch, relaxing deeper into my orgasm until finally, the intense pulses start to fade and he slows his tormenting thrusts. He steps closer to me just as my hold on the bar falters, and I fall heavily into his strong arms. His lips come back to my throat, giving me a second to catch my breath as his thick cock remains buried deep inside my pussy.

"That—" pant, "was—" pant. "So fucking good."

This mysterious stranger chuckles against my skin, and the sound is something that I'll forever remember. There's something so comforting and warm about it. It reminds me of—nope. I need to stop going there. This isn't Izaac. This is a perfect stranger—one who just happens to know exactly what a woman needs.

"You think it's over, Little Birdy?"

My back stiffens, and I snap my gaze to his, despite not being able to see his face in the darkness. "It's not?"

"No. I don't come until you're completely spent, and Little Birdy, you still have another one in you."

A shiver of anticipation shoots down my spine when I try to think through the haze of post-orgasm bliss, remembering the way his body shuddered when I was coming. "But I thought you did," I say with a breathy whisper, not able to find enough strength to project my voice much louder over the electrifying music.

I feel him shake his head. "Your pleasure comes first, Birdy. Now let me show you what you've been missing."

With that, he pulls me away from the wall and strides across the room, every step making his cock bounce and move within me. I clutch my arms around his neck, holding on with what little energy I have left, but the thought of getting to be fucked by this incredible stranger again has a burst of newfound life burning through my veins.

I need to feel how he'll fuck me, need to feel his electrifying touch all over my body.

I'm placed down on a low-lying table and my body trembles with disappointment as he pulls back, his thick cock falling from my spent pussy. His hands roam down my thighs, finding the top of my boots and working them down my legs until they're gone.

"Turn around, Birdy," he says, once my boots have turned into a distant memory. "On your knees."

My brows furrow, but I do as I'm asked, swiveling around on the table and getting up to my knees. I feel him step in behind me, his thick cock dancing across my ass and that delicious piercing tormenting me, teasing me with what it can do.

The anticipation is too much and when his hands circle my body, one roaming up to my tits while the other travels south, dipping between my legs, my body shudders again. His touch is so perfect, so sensual and erotic. How could any other man touch me again and it ever compare to this?

His lips are at the back of my neck, his chest pressed right against my back. “Bend over, Birdy. Offer me that sweet cunt.”

I swallow hard. It’s one thing being fucked up against the wall, but like this? Holy shit, this is hot.

I immediately drop down, my chest pressing against the cool table as my ass remains high in the sky, offered to him like a buffet. Butterflies swarm through the pit of my stomach, and impatience burns through me as his hand circles over my ass before dropping between my thighs and cupping my pussy.

He pushes a finger inside of me from behind. “Spread your knees,” he says in that deep, rumbling tone, making me shudder.

Without hesitation, I push my knees as far as they’ll go, opening myself to him as he continues plunging his fingers deep inside of me. In and out, spreading my arousal.

I arch my back, offering him more, but he pulls out of me, making me whimper with need. His hand returns to the curve of my ass, and just when I think he’s about to plunge that thick cock back inside of me, I feel the warm swipe of his tongue against my clit.

My hips jolt, my body instantly turning into a quivering mess, still so sensitive from my earlier orgasms, but he doesn’t stop there, taking it higher and swiping his tongue over my entrance, plunging it inside of me, and lapping up my arousal.

I push back against him, needing more, but he pulls away, and I feel him get back to his feet. “So hungry for me,” he says with approval, and in response, I push back again, desperate for him to take me. "Touch yourself, Birdy."

Nervousness trickles through me, but nowhere near as bad as earlier. I've never touched myself in front of a man, but considering the darkness and the fact that he's already been inside of me, there's nothing holding me back.

Snaking my arm beneath my body, I press two fingers to my sensitive clit, slowly rolling them just the way I like it, and my body immediately begins to quake. My breath shakes, and he steps in close behind me. "Just like that," he murmurs as I feel that delicious piercing skating through my wetness before stopping at my entrance, the height of my cunt lining up perfectly with his thick cock. "Don't stop."

Never.

Without another word, he plunges inside me. I cry out, clutching the side of the table with my free hand. My walls immediately stretch around him as he bottoms out, and in this position, I'm somehow able to take him deeper.

"Oh, fuck," I cry, pushing back for more.

He doesn't hesitate, thrusting again as he takes my hips to hold me still, and I furiously pick up my pace, the lazy roll over my clit turning into tight, desperate circles.

He drives into me again and again until my legs shake. I'm immobilized in this position, unable to do anything except take his deep thrusts as my body becomes reliant and obsessed with his every touch.

His balls slam into my fingers as I work my clit, and as he rolls his hips, taking me at a new angle with deep, long thrusts, I cry out for more. My walls clench around him, completely captive to his every move, and as that familiar coil deep inside my core begins to tighten, I realize that this is going to be my most intense one yet.

"I'm going to come," I warn him.

His hand comes down over my ass in response—the most erotic spank I've ever felt, and my pussy shudders for more. "Good girl," he grits through a clenched jaw. "Squeeze me."

I clench around him, squeezing as tight as I can, the intensity rocking through my body and sending me into a quivering mess. My eyes flutter closed as I grip the side of the table, desperately trying to hold on to it, but it's no use. He has a chokehold on my body, every wish is his command.

"Let it go, Little Bird," he demands with a deep growl. "Let me feel you."

His words are my undoing, and as if on command, the tight coil springs free, and my orgasm detonates from within. I shatter like glass. My body trembles and quivers with intense waves, sending bursts of undeniable pleasure rocking through me as my pussy spasms around his thick cock.

I cry out, tears springing to my eyes, and he continues drilling into me. Thrust after thrust, his fingers tightening on my hips. I keep working my clit, drawing out every ounce of pleasure, when he drives into me one more time with a loud roar that rings in my ears.

He stills, his hips jolting against my ass as he empties hot spurts of cum inside of me, and it only hits me now that I forgot to ask for a condom, but I can't find it within me to care. The idea of his warm cum inside me makes it that much hotter.

The intensity is too much, so I pull away from my clit, unable to take it any longer. Then when my orgasm finally begins to ease, I turn to Jell-O on the table.

He doesn't dare pull out of me, but his hold relaxes on my hips, slowly rocking his hips as if helping me come down from my high. But when his hand lifts and slowly trails up my spine, a shiver sails across my skin.

I close my eyes and savor his gentle touch. It's absolutely everything I didn't know I needed, and it makes me feel like so much more than just a random fuck in a dark room. There's an intimacy about it, and just like that, I've been ruined for any other man.

"You okay?"

"Better than okay," I breathe.

He finally pulls back, easing his thick cock out of my spent pussy, and his hot cum immediately drips out of me. I sense as he walks away, and I adjust myself on the table, and by the time I push off and get back to my feet, he's right there, pushing me back against the table, catching my weight.

"Take it easy, Birdy," he says, his tone low as I notice he somehow managed to find his pants in the darkness. "Your legs will be shaky after that. Take a minute."

I swallow hard when he presses a warm cloth to my inner thigh, slowly trailing it up to my core, and every touch is just as sensual as the ones before. He cleans me up, and when he's done, he curls his hand around the back of my neck and into my hair. He tugs, pulling my head back until my chin is lifted, and I sense his gaze on mine.

His breath brushes across my lips, barely an inch away, but he doesn't dare close the gap. Somehow, despite everything we've done tonight, I feel that would be too personal. "I hope you visit me again, Little Birdy," he rumbles before dropping his lips to my cheek. He pulls back just an inch, releasing his hold in my hair. "I'll give you some privacy to dress. There's ice water by the door, but there's no rush to leave. The room is yours for as long as you need."

"Okay," I breathe, still trying to ease my racing heart.

"I'll turn the lights on as I leave so you can see what you're doing."

And with that, he walks away.

I sense every step he takes across the room until the distinct sound of the door opening catches my attention. A small shaft of light gleams against the dark floor, but it's gone a second later as the man's tall, broad shadow passes through the door and it snaps shut behind him. The overhead lights flicker on, slowly filling the pitch-black room with a dim light that's just enough to see my clothes where I left them.

Testing my weight on my shaky legs, I trudge across the room and dress, desperate to stay here and dwell on everything that just went down, but I'm also desperate to get back out there and tell Becs all about it. I find my boots by the table I was just fucked on, and after pulling them back into place and having a small glass of water, I finally curl my fingers around the door handle.

A strange nervousness settles into my chest, and as I pull the door open and step out into the VIP lounge, my gaze immediately locks with

Becs' as she sits at the bar. As if knowing exactly what just happened, a slow, proud grin tears across her face, and I grin right back, more than ready to tell her every last detail.

4

ASPEN

The early morning sun creeps through my bedroom window, and despite the time and the delicious ache between my thighs, a smile spreads across my face.

That was hands down the best night of my life.

Becs and I didn't get home until three in the morning, and while I didn't indulge in any more of the incredible men on offer, I still had an amazing night. There's a new air about me. I suddenly don't feel like a child flailing about in the real world. I feel like a woman, and what's better, I don't have one of those shitty stories where I was drunk and ended up losing my virginity at sixteen in the back of some guy's car while he was too drunk to figure out what goes where. No, I was fucked by a real man who knew exactly what he was doing, and

I'm so damn pleased I waited.

I wonder if Izaac fucks like that. I bet he does.

I've always viewed Izaac as a real man, ever since I was a kid. He's always been larger than life, and the few times I've accidentally caught a woman sneaking out of the guest room after one of my brother's ridiculous parties, they've always looked more than satisfied.

Shit. I shouldn't be thinking about him like that, but ever since last night, when his stupidly gorgeous face popped into my head, I've found myself imposing it onto the body of the man from Vixen. How fucking stupid is that?

God. All I've done is make this ridiculous crush even worse.

Why does it have to be Izaac? He's the one man I'm not allowed to want, the one man I *shouldn't* want.

To me, Izaac Banks is everything.

He was adopted by a wealthy couple at a young age, and the second he was enrolled in the same school as my brother, they were tied at the hip. He's kind, sexy, attentive, and is one of the few men I've met who actually give a shit about the important things in life. He knows how to dominate when it comes to business, and that's clear with the three successful nightclubs he owns.

He's always pushing himself to be better, always showing up for his family and friends. The only thing he's missing . . . is someone to love him unconditionally—someone who'll never be me.

I groan, my good mood suddenly plummeting.

I'll never get to stand at his side, never get to feel his touch on my body, his lips on mine. The night I shared with that perfect stranger is a night I will never get to have with Izaac, no matter how many times I pretend it was his face on the stranger's ripped body.

With the realization that the night I just shared in that dark room is a night I will never get to experience again, I let out a heavy sigh. Hell, the only way I'll ever experience something so intense is if I were to go back, but then, who am I supposed to ask for? Despite his invitation to return, I know nothing about him.

A heaviness presses down on my chest, and I yank my blanket up over my head, more than ready to wallow in a pit of self-inflicted misery when my phone screeches to life on my bedside table. I groan, letting out a heavy breath as I throw the blanket back and scramble for my phone before I miss the call.

It's probably Becs checking in and making sure I don't regret anything that went down last night, and I don't. My only regrets are that I won't get to do it again and that the memory of the man who I happily gave my virginity to is nothing but a faceless figure locked away in my imagination. If I saw him on the street, I'd never know it was him.

Scooping up my phone, my brows furrow, finding my brother's name flashing across the screen. That's odd. He never calls me this early.

"Whatdoyawant?" I rumble through a yawn as I scooch back in my bed and flop against my pillow.

"You on your way? You're late."

I fly up into a sitting position, probably looking like one of those possessed characters from a scary movie. "Huh? What are you talking about?" I ask, pulling my phone away to look at the time on the screen. "I have ages. It's only—OH FUCK!"

Shooting out of bed, I barge through my apartment in a mad rush to get to the bathroom, trying to strip off my clothes as I go. Mom is going to kill me!

Austin laughs, always having found the utmost joy in my misery, especially when that misery means my parents will be too busy scolding me to bother pestering him about his love life . . . or lack thereof.

"Mom only turns fifty once," Austin reminds me as I put the phone on speaker and barge through the door of my bathroom, tossing my clothes across the room. "The only thing she asked for was for us all to be on time for once."

Shit. Shit. Shit.

I lean into the shower and turn on the taps before noticing the red and white wristbands still braced around my wrist, and as the water warms, I whip around and search through my makeup bag for my tiny nail scissors, desperate to cut them off. Though, would it be weird if I kept them? Maybe hidden away as a secret memento to remember my night with the wild caveman who fucked me all night and made me come three times? Yeah . . . maybe that'd be weird.

"First off, Mom is turning sixty. Not fifty. And I'm not *that* late. Just tell her I'm right around the corner and then she'll be happy and get distracted asking how the restaurant is going. I'll slip through the back door. She'll never know."

I hear Austin's cringe through the phone. "If only it were that simple. I'm still an hour out."

"WHAT?" I shriek, finally getting the wristbands off and dumping them in the top of my makeup bag. "Ahh shit. We're both fucked. It's going to be like last Christmas all over again."

Austin groans. "Shit."

"Wait," I say, stepping into the shower and keeping the door open so I can continue my conversation. "How'd you know I was late if you're not already there?"

"Because you're Aspen. You're always late."

"Am not!"

Austin scoffs. "Just hurry up, dork. I'll see you later."

He doesn't bother with a goodbye, simply ends the call as I reach for the shower door and pull it closed. I do what I can to race through my shower, scrubbing all the important bits and trying to remember if I washed my makeup off when I got home in the early hours of this morning.

I lather up my loofah and get to work, sailing down my legs and back up, detouring through the center and sucking in a breath, finding myself still a little sore from my wild night, but fuck, it's a welcome feeling. I put it to the back of my mind, determined not to get carried away.

It's already ten in the morning. I don't know how I managed to sleep through my alarm. Actually, I know exactly how I managed that, but what's important is that Mom's birthday lunch is at twelve. If it were any other lunch, to Mom, that'd mean we would all need to be there by ten thirty at the latest. Considering it's her sixtieth birthday, arriving any later than ten for a midday lunch is already considered late.

Thankfully I washed my hair and shaved all the important bits before Becs dragged me out last night, so it doesn't take too long to get myself all squeaky clean. After stepping out of the shower, I quickly towel dry before pulling on a cute summer dress—my baby green, spotted backless one, the one I know Mom has always loved. Then because I know there's a good chance that Izaac will show up, I pull the sleeves down over my shoulders, showing off just enough skin to remind him I'm not a child anymore . . . not that my tricks of the trade have ever worked before, but there's always hope.

I pull my hair up into a long ponytail and add all my favorite jewelry before rushing through my makeup routine. I give myself a golden not-so-natural glow and hit my lashes with just enough mascara to make my eyes pop. Finally, I grab my overnight bag and shove everything I need into it.

I live close to campus, but it's still a twenty-five-minute drive back to my parents' place. Considering it's only a quarter past ten, I'll still beat Austin there, and that's all that matters. I'll be the favorite child today.

Hurrying out of my small apartment, I quickly lock up before making my way down to the parking garage and getting on my way. I crank the music to ease my nerves.

Going home is such a simple task, but knowing Izaac will be there creates such a stir in me. Since being in college, I haven't spent much time at home outside of birthdays or holidays, and since Izaac is Austin's chosen brother, he never misses a single family event.

His family is our family, and our family is his. It's been this way since the moment he and Austin met as kids, and I grew up right alongside them.

After making great time on the highway, I park my car and slip in through the back door. Mom is busy slaving away in the kitchen. "Hey, Mom," I say, walking straight into her and wrapping my arms around her. "Happy birthday."

"Oh, my sweet girl. Thank you," Mom says, locking me in a warm hug. "When did you get here? I didn't hear you come through the door."

I grin to myself, my plan working like a charm. "I got stuck talking to Nancy from next door. She was admiring your rose bushes," I tell her. "But I don't blame her. They're looking incredible. What are you feeding those things?"

Mom laughs and pulls back, determined to get back to her cooking, but I quickly step in and take over, wanting her to relax on her birthday. Only Mom isn't one of those women who can handle standing around, and she gets right to work on something else. "I got myself a new garden boy," she tells me like it's some kind of secret. "He's not very good at the lawns, but when he prunes the bushes, he prunes them well."

I can't help but laugh. "Mom!"

"What? He's a very handsome young thing. Maybe I should give him your number," she muses. "You know, he likes to work without his shirt, and he's got quite a fit body, very muscly, and has one of those V thingies. You know, like an arrow pointing right to his—"

"MOM!" My cheeks flush. "I'm sure your new gardener's dick is as impressive as they come, but I really don't need to hear about it."

"Ugh," I hear my father's tone as he walks into the kitchen behind us. "Why is it that every time I walk into a room, I have to hear about someone's dick?"

I smirk, not sorry in the least. Now, if he really wanted to hear about impressive dicks, I know of one I can tell him all about. Though for some reason, I doubt he'd want to hear about what said dick did to his little girl all night.

Dad steps into my side and wraps his arm around me, pressing a kiss to my cheek. "Hi, sweetheart."

"Hey, Dad," I say, offering him a smile. "Do I want to know who else has been talking about dicks around you?"

"Your mother," he states with a heavy sigh. "Always your mother."

I can't help but laugh as Dad collects the tray of meat and waltzes out the back door, ready to start grilling, as Mom keeps herself busy. "What time do you call this?" she mutters, sparing a second to glance at the clock—a clock that now reads eleven. "Where's that brother of yours? I swear, he's always running late."

"Tell me about it," I say, more smug than I've ever been in my life. "He needs a secretary who can keep him on time. I swear, he'll be late to his own funeral."

"I heard that," comes my brother's booming tone from deeper in the house—the back door precisely.

He comes waltzing through the house before appearing in the kitchen to face down my mother. She stands with her hands on her hips, glaring at Austin. "If I find out that you were trying to sneak through the back door so that I didn't notice you were late to my birthday lunch, Austin Ryder, your lunch will be served with a smackdown."

I can't keep the snicker from bursting from my mouth, having to smother my hand across my face as Austin shoots a glare at me. God, it's nice when my mother's wrath isn't aimed at me. "I would never do that to you, Mom," Austin says, walking straight into her and pulling her into a hug. "Did I mention you look beautiful? What's this birthday? Forty-three?"

Mom chuckles and can't resist finally pulling her son into her arms. "Oh Austin," she coos, turning to Jell-O at Austin's exaggerated flattery. "You know I'm fifty today."

Dad's scoff is heard from all the way outside. "And the rest!"

Mom rolls her eyes and lets out a loud huff before focusing her attention on Austin. "Will we be seeing Izaac today?"

"He hasn't missed a single one of your birthdays in the last twenty years. He's not about to miss this one."

Mom smiles before her gaze lifts to the clock again. "Oh, well he must be running a little—"

I shake my head, trying not to be obvious about the way my body reacts to just the mention of his name. "Izaac's not your son, Mom. You can't get angry at him for not showing up two hours early for lunch. You know, when you say lunch is at twelve, the general population believes that lunch is actually at twelve."

Mom rolls her eyes. "Just because I'm not technically his mother doesn't mean I don't consider him my son. Izaac's been around long enough to know the rules."

Oh, geez.

Austin scoffs. "In that case, you need to hold him to the same punishments I get. He better be served a smackdown with his lunch too."

"Oh, he will," Mom declares. "Now go and help your father with the grill. You know how he likes to burn things."

Austin scrambles, leaving me with Mom, and the second she turns to me with her eyes sparkling, I immediately dread whatever's about to fly out of her mouth. "So," she says, her tone suggesting I should run for the hills. "What's going on with you, honey? Any men on the scene that I need to know about?"

"Mom," I groan. "You know damn well I haven't had time to go out and find myself some guy."

Mom scoffs. "Oh, of course, with all that sitting on the couch and binge-watching TV shows you've been doing."

"What? I have not. I've been busy. Graduation is in a few months."

"Perhaps you've forgotten that you're a cheapskate and have been piggybacking off my Netflix account? I know exactly how much spare time you have, Aspen. Which begs the question, why the hell can't you find a spare minute to drop in every now and then? You know, your poor momma is getting old."

"You're not old," I scold, knowing damn well age is nothing but a number to her. "Austin wasn't kidding. You look like you're in your forties, plus you do yoga four times a week. You're fitter than I am."

"Flattery will get you nowhere," she warns.

"Bullshit! Flattery got Austin off the hook."

"The hell it did. That boy's got another thing coming if he thinks he's off the hook, but if he thinks complimenting his mother is the way to go, then who am I to discourage him?"

I roll my eyes, a smirk playing on my lips. "You've always been able to see right through our bullshit."

"Damn right, I have," she tells me. "Which is exactly how I know that you snuck through the back door too. You really think I'd buy that crap about Nancy from next door liking my rose bushes? That woman can't stand my rose bushes. She's been jealous of them for ten years."

Ahhhh shit.

"Speaking of being able to see right through your bullshit," she continues. "Don't tell me the reason you're not putting yourself out there is because of this ridiculous crush on Izaac."

I blanch, my gaze quickly shooting around the room in a panic. This insane crush has been the worst-kept secret for as long as I can remember. My family has teased me relentlessly for it over the years, but since I turned eighteen, it's become a taboo topic, especially with Austin.

My brother hates it.

The second it's brought up, he shuts down, and so I make a point not to mention anything about Izaac when Austin's around. We've never actually had a conversation about it, and he hasn't given me the time of day to actually explain why he's so against the idea. But I suppose it doesn't matter anyway. Izaac knows I'm off-limits just as much as I know that he is. Only difference is, Izaac has never looked at me as anything more than a little sister.

"Mom," I scold, lowering my tone. "Do we really have to talk about this now? Austin could walk in at any moment."

"Please," she scoffs. "Your brother won't be coming back in here any time soon, not now that he's terrified of facing my wrath for being late. Now, tell me what I need to know, or I'll have no choice but to keep asking, and who knows, Izaac will be here soon, and the question might accidentally slip out of my mouth right in the middle of lunch."

I level her with a hard stare. "You wouldn't."

She stares right back, her gaze just as ferocious as mine. "Want to make a bet?"

Shit.

If there's anything I've learned over the past twenty-two years, it's don't challenge Momma Ryder, because I will lose. Every. Damn. Time.

Letting out a heavy breath, I fall back against the counter, peeling the layers of my carefully placed mask back and letting her see the real pain in my eyes, the agony of being so desperately in love with someone but not being able to scream it from the rooftops. Not being able to feel their touch, their love. It's the most agonizing thing I've ever felt, and I know without a doubt that it will never go away.

"It's not some little girl's ridiculous crush, Mom," I murmur. "Not anymore. I've been deeply in love with him since before I can remember, and I don't know how to make it stop."

"Oh, honey," she says, stepping into me and pulling me into a warm hug.

"I know it's never going to happen, that it can't happen, but I don't know how to move past it. How do I train my heart not to love something I've always wanted so much?"

"I'm sorry, sweetheart. I really wish I had the answers for you," she tells me, her hand moving up and down my back just like she used to when she was trying to soothe me as a little girl. "All I know is that you need to try. You need to find a different version of happiness. It's out there for you somewhere. The journey is in discovering where, but the true adventure is what happens once you find it."

5

IZAAC

Making my way up the long driveway of the Ryder estate, I look up at the home I was practically raised in. Every holiday, birthday, and event, I was here, not to mention every minute of my spare time. After school, I came here. After football practice, here. After I fucked up my first date, here. Don't get me wrong, there were plenty of times Austin and I hung out at my place, but my family home is cold whereas the four walls of the Ryder estate . . . that's a real home.

My parents are great. They adopted me when I was six years old, gave me a warm bed and a home, and they loved me in the best way they could, but with them, work always came first. They instilled the importance of being a beast in the boardroom, but when it came to teaching affection and the importance of family, I got that from the

Ryders.

My father built his brand from the ground up and became exactly what he always wanted me to be—a killer in business. He owns a huge vineyard out in Napa Valley that was responsible for our family's wealth, and from there, my father's legacy has become unlike any other. He has worked himself to the bone, and I'm quickly following in his footsteps, putting all of my efforts into building my brand as the top nightclub owner in the country. I still have a fair way to go, but I've always been taught to dream big. The sky is the fucking limit and all that shit.

As for Mom, I don't even think she knows what she does. She lives the life of a socialite and thrives as the head of the women's committee at the country club. But honestly, I think it's a made-up group their husbands created to give them something to do while they drink and play golf.

By the time I was thirteen, my parents had all but forgotten I lived in their home. But it was fine because I preferred being here.

I've always preferred being here.

This place is my second home, even now as a grown man, I wouldn't have it any other way. It didn't take long for Marc and Angella to accept that I was a permanent fixture in their home. The second Austin and I bonded over ice hockey, it was set in stone.

My Escalade rolls to a stop at the top of the circular driveway, right between Austin's Range Rover and Aspen's white Corvette—her twenty-first birthday present from her parents. I can't help but grin as my gaze sails over the car. There's no denying it, it's a nice car. It's been

Aspen's dream car since before I can remember, and the day she got it . . . fuck. My ears are still ringing from the way she screamed. I still remember her face-splitting grin. I've never seen anyone light up like that.

Getting out of my car, I make my way up the front steps of the Ryder estate, making a point to glance at Angella's roses, knowing damn well she's going to ask me what I think. She's been obsessed with those damn things since the day they were planted when I was a kid, and though they've thrived in her garden, they look the same to me as they did ten years ago.

When I get to the front door, I walk straight inside and follow the noise. I hear the familiar sound of plates shifting around in the dining room, and I spare a glance at my watch, double-checking that I'm not late, but it's still a quarter to twelve. I'm right on time.

Striding into the dining room, I find Aspen with plates piled high in her arms, and I pause, taking her in, my breath caught in my throat.

Fuck, she looks good in that green dress.

My gaze sails over her, taking in the way her short sleeves rest low on her shoulders, showing off her creamy skin, but the way it dips down in the back . . . fucking hell.

I avert my gaze. What the fuck am I doing? I can't be looking at her like that. She's practically a kid. If Austin caught me checking out his little sister, he'd castrate me.

It's no secret that she's had a crush on me since she was a kid. I always thought that as she got older and hit her late teens, she would have grown out of it, but she never did. Instead, she learned how to disguise it . . . not very well, but I appreciate that she's always tried. I've watched over the past few years as she slipped a mask into place every time I walked into a room. She's too careful around me, not the carefree kid she used to be. She watches what she says and is careful not to get too close.

I've never reciprocated that crush or looked at her as anything more than Austin's little sister, but if I ever did make a move on her, Austin would never forgive me. Not that it matters. Despite how fucking gorgeous she is, that's a line I would never cross. I'm always on my best behavior, never letting my hands or eyes linger too long, and I certainly don't hide the details about the women I'm with. I notice the hurt in her eyes when she overhears my conversations with Austin, and I fucking hate to hurt her, but it's important that she knows where the line is drawn.

Austin's protective of her, and though we've never spoken about it directly, he's made it clear that I'm not good enough for her, and I agree with him. She's a shy girl, quiet and timid. While she likes to have a crazy night out of wild drinking every now and then, she prefers a quiet night at home in her ridiculous Grinch pajamas with a pint of ice cream and a good series to binge-watch. On the other hand, I live for my work. I spend my days dreaming of how I can expand and my nights living it up in my clubs.

Aspen and I . . . we're not the same.

We're not compatible.

Striding into the dining room, I act as though the very sight of her doesn't blow me the fuck away. Just because I don't want to get in bed with her doesn't mean I haven't noticed how fucking breathtaking she is.

"Hey, what's going on?" I ask, watching how she stacks dishes high, balancing them as best she can, and while I might not know much about hosting fancy lunches, I'm almost damn sure she's un-setting the table that hasn't been eaten at yet.

Aspen's head snaps up at the sound of my voice, and a dazzling smile cuts across her face. Fuck, she truly is gorgeous.

I continue around the large table toward her, unable to keep from noticing that there's something different about her. Something different in the way she carries herself. There's a glow—a happiness that screams of confidence, and it looks fucking good on her. She's always been on the shy side, but not today. She looks as though she's broken out of her shell, and for just a moment, I'm caught off guard, rendered speechless.

That dazzling smile falls, replaced by the fake one she always tries to use around me, and she casually loads up another dish. "Even at sixty, my mother's still capable of driving me insane," Aspen says, rolling her eyes and letting out a heavy sigh. "She spent an hour working on her table setting, then took one look out the window fifteen minutes before lunch was due to be served, and decided that she wanted to eat outside."

I laugh, finally reaching her and stepping into her side. I immediately hook my arm around her, place my palm in the center of her back, and press a swift kiss to her cheek. "How're you doing?" I ask, lowering my tone as I pull back, noticing the way a wave of goosebumps dances across her skin.

Aspen seems to think it over as if wondering what kind of response she wants to give when her cheeks begin to flush and she worries her bottom lip. A softness flutters in her eyes, and as she looks up at me, I'm fucking floored by her beauty. "I'm really good," she tells me, and damn it, now I'm certain that something has changed.

Is she seeing someone? Maybe she's finally fallen for someone else. That's what I've always needed from her, but the thought of it doesn't sit right with me. Perhaps Austin and I need to do some digging. Just because I'm not good enough for her doesn't mean any other fucker is.

I nod, not sure how to voice a proper response without the deep curiosity showing in my tone. So instead, I reach for the dishes in her hands. "Here, let me help you."

"Thanks," she says, handing them to me and grabbing more. I follow her out of the dining room, through the kitchen, and toward the back door. "You should be warned though, Mom is on the warpath."

My brows furrow, hoping nothing is wrong. "Why? Something happened?"

"*You* happened," she says with a smug smirk.

The fuck? "Did I miss something?"

"Lunch," she confirms. "It starts at twelve."

"Okay. I'm definitely missing something," I say, pausing by the back door, not willing to go out there without a little heads up when Angella is on the warpath, especially if it's coming my way. "It's not twelve yet. I'm still on time."

"Are you though?" she questions, glancing back at me, her lips quirked into an amused grin before barely managing to get the door open. She steps outside but pauses again. "You know how Mom is. When there's a lunch, there's an unspoken rule to get here ridiculously early, but when it's a big birthday . . ."

She lets her words trail off, willing me to put the pieces together myself, and the second it hits me, my eyes widen. "Oh fuck," I breathe, glancing past Aspen to Angella, who's standing out back, busily fussing over the outdoor setting. "I'm screwed."

"That you are," Aspen laughs. "I knew today was going to be a good day."

She sashays away, and I refrain from dropping my gaze to her ass, repeating the mantra that's been showing up more often than not—*she's my best friend's little sister. I will never cross that line.*

Making my way outside, I meet Angella's haunting stare, and I put all the plates down before stepping right into her. "I'm sorry I'm late, Angie," I tell her straight up, knowing she can't resist it when you come straight out with the truth instead of trying to make up some bullshit excuse like Austin and Aspen do.

She fixes me with a hard stare, and I pull her into my arms, dropping a kiss to her cheek. "Happy birthday, Mom."

She sobers immediately, and before she even says a word, I know I've been forgiven. She's always loved it the few times I've called her Mom. The first time, it was an accident. I was only a kid and it spurted out, but the warmth in her eyes when it happened has always stuck with me, and despite not being one of her biological children, I know she's always loved me as a son.

"Thank you, Izaac, but like I said to Aspen, no amount of flattery will save you," she tells me, pulling back. "You and Austin are on dishes, and the dishwasher is off-limits."

My face falls, horror booming in my chest as I glance at the table while recalling just how many dishes are still inside. Angella must have used every single dish in the house. "You mean . . .?"

"Yep, you've gotta scrub the good china by hand. And I'll tell you what, there better not be a single mark left on those plates."

"Shit," I say with a heavy sigh.

Ten minutes later, after checking in with Marc and Austin and helping Aspen with the rest of the table setting, we all sit down to lunch, basking in the sunlight. It's a great day made even better by greater company, even if it means spending the rest of my life scrubbing dishes.

Marc sits at the head of the table as usual, his wife directly to his left and Austin to his right. Aspen sits beside her, putting her directly in front of me, and as she eats, I can't help but watch her with that same curiosity I felt earlier, sensing that change again and driving myself insane trying to figure out what it could be.

The dating suspicion is definitely plausible. Any man with a pulse would want her, but if she were with someone, Austin would have mentioned it, only because it would have driven him insane. He wouldn't be able to keep it to himself and would have turned into a sixteen-year-old girl stalking some asshole online until he figured out what color underwear the guy's mother prefers.

I need to figure this out, but on the other hand, why the fuck do I care so much? It's none of my damn business if she's dating someone, and she already has an overprotective brother to sniff out the losers. This isn't my problem unless Austin says it's *our* problem, right?

Before I can stop myself, my leg stretches out under the table, brushing against hers until her gaze snaps up, and I watch her carefully. Her eyes meet mine, and despite her brother sitting right beside me, I wink . . . and then I wait.

My gaze lingers on her full cheeks, waiting for that deep blush that always takes over every time I touch her.

I wait a second, then ten . . . twenty, and nothing!

What in the ever-loving fuck?

No blush?

Since when does Aspen Ryder not blush when I touch her, accidental or not? Hell, her cheeks should be burning with a wink like that. Something is definitely going on.

She has to have met someone, and despite how Austin and I feel about her being too damn good for any man roaming this earth, I have to somehow convince myself that this is a good thing. Maybe if she finally moves on and finds whatever it is she's looking for, I won't have to constantly wonder if I'm sending the wrong signals. Things could finally be easy between us.

"How're those clubs of yours going?" Marc asks from across the table.

My gaze snaps to Marc's, needing a minute to repeat his comment inside my head to actually figure out what the fuck he's asking me as I try not to think about the prospect of his daughter fucking some random asshole.

"Good," I tell him. "I was at Scandal most of the night looking over a proposal for a new club."

"What?" Aspen breathes, her gaze snapping to mine as she gapes at me. "Another one? Didn't we only go to Scandal's grand opening like . . . eight months ago?"

I nod, pride swirling in my chest. My nightclubs—Pulse, Cherry, and Scandal—are my fucking babies. "Sure did."

"Wow. That's really impressive," Angella says. "You must really be making a name for yourself in the industry. Before you know it, you'll have a club in every state and your name will be hailed among drunken college kids across the country."

A smirk pulls at my lips. "That's the plan."

"Really?" Aspen questions, her eyes flashing with awe. "You really want to expand across the country?"

"Yeah. At least, that's the long-term goal. Short term, I just want to get my current clubs running to the point where I'm not needed to overlook the day-to-day bullshit. After that, I can focus on growth."

Austin scoffs beside me, nudging his elbow into my ribs. "You sound like your father."

"That a bad thing?"

"Nah. I just wish some of that business sense would have rubbed off on me over the years," he says. "I could have used it this week."

My brows furrow, needing to know what the hell he's talking about, but Marc beats me to the punch. "What's going on? I thought everything was going well with the new restaurant. The kitchen was going in this week, right?"

"It was," he says, glancing at his father, disappointment heavy in his tone. "We were set to start building yesterday when the architect was going over his designs and realized he miscalculated where the gas lines run, and now the whole fucking project is at a standstill. We'll probably need a complete redesign, which would put us back months, and until then, the restaurant will be nothing but an empty shell."

"You can't just move the gas lines to match up with the kitchen layout?" Aspen asks.

"Technically, yes," Austin says. "But I know what you're thinking, and it's not quite that simple. There's a lot to consider with the age of the building and just how much destruction we'd have to do in order to move them. Even though it would be a good fix that'll keep me on track with the original design and save me from having to put in a new custom kitchen order, it could also turn into a really big pain in my ass."

"Shit," I say. "That bad, huh? Let me put in a call with my team. They're on other assignments right now, but I'm sure they could spare an afternoon to come down and help you figure out your best course of action. I assume you're in the market for a new architect too?"

"Yep. Didn't even need to fire that asshole, he just knew it was time to pack up his shit and leave."

Angella reaches across the table and takes Austin's hand. "I'm sorry, love," she says. "Is there anything we can do to help?"

Austin offers his mother a small smile. "Thanks, but between me and Izaac, I think we can get it handled," he says as his small smile turns into a full-blown smirk. "Unless not doing the dishes is in the cards?"

Angella sits back in her chair, pulling her hand away from Austin's and rolling her eyes. "No chance in hell," she says, sparing a knowing glance toward Aspen when her brows furrow. Her gaze locks onto something, and she reaches for Aspen. "What on earth is that?" she demands in horror. "Did you . . . did you get a tattoo?"

Every eye at the table shoots toward Aspen in shock as Angella grips her wrist and gapes at the gold moth that's all too fucking familiar.

My chest constricts, my eyes widening as Austin freezes beside me, knowing exactly what that gold moth is. Hell, I was the one who hired the designer to create it, but how the fuck did it end up on her wrist?

"What? No," Aspen says to her mother, clearly unaware of the horror drumming through my veins. "It's just one of those nightclub stamps. Becs dragged me out last night, and I completely forgot it was there. I rushed through my shower this morning, and I suppose I forgot to scrub it off."

That fucking liar. *Just one of those nightclub stamps?* Bullshit.

Angella narrows her gaze on Aspen, dipping her finger in her water and scrubbing at the stamp, just to make sure she's not lying, and when the stamp begins to smudge across her slim wrist, both Marc and Angella relax.

Only Austin and I don't.

Because that stamp isn't just a stamp to any nightclub like the three I own. It's the exact stamp to the exclusive, underground sex club I make sure people have no fucking idea that I own. A stamp that would put her in the VIP lounge. The very same lounge where, just last night, I spent hours indulging in a beautiful woman, touching her in ways she'd never been touched before.

It's not a club for the faint of heart. I built it specifically for members to explore their sexual fantasies, push their limits, and be free to do things they wouldn't get the chance to do in the privacy of their own homes. A place where they can find willing partners who will do the things a loving partner maybe isn't comfortable with.

In some ways, it's fucked up, but in others, like last night, it's never been so fucking right. But one thing is for sure, Vixen is the kind of club that a sweet, innocent soul like Aspen Ryder shouldn't know a damn thing about.

But if she does, then perhaps she's not quite the sweet, innocent soul I've always assumed her to be. And suddenly, I'm willing to cross every fucking line to find out.

6

IZAAC

Grabbing the dish towel, I blindly dry Angella's good china as my gaze remains locked out the window, watching Aspen as she makes her way out to the pool, wearing a swimsuit that has me weak at the knees, the firm globes of her ass staring back at me as if begging me to take a bite.

But all I can think about is that fucking stamp.

Actually, scratch that. Make it two things.

That stamp and whatever it is that's changed about her. I've never seen her like this, so full of confidence. She's fucking radiant, and while it looks absolutely stunning on her, chances are good she's dating someone, and I bet that asshole is the one who brought her to Vixen last night. She said her friend Becs was the one who dragged her out, but I doubt it. Over the past twenty minutes, sitting across from her and feeling the tension rolling off Austin, I suddenly found myself wondering if I truly know her at all.

Fuck. What the hell is wrong with me?

Austin slams a plate down on the drying rack before grabbing another and dunking it into the sink, not even bothering to look if the plate is getting clean. His gaze is locked out the window, just like mine. Only I can guarantee he's not staring at his sister's ass like I am.

"What the fuck was she even doing there?" he hisses, keeping his voice low so that his parents can't hear us from the living room.

"What do you think she was doing there?" I throw back at him. "It's a *sex* club, Austin. You've been there plenty of times. You know the drill. She was obviously—"

"STOP!" he grits through his teeth, almost breaking one of his mother's fancy plates. "Don't even think about finishing that fucking sentence."

I roll my eyes. Is he that delusional that he doesn't think his sister is having sex? Hell, she's a senior in college, she's probably fucking more than Austin is. He lost his virginity at fourteen to some cheerleader who ended up breaking his fragile little heart, and as for Aspen, she's twenty-two now. I can guarantee that ship sailed a long time ago, but that's not exactly something I should remind him of right now. Actually, ever. Not unless I want to spend the rest of the weekend nursing a concussion.

I watch Aspen take her long chestnut hair and curl it up into a bun before reaching for her cocktail glass. She takes a sip, every movement done so slowly as if knowing she has my full attention.

I'm on the fucking edge. I need to get a grip.

Putting the plate down, I grab the next, furiously drying it as though it personally offended me.

Austin lets out a heavy sigh. "You were there last night, right?" he questions. "Didn't you see her? You always check the logs. You must have seen her name."

I shake my head. "Trust me, if I fucking saw her, I would have marched her ass right out of there," I tell him, knowing damn well I'm lying. Morbid curiosity would have had me watching every fucking second, watching how she moved, how she liked it, and the way her face scrunched up when she came . . . and then, I probably would have jerked off in the bathroom like a fucking horny teenager. But Austin doesn't need to know that. Just because physical lines have firmly been drawn doesn't mean my mind hasn't wandered once or twice. "Besides, I was only there for a few hours before heading to Scandal, and for those few hours that I was there . . . I wasn't exactly catching up on my paperwork."

"FUCK!"

Austin drops the plate back into the sink before clutching the side of the counter and glaring daggers at his sister outside. "I want her scrubbed off all of the security footage and banned from the guest list. If she shows up again, she's to be turned away."

"Already made a note to do it."

"It's gotta be you," he says. "I don't want your security team looking up that footage and watching her like that."

Fuck. As curious as I am to see her like that, I know I shouldn't, but my back is against the wall. He's right, I'll be dead and buried before I allow anyone else to see that footage of her. But there's no denying it, seeing it for myself is going to cross boundaries I won't be able to come back from. I won't be able to look at her without remembering what I saw, and if I like it . . . well, fuck.

"Alright," I finally agree.

Letting out a heavy breath, I glance back out the window, watching as Aspen makes her way across the pool and settles at the far side, hooking her arms over the waterfall edge and gazing out at the afternoon view as she sips her cocktail.

"You've gotta ask her about it," Austin says after a moment.

"What?" I demand, my eyes going wide, horror filling my chest. "I'm not asking your fucking sister about what she did at my club."

"No, not . . . I don't want to know that shit," he says in disgust. "I just need to know what she knows. Like if she knew where she was going or if that friend of hers sprung it on her and dragged her in before she got a chance to figure out what she was getting into."

"Either way, you know my hostesses vet everyone who walks through the door. Whether it was her first time or not, she would have known exactly what she was walking into before entering the main club."

He takes a shaky breath, looking as though he's ready to fucking burst. "Just fucking ask her, okay?"

"Why me? She's your sister. I don't want to be asking her that shit."

"And you think I do?" he throws back at me, gripping another plate in a chokehold. "But like you said, she's my sister, and there are just some things a brother can't talk to his little sister about, and her participation at an underground sex club is one of them. So, man the fuck up, Izaac. You're taking point on this one."

"Damn it," I groan, hating how right he is. It has to be me.

I blow my cheeks out, not having the faintest idea how I'm supposed to broach this topic with Aspen. I make a point not to talk to her about anything real, specifically to avoid emotion entering the conversation. But now this? Asking about her sex life? That's diving right into the deep end of a pool I know I'll drown in.

I'm not ready for it, but the truth of the matter is, if she's fucking around at my club, I need to know, and there are certain things she'll need to know in order to feel comfortable there. I'm sure if she knew I owned Vixen, it would have been the last place she would have gone. But having said that, if participating at sex clubs is what she's down for, then I'd prefer she spend her time at Vixen because I can personally guarantee her safety. All of our members and employees have background checks, and on top of that, they go through regular health screens to make sure no diseases are spread throughout my club. As for the other clubs scattered around the city, they don't offer the same high standards.

I find myself watching her again as I silently dry the dishes, making a nice stack of clean plates beside me. We're halfway through when the question that's been bugging me all day slips out of my mouth. "Do you think something's up with her?" I ask, the curiosity far too obvious in my tone, but thankfully for Austin's sour mood, he doesn't pick up on it.

"I haven't noticed shit," he says. "What are you talking about?"

I shrug my shoulders. "Don't know. She's just acting differently. You think maybe she's seeing someone?"

"Right," he scoffs. "Because she clearly loves telling me all her dirty little secrets."

There's a note in his tone, and as I glance toward him, I realize he's hurt, and while I'm sure he was blindsided about finding that stamp on her wrist, she's usually an open book, with him at least. They've always been close, but the idea of her seeing someone and not talking to him about it doesn't sit well with him. Though, I can't exactly blame her. Austin isn't known for taking that kind of news very well. Perhaps she's learned from previous experiences, or perhaps she just doesn't care to splash her business all over the world for everyone to see.

I take the plate out of his hand. "Alright, if I talk to her about all of this shit, would you promise to chill out? It's your mom's birthday, and I don't want you fucking it up for her."

"Yeah, whatever," he mutters under his breath before motioning toward all the ingredients Aspen left on the counter for her cocktail. "You wanna get her talking, then make her another one of those, and make it strong."

Once all the dishes are washed and put away and Austin is sulking in his childhood bedroom, I take a shaky breath, feeling like a fucking pervert as I stride toward the pool with two cocktails in my hands.

What kind of asshole asks his best friend's little sister about her experience at a sex club?

Fucking hell. I've never dreaded anything more.

My gaze remains locked on her back as she continues gazing out at the incredible view, and I notice the exact moment she realizes I'm here. Her body tenses, her back stiffening as the soft muscles in her arms tighten. She glances back over her bare shoulder, those deadly green eyes coming right to mine just as I step up to the side of the pool.

"Figured you might need another one of these," I say, holding out the cocktail toward her.

"God, yes," she says in a deep, gravelly tone that somehow reminds me of the innocent woman I was with in the private room last night. There was something so pure about her, so vulnerable and trusting, and for the first time, it made me stop and think about who I was with. I've never invited a woman to come back for more. My club is about other people and their needs, but I needed to taste her again, needed to feel the way her sweet pussy pulsed around me.

I've never nicknamed a woman at the club, but the second I touched her and felt that pure innocence about her, the name Little Birdy formed in my head, and the second the words fell from my lips, I couldn't stop myself.

It felt right.

Aspen makes her way to the edge of the pool and reaches up to take the glass out of my hand before taking a hesitant sip and scrunching her face. "Holy shit. Is this just straight tequila?"

I grin. "Pretty much."

"Jesus. And to think you own three clubs."

Four.

"Just because I own them, doesn't mean I know shit about mixing drinks," I say, loving the easy conversation between us and how it seems so refreshing. "You want a beer, I got you, but the second you start ordering the girly shit, I'm out."

Aspen laughs and moves back to the edge of the pool where her finished glass and her phone sit patiently awaiting her return. I put my full glass down before reaching behind my neck and shrugging out of my shirt. I toss it to the ground as she turns back and stares at me. "What are you doing?"

"Uhhh . . . going for a swim."

Her gaze narrows with a deep suspicion. "I've known you all my life, Izaac, and I don't think you've ever come for a swim with me."

"Bullshit. We swim all the time."

"Without Austin?" she challenges. "I'd go as far as to accuse you of purposefully avoiding swimming with me."

She's not wrong.

Her eyes sparkle, and for just a second, I could have sworn she was flirting with me. But that couldn't be right. She's too careful around me. She puts real effort into not crossing that invisible line. But then again, she's on her second cocktail after demolishing a whole bottle of champagne with her mom over lunch.

"Don't know what you're talking about," I grin, not prepared to admit that she's right despite both of us knowing damn well she is.

"Sure," she scoffs, and with that, I dive into the huge pool.

I glide under the water, not coming up until I'm right next to her, and when I do, I find her curious gaze locked on me. I shake my head, droplets of water dancing across the pool as I move in behind her, being careful not to brush against her as I reach around and pluck her glass from the edge of the pool.

"Hey," she snaps, but it's too late, the glass is already at my lips.

I take a step back, putting some space between us before almost choking on her drink. "The fuck is this shit? That's terrible."

"You made it," she laughs, taking the glass back and having another sip before splashing water up over me, the smile across her face making something ache inside my chest.

I can't help but stand back and watch her, holding her green stare and getting lost within it. "There's something different about you today," I tell her.

Something sparkles in her eyes, and judging by the knowing grin creeping across her face, she knows exactly what I'm talking about, only she's keeping it to herself. I knew she wouldn't make this easy on me.

"Did you find yourself some hotshot lawyer at that fancy school of yours?" I question, the curiosity killing me.

"Ha. Don't you think Mom would already be trying to plan my wedding if I was hooking up with some hotshot lawyer?"

"Good point," I laugh, slowly moving back toward her as a strange relief pounds through my veins. Okay, so if she's not dating anyone, then what the fuck has gotten into her?

Deciding it's none of my business, I shift gears and get into the reason why I'm actually here. "So, lunch was intense."

Aspen groans. "You mean with Austin?" she asks, glancing at me over her shoulder. I nod and she goes on, focusing her attention back on the view. "I don't get his problem. Surely he's not pissed because I went out to some club. He of all people should be down with it. Maybe he was too drunk to remember, but I was the one picking both of your stupid asses up when you could barely walk a straight line, and he knows I'm not nearly as irresponsible as you two were. Besides, it's not like I'm some sixteen-year-old teenager sneaking out of my bedroom window. I'm an adult."

I laugh to myself, wondering how the hell this got so off track. Forgetting all about the line I said I would never cross, I find myself stepping right into her back, so much closer than I was before.

What the fuck am I doing?

Aspen stiffens, her bare back pressed against my chest. My hand automatically comes to her waist as my other trails down her arm, leading down to the stamp at the base of her wrist. I hear her soft gasp, and that one sound throws me back into the private room at Vixen when I searched out the two wristbands on the woman's arm. It was so eerily similar to this moment.

That's twice she's reminded me of her.

My hand tightens on her waist, and Aspen sucks in a breath as my fingers trail right down to her wrist, my thumb stroking over the gold moth. "You and I both know this isn't an ordinary club stamp," I murmur in her ear, her whole body trembling under my touch. Fuck, why the hell do I like it so much? Austin would murder me if he glanced out his bedroom window right now. This isn't a risk I should be taking. "I know every fucking club in this town, and there's only one with a stamp like that."

My hand continues down, my fingers gripping her hand, and she closes her fingers around mine, clutching it like a lifeline, as if her basic instincts are to hold on to me and never let go. "Don't know what you're talking about," she says, her voice shaky as she repeats the exact words I'd said to her only a minute ago. Only I was lying then, just as she's lying now.

"Uh-huh," I rumble. "What were you doing at Vixen, Aspen?"

"Nothing," she finally says. "I was just checking it out. Becs scored an invite with a plus one and asked me to come along. Up until we walked down the stairs and some woman handed me a menu of . . . *experiences,* I thought we were going to some exclusive nightclub."

"So, you were just checking it out?"

"What's it to you?" she asks, her voice becoming breathy as her bun comes loose. Her long chestnut hair unravels, tumbling down between us, the tips plunging into the cool water. "How do *you* know about that club?"

"I make it my business to know about every club in the city."

"And Austin? I suppose you're going to try and tell me that you both know about this mysterious club and aren't frequent flyers?" she asks, releasing my hand as her chest heaves with heavy breaths.

"What Austin does with his spare time is his business," I say, releasing her waist as I take hold of her long hair to pull it out of the water, only I'm struck with another memory of the woman, of winding my hand into her thick hair—hair that was up in a long ponytail just like Aspen's.

I scoop her hair over her shoulder, leaning forward just enough to be hit with the scent of her perfume, and I pause, recognizing that smell, only the last time I smelled it, it was mixed with the scent of arousal.

Her arousal?

"And you?" she goes on, not noticing the way my body stiffens with horror as all the fucking pieces begin to fall into place. Her hair. Her waist. Her wrist. Her perfume. There are too many similarities to be coincidental.

My heart lurches in my chest, horror gripping me in a chokehold.

Holy fuck. What have I done?

Aspen wasn't just checking out the club last night. She was the woman in the dark room. She was the woman I spent the night sinking into. She's the woman who had me falling apart, who had me coming harder than I ever had before.

No.

I take a hasty step back, my heart pounding so fucking hard in my chest, it threatens to destroy me.

Not only did I fuck Aspen Ryder, *my best friend's little sister,* I took her virginity. I clutched onto the two wristbands—white and red—and shamelessly claimed them both.

How could I not know it was her?

I start retracing every second of last night, wondering how the fuck she ended up in my private room. Out of all the women who could have wandered in there last night, why did it have to be her?

And why did being inside her have to be the best fucking feeling in the world?

The way she fit me, the way she took me.

Fuck.

We've crossed a line, one we can't come back from. I thought viewing her through the security feed was going to destroy me, but actually knowing what it *feels* like to be inside her, how it feels when her tight little cunt shatters around me, how she tastes and sounds when she comes . . . FUCK!

Aspen turns, looking up at me with those trusting eyes, and it's clear she has no fucking idea the man she was with last night was me. That change in her today, the reason she's filled with newfound confidence and glowing like a fucking angel is because of me, because I took something from her—her purity. Her virginity. I took it without a second thought.

Stolen in the dead of night. I robbed her blind.

How the hell could I let this happen?

A moment that she's looking back on with absolute bliss is anything but. It's a lie. A betrayal.

I fucked her raw, made her come three times—once on my tongue and the others on my cock. I robbed her of her virginity and then bent her over and emptied myself inside of her without a second of hesitation.

Shit!

Aspen is my innocent Little Bird.

Austin is going to kill me.

Aspen inches toward me, her brows furrowed, and with every step she takes, my heart thunders just a little bit faster. "Are you okay?" she asks, deep concern flashing in her eyes, and I realize that I can never let her know. It's one thing for her to explore her sexual boundaries in my club, but if she ever found out that we were together, that I was the man she gave her virginity to, things will never be the same.

I will go on knowing that I will never find a woman who can compare to the way she made me feel last night, but I don't want that for her. We were like fire together. The chemistry that burned between our bodies was like nothing I've ever experienced. She responded to my every touch as though we were made to fit together. But it can never happen again, and she can never know.

If she found out, she would feel betrayed, and she'd have every reason to. She offered her virginity to a faceless stranger in a club, not to me. And while I had no idea that it was her, I feel a responsibility for her. I've always wanted to protect her, but this . . . I've taken something from her that didn't belong to me.

She deserves so much better, and I'm going to make sure she gets it.

"I uhh . . . just realized I was supposed to submit some applications for Scandal by close of business last night and it completely slipped my mind."

"Oh, you better get that sorted out," she says, retreating back to her glass and drinking what's left in the bottom.

I nod before pointing to my full one over by the edge of the pool. "Help yourself to mine," I tell her, turning away before finding myself pausing. "Hey, listen, I booked out that restaurant your mom loves for your dad to take her out tonight and figured while they were out, we should hit up Pulse. I've gotta check in with a few things, and I know with all the bullshit going on with Austin's restaurant, he could really use a night to relax. What do you say?"

Aspen glances back to the view, clearly conflicted. "I don't know. I had a really late night. I'm working on only a few hours sleep."

"We don't need to leave for a while. Take a nap."

Her face scrunches again, and I have to force myself to take another step back to keep from remembering the way it felt as I pushed inside of her and the way she whimpered when her walls stretched around me.

Fuck. I need to erase this from my mind.

How could I not know it was her?

"I don't know," she murmurs. "Could I bring Becs?"

"By all means, but if she starts dancing on my bar again, I'll put her in an Uber and send her ass home."

A grin stretches across Aspen's face, and just like that, I know she's in. "Alright, fine," she finally says. "But if you and Austin are boring, we're out. You're not taking us out just to sit around in some lousy booth, talking about the good old days when you used to do crazy shit. If we're doing this, we're doing it right, and we're all getting fucked up. I want at least three of us hurling in Mom's rose bushes."

"She'll kill you."

"She will," Aspen agrees. "But it'll be worth it."

I laugh, and with that, I walk away, wondering how sick I must be to want to fuck my best friend's sister all over again.

7

ASPEN

"Damn, Aspen. Your brother is looking like a snack," Becs says as we arrive at the first club Izaac built, Pulse. We haven't been here for a while, and despite only celebrating its fifth anniversary last month and still being considered new in the grand scheme of things, I can't help but gape at the renovations. I've gotta give it to Izaac, he knows how to keep his clubs relevant, and damn, he does a great job of it.

"Don't even think about it," I tell her as my gaze sails over the upgraded bar and the new mezzanine level that overlooks the sprawling dance floor. "I don't care if you were the last two beings on earth and it was up to you to keep the human race alive, you're still not sleeping with him."

"Why does he look so . . . feisty?" she murmurs, her gaze sailing up and down his body as he stands with Izaac by one of the many bars. He's been an ass ever since Mom so kindly pointed out the gold stamp on my wrist during lunch, and it's clear he knows exactly what it means. Hell, when Izaac pointed it out, I couldn't have been more humiliated. It's one thing for Izaac to know how I spent my night, but Austin . . . shit. I was hoping the night out and a few beers would help him calm down, but judging by the look on his face, either someone just accidentally kneed him in the balls, or he's still pissed. "Whatever you did to piss him off, I approve. I bet he'd fuck like an animal in a mood like this. He needs a distraction, and that distraction is going to be me."

Damn. There's no denying that giving Austin a distraction would make my night so much easier. But still . . . I can't allow it to happen.

"I call girl code," I tell her. "He's been an asshole about my feelings for Izaac since I first sprouted a pair of tits. He would blow up every time someone even joked about it, and now I break out in a sweat whenever anyone even mentions Izaac's name around Austin. So no, on principle, you don't get to make him your project tonight. If I can't even be allowed to like Izaac, then he sure as hell does not get to sleep with my best friend. Find some other desperate loser to screw in the back alley. I'm sure it won't be hard."

"Ugh," she groans. "Don't be a party pooper! Just think about it, if I'm keeping Austin busy, then you and Izaac . . ."

She trails off, leaving her suggestive words to hang heavily in the air between us, tempting me with insinuations that are only going to get me in trouble. But damn it, there's no denying that she has a point. If Austin and Becs are busy . . . doing whatever they might be doing, then I'll have all the time in the world with Izaac. Not that it'll actually go anywhere. Though, he was certainly forward in the pool after lunch. He's never touched me like that before. The way he moved in behind me, pressing his wide chest against my back, and how his big hand curled around my wrist and roamed over the shimmering gold stamp. My body came alive with his touch, but deep down, he was only trying to coax information out of me the best way he knew how, and it worked like a charm.

I scoff, trying to downplay just how much I wish things could be that easy. "I could be standing in front of Izaac in the nude, wearing nothing but a pair of black heels and a big red bow, and he still wouldn't notice," I say, starting to lower my voice as we approach the guys. "So, no. If I don't get to have a wild night with my brother's best friend, then you don't get to have a wild night with your best friend's brother."

"Damn," she sighs. "Can I at least flirt just a little?"

"To your heart's content," I laugh.

Becs grins back at me, her arm looped tightly around mine as we finally meet up with the guys, and just as always, when Izaac's gaze lifts to mine, my knees turn to Jell-O, and I have to pause to keep myself from crumbling.

"About time you ladies got here," Izaac says in that deep tone that stirs something wild within me. His gaze roams over my face, rendering me speechless as something wicked flashes in his eyes, something I've never seen before, but damn, the way it has my pulse racing has me desperate for more.

He's been weird since the pool this afternoon, like something rattled him, and I don't buy his excuse about submitting papers for Scandal. The thing about wanting someone for so long in the way that I've wanted him, you learn about them. You learn what makes them tick, what gets under their skin, every single one of their tells, and when it comes to Izaac Banks, I know everything. He was lying. There was no application he needed to submit, something else rattled him, and I can't help but wonder if it was me.

"Can't rush perfection," Becs says, indicating our bodies and the stunning outfits she pulled together while also saving me from awkward silence.

Izaac's gaze drops down my body, slowly dragging over my chest and waist before sailing right down past my thighs and to my heels. He leisurely makes his way back up, a knowing smirk lingering on his lips before meeting my stare with a deep appreciation in his dark eyes. "No, you can't," he rumbles.

Oh fucccck. Why is there suddenly a fire burning between my legs? And why the hell is he looking at me like that, especially in front of Austin? He's purposefully gone out of his way not to look at me like this over the past few years.

Izaac holds my stare as my heart beats right out of my fucking chest, and when Becs clears her throat, the spell is suddenly broken. I look away just in time to catch Austin rolling his eyes as an irritated scoff tears from the back of his throat. He grabs his glass and takes a swift drink, chugging nearly half of it before slamming it back down on the bar, way too roughly to be considered safe.

He doesn't say a word, but I know my brother well enough to know that he's not going to be able to let this go. He's going to ruin the whole night if I allow him to, and I didn't give Becs full authority over my outfit only for my asshole brother to let his bad mood rub off on me.

"Ugh, seriously?" I groan. "It wasn't enough for you to ruin Mom's birthday lunch, now you have to ruin tonight as well?"

Austin's head whips back toward me, fury pulsing in his eyes. "You're fucking kidding me, right?" he demands. "I'm the one who ruined Mom's lunch? Get fucked, Aspen. I love you, but you're fucking delusional. You're the one who showed up with the Vixen stamp on your wrist. All this bullshit today, this is on you."

"Fucking hell, Austin. You're such a hypocrite."

His eyes practically bulge out of his skull. "A hypocrite?" he sputters.

"You heard me," I throw back at him. "You knew exactly what that stamp was, and considering the club's exclusivity, the only way to know is if you had been there yourself. Which means, Austin. You're a fucking hypocrite. Why is it okay for you to go and not for me?"

He gives me a blank stare. "Because you're . . . you're a good girl. You don't do shit like that. You're supposed to be better than me."

I scoff. "You're not making it hard."

"Oooooh shit," Becs says, sucking in a breath.

Austin shakes his head, looking at me like I'm a stranger. "Low fucking blow."

"You wanna talk low blows?" I demand, inching closer and putting myself in front of Izaac to get closer to my brother, anger rolling through me. "A low blow is suggesting that just because I might have got a little freaky one night suddenly means I'm no good. Fuck you, Austin. I'm twenty-two. I'm not a fucking kid anymore. So what if maybe I like being fucked by a bunch of men in a room full of strangers."

"FUCK!" Fury ripples across his face and he flies to his feet, his dark gaze shooting to Izaac's with a strange betrayal that I can't for the life of me begin to understand. It's gone just as quickly as it came, but I don't have time to process before that fury is aimed at me. He steps into me, moments away from breaking. "Tell me you didn't."

"So what if I did?" I spit at him, knowing damn well I'm only making matters worse, but the fucker deserves it. "Does that make me a whore for enjoying sex just like every other fucking human being in this place? Just like I'm sure you do. I'm still your little sister, Austin. I'm still the same person I've always been. But what it comes down to is that my sex life is none of your damn business."

His jaw clenches when a big arm locks around my waist and I'm lifted off my feet. "Alright, that's enough," Izaac says, pulling me away before I get the chance to gouge my brother's eyes out. "You two are not about to have it out in the middle of my club."

"Let me at him. I'm going to tear his balls right off his body."

Izaac scoffs, placing me back on my feet and giving me a shove to get me moving. "Is that a newfound kink of yours?" he murmurs in my ear, and if I wasn't so worked up over Austin's disapproval, I'd be a mess at just the thought of Izaac Banks saying the word kink anywhere near me.

Instead, I shove my elbow back into his stomach. "My brother's balls and the word kink should never be mentioned in the same conversation."

Izaac laughs, his hand dropping to my lower back and leading me to the other end of the massive bar. "Do you think you can manage sitting your ass down without getting into a fight with any of my paying customers?"

I roll my eyes and drop my ass onto one of the barstools as Izaac steps around me and makes his way to the other side of the bar. "He's an asshole," I remind Izaac, just in case he might have forgotten in the last ten seconds.

"He's overprotective and in shock. There's a difference," he says, grabbing a glass and throwing something together, though I hope that's not for me because the drink he made me this afternoon was terrible. I can't imagine this would be any better. "He would have been less surprised if you'd come home and announced you were marrying an Egyptian prince. Learning your little sister went to a sex club . . . that takes a minute for a man to process. Besides, you and I both know you were baiting him."

"I was not."

"You were, Aspen," he chides, his gaze darting back down the long bar to where Becs flirts animatedly with Austin, instantly getting under my skin, despite how I'd told her to flirt to her heart's content. I suddenly don't feel so generous. "Besides, no hate to Becs, but between the two of you, if someone were having a wild orgy in front of a bunch of strangers, it'd be her. Not you. That's not your thing."

"Oh," I say, my brow arching. "And you suddenly know what my *thing* is?"

A smirk stretches across Izaac's lips, and he glances up at me through a thick row of dark lashes, and something clenches deep in my core. He doesn't say a word, but the look in his eyes suggests he knows exactly what my thing is.

Izaac holds my stare a moment too long before finally dropping his gaze and breaking the hold he has over me, giving me just a moment to breathe.

What the hell has gotten into him today? Perhaps he fell and smacked his head and is currently nursing a concussion. This bold, handsy version of him is messing with my head. The Izaac I know goes out of his way to remind me nothing will ever happen between us, but the way he keeps looking at me and making excuses to touch me . . . shit. I don't know what to make of this. He's making me feel things he and I both know I shouldn't be feeling, but the more attention he feeds me, the hungrier I get.

"Here," he finally says, handing me the drink he's been busily working on. "Drink this and wait here while you cool down. I need to meet with my bar manager and figure out what's going on with our stock. I'll be ten minutes tops. Do you think you can keep yourself out of trouble for that long?"

A smirk lifts my lips. "Who knows? I've been feeling a little . . . wild since last night," I say, baiting him as I turn to look out at the people who've come to have a great night. "I might need to find someone to throw me up against the bathroom wall."

"Fucking hell," Izaac mutters under his breath. "You're gonna get me in trouble."

I glance back at him just in time to catch his eye before he turns and walks away.

Now, why the hell would the idea of me screwing some random guy get him in trouble?

I watch as he leaves, stopping by some woman and pulling her aside. She grabs a folder from under the bar and starts flipping through the pages, but I can't help but notice how often Izaac's gaze wanders back to me. Is he trying to watch out for me to make sure I'm okay? Or is he making sure I'm not running off with some stranger and fucking on his dance floor? I can only imagine what Austin would have to say about that.

At the mere thought of my brother, I grab my drink and lift the glass to my lips, taking a hefty sip, and I'm surprised to find it's not too bad. I keep sipping, and as I do, my gaze lingers on Izaac as he works. He's the perfect definition of a woman's wet dream in his dark button-up shirt. It's been left undone at the top, showing off the perfect amount of his muscled chest, and every time my gaze dips down and lingers there, my mouth begins to water.

He could be Greek or Italian, we don't really know. There were no details in his adoption papers, but he likes to think he's some kind of Greek god, so we've always rolled with that. Every inch of his body is perfected. He's so tall with broad shoulders and bulging muscles. I've never wanted to sink my nails into him more, and with the dim lighting in the club catching on the ridges of his toned body, he's simply delicious.

My drink is practically gone by the time he wanders back across the bar, and seeing my nearly empty glass, he swipes it off the bar and starts working on a new one. "You liked that one, huh?"

I smile. "I suppose your bartending skills aren't as bad as you pretend they are."

Izaac grins before handing me my new drink. He takes another glass and starts working on something for himself. "You calmed down enough to bite your tongue around your brother? Because if not, I'm gonna need to make this a double."

I roll my eyes. "I'm fine," I say. "Besides, from what I can tell, it looks like Becs has sunk her claws into Austin. If she keeps flirting like that, he won't even remember who I am."

Izaac laughs, his gaze lingering on mine. "Not possible," he murmurs before striding around the bar and stepping into my side. "Come on. You said you wanted to get fucked up, and that's exactly what we're going to do."

Getting fucked up with Izaac Banks? Count me the hell in.

We make our way back over to Austin and Becs, and as I step up in front of them, I find Austin settling a heavy glare on Becs as she looks at me with a wicked grin. My brows furrow, wondering what the hell Becs could have done to warrant such hostility from my brother. She turns to him with expectancy. "Don't you have something to say?"

Austin's lips pull into a tight line, anger rolling through his stare as he turns his attention to me. "I'm sorry for being an asshole," he states.

"What you do with your body is none of my business, and I never had the right to question it or make you feel less than because of it."

Both Izaac and I stare at Austin completely dumbfounded. I don't think I've ever heard my brother give a sincere apology to anyone who isn't our mother in his whole life. "The fuck?" I blanch.

"And?" Becs prompts, clearing her throat and giving Austin a nudge.

He lets out a heavy sigh. "And I hope you can accept my apology in the form of shots."

My jaw drops, still gaping at my brother. "Are you ill?" I question, hastily stepping into him and pressing my hand to his forehead. He's not running a fever.

"I'm fine," he mutters, shoving my hand away and rolling his eyes. "Do you want the damn shots or not?"

"Uhhhh, of course. Is that even a real question? But I'll only accept the shots as an apology if you actually pay for them," I state, my chin held high in defiance.

"But I—"

I hold up my finger to silence him. "Telling the bartender to put them on your tab when you know damn well that Izaac is going to wipe it at the end of the night doesn't count. You need to hand over that cold, hard cash brother."

Izaac laughs from behind me, clearly amused as Austin's shoulders sag. "Fine," he mutters, his gaze flicking back to Becs as if seeking some kind of approval. I watch them closely, not sure how she managed to sink her claws so deep in such a short amount of time.

"Now," Becs declares. "Hug it out."

Both Austin and I blanch. Hug? She's got to be kidding herself. Don't get me wrong, I love my brother more than life, but we draw the line at showing any form of physical affection. His way of telling me he loves me is by crash-tackling me onto the couch and sitting on me. There's certainly no hugging.

Austin cringes and turns his gaze back to mine before making a move to get up. He looks as though he just sucked a lemon by accident. He makes a move toward me, his arms going wide and looking just as horrified as I feel when I fix him with a hard stare, crossing my arms over my chest. "If you even think about putting your stanky arms around me, Austin Ryder, I will drop you to the ground so damn fast you won't even know what century we're in."

"Oh, thank fuck," he says with a heavy sigh, retreating so damn fast that it all could have been in my imagination. He holds my stare, relief flashing in his eyes. "That was a close one."

"Tell me about it," I murmur, moving in closer to the bar. "I'm gonna need those shots now."

"Coming right up," Austin says before getting the bartender's attention, and considering Izaac is with us, the bartender immediately caters to us despite the busy lines, making us their most valued VIPs for the night.

As our shots are poured, I glance up at Becs. "What the hell did you do to my brother?"

"Oh nothing," she coos, a smirk pulling at the corner of her lips that has her eyes flashing with silent laughter. "Just helped him to see the error of his ways is all."

"I think you just became my hero," I laugh.

Becs grins, and not a moment later, we're each handed a shot, and I watch with undeniable delight as Austin digs into his wallet and pays. Izaac reaches between me and Austin, scooping up the final shot off the bar. "Wow, never thought I'd see the day you paid for your own drink," Izaac teases Austin as laughter bubbles up my throat.

"Shut up and take your shot," Austin says, and with that, I lift the glass to my lips and tip every last drop down my throat.

8

IZAAC

My arm loops around Austin's back as we climb out of the Uber, trying to hold his drunk ass up as Aspen rushes around his other side, laughing as she mimics my hold. "Okay, maybe he took the whole getting fucked up thing a little too literally," she snickers as Austin tumbles over his feet.

"Ya think?" I mutter, dragging him toward the front door of the home we all grew up in.

"Hey," Austin slurs. "I'm not drunk. I'm just . . . Uh-oh—"

Aspen pauses in the middle of the driveway, bringing us to a halt as she gapes at her brother. "You don't look so—"

Vomit surges from the deepest pits of Austin's guts, redecorating the driveway and narrowly missing Aspen's heels as she hastily jumps away. “Gross, Austin,” she screeches in pure disgust as he doubles over, practically dislodging my shoulder in the process.

Vomit goes everywhere, splattering all through Angella’s rose bushes, and I cringe as I hold my breath, the smell instantly assaulting my nostrils. “Fuck, man. Your mom is gonna kill you.”

“Nah, she loves me. It’ll be fi—Awww fuck—” he starts round two, violently heaving and throwing up every last drop of alcohol lining his stomach, cutting off his delusional words about how his mother isn’t going to tear him a new asshole first thing in the morning.

Aspen makes a wide circle around Austin, putting herself on my other side, and as she stumbles, my hand whips out, catching her by the waist. She clutches my arm, keeping herself upright before laughing at herself. I can’t help but grin. She’s been so carefree tonight. I haven’t seen her like this since . . . Well, I can’t even remember. She danced and fucked around with Becs, the two of them having the night of their lives, and the whole fucking time, I couldn’t take my eyes off her.

I’ve gotta get a grip, but last night at Vixen . . . I can’t get it out of my head, and now every time I look at her, I remember how it felt being inside her, how fucking tight she squeezed my cock when she came.

She can never know. It’ll destroy her. She’ll feel betrayed and violated, and yet watching her move on the dance floor tonight, I wanted her in a way I’ve never wanted her before.

Once Austin is safe to keep walking again, the three of us trudge up the stairs, and I watch with amusement as Aspen fishes through her bra and digs out her front door key. She tries it in the lock at least a hundred times, all while wobbling on her feet, and when I step into her side to take the key out of her hand, she fixes me with a hard stare. "I can do it," she announces before trying again and failing.

"Ugh. Move over," I groan, shoving Austin against the wall and balancing him before stepping into Aspen and taking the key out of her hand. Only being this close, I can smell her, and that heavenly scent does wicked things to me, making me wish I could bend her in a million different ways and take her deep until she's screaming my name.

FUCK!

She's Austin's little sister. I need to forget how fucking wet she was for me, need to forget how sweet she tasted on my tongue.

After finally unlocking the door, I shove it open and collect Austin, who's half asleep against the wall. He sways and trips over his feet as Aspen tries to muffle her laughs. I get him through the living room and past the kitchen where Aspen stops and starts rifling through the cupboards.

After what feels like a fucking hike through the Grand Canyon, I reach Austin's room, shove the door open, and let him tumble right in. He crash lands against his bed and within seconds, he's sound asleep.

I shake my head. This is why he can never take a girl home when he's been drinking. The second his head hits the pillow, it's lights out.

Glancing over him and deciding he's going to be just fine, I switch out the light and turn to step out of his childhood room when I walk right into Aspen. She lets out a soft yelp as she tumbles back, and I quickly reach for her, catching her around the waist.

"Holy shit," she breathes with wide eyes, the glass of water in her hand sloshing around and splashing over the rim. Her gaze rests on mine, and with each burning second between us, my hand tightens. We're locked in each other's stare, and the tension quickly thickens in the air around us.

I feel my heart booming out of my chest, daring me to make some kind of move, and I inch closer, watching as her chin tilts higher, welcoming me in. God, what it'd be like to feel her lips against mine.

"I, uhhh," she starts, her voice low and breathy. "I was just gonna get Austin some water and Aspirin for when he wakes up."

"Austin. Right."

The sound of his name coming out of her mouth is like having a bucket of ice water poured over my head, and I hastily step back, my hand dropping from her slim waist. "Umm . . . yeah. Good idea. Knowing him, he'll need it."

Disappointment flashes in her eyes, but she quickly recovers before giving me a beaming smile and rocking right into the wall, reminding me just how much she drank tonight. Fuck, when the Ryder siblings say they're getting fucked up, they mean every damn word.

"Give me that before you spill it everywhere," I say, reaching out and taking the glass from her hand. I walk back into Austin's room as Aspen follows me in, and I set the glass of water down on his bedside table. She drops the Aspirin beside the glass, and I shake my head, watching as they roll right off the table.

I quickly scoop them off the floor and put them back on the table before finally walking out of Austin's room. Aspen strides out into the hallway, and I close the door behind me. "You good to get to your room without hurting yourself?" I ask.

A smirk stretches across her face, and she steps into me, her hand falling to my chest as she looks up at me, those big green eyes lingering on mine. "If I didn't know better, it would sound as though you were asking if I needed you to take me to bed."

I blanch. "I uh . . . no. I umm. That's not what I—"

Aspen's shrill laughter cuts off my panic, and as she pulls away, I gape at her. "Holy shit, Izaac. The look on your face is priceless. I'm only teasing," she says, turning around and sashaying down the hall. Only she glances back over her shoulder, her gaze hooded and filled with a fire that has a burning desire pumping through my veins. "Unless I'm not."

What the ever-loving fuck?

Aspen disappears down the hall and into her room, and all I can do is stare after her. Did she just invite me to her room?

Holy fuck.

My cock springs to attention, and realizing I'm standing in the middle of the Ryders' hallway with a raging erection, I scurry across the hall and lock myself in the guest room.

She's Austin's little sister. Austin's little sister.

The words play over and over in my mind, yet they do nothing to ease the intense hunger within me. How the fuck does she keep doing this to me? It was one night. I shouldn't want her this way, yet the thought of never getting to taste her again leaves me in physical pain.

After dropping my shirt to the ground and stepping out of my pants, I crash against the mattress, listening to the soft sounds of Aspen moving around in the room directly beside mine. She fumbles and catches herself against the drywall, and as she peels off her boots, there is a familiar thud as they hit the ground. The memory of last night floods my mind again, and I can't stop picturing her dark silhouette propped up on the table as I took those very same boots off her quivering body. A few groans and grunts sound from the wall we share, and judging from the tone of her voice, I can only assume she's trying to get herself out of her dress.

I wonder if she needs help.

FUCK! I need to stop.

Grabbing the pillow from under my head, I yank it out and slam it over my face, trying to block out the sounds coming from her room, only when I hear the familiar sound of her flopping against her bed followed by a low groan, I find myself listening more intently.

She tosses and turns, clearly trying to get comfortable when a soft hum sounds through the room . . . some kind of vibration.

My whole body stiffens. What the fuck is that?

Aspen groans and my dick turns to fucking stone. Either she's brushing her teeth in bed with an electric toothbrush . . . or she's using a vibrator.

Fuck. Fuck. FUCK!

I'm a goner.

Before I can stop myself, my hand shoots inside my underwear, and I fist my heavy cock, squeezing hard and willing myself not to be so fucking turned on by the woman in the next room, but it's impossible.

I've been aware of her all night. Every roll of her body on the dance floor, every brush of her skin against mine as she moved past me.

It's as though she knew how on edge she's had me, but that's not possible. She couldn't know.

"Oh, God," I hear whispered through the walls, and my mind goes crazy, picturing her fucking herself.

What the fuck is wrong with me?

The sweet temptation is too much, and my fist starts moving up and down my thick length, barely able to grip it in my palm, and I let out a shaky breath, unable to keep from picturing her. Her mouth. Her hand. Her body. Everything I shouldn't want.

Then in a moment of pure insanity, I take my phone and open a new text, and with every word I painstakingly write out, I grit my teeth.

Izaac - A lot of noise coming from in there. What are you doing?

I hit send before my brain is capable of reminding me of all the reasons I shouldn't, and not a second later, I hear the soft *ding* of her phone. She scrambles around, and I hear her soft intake of breath as she reads my text and then there's nothing but silence.

Fuck.

That was stupid. I crossed a line . . . again, and now she probably thinks I'm a fucking perv, but isn't that exactly what I am? Listening to her get herself off in the next room.

My phone buzzes in the blankets, and my heart races. This is it.

This is the moment she calls me out on my bullshit. I almost don't want to look.

My hand hesitates over the phone before finally finding the balls to pick it up and swipe my thumb across the screen. My gaze sails right to the words she's written, and with a sharp intake of breath, my grip tightens on my cock as a strange feeling circles the pit of my stomach.

Aspen - I don't think you're ready to know what I'm doing in here.

Fuuuuuuck.

How am I supposed to come back from that?

I hear a laugh from the room next door, and suddenly the humming goes from a slow pulse to a rapid buzz. "Oh fuck," she grits out, her words taking me captive as my fist works up and down, tightening at my tip and trying to keep myself in control. But fuck, there's no denying it now. All sense of control slipped away the second I figured out she was the woman from Vixen last night.

My fingers have never moved across my screen faster.

Izaac - Need a hand?

Aspen - You wish!

A wicked grin cuts across my face. I had no intention of going in there. We're both drunk, and giving in to my impulses now would be fucking reckless, but nobody said I can't have a little fun with it.

Besides, I've already crossed the line. What's the point in trying to backtrack now?

Izaac - Who do you think of when you fuck yourself, Aspen? Is it me? Do you picture the way I'd bend you over and slam into your tight little cunt, taking you so fucking deep that you feel me in your throat?

Ding.

My fist jerks furiously, my hips jolting with excitement as I listen while Aspen scrambles for her phone again. She groans, and as I look at my screen and watch as the read receipt appears below my text, I grin.

"Holy fucking shit," I hear murmured through the drywall.

The three bubbles appear at the bottom of the screen, letting me know she's responding, then they promptly disappear. A second passes, and they show up again, but just like before, they disappear again.

Izaac - Answer me, Aspen.

Izaac - Now.

Izaac - Do you think of me when you fuck yourself?

I've never been so impatient for a response, and then finally, when the three little dots appear, they don't fade away until there's a new text appearing below mine.

Aspen - And if I do?

Aspen - Does the idea of me thinking of you get you hard? Are you fucking yourself right now and wishing it was my mouth on your cock? My tongue working over your tip?

Fuck. And here I thought I was the one being bold. But how the hell am I supposed to answer that? I can't be honest. I can't tell her the filthy things that have been going through my head all night.

Izaac - No.

Aspen - Don't lie to me, Izaac. You might be able to hear me, but that doesn't mean I can't hear you. These walls are paper thin, and you've stayed in that guest room more than enough times for me to know exactly what it sounds like when you're getting yourself off.

Well, shit.

I guess there's no point denying it then.

Izaac - Checkmate.

Izaac - Tell me exactly what you're doing. I need details.

There's a slight pause before she starts typing again.

Aspen - My fingers are brushing over my skin, right at the apex of my thighs, while my vibrator works my clit. It's so fucking

sensitive. I wanna come, but I can't. I'm so fucking desperate, but it's not enough. I need more.

Izaac - Ride your fingers, Aspen. Picture me as you push them inside your sweet little cunt.

"Oh, God," I hear from next door, the hum of her vibrator getting more intense as she works through the levels. My hips jolt, my fist tightening around my cock as I furiously fuck my hand. I clench my jaw, needing this moment to last a lifetime, but knowing that it will never compare to how good it felt while actually being inside of her.

She's the forbidden fruit, and I'm the snake in the garden, all too willing to take what I can't have.

Aspen - Or...you could just come in here and I'll ride you instead.

Izaac - Don't fucking tempt me. If I walk in there right now, we both know what's going to happen, and that's not a line either of us is willing to cross.

The sound of her vibrator fades away and my movements slow, wondering if I've just fucked this up.

Izaac - Don't stop, Aspen. I'm not coming until I hear my name on your lips. Now ride your fucking fingers and think of the way my cock would fill you to the brim, stretch your walls until the point of pain. I know you've wondered how fucking big

I am. Now picture the way I would take you.

The read receipt appears and the vibrator starts again, setting a wide grin across my lips. My breath becomes labored as just the thought of what she's doing pushes me right to the fucking edge. Her needy groans and pants sound through the wall, pushing me further.

Aspen - Holy fuck, Izaac. If you had any idea how wet you've made me…

Izaac - I told you not to fucking tempt me.

Aspen - I'm going to explode…

Izaac - Do it, baby. Let me hear you come for me.

"Oh, fuck," she cries, and there's a thud as something tumbles to the ground. She's panting so heavily that it sounds like she's right next to me, and I raise my hips, feeling ready to explode right along with her. Not a second later, the sweetest sound rocks through the wall between us. "Oh, God. Izaac. Yes!"

I come hard, shooting hot spurts of cum into the palm of my hand as Aspen rides out her high. I close my eyes, my head tilted back against the pillow as I just lay there, my chest heaving with a handful of cum. This really isn't how I anticipated my night to go, but now that it's happened, I can't bring myself to regret it.

I lay in silence, listening to Aspen's breathing slow down until it fades completely, and then after hearing her place something on her bedside table, the three little dots appear on the screen again.

Aspen - He can never know.

I've never agreed to anything so fast in my life.

Izaac - Never.

9

ASPEN

My head pounds as I wake in my old childhood room, last night's extracurricular activities coming back to me in screaming color. Did I really get off while Izaac listened in the next room over, texting me every dirty thing I've always dreamed he would?

I've always wondered if he had a filthy mouth while in the moment, and there's no need to question it any longer. Izaac Banks has got the filthiest mouth I've ever heard . . . or read.

And I fucking loved it.

Only now that the alcohol is no longer buzzing through my veins and my brain cells seem to be waking out of their alcohol-induced fog, last night suddenly doesn't seem as exciting as it had before. It feels like nothing but cold, hard regret.

Why did I allow that to happen? I should have shut it down the second his first text came through, but I've wanted him for so damn long that I couldn't bear the thought of not seeing it through. Now, I somehow have to get out of bed, take a shower, and face him while knowing exactly what's running through his head.

I'm screwed.

How the hell have I gone from practically joining a nunnery to having two insanely crazy sexually-filled nights in a row? Is this what it's like to have finally found my sexual freedom? Or is this just what others like to call insanity? Surely texting my brother's best friend while I was getting off is the kind of bullshit that should have me committed.

Throwing my blanket back, I let out a groan, unsure if it was from the humiliation of having to face Izaac or the killer hangover that pounds through my skull. Grabbing a dress for the day and my makeup bag, I trudge down the hall, being as quiet as possible. Izaac's bedroom door is still closed. The last thing I need is to wake him and have to face the humiliation of what I did so early in the morning. I need at least a double shot of coffee before I'm capable of facing any of that bullshit.

I hurry through a shower, trying to get the remains of last night's spilled drinks off my body before doing what I can to look somewhat human. After drying off, I pull on a pair of loose pants and a cropped tank before working on my hair. I dig through my makeup bag and cover up the dark circles under my eyes from the two late nights in a row before finally glancing over myself and deciding this is as good as it's gonna get. It's certainly not my most daring or breathtaking look, but it'll have to do.

Wanting to be as far from the bathroom as possible when Austin wakes up and goes on another vomit rampage, I grab my pajamas and shove my makeup bag on top before heading for the door. I grab the handle and yank it open, only to find myself barricaded in, a half-naked Izaac standing on the other side, his strong arms gripping the door frame above my head.

My eyes widen, humiliation and horror blasting through my veins. I'm not even close to being ready to deal with what happened last night. I need to make a break for it, but damn, he smells so good, and that body . . . shit. His chest and abs are so defined, and my mouth waters, desperate to reach out and touch him. Hell, I wouldn't mind taking a bite either.

The things I would do to this man . . .

His gaze slowly begins to drop when he lingers on my makeup bag. Confusion brims in my chest when his hand falls from the frame and he dips his fingers into my makeup bag, pulling out the two wristbands I'd shoved in here yesterday morning before I left for Mom's birthday lunch—the very wristbands that tell him exactly just how much sexual experience I have.

He rolls them between his fingers as that dark gaze lifts back to mine, a knowing glimmer flashing in his stare. "Interesting . . ."

Hooooly fuck.

Humiliation slams through me like a fucking wrecking ball, and I snatch them back faster than lightning. I shove the wristbands right back into the bag, feeling the blazing blush burning across my cheeks.

"Is there something you need?" I ask, doing my best to recover, but let's face it, there's no recovering from that because suddenly Izaac Banks doesn't just know that I had sex with a stranger in a club, but that stranger took my virginity—at twenty-fucking-two years old.

Just fucking great.

His dark gaze lingers on mine, every passing second seeming to suck the oxygen right out of the air around me. My stare drops to the space between the door frame and his body, wondering if I'm small enough to slip through and make my escape, but his hand shoots out and comes to my chin, gently lifting and forcing my gaze back to his.

A moment of heated silence passes between us when he narrows his stare, instantly putting me on edge. "You've really been able to hear me through the wall every time I've gotten off over the past . . . fuck, I don't even know how long?"

Shit.

It's one thing being drunk and bold enough to admit such things in a text, but having to actually talk about it face-to-face with the man I've been in love with my whole life? Fuck, I am not even a little ready for this conversation, but judging by the demanding stare in his eyes, I don't think I have an option.

I feel my cheeks begin to flame, but I refuse to let it eat at what little confidence I have. Instead, my lips twist into an awkward cringe. "I was hoping that you were too drunk to remember anything that went down last night."

Izaac scoffs, amusement dancing in his eyes. "No chance in hell," he murmurs, keeping his tone low in case Austin decides to wake anytime this century, but he doesn't dare look away, holding me captive with his stare alone. "Answer the question, Aspen. How much have you heard?"

Nerves pound through my body, paralyzing me while knowing I don't have the guts to be as forward as I was with him last night. Things have shifted. For some insane reason that I can't even begin to work out, Izaac is noticing me in a way he's always refused to in the past. All the winking and subtle touches. The way he moved in behind me in the pool yesterday and at the club last night. I felt his stare on me all night, dragging hungrily up and down my body as if he only just realized that I'm no longer a scrawny teenager.

What if this is my chance? I can't afford to fuck it up. But what if I'm wrong? What if I'm reading into this too much and imagining things that simply aren't there? I could seriously fuck up the dynamics between us, and not to mention Austin. If he even heard a whisper of what went down last night, my world would crumble at my feet.

Deciding I can't risk letting this opportunity slip through my fingers, I step over the threshold of the bathroom and right into Izaac's personal space. Keeping my chin lifted, I hold his gaze and lower my voice to a seductive whisper while pummeling the nerves out of existence. "The things I've heard you do . . . " I start, reaching out and gently brushing my fingers across his tight abs and loving the way his muscles tense under my touch. God, I've wanted to do that for so long. "I've heard everything so clearly that it was like being in the room with you. I know the way your breath catches right before you come. How you growl when you're frustrated and desperate for a release. I even know the difference between the sounds you make fucking some random woman and how you sound when you're jerking off all alone. But last night . . . that sounded different. Last night was full of a desperation I've never heard from you before."

He just stares at me, appearing dumbfounded, and I don't know if he's shocked that I actually answered him or if he's horrified by the realization of what I've just told him. Either way, it makes me feel like a fucking goddess, and for the first time, it feels as though I'm the one who finally has the upper hand between us.

A raw smugness filters through my veins, furiously pounding through my body, and I bite down on my lips, feeling heat pool between my thighs. "Are we done?" I whisper. "Is there anything else your perverted little soul needs to know, or have I answered all of your burning questions to your satisfaction?"

Izaac continues to stare, and my lips lift into a wicked smirk. I push against his abs, forcing him to back up, and without another word, I finally make my escape, striding back to my room with newfound confidence.

The second I get to my room, I throw myself over the threshold and hastily close the door behind me. I lean back against it as though the solid wood can offer me some form of protection from the curious stare of Izaac Banks.

What the fuck was that? I don't think I've ever seen Izaac lost for words.

I give myself a second, waiting for my racing heart to finally calm before finding the courage to peel myself off the door. I listen out in the hallway and hear the distinct sound of the shower running, and I let out a heavy sigh of relief before finally stepping out into the hallway again.

I make my way to the kitchen, tiptoeing past the bathroom as though he'd somehow be able to hear me passing. Only as I turn the corner and walk into the kitchen, I come to a halt, finding Izaac standing by the island counter, an apple clutched in his hand, hovering in the air in front of his mouth.

Shit. It must have been Austin in the shower.

Izaac's gaze comes straight to mine, pausing just as I do, and just like that, every fiber of my body is buzzing with an intense awkwardness.

Fucking hell.

Why did he have to choose last night to text me, knowing that we were going to see each other the very next morning? Any other night would have been fine.

I try to recover, quickly clearing my throat and raising my chin as though I barely even notice he's in the room. Only zoning him out has always been an impossible task, especially now that he seems to be just as hyper-aware of me as I am of him.

How am I supposed to pretend it never happened?

Izaac tracks every step I take, and when I lift my gaze to swiftly catch his eye, his gaze darkens, and there's no doubt in my mind what he's thinking about. I start to sweat. Heat pulses through my veins. Surely he can see the hunger firing through my body, the desperation eating at me.

Trying to hold on to that tiny sliver of control, I stride through the kitchen, taking the long way around the island counter, and settling myself in front of the coffee machine. Reaching up into the cupboard, I grab a mug before placing it beneath the nozzle.

After making all my selections and putting a new pod in, I hit start and wait as the mug slowly begins to fill with steaming coffee, silently willing it to hurry up. A body moves in behind me, and I hold my breath, my hands shaking against the counter.

Why does he keep doing this? Doesn't he know how hard he's making it?

"Aspen," he says, his tone lowering, but not the good kind. This is filled with regret and hesitation, and before he's even said a word, I know exactly what's about to come out of his mouth.

I've dealt with his silent rejection for years, and every time it comes around, it guts me, but to have him openly tell me how this was only a little bit of fun and something that will never go any further . . . Well, shit. I know damn well I won't be able to handle the agony that comes along with it.

So instead of waiting for the agonizing torment, I beat him to the punch.

Turning around, I hold my hand up, stopping him before he gets a chance to speak. "Don't," I say, hoping he can't hear the hurt in my voice. "I know exactly what's about to fly out of your mouth, and I agree. It was just a little drunken fun. Meant nothing. So instead of having all of these awkward encounters in the hallway and kitchen every time we pass each other, we can just pretend like it never happened. You're still the unattainable Izaac Banks, and I'm still your best friend's little sister. Nothing less. Nothing more."

He cringes as those last words fly out of my mouth and nods. "That's not exactly what I was coming over here to talk to you about, but I—"

My face twists with confusion. "It's not?"

"No. I was more curious about just how long you've been hearing me through the walls, but there's no denying that everything you just said is true. Texting you like that . . . I shouldn't have. You were drunk and . . . I don't know. Like you said, you're Austin's little sister, and that's not a line I'm willing to cross."

Something flashes in his stare, but I'm not willing to delve into it right now. "Yep," I say, hastily turning so that he doesn't see the way his words tear me to shreds.

Finding my mug filled almost to the brim, I scoop it up and lift it to my lips, taking a desperate sip and hoping the deliciousness can somehow make this conversation easier. Then, taking my mug with me, I make my way back around to the other side of the island counter, pulling out a stool and taking a seat, doing everything in my power to avoid his stare. "So, this whole shared bedroom wall thing," I state. "I thought we covered that earlier in the hallway."

"We did," he says, clearing his throat as though the topic alone has the walls of his throat closing in on him. "But after you took off thinking you achieved something, it occurred to me that I've had my own place for years, so you could have only been referring to the times I stayed here in college."

I avert my gaze, feeling the awkwardness beginning to creep up, threatening to swallow me whole. "Uh-huh."

"I finished college at twenty-two, Aspen."

I lift my mug, half hiding my face with it, still unable to meet his eye. "Yep."

"You were barely sixteen."

I scoff, arching a brow and finally glancing up. "And to think, you were a high school junior when I first started hearing things through the wall."

His expression changes, and the color quickly drains from his face. "Fucking hell," he mutters under his breath, gripping the edge of the counter and hanging his head. "You were a fucking kid."

I nod. "I would have been around ten the first time I heard you, but it wasn't until I was maybe thirteen or fourteen that I actually understood what was going on in there."

"Shit, Aspen. I'm sorry," he tells me with a cringe. "If I knew you could hear all of that shit, I never would have—"

"Don't" I say, cutting him off again. "Don't start beating yourself up over it. It's not a big deal. Besides, by the time I was older and more aware of . . . myself, you were away at college. So it's not like I was . . . you know, not like last night."

Izaac gives me a hard stare, his brow arching as if knowing damn well I'm talking shit. "Austin and I had a fuckload of wild parties here during our college days, Aspen. Just because I was away at college, didn't mean I wasn't staying in that room just as much as I always did."

Lifting my mug to my lips, I glance away again, trying not to grin. "Yep."

During his college days, I used to love when he came home. Even if it meant he was screwing some random girl, it still meant that I got the slightest window into what it would be like to be with him, and I fucking loved it. But I'm not about to admit that to him.

No wonder I've struggled to get over him. When it comes to sex, I've always associated it with Izaac.

"FUCK!"

Izaac grips the counter again, his knuckles turning white, but all I can do is silently laugh, smothering my hand over my lips.

His gaze snaps up, looking at me in horror. "Are you seriously laughing at this? I was unknowingly corrupting you as a kid."

"Cool your jets, Izaac. It's not like I had a secret glory hole in the wall and was using it to watch you fuck your way through the female population. Though, one thing is for sure, when you've been drinking, that stamina of yours . . ." I make a whistling sound, starting high and getting lower with every passing second, and just for good measure, I make an arc with my finger, starting up by my head and finishing way down past the counter.

Izaac scoffs, amusement flashing in those dark eyes that have always held me captive. He presses his elbows on the counter and leans in, bringing himself a shitload closer and holding my gaze. "If you've really been listening through the wall as intently as you say you have, then you know damn well that's not true. I fuck like a god, Aspen."

I swallow hard, my heart racing a million miles an hour as my core clenches. I've heard him through the wall more than enough to know he likes to take his time. He fucks a woman until she can't possibly take it anymore, no matter how intoxicated he might be. There's no denying it, Izaac Banks certainly does fuck like a god. Just like the perfect stranger from Vixen. Now, if Izaac were to fuck me the way my perfect stranger did . . . Good God! I'd be ruined forever.

A shiver sails down my spine, but all I can do is stare back at him, hunger pooling deep in my core.

I need to get a grip.

His gaze darkens as if knowing the effect he has on me, and when his lips kick up into a wicked smirk, he pulls away. He's so fucking smug. It's as though making me sweat has just become his new favorite game, and for the most part, I'm so here for it. Only this is one game I don't think either of us will win.

Izaac wanders around the kitchen, collecting a bunch of things from both the fridge and pantry before spreading it out on the counter. I watch him grab two bagels, and as he cuts them open, I silently sip my coffee, watching his every move.

There's something so peaceful about it. It's rarely just me and him. Austin goes out of his way to make sure of it, but at times like this, I do what I can to soak it up. It would be so easy between us . . . If only he ever saw me in that way.

Izaac spreads cream cheese across the bagel before quickly glancing up at me. "You heading back to campus today?"

"Yeah," I say, grateful for the change of topic that allows me the chance to actually breathe. "I've got a big assignment due this week, so as soon as everyone is up, I'll probably say goodbye and get out of here."

A playful grin stretches across his lips sending butterflies storming through my stomach. "Let me guess, you haven't started it yet?"

I laugh, trying to play off the way his gaze makes me squirm in my seat. "I have . . . mostly."

"Uh-huh," he says with a smug grin before putting the top back on the bagel and sliding it onto a plate. "Here. Eat this. If you have any hope of concentrating after the night you've had, you're gonna need your energy."

Izaac hands me the plate, and without leaving a single crumb, I annihilate my bagel, knowing it tastes even better just because it was made by the capable hands of a sex god.

10

IZAAC

What the fuck was I thinking?

I shake my head as I stride through the service entrance of Vixen on Tuesday afternoon, doing my best to ignore the strange feeling fluttering through me at the thought of Aspen having been here with me.

Ha. If only she knew.

She'd fucking hate me for keeping this from her. She consented to be with someone she thought she'd never see again, and there's comfort in the anonymity of Vixen's dark rooms. If I had known who she was, it never would have happened, but telling her the truth now would only ruin her fantasy.

She deserves to know that the stranger who bent her over the table and slammed into her sweet little cunt isn't a stranger at all, but someone who has known her since she was a baby, but if she knew that every time she walks into a room, I remember the way she tasted on my tongue . . . fuck. That's different, and every second I don't tell her is another second of deception. She deserves to know.

Going out to Pulse on Saturday night was a bad idea, but getting drunk with her was even worse. After spending the afternoon obsessing over her every fucking move, I should have known better than to put myself in that position. And yet, I can't bring myself to regret it.

Those texts . . . fuck.

I'm not going to lie, I've reread them more than enough times to be considered fucking perverted, and the fact that I'm generally rock hard and jerking off while doing it . . . Yeah, there's something profoundly wrong with me.

She's off-limits. Austin would beat the shit out of me if he knew it'd already gone this far, if he knew the vile things I wanted to do to his little sister.

Fuck me.

I can't want her like this. I *shouldn't* want her at all. Yet, I've never wanted to bury my face between those sweet legs more. I want to feel the way her walls stretch around me, bury my cock deep into her over and over until she screams my name, and what's more, I know if she were given the chance, she'd take it without hesitation. I need to be the one in control. I need to keep these urges to myself and delete those fucking messages. If I make one wrong move, it could ruin everything.

There's too much at stake. My relationship with Austin and his parents, not to mention Aspen. If I allowed myself to go there, I would destroy her. She's always wanted so much more, and that's not something I can or want to give her. It would be about sex. Raw, wild, and desperate sex. Nothing more. And I know without even needing to really consider it that I would shred her fragile heart to pieces.

Striding through my club, I look over the layout, my mind constantly going over ways that I can improve, and for once, I've got nothing. Vixen is in pristine condition, unlike Pulse and Cherry which seem to always be in the market for upgrades. Scandal on the other hand, while it's only eight months old, is holding up well, but I'm starting to notice some slight wear and tear in the floors and bars. They'll be okay for another few months, but then they'll be seeing some upgrades too.

My nostrils burn from the fumes left over by the cleaning crew. Vixen closes its doors at four in the morning, and by five, the cleaning crew is rocking up. They do a deep clean every day, no matter if the room has been used or not. There's no telling just how far DNA can spread, and my club won't be the reason for its members catching any diseases. The cleaners are generally done by midday, and when my bar staff comes in to restock the bar, one of them is responsible for opening up the doors and letting the fumes out.

I've beaten everyone in today, needing uninterrupted access to my security feed. I'll be scrubbing any evidence of Aspen off my system before any of my security team happens to come across it. Don't get me wrong, I have the best security team I could ask for, and I trust them implicitly, but that doesn't mean I want them feasting their eyes on what's mine—fuck no.

I mean . . . shit.

Aspen Ryder is not mine. She's far from it. She's mine in other terms of the word. Mine to protect, mine to make laugh, and mine to care for, just as she is to Austin. But she's certainly not mine. If anything, I should view her as a little sister. Nothing more.

Making my way through the club, I push through the employees-only section and down to the security office before hashing in my personal access code and opening the heavy metal door. The system is on and ready to go, and without skipping a beat, I sit down and search through the files from Friday night.

A strange nervousness pulses through me. It's one thing reliving that night over and over in my head and reading those texts, but to actually see it play out before me . . . fuck. I don't know if I have the strength to hit delete. Hell, what if it was all in my head and she wasn't the girl in the dark room at all?

I bring up the footage from the main entrance, fast-forwarding until I see a familiar face appear at the end of the alley. A grin pulls at the corner of my lips, and I watch as Aspen loops her arm through Becs' and the two of them make their way toward my club.

There's no sound, but it's clear they're having a conversation, and judging by the look on Aspen's face, she doesn't seem down with walking down a dark alley in the middle of the night. I suppose Austin and I have taught her well over the years. Though, one could argue that maybe we haven't, seeing as though she was easily swayed to do it anyway.

They reach the door, and I watch as the girls make their way inside and disappear from the camera's range. Then before I move to another camera, I make sure to delete the footage. Changing to the main entrance feed, I watch as they move through the dimly lit hallway and make their way down the stairs and to the reception area. The dim lights catch against Aspen's sequined top, and I can't help but laugh. If Austin knew she owned a top like that, he would have stolen it and burned it. Hell, maybe I would have helped him, but now that I've seen how it looks on her, maybe I'll keep my mouth shut about it.

The girls talk to Casey in reception, and despite nothing interesting happening here, I find myself intrigued by Aspen and watching her facial expressions as she figures out what Vixen is all about.

They get their wristbands, and when they make their way onto the main floor of the club and disappear out of the frame, I hit pause and delete. The routine goes on, and with every frame they move out of, I erase any evidence of their night. Only as Aspen hovers by the bar and she's approached for the first time, my blood runs cold, and I find my hand pausing on the delete button.

The man in question is Ryatt Markin, and I can guarantee that the second Aspen walked through the door, he would have zoned in on the white wristband dangling around her delicate skin. He's a CEO of a big corporate company and gets off on being an asshole when it comes to his business negotiations, but what really gets him off is his fetish for virgins. Hell, they don't need to actually be a virgin to catch his eye, they just need to look pure and innocent, just like Aspen. I can't say I've ever taken the time to sit down and chat with the guy, and I could be way off base, but I don't like him, and it has nothing to do with the fact that he approached Aspen.

I've had my eye on Ryatt for a while. He's not someone I would ever want Aspen getting caught up with, and the fact that he's sitting beside her at the bar makes my skin crawl. He's charming and plays the part, effortlessly getting women to fall for his game. It usually doesn't take long before he's taking a woman's hand and leading her into a private room, and every single time, without fail, those women have left with him afterward. I can't put my finger on what it is about him that gets under my skin, but let's call it a gut feeling.

I don't like him, and the second I catch him breaking even the slightest rule of my club, he'll be out.

Relief drums through my veins as I watch the stiff way Aspen holds her shoulders. She engages in conversation with Ryatt, but while she's smiling and being polite, she's not falling at his feet, and it's not long before Ryatt bows out, clearly not up for the chase.

I need to keep my eye on Ryatt when it comes to Aspen, but let's face it, she won't be coming back here. Not if I have anything to do with it.

Once Becs and Aspen disappear from the screen, I delete that footage and follow their trail to the VIP area. A strange bubble expands right in the center of my chest, and I try to shake it off, not understanding it. It's not as though I don't already know what's about to go down.

The second the girls reach the floor of the VIP area, Caesar Eros moves in behind Becs, his hand plunging between her legs, and my heart kicks into gear, only after a short conversation, Caesar ushers

Becs away, leaving Aspen to explore on her own. I make a note to come back to Becs, feeling that it's only right for me to delete that footage as well.

I fast forward through the footage as Aspen sits at the bar, and the more she sips on her drink, the more confident she appears. It's not long before someone approaches her and as he puts his hands all over her, mine clench on the table.

I have no right to get fucked up over that, and yet here we are.

My irritation is short-lived when something catches her eye and she stares off across the club. Her attention is gone for only a second, but it's enough to put her in motion. She steps right out of the guy's arms, and judging by the direction she walks, I know this is it. Hell, I remember walking that way and disappearing into the dark room. I hadn't expected anyone to come in so soon, but the second she did, a strange chill swept across my body.

There's a determination in her stride as she steps into the dark room, and I mentally high-five myself for making sure my security system was fully equipped with night vision. I see the nervousness in her eyes, but I don't need to see it. I *felt* it radiating off her and could sense her determination. She was there to do one thing and one thing only, but I was also determined—determined to make her come alive and discover just how fucking good it gets.

I feel like too much of a fucking perv watching it, so I put it in fast forward and skip through the best fucking night of my life, watching as I press her into the wall and taste her before having her hold the bar above her head and drilling into her.

Had I known that was Aspen, maybe I would have done things differently, taken it slower and been gentle, but I've never been the type to hold back when it comes to sex. I give my all, every fucking time.

I watch as Aspen comes for the second time, and it takes everything in me not to stare as her tits bounce with every thrust of my hips. My cock twitches in my jeans, painfully hard, but it's practically been that way since the moment I walked in here.

The footage goes on and on, yet I'm painfully aware of the fact that I haven't put it in triple speed yet. As the scene plays out and I carry her to the table and sit her down to remove her boots, my phone rings loudly in my pocket.

I hit pause on the tape, the angle of Aspen's leg as I remove her boot perfectly showcasing her glistening cunt, and despite calling on my every last shred of willpower, I can't find it in me to look away. Not anymore.

Answering the phone without looking at the screen, I lift it to my ear, squishing it between my shoulder and face to free up my hand. After all, I'm getting really fucking close to needing it wrapped around my cock.

"Yo, you done it yet?" Austin's voice booms through the phone, sending a wave of horror blasting through my chest, and out of sheer fear for what he would do to me, I tear my greedy stare away from the screen.

"Working on it now," I say, needing to clear my throat.

"Oh. So you're—"

"Currently watching footage of your sister in my club," I confirm, not bothering to sugarcoat it. After all, he was the one who asked me to do this. Surely he had to have known what it entailed.

"Fuck," he grunts before pausing, and I can imagine the way he would have sat on the edge of his couch and dragged his hand down his face. "Who was she . . . umm . . . you know?"

"You're fucking kidding me, right?" I almost laugh. "I'm not telling you that shit."

"The fuck? Why the hell not? I need to know which bastard put his fucking hands on my sister."

"You know damn well how it works at Vixen, and besides, no one put their hands on her without her consent."

"Izaac," he groans, his tone hitching higher with a clear warning not to fuck with him right now, but he's got another thing coming if he thinks I'm about to betray her privacy like that.

"You really want to know?" I ask him.

"Of course I don't *want* to know," he spits back. "I never wanted any of this. If I could somehow go back and make sure she never stepped foot in that club, I would. But she's left me no fucking choice, and now I need to do damage control and make sure—"

"Austin," I say, cutting him off. "Respectfully, the only thing you need to do is shut the fuck up. I'm here deleting any footage of her. This is all the damage control that needs to be done. Nothing more. Like she said at Pulse, she's a fucking adult, and if she wanted your input on her sex life, she would have asked for it."

"Whose fucking side are you on here?"

"Are you hearing yourself? So what she went to Vixen. She sat at the bar and had a drink with her friend. She had a good time. You should be happy she's not doing this shit with random assholes in back alleys. She was in a clean, controlled environment with security."

Austin scoffs, clearly not happy, and I can't help but shift my gaze back to the paused screen, my tongue involuntarily rolling over my bottom lip. "Do you have any idea how fucking messed up that is? This is Aspen, Izaac. Are you not getting that?"

"Oh, I'm fucking getting it, but from where I'm standing, you're the one who's not getting it," I throw back at him. "Get off her fucking back about it. She did nothing wrong, and from what I've seen in this footage, you have nothing to worry about anyway. She's not whoring herself out. She's not getting drunk and letting assholes take advantage of her. She knows her fucking limits and is being respectful of herself. But if you really need to know what she's doing, then I'll tell you, right after I call her and tell her in explicit detail every fucking vile thing you've done within the walls of my club. Is that what you want? Because I'm not violating her privacy without violating yours. So, what'll it be?"

"FUCK!" Austin roars. "I really fucking hate you right now."

"Yeah, I can live with that," I say. "But can you live with yourself if you were to destroy your relationship with your sister? Because let me tell you, you're already heading down that road, and you're not just walking down it, you're going a hundred miles per hour. I know Aspen is forgiving when it comes to the stupid shit you do, but there are some things that not even she could forgive."

I'm met with a long silence, the only tell that he's still on the line is the sharp intake of breath as he tries to calm himself. "Just . . . Just delete the fucking footage and make sure she's turned away if she shows up there again."

"You know I will."

He lets out a barely audible huff before the line goes dead, and I pull my phone away, tossing it onto the table before letting out a heavy sigh. I hate getting into it with Austin like that, especially when it comes to Aspen. Nine times out of ten, I'm on his side, but the times when his over-protective brotherly bullshit comes into play, I have to call him on it, and it rarely goes well. But we'll be good in a matter of days. He just needs time to cool off. I just wish this shit wasn't coming at the same time as his restaurant nightmare, but it'll pass. He's got a good team, and I've made sure my architect is heading out there at the end of the week to offer his help.

My gaze swings back to the screen, and a wave of guilt crashes through me, but this time, my gaze doesn't dare drop to the apex of Aspen's thighs. Instead, I put the footage in triple speed and quickly make my way to the end before promptly hitting delete on everything that happened in the dark room.

Then just to be on the safe side, I watch as she meets up with Becs and keep my eye on her until she's finally back in an Uber and speeding away from the club. Once all evidence of Aspen and Becs ever being here is gone, I pick my phone up off the table and send Austin a text, knowing he'll be waiting for confirmation.

Izaac - It's done.

Austin - All of it? Make sure she's permanently banned. I want her face plastered to Casey's desk so she can't slip through the cracks.

I grit my teeth. I know I agreed to have her banned, but it doesn't sit right with me. Not even a little bit. If she wants to return to Vixen, she should be able to, but on the other hand, if she were turned away at the door, it would take the temptation away right along with her, and there's no denying the benefits of that. Then out of the sake of protecting my relationships with both Austin and Aspen, I agree.

Izaac - Consider it done.

11

ASPEN

Mindlessly swiping through the less-than-appealing options on Tinder, I try to find someone who might be able to come close to making me feel the way my perfect stranger did at Vixen last week, but I know deep down that nothing will compare to what I experienced with him. Not even a little bit.

It's been a busy week, and after spending every night working on that damn assignment and forcing myself to concentrate, as opposed to thinking about things I shouldn't have been, I was finally able to hand it in. Every day was a headache. My perfect stranger has left me needier than ever, and now that I know just how good it can be, I'm desperate for more. Every toy in my bedside table has been overused and abused this week, and now, late on Thursday night, I've never been so sexually frustrated.

With one hit, I've become his greatest addict.

Nothing will compare, and something tells me that no matter how high and low I search, no other man will be able to make me come the way he did.

Getting to be with the mystery man from Vixen was like finding a complete checklist, and getting to tick them off along the way was the best fun I've ever had.

Tall - Must be tall enough to have childhood trauma from people constantly telling them 'You should play basketball'.

Hot as fuck body - MUSCLES! MUSCLES! MUSCLES! If he's not capable of throwing me around, I don't want it!

GINORMOUS MONSTER COCK!!!! - Must be both thick and long for extra deep penetration, and if he can't stretch those walls, forget it! I WANT TO CHOKE ON THAT GIRTH!

Dick piercing - Every girl loves a little bling!

A tongue that could send a woman to an early grave - Do these come with vibration mode? Asking for a friend.

Skill set - Hasn't learned everything he knows from watching porn.

A filthy mouth, and I don't mean bad hygiene. He should know when to call me a dirty little slut and when he shouldn't.

KNOWS WHERE THE CLIT IS AND WHAT TO DO WITH IT!!!!!

Okay, so maybe my list is describing the rarest of men, but I don't think it's that much to ask for, right? Sure, I might find a guy who has a few of those qualities, but what's the likelihood that I'll find one who has them all? It's not possible. Besides, if sheer luck happens to see one fall willingly into my lap, there's no way I'll be able to hold on to him. Now, a girl like Becs, she could. But me and my lack of . . . everything? There's no hope for me.

It's time to face the music. Mystery Vixen man has ruined me.

Disappointment floods through me as I continue swiping through my Tinder options. They're really not looking good, and honestly, the few who might have just a little potential have been skipped past too because deep down, I know it's pointless.

But that fucking itch that needs to be scratched! I can't live like this! I need to be thoroughly fucked by something that isn't battery operated.

Damn it!

I can't take it anymore.

Swiping through the Tinder options, I demand myself to stop on the next guy who shows just a fraction of potential and open his profile.

Colton Firebird.

My lips twist with distaste. There's no way that's his real last name, but he's also kinda cute. Dark hair and a sharp, chiseled jaw, and with that cocky smirk, he looks like he eats, sleeps, and breathes pussy. His profile says that he's six-four, but also specifically states that he's only looking for a booty call. He's not looking for a girlfriend or anyone who won't be able to say goodbye at the end of the night.

Maybe this is what I need. I'm definitely not looking for a relationship with this guy, but he might be able to tick off at least four or more of the requirements on the checklist, so it wouldn't be a complete fail . . . right?

Shit.

Then without giving myself a second longer to think about it, I swipe right on Colton Fakelastname, and the moment I do, my stomach sinks with nerves. I can't do this. What if I was only able to be physical with the mystery Vixen man because it was pitch-black in that room? I've never had the courage to sleep with a man before that, so what if there's something fundamentally wrong with me? What if, in a real-life setting, I don't actually have the guts to welcome someone into my bed?

My nerves quickly turn into a full-blown panic when my phone chimes with a notification, and my gaze snaps to the screen, finding that Colton has matched with me.

Well, shit.

Now what?

Almost immediately, a new message appears in my Tinder chat, and I open the notification.

Colton - Your cute

I let out a sigh. He's forward, I like that, but he clearly doesn't know the difference between *your* and *you're*. Though, it's not as though I'd be meeting up with him to discuss his knowledge of the English language.

Aspen - You're not so bad yourself.
Colton - It's your****

The fuck? Is this guy for real?

Aspen - It's really not.

Colton - HAHAHA I'm just fucking with you. Needed to see if you could take a joke. You can tell a lot about a girl by how she responds to this shit.

Colton - You're profile says your close and your 22. I'm assuming that means your at the college? A senior maybe?

I scoff, reading over his message, shaking my head at the blatant incorrect uses of your and you're again, but now I really don't know if he's actually screwing with me, or if he was trying to play it off that he was. Either way, it's not exactly a turn-on. Buuuuut, maybe I'm being too judgmental.

Aspen - That's right. I'll be graduating with a journalism degree in a few months.

Colton - Sounds cool. I'm halfway through my business degree. Been a tough week though. Could really use a pick-me-up. What do you say we meet up and let off a little steam?

Aspen - What do you have in mind?

Colton - Your call. We can meet somewhere, grab something to eat or just head back to you're place. Whatever your down with.

Truth be told, I'm not really down with much when it comes to this guy, but that doesn't change the fact that he's cute and I'm curious to find out if I'm actually capable of being physical with someone who isn't a faceless man in a dark room. Call it an experiment.

A grin tears across my face as I imagine what Becs would say to all of this. She'd throw me a wild party and would probably offer to vajazzle my vagina for good luck.

Aspen - Count me in. Tomorrow night work for you? Kinda been craving a good kebab. Haven't had one in ages.

Colton - Tomorrow is perfect. I know a place about ten minutes from here. I can swing by and pick you up.

Aspen - Perfect!

I give Colton my details, and before I know it, I have a glass of wine and I'm curled up on my couch, ready for a night filled with Grey's Anatomy. Then wanting to jump straight into the drama, I skip ahead to the double episode at the end of season six and watch as McDreamy goes down.

I'm halfway through when my phone chimes with another text. I dive for it, feeling around in the cushions, not capable of taking my eyes off the screen, only when I hold up my phone and see Izaac's name, suddenly watching Meredith demand to be shot doesn't seem so important.

Every bit of my attention falls to my phone, and I shift back on the couch, snuggling up on the cushion, almost too scared to open the text. I don't know what he could possibly want. He makes a habit out of never texting me . . . apart from the other night. I think that was the first message I've received from him in over a year. Either way, Saturday night's texts were a far cry from anything I've gotten from him before. Usually, they sound like *Austin needs* or *Austin was wondering*. His messages are never *let's secretly get off together through the paper-thin walls.*

A shiver sails down my spine from the memory. Easily the best night of my life . . . right after my wild night at Vixen, of course. Though, I can guarantee I won't be that lucky again.

Preparing for a random rejection message just to remind me of my place, I cringe as I open the text, but as I read the words, I simply just stare. I'm not really sure what I expected, but it definitely wasn't this.

Izaac - What are you doing?

My brows furrow. Since when does Izaac Banks ask me what I'm doing?

Aspen - Not much, just organizing my bi-weekly orgy. You?

Izaac - Dusting off my old collection of strap ons and ball gags. Figured you'd get more use out of them now that you're a raging sex addict and all.

A snort tears from the back of my throat, and I scooch down further on the couch and pull my blanket up as I type out a response, giggling at my phone like a love-sick schoolgirl.

Aspen - I haven't got a clue what you're talking about!

Izaac - Uh-huh…

Aspen - Is there something you needed?

Izaac - Just checking in is all.

Aspen - Bullshit. I've known you all my life and you've never just checked in.

Izaac - Maybe…and this is a big maybe, but maybe I was just replaying the other night in my head and thought I should see how you were doing.

Aspen - …

Aspen - I thought we agreed that nothing happened.

Izaac - We did. Nothing happened.

Aspen - So then there shouldn't be anything for you to replay in that ridiculous head of yours.

Izaac - Like you haven't thought about it.

Damn. Of course he knows I have, but what's the point in bringing it up? He's already made it clear that we're not something that will ever happen. There's a million metaphorical lines drawn between us, keeping me from even thinking about a potential future, so all he's doing now is fucking with my head.

I need to quit while I'm behind. I can't allow him to let me hope for something that's never going to happen. Only one of us is going to end up hurt here, and it's not going to be him.

He needs a reminder of what's at stake. He needs a reality check.

Aspen - You're giving me whiplash. Which is it? Are we pretending it never happened or are we sneaking around behind Austin's back and doing something you and I both know we shouldn't?

There's a slight pause, and I watch as the three little dots appear at the bottom of the screen, and I find myself holding my breath, anxiety bubbling through my veins.

Izaac - Fuck. You're right. I'm sorry. Austin would have my balls for this, but the other night...lines got blurred. You're not a kid anymore.

What in the ever-loving fuck is that supposed to mean? I'm not a kid anymore? Of course I'm not a kid anymore, but what does he mean by that? Has he suddenly taken notice of me? Or is he seeing me in a new way since Saturday night? Though one thing is for sure, the lines really did get blurred, but we have no choice but to unblur them. Me and Izaac . . . nothing can happen. Despite how desperately I might want it to.

Aspen - Have you been drinking?

Izaac - No…

Aspen - …

Izaac - Okay. Maybe a little. Or a lot…

Aspen - Where are you? Do you need me to come get you?

Izaac - Not unless you want me to throw you up against a wall and fuck you until you can't walk.

Holy fucking shit. I think I just came.

Aspen - Okay, sex god. Whatever you say.

My phone starts to ring as my eyes widen in horror, and I throw it down as though it could physically burn me. I gape at Izaac's name in bold letters across my screen. What the hell does he think he's doing calling me like this?

My heart pounds as my hands begin to shake, terrified of what an actual conversation could mean. Does he just want to talk shit while he's drunk or does he plan to bring up Saturday night again? Because when he makes comments like, *You're not a kid anymore,* I don't think I'm capable of responding without begging him to come fuck me.

The phone continues to ring and before I give myself a chance to think it over too much, I hastily scoop it up and hit accept, immediately putting the call on speaker.

"Izaac," I say in warning. "You and I both know you shouldn't be calling me."

"You really think I'm a sex god?"

"No," I laugh as a fire burns in the pit of my stomach at just hearing the word sex fall from his mouth. "I think you're drunk and therefore, you think you're a sex god. Or do I need to remind you of what you said to me in the kitchen the other day?"

Izaac laughs. "According to you, we never had any conversation the other day. We never did anything, and I sure as fuck didn't hear you groan my name when you came on your fingers."

My cheeks flame, and I clear my throat, not trusting my voice to not come out all squeaky and obvious. "Is there a reason for your call, or do you just get off on making me squirm?"

A soft chuckle sounds through the phone before I hear the familiar sounds of him flopping back against the couch and getting comfortable. "You never told me what you were doing."

"I did," I argue. "I said I was organizing a wild orgy."

"Cut the bullshit. What are you really doing?"

I let out a heavy breath, pressing my lips into a tight line. "You really want to know?"

"Would I ask otherwise?"

"Who knows? You seem to be saying a lot of things you don't really mean."

"Just answer the fucking question."

My shoulders sag, and despite my better judgment, I give him the cold hard truth. "I was sick of contemplating if I was broken, so I was distracting myself with reruns of Grey's Anatomy."

There's a short pause before his voice comes back, only it's much softer. "Why the fuck would you be broken?"

"Because . . ." I pause, a heaviness weighing down on me. "You saw those wristbands. I was a twenty-two-year-old virgin up until last week, and it's not for lack of trying. I'm just not . . . I don't know. Brave enough, I guess."

"The fuck are you talking about?"

I feel the blood rush to my cheeks, humiliation washing through me, but at the same time, I feel as though this is the most honest conversation I've ever had. Despite Izaac being drunk, I know I'm not being judged. "I've been presented with plenty of opportunities to rectify that particular . . . virgin issue, and every time, I chicken out. Then Friday night comes along, and I walk into a pitch-black room, and without a second thought, I let some perfect stranger do whatever the fuck he wanted to me."

"And?" he prompts.

"And what?" I ask. "It was incredible. One sexual experience, and I'm ruined for any other man. Nothing will ever compare to what he did to me. No amount of toys, fingers, or imagination has ever come close, and now I'm frustrated because there's an itch that only one person can scratch, and I don't even know who he is."

Izaac scoffs, but I hear the grin in his tone. "That good, huh?"

"Mm-hmm," I murmur.

"So what are you gonna do about it?"

I shrug my shoulders, despite knowing he can't see me. "I don't know. The best plan I've got is to screw my way through campus and see if anyone can even come close, and then I suppose I'll have to settle for that guy while always knowing he'll be second best."

"You're gonna do what?" he blurts out in horror.

"You heard me," I say. "I'm meeting up with some Tinder guy tomorrow. I guess I'm officially entering my whore era. Austin will be so proud."

"You're fucking with me, right?"

"What's it to you? I've gone out with plenty of guys before, and you've never cared about them."

"Yeah, well, you've never declared that you were about to fuck them all," he mutters, anger lacing his deep tone.

"So?" I throw back. "Up until now, you probably assumed that I did anyway."

"But up until now, I didn't know how you sounded when you came."

Holy fuck.

My heart lurches out of my chest, racing a million miles per hour. "Fuck, Izaac," I groan, closing my eyes as I brace my elbows on my knees. "You can't say shit like that to me. You're gonna have to start blocking my number before you go out drinking."

A thick silence follows, just long enough for me to wonder if maybe he fell asleep. Finally, I hear his low tone. "You're really gonna fuck this guy?"

"I don't know," I say truthfully. "We're going out to eat, but if it feels right, then maybe. But honestly, what's the point? He'll never live up to—" I cut myself off, my eyes widening with horror, realizing what I was about to say. *He'll never live up to you.*

"He'll never live up to what?" Izaac prompts.

"It's nothing. Don't worry," I say. "I shouldn't have said anything."

"Aspen, I—"

"Don't," I whisper. "If you're about to say something you know you're going to regret tomorrow, then just don't say anything at all."

"But—"

"No. You're the one who's gone out of his way to make sure that I know nothing will ever happen here, but this past week, it's as though you're determined to fuck with every line you've ever drawn between us. I can't do this. You're fucking with my head. You don't want me, Izaac. Not how I've always wanted you, so just . . . stop. Please."

I'm met with that same silence again, only this time, I can hear him take a deep breath. "You're right," he finally says. "It's not my intention to fuck with your feelings like that. I just . . . I think over the weekend I realized that maybe I didn't know you as well as I thought I did. You're not the same girl I remember."

"I'm not a girl at all," I agree. "I'm a grown woman."

"That, you are," he mutters, sounding deep in thought. "I've spent the last few years purposefully pulling away from you, and I've missed out on getting to know the person you've become."

"I know, but it's fine. I understand why you did it, and it was better that way. I was young. I needed the boundaries."

"You're not young anymore."

"Don't be thinking about me in ways you're not prepared for," I warn him. "Unless you're ready to risk it all with Austin, then you need to put those boundaries right back in place. I'm not about to become some dirty little secret."

"Why not?" he laughs. "Don't you think it'll be fun?"

"Izaac!" I scold.

"Alright, alright," he mutters. "I'll leave you alone. But tomorrow night, when you're fucking your new little Tinder date, just know that when he slams inside that sweet little cunt of yours, you and I both know that you'll be wishing it was me."

I suck in a gasp, seeing red. "HOLY FUCKING SHIT, IZAAC! I'm gonna kill—"

The line goes dead as I hear the echo of his laugh booming through my skull.

That asshole. I don't know whether to be mortified or to just laugh. But there's no denying that he's right. When it comes to me, there's only ever been one man that I've wanted.

Izaac fucking Banks.

12

IZAAC

Who the fuck gets drunk alone on a Thursday night? This fucking loser.

Since the moment I discovered that I stole Aspen's virginity, I've been a mess. Every fucking line has been crossed. The things that have circled my mind over the past few days would guarantee a death sentence from Austin, but no matter how fucking hard I try, I can't make it stop.

I need to get a grip. I'm risking everything. The Ryders are my family. They trust me implicitly, and with every passing second that I picture their sweet daughter on her knees, I'm betraying it all.

If Austin knew what happened at Vixen and understood that I had no idea it was Aspen, he might be able to forgive me. It would take time, but he'd eventually come around. But if I were to admit that I haven't stopped thinking about her since, or if I actually fucked her again, the friendship we've built over the past twenty-two years wouldn't mean a damn thing.

There'd be no coming back from that, so tell me why the hell the thought of Aspen going out on her stupid date tonight is fucking with me so bad?

One date isn't going to make a difference in how she feels about me. Unless he has a golden cock and a magical tongue gifted to him by the angels of heaven, but even then, her desires will still be with me.

Aspen took me perfectly at Vixen, and she was right on the phone last night, there's no comparing to something so fucking good. Aspen and I . . . we just fit together. Call me cliché, but it's as though her body was made just for me. I've never had a woman take me so well, and for it to feel that fucking good. Even before I knew it was her, I already considered her to be the best I'd ever had.

Last night over the phone, she boasted about how good her faceless stranger was, how he ruined her for every other man, and no matter how hard she tries to fuck herself with toys, nothing will ever compare. Pure fire flooded my veins as she told me what I already knew. She felt just as good as I did . . . fuck. I don't even have the words for it.

It was almost impossible to keep my mouth shut, to not roar at the top of my lungs that the man she's been dreaming of is me. But I stand by what I said. Letting her know would destroy everything.

It's Friday night, a week since I first got to taste her, and I was supposed to be at Cherry an hour ago, only instead of getting my shit together, I'm pacing my fucking living room and trying to convince myself not to ruin her date.

If she fucks this guy, then that's her business, but all he'd be doing is using her to get off, and she's better than that. She deserves so much better. Besides, she knows he won't fuck her like I could . . . or at least like her faceless stranger would.

A strange desperation pulses through me, and it suddenly occurs to me that I could be . . . no. Surely not. Am I jealous? Is this what it feels like?

Holy fucking shit.

This is not okay.

I'm jealous. And yet, I don't have a single fucking right to be.

I need to get a grip. I need to get my ass to Cherry and get my shit under control. Only the second I fly out of my home and hit the gas, it's not my club I'm heading toward.

I pull up outside the familiar property before making my way to the door and slamming my fist against the hardwood. I shouldn't be here, but the second the idea formed in my fucked-up mind, I couldn't take it back.

The door opens barely a moment later, and before Austin even gets a word out, I storm past him into his home. "The fuck are you doing here?" he demands, still not having forgiven me for threatening to spill his dirty Vixen secrets to Aspen.

"You need to call your sister," I rush out, hovering in his foyer. "I think she's about to get herself in trouble."

His eyes widen, and his body stiffens, panic flashing in his eyes. "What the fuck are you talking about?"

"I was checking in with her last night after all the Vixen bullshit," I start.

Austin's sharp gaze snaps to me. "You were texting my sister?" he questions, cutting me off.

I shake my head as though that could somehow help. "That's not important. She said she was meeting up with some guy she'd never met."

His brows furrow, horror flashing in his gaze. "The fuck are you talking about?" he demands, his mind clearly racing a million miles per hour. "What guy?"

"Don't know, man. She just said something about entering her whore era. I think she's going to try and sleep with this guy, but she knows nothing about him," I say, adding an extra hit of urgency to my tone. "What if he's a convicted felon or tries to fucking rape her? She's not thinking straight. You have to do something about this."

Austin clenches his jaw, shaking his head with frustration. "You're fucking kidding me," he grunts, his hand digging into his pocket and pulling out his phone. "What the hell is she thinking?"

I don't respond. Instead, I stand back and watch what siblings do best—fight. But there's one thing I can always count on, when Austin thinks he's protecting his little sister, he'll go to the end of the earth. They'll be okay though. They always are. She'll get snappy and tell him to mind his own business, but in the end, he'll force her to see reason, and going out with this loser—where's the fucking reason in that?

Austin storms through his home, the call already connecting to Aspen, and I follow him into his living room. "Hello?" Aspen's voice answers after the third ring as Austin falls heavily onto his couch.

"What the fuck is this I hear about you trying to hook up with some random asshole you've never met? Are you insane? Do you have any idea how fucking stupid that is?"

"What? How did you—fucking Izaac," she grunts, clearly irritated as a wide smirk stretches across my lips. "What did he tell you?"

"Doesn't matter what he told me, only that you're trying to fuck some loser you've never met."

"I swear, Austin. When in the ever-loving hell will you learn to mind your own goddamn business?" she demands, her tone hitching higher. "My sex life has got nothing to do with you. It doesn't matter if I wanted to fuck my way across the country or spread my legs for a fucking stadium of assholes. Your only job is to love me—"

"The hell it is," Austin throws back. "It's my job to protect you, and right now, you're making that very fucking hard."

"I'm not a kid. I don't need your protection."

"Oh, right. Because hooking up with some stranger clearly shows how responsible you are. How could I have been so blind? My bad!"

"Fuck off, Austin. I'm really not in the mood for your bullshit."

Austin groans, falling back against the couch as I sit on the edge of the coffee table, my brows furrowed, not liking the tone in her voice. Is something wrong? Usually, she's all for a fight with her brother. It's their favorite thing to do.

As if sensing the same thing I do, Austin finally lowers his voice and takes a new approach. "Just tell me you'll reconsider?" he begs. "I'd never forgive myself if something happened to you. You're my only sister, Aspen, and I know we fight all the time, but I love you."

Aspen lets out a heavy sigh. "I've already told him to fuck off."

My brows furrow, and I lean closer to the phone. "Huh?" I grunt, my gaze darting to Austin's, both of us just as confused as the other.

"Fuck. Izaac's there?" Aspen questions. "Jesus, Austin. You could have warned a girl. Take me off speaker."

"Lay off him," Austin says. "He was just concerned about you, and apparently, he had every right to be. I swear, Aspen. What has gotten into you lately? Vixen last week and random hookups this week. Is this some kind of cry for attention?"

I cringe, knowing that's not going to go down well, and considering the look on Austin's face, he clearly regrets his choice of words, but when these two fight, there's usually not a lot of thought put into the bullshit they say to each other.

"The fuck?" Aspen demands. "A cry for attention? Why don't you come over here and say that? I'll show you a fucking cry for attention."

"Chill out, Aspen. Just . . . fuck. We're getting off track here."

"Ya think?" she grunts. "This whole call is off track."

"Just . . . What did you mean you've already told him to fuck off?" Austin asks, making an effort to calm his tone.

Aspen lets out a heavy sigh, and I have to refrain from scooping the phone out of Austin's hand and taking over. She sounds so disappointed, broken almost, and I want nothing more than to drive over there and make sure she's alright. "He came by an hour ago. We were supposed to go out to eat, but according to him, I wasn't worth the meal, and he thought we should just fuck instead."

"The fuck?" I grunt as the same disgust flashes in Austin's stare.

"Despite what you two clearly think of me, I'm not a complete lost cause," she says. "I have respect for myself, and believe it or not, my standards are a shitload higher than yours. Besides, I highly doubt either of you can honestly say that you haven't had a random one-night stand before, so why is it such a big deal if I do?"

"Because like you just pointed out, you're better than us," I tell her. "You have higher standards for yourself, and I don't want to see you screwed over by losers. Neither of us do."

Aspen groans. "I'm hanging up now."

"You're okay though?" Austin asks.

"I'm fine," she mutters, her tone suggesting she's anything but.

"He's wrong," I tell her.

There's a short silence before her tone sails through the small speakers again. "What?"

"That you're not worth the meal. He's wrong," I tell her, ignoring the strange stare I receive from Austin. "You are. You're worth so much more than that, and I'm glad you had the self-respect to tell him to fuck off. Though, we do need to have a chat about giving out your address to assholes you've never met."

"And we need to have a chat about your need to tell my brother my business," she says with a heavy sigh. "You're an asshole, Izaac."

"He was just concerned about you," Austin says, always having my back.

"Right," she says slowly. "*That's* what he was concerned about."

My heart lurches in my chest, panic blasting through my veins as Austin's brows furrow, clearly having no idea what Aspen means by that, but he's too worked up to put much thought into it. "Just . . . promise me there will be no more random hookups with strangers."

"It wasn't a hookup," Aspen groans. "It was a plan to grab something to eat with the possibility of hot sex afterward. You know, after I'd gotten to know him a little bit. But it doesn't matter anyway. He's gone, and my legs are practically superglued together, so why are we still discussing it?"

"Yeah, okay," Austin says. "I guess I'll talk to you later."

"Whatever," Aspen says before the call goes dead.

I cringe, that definitely could have gone better, and sure, I feel like an ass for dropping her in shit with her brother, but on the other hand, she's not fucking random strangers. I'm the only random stranger she'll be fucking . . . or fucked. Past tense because it's definitely not happening again. But I suppose the real question is, why the fuck am I thinking about this while sitting barely a foot away from her brother?

"Fucking hell," Austin mutters. "That was a close one."

"Right," I agree. "But she's good though. Seems she's making better decisions than we did in college."

Austin grins. "Fuck, those college days were wild."

"Exactly my point."

He nods. "Yeah, well, thanks for letting me know. I mean it, if something had happened to her, I'd never be able to forgive myself. I know she thinks I'm too hard on her and always butting into her business, but I just want her to be safe."

"I know, man," I say, reaching out and dropping my hand to his shoulder in encouragement. "Now, tell me about this restaurant. Did my architect make it out today?"

"Yeah," he sighs with relief, his whole demeanor shifting as a wide grin stretches across his face. "That man is a fucking miracle worker. He's got a few ideas that could get me back on track. He'll be drawing it up first thing Monday morning, and we'll go from there."

"Thank fuck for that," I say, getting up from the coffee table and meeting his stare. "I've gotta get out of here. I was supposed to be at Cherry ages ago. You wanna come for a drink?"

"Nah, man. I'm gonna call it a night. It was a fucking huge day."

"Alright. Suit yourself," I say, and with that, I head for the door.

I make my way out of Austin's home, and by the time I'm settling in behind the wheel of my Escalade, my phone is buzzing with an incoming text. Digging into my pocket, I pull it out before glancing down at the screen, and within seconds, a smug smirk cuts across my face.

Aspen - You're an asshole.

She may be right, and telling Austin about her plans was definitely overstepping, but there's no denying that when she's feisty like this, I can't fucking resist her. As I sit in Austin's driveway, I get to work, texting his little sister back.

Izaac - You're welcome.

13

ASPEN

Frustration burns through me, and honestly, I don't know if it's irritation with my brother's need to butt into my business, annoyance with Izaac for all his whiplash and mixed signals, or if I'm just sexually frustrated for not being able to get myself off well all week. Don't get me wrong, I've definitely tried, and no matter how long it takes me, I always reach the finish line, but it never hits the spot. I'm always left disappointed and even more on edge than when I started.

Who would have thought that one sexual experience would leave me so wound up and sex-crazed? I've barely been able to concentrate all week, and now that my plans for the night have fallen through, I'm left with nothing to do but sit on my couch and stare at the wall.

Fucking pathetic.

Unless . . .

My mystery Vixen man made a point to invite me back. Technically it would be rude not to accept, right? And I'm not in the business of letting other people down. But does that officially mean that I'm desperate? Am I that much of a loser that the only way I can get what I need is by visiting a stranger in a sex club?

Shit.

Let's face it, despite how pissed off I am with Izaac right now, I'm still desperately in love with him, and I really doubt that I'll be capable of meeting someone who could possibly have my feelings for Izaac fading, and I also doubt that I'll be attempting the whole Tinder date thing again, so I'm screwed.

I need sex, and I'm not too ashamed to admit that I'm more than just desperate.

I need my mystery Vixen man more than my next breath, and now that I suddenly don't have any plans for the night, what the hell is stopping me?

Determination pulses through my veins, and before I know it, I'm grabbing my phone and flying out the door. I'm already dressed and ready due to my failed date, so all I need is a little liquid courage, which I can find at Vixen's bar.

A thrill blasts through me, propelling me ahead, and within seconds I drop into my car and hit the gas. I have to really concentrate to remember which roads to take, but within the space of twelve minutes, I pull up exactly where the Uber driver had dropped me and Becs off last week.

Holy shit. I can't believe I'm actually doing this.

Maybe I should have texted to let her know I was coming. She had such a great time last week, I'm sure she would have loved to come again, but then I would have had to explain why I was here, and honestly, I'm not sure I'm ready for that conversation.

The moment I step out of my car, a wave of nerves settles in the pit of my stomach, but I do my best to ignore them as I walk a little up the street. As the opening of the alley appears before me, I peer down into the darkness, and my nerves turn into regret.

Maybe I didn't really think this through.

It's one thing walking down a dark alley with Becs at my side—a woman who wouldn't hesitate to throw hands—but to do it alone when I'm scared of my own damn shadow . . . What the hell was I thinking?

The promise of a great time and a killer orgasm keeps me moving, one foot in front of the other. My hands shake the whole way down the alley, and my paranoia insists that the dark shadows are watching me with every step.

Reaching the familiar black door, I yank it open and hurry inside, barely getting the slightest flash of the Vixen logo above the door before I pass beneath it.

The heavy door closes behind me, and I make my way down the long hallway to the stairs, the dim lighting offering just enough light to help me relax. I make my way down, clutching the handrail before finally stepping out into the reception area.

I recognize the same girl that I saw here last week and curse myself for not being able to remember her name, but in my defense, there was a lot to take in.

She gives me a beaming smile, her eyes quickly darting to something behind her desk before coming back to me. "Hi there, you're Aspen, right? You came in with your friend last week."

"Yes, that's right," I tell her before cringing. "I'm sorry if this isn't how things are usually done, but I met someone last week, and he invited me to come back, and I . . . shit. This is embarrassing. I don't even know his name or what he looked like, or if it's even okay for me to be here."

The woman laughs. "It's okay. You wouldn't believe just how common that actually is. Let me put in a call and see what I can do."

She gives me a sugary-sweet smile, and I take a step back from her desk as she picks up her phone and dials a number. There's a short silence in the reception area, and as she waits for whoever to answer the call, it occurs to me that she could be waiting for *him* to answer.

My stomach twists with nerves, but I try to keep any evidence of it from my face as her tone cuts through the silence. "Hey, it's Casey," she says, her gaze flicking to something behind her desk before glancing up at me once again.

There's another pause. "Yes, that's right." She starts typing something into her computer, a strange curiosity flashing in her eyes. "But I thought you said—Oh, okay. Sure thing. I'll send her through."

Relief pounds through my veins, and as Casey hangs up the phone, her gaze sweeps to me again. She stands behind her desk with a fake smile and lifts her hand. I recognize the stamper for the gold moth pinched between her fingers. "Your wrist please."

I step into the side of the reception desk and immediately offer my wrist. She presses the gold stamp to my skin, and I can't help but watch as she pulls it away, leaving the perfect imprint of the moth against my wrist. A small smile pulls at my lips. The last time I wore this stamp, Austin and Izaac were staring at me in horror. It's insane to think how much has gone down since then.

Casey puts the stamper away before moving out from around her desk. "Right this way," she says, waving toward the main entrance to the club.

"Oh . . . umm. Don't I need to sign paperwork and get a wristband?"

"That won't be required today," she tells me, her smile faker than the Rolex Austin wears. Maybe I was so caught up with everything last week that I didn't take the time to notice how insincere she seemed. "When you enter the club, please head down to the VIP bar and make yourself comfortable. Perhaps try one of our frozen Daiquiris. We're trialing a new recipe and in my opinion, they're absolutely delicious."

"I uhh . . . yeah. Okay."

"Wonderful," she says, striding to the door and reaching for the handle. She pulls it open and waves me inside, but I find myself pausing.

Glancing back at Casey, I cringe, feeling like an idiot. "You don't happen to know his name, do you?" I ask. "I feel so stupid. I was so caught up in the moment last week that I didn't even think to ask, and before it even occurred to me, it was already far too late."

Casey gives me a tight smile. "Unfortunately, I can't disclose the information of our members. I'm sure you understand."

"Yes, of course," I say, shaking my head. "I'm sorry."

"No need to be sorry, just go in there and have a good time."

Not wanting to waste another minute, I walk through the door and into the main club, the loud, pulsing music instantly vibrating through my chest. A smile pulls at my lips. How is it that I've only been here once before and already it feels like home? There's just something so right about it.

Up until I found this club, my life was predictable and boring. I lived within the confines of what my family expected of me, but here, wrapped in the glimmering lights and seductive music, anything feels possible. My only limitations are the boundaries I set for myself, and nothing has ever excited me more. Walking this club and taking it in only ramps up the tension that I'm so desperate to release, and despite not having Becs by my side, I'm more comfortable knowing exactly what's in store for me.

My gaze sweeps through the club, taking in the insane scenes filling every corner. The threesomes. The orgies. The woman taking a cock so deep down her throat it's practically in her stomach. And instead of stopping and chilling at the bar as everything unfolds around me, I head straight to the stairs leading down to the VIP lounge.

After flashing my gold moth stamp, I head down the stairs, and just like last time, I notice the shift in the music. There's something so electrifying about it that I feel it deep in my soul. Then just as Casey requested, I make my way over to the bar and take a seat, only I skip over the frozen Daiquiri and order a Cosmopolitan.

With a drink in my hand, I swivel on the barstool and gaze out at the VIP lounge. It's busy, just as I expected, and I can't help but glance toward the dark room I was in last week. There's no sign of my mystery stranger, but the buzz that pulses through my veins tells me that he's definitely here somewhere. I can feel it.

I barely get to sip my Cosmo before a familiar face moves in beside me. "You were here last week," the man says, his suit fitting him just right. I can't help but drag my gaze over him. If I were into older men who looked as though they could turn a board meeting into their bitch, then he'd be the man I'd sneak off with tonight, but just like last week, he's not going to scratch that particular itch.

"Hi, yes. I was," I say just to be polite.

"All alone?" he questions as something flashes in his eyes.

Alarm bells sound in my head as metaphorical red flags sprout up all around him. Why does he need to know if I'm alone? Quite frankly, that's none of his business, and honestly, it sounds like the kind of question that would come from a serial killer textbook. "No actually. Just waiting on a friend."

"Ahh, I see," he says before offering his hand. "The name's Ryatt."

I give him a tight smile, not daring to take his hand. Last week I put in more effort to appear approachable, and he easily picked up that I wasn't interested, but tonight, I'm barely even polite, some would even accuse me of being rude or cold, yet he's still sitting here as though he might have a chance.

"Aspen," I say, glancing past his shoulder to the opening of the dark room, seeing no sign of my perfect stranger, not that I would have even a clue what to look for. I have no idea what he looks like or even the color of his hair. Just that he's tall and stacked with muscle. Though if there were a lineup of dicks put out before me, I'm sure I could figure out which was his. There's no mistaking that girth and length, not to mention the piercing that drove me crazy.

Ryatt tilts his head just a fraction, putting himself right in my line of view, a cocky smile pulling at his lips. "Aspen," he says as if trying my name out on his lips. "Beautiful name."

"Thank you."

I fill the weird silence by taking a sip of my cocktail, and when he reaches for my elbow, the bartender clears his throat from behind me. I whip back to catch his friendly smile. "I'm sorry to disrupt," he says. "However, your presence has been requested in the dark room."

A thrill shoots through me, and a heavy throb pulses deep in my core. "Wonderful," I say, getting to my feet. I give the bartender a slight nod of thanks before turning to Ryatt. "It was a pleasure seeing you again."

"Of course. Perhaps next time you and I could get to know each other a little better."

Doubtful.

"That would be nice," I say. "Now if you would excuse me . . ."

I let my words trail off. I don't owe him any explanations about what I intend to do or where I'm going, so I simply walk away, clutching my Cosmo between my fingers. I take a few desperate sips, unsure why the nerves have decided to make another appearance. I know exactly what's going to go down in there. I know he's not going to hurt me and that he's going to make me feel comfortable. I have nothing to worry about, and yet . . . the bundle of nerves in the pit of my stomach continues to grow.

In the short walk from the bar to the door of the private room, my drink almost disappears, and when I finally reach it, I find myself pausing. I take a calming breath, and as the excitement builds within me, I realize it wasn't nerves at all. It was raw anticipation.

I've been waiting for this moment since the second he finished with me last week. I've thought about it nonstop, and I've pictured just how good it would be until nothing else could do the job, but what if last week was a fluke? What if he was on a roll and was doing everything right and tonight doesn't live up to my expectations? I'll be crushed. But what do I have to lose? There's a man standing in this room who's willing to do whatever it takes to make me see stars, and I'd be a fool to walk away now.

Scrounging up every last shred of courage, I step over the threshold to the private room, and the moment I do, the anticipation shifts into an electrifying buzz that sets my body on fire.

Despite the darkness that surrounds me, I sense him in the room. "Close the door, Little Birdy."

Hooooly fuck.

Just the sound of those words makes something melt within me. Shivers sail down my spine, and without a second of hesitation, I close the door behind me, then remembering the small table by the entrance, I finish off the last few drops of my Cosmo and place the glass down.

"Come to me."

Just like last time, the music is so loud that it's nearly impossible to hear his smooth tone over the sound, but every word he speaks is as though it's directed right into my soul. I drift toward the center of the room, taking my time. I don't see him, but I can feel him here. The air between our bodies crackles with desire and need, and the tension builds with each step I take toward his voice.

I come to a stop when I smell the familiar scent of his cologne, and not a moment later, I feel his hand at my waist. He pulls me in hard, spinning me at the same time until my back is pressed against his bare chest. A gasp tears from my throat, and when his fingers brush across my jaw and drop to my chest, I have to remind myself how to breathe.

"What are you doing here, Birdy? What do you need?"

I swallow hard, not really sure what I need, just as long as he's the one giving it to me, then I don't really care. "The women in this club, they come here to explore their kinks, to push their boundaries and try things they maybe wouldn't be brave enough to try somewhere else. But you . . ." I pant, needing to pause as I try to figure out what I'm saying. "Since last week, you have become my kink. Nothing has been able to compare to the way you touched me, and now . . . I don't even know what I need from you, just that I need it to be you."

A deep growl of approval rumbles through his chest as his hand dips low between my thighs. He cups my pussy through my jeans and grinds the heel of his palm against my clit, making my hips jolt as though being struck by lightning. "You need me to fill you?" he questions. "To stretch that sweet little cunt to its limits?"

"Yes," I breathe.

"To fuck you," he continues, "hard and deep until your legs start to shake?"

I suck in a breath as his other hand skims over my trembling body. "Yes. I need you to touch me. Ruin me."

Without warning, his hand twines into the back of my hair, and he pulls my head to the side as his hungry lips come down on my neck. His tongue roams across the sensitive skin as my knees immediately try to give out beneath me.

I groan, gripping his strong forearm and digging my nails into his skin. "Oh, God," I moan, my eyes rolling as he continues to grind his palm against my pussy. "I need to feel you inside me."

"Patience, Sweet Bird."

I'm losing my fucking mind, my pussy is already soaking with need, and when his hand releases my hair and skims down my body to the hem of my silk top, the anticipation intensifies. He pulls the dainty fabric over my head and drops it to the ground before reaching for my bra. He effortlessly unclips it with barely a flick of his fingers, and by the time that hits the ground, his hands are already at the waistband of my jeans, quickly working the button.

My hands start to roam, reaching up behind me and hooking my hand around the back of his neck as he works his lips across the base of my throat. I've never felt so alive, and he's barely touched me yet.

He pushes my jeans down, taking my thong with them, and the second I kick them off my feet, he whips me back around and grabs me by the ass. I'm lifted into his strong arms, and my legs hook around his waist, holding on for dear life as my body molds to his.

The sweet torture of his tongue on my neck doesn't stop as he strides across the room. He places me on the edge of something soft. It's too wide to be a couch, and there's no backrest, but it's definitely not a bed. Either way, it's deliciously comfortable as my body sinks into it.

He stands between my legs, his crotch right at the perfect height if he wanted to fuck me right here and now, only something tells me that he's not quite ready for that yet. His hands grip my thighs, his thumbs rolling over my smooth skin as he pulls them up so that my feet rest against the cushion, keeping them spread wide.

"Do you smell the sweet scent of your arousal?" he rumbles, bracing his knee between my legs and leaning toward me, then without warning, he closes his mouth over the sharp peak of my nipple, flicking his tongue over the sensitive bud. "You're addictive."

I arch my back off the cushion, trying to offer more of myself to him, but I'm at his mercy and can only take as much as he's giving.

His tongue continues working over my nipple when I feel his hand slide down the inside of my thigh, and my breath catches, my body jolting as he reaches my drenched core. Hunger pulses through my body, and desperation keeps me on edge as he slowly pushes two thick fingers deep inside me, taking me inch by inch.

My body squirms beneath him, but he doesn't relent, doing it again and again, curling his fingers inside me before pulling them free and rolling them straight over my clit. I gasp, already trembling as my hips jolt against the cushion. He does it again, this time adding more pressure as his fingers rub smaller, tighter circles. It's everything.

His other hand roams across my waist, exploring my skin, and every brush of his fingers sets me on fire. It's different from last week. That was crazed desperation, but there's something so sensual about this. It's as though he's committing every inch of me to memory, and I fucking love it.

Not wanting to waste an opportunity, my hands explore, touching every inch of him. Grazing my nails across his chest, his abs, and his strong arms before reaching higher and brushing my fingers across the stubble on his sharp jaw. Even in this darkness, it's clear that he's attractive. How could he not be? The confidence of this man can only come from someone who's capable of making women fall to their knees, and despite knowing he must have been with countless women, I'm proud to be one of the many.

He works my body right to the edge, pushing his fingers back inside of me as he uses his thumb to keep working my clit. I'm so close, but I need so much more. I need to feel him. Then understanding my wild desperation, he doesn't try to stop me when I reach for the front of his jeans. Instead, he pops the button with ease and frees his massive cock as he shifts higher, his lips coming back to the base of my throat.

I feel that addictive piercing as his cock falls against the inside of my thigh, and I can't resist curling my hand around him, gently squeezing and roaming my fist up and down. I can barely fit my whole hand around him, and just as I stretch my thumb across his tip, he plunges his fingers deeper.

My body spasms as my orgasm blasts through me like a fiery explosion, and the sound of his hiss as I circle his tip somehow makes it stronger. "Oh, God," I groan, my grip tightening on his thick cock as my walls convulse around his fingers.

I can't hold still. My whole body squirms with the sweetest pleasure. "Yes, Little Birdy. Just like that. Show me how you come on my fingers."

I still, unease derailing me like a freight train.

With his lips so close to my ear, I hear him loud and clear, and that tone . . . I know that fucking tone better than I know the reflection that stares back at me every morning in my bathroom mirror.

Horror slams through my body, and without a single second of hesitation, I release my hold around his cock and bring my foot up, slamming it against his chest and forcing him as far away as I possibly can.

That voice could only belong to one man.

Izaac fucking Banks.

14

IZAAC

No. No. No. No. No.

How could I have let this happen?

My chest aches from when she shoved me away, but I barely even notice it as she scrambles to get to her feet, hastily climbing off the large ottoman.

She knows. She fucking knows.

I hear her feet against the floor as she strides toward me. "It's you, isn't it?" she demands, her voice shaky and filled with deep betrayal. She brushes her hand against my cheek as if tracing the lines of my face that she committed to memory by the time she was ten years old.

"Aspen," I breathe, not knowing what to say or how to fix this, all I know is that I fucked up, and now, hearing that thick betrayal and fear in her tone, there's no denying it. Things will never be the same again.

Hearing her name on my lips is all the confirmation she needs, and she hastily pulls away. "FUCK," she cries out, and without being able to see that beautiful face, I know there are tears streaming down her cheeks. "How could I be so stupid?"

"Aspen, please," I say, reaching for her, my hand falling to her waist.

She slaps it away as though it physically pains her. "Don't touch me," she seethes, her voice shaky and raw. "Don't ever fucking touch me."

"Aspen."

"Turn the lights on," she demands.

"Are you sure?"

"Turn the fucking lights on, Izaac. I need to see you for myself. I need to know that the man standing before me isn't the man I think he is because the Izaac I know, the one I've been in love with my whole damn life, would never betray my trust like this."

Guilt tears through me, and I feel the exact moment my heart cracks down the center. I should have made Casey turn her away. That was the whole fucking point of banning her from the club. Her picture was put at reception, and I gave Casey specific instructions to call me if Aspen were to show up again. I thought maybe she would in a few months out of sheer curiosity, but when Casey called and said Aspen was standing in reception, I couldn't resist telling her to send her down to the VIP lounge.

The second the words were out of my mouth, I knew it was wrong.

I wasn't just betraying her trust by letting her walk through the door, I was betraying Austin's as well. But the idea of getting to be with her again, especially after spending all day thinking about her entering her whore era with some loser from Tinder . . . fuck. I had to remind her just how fucking good it was between us.

I'd only just arrived at Cherry when Casey's call came through, and before I even made it through the door, I was right back in my Escalade, speeding toward Vixen. It's an eight-minute drive at this time of night, but I did it in five, and the whole fucking time, all I could think about was all the other assholes who were watching her at the bar while I sped toward her.

What the fuck is wrong with me? It's one thing accidentally fucking my best friend's little sister, but to take her intentionally . . . I've not just crossed the line, I fucking destroyed it.

Not wanting to keep her waiting, I move across the room and hastily tuck my dick back inside my pants before finding the tablet against the wall. I turn on the lighting and the room fills with a dim glow.

I'm almost too fucking scared to turn around.

Despite the noise and the distance between us, I can hear her gasp as she finally sees me, or maybe I'm just so in tune with her now that the agony in her tone just spears right through my chest.

I slowly turn and lift my gaze to hers, making a point not to linger on her body. She wouldn't want that. It's clear in the way she tries to cover herself, hiding the body from me that I'd just had my hands all over, my fingers buried deep inside, and my mouth roaming over those sweet nipples. But something tells me that's a gift I'll never receive again.

Regret rests heavily on my shoulders. How could I let it get this far? She's never going to forgive me, and she shouldn't. Last week was sheer coincidence, but tonight . . . This was a clear betrayal. A violation of her trust, and I'm fucking disgusted with myself.

"I . . . I don't understand how this happened," she says, shaking her head.

I inch toward her, my gaze not moving from hers as she stands there and watches me with the greatest sadness. Tears well in her eyes and slowly roll down her cheeks. She fucking hates me. "Aspen, I . . . I'm sorry," I tell her. "I never intended for it to happen this way, and when I figured out the girl from last week was you, I just . . . I'm sorry. You have to know how fucking sorry I am."

"You're sorry?" she scoffs, her voice breaking with despair. "You were *inside* of me, Izaac. You took my virginity, and then you let me walk right back in here without saying a goddamn word. You're supposed to be my family. You're supposed to protect me from the people who want to use me like you just did. Isn't that why you told Austin about my date today, or was it just so you could take advantage of me yourself?"

"Fuck, Aspen. It's not like that. I just—I'm so fucking sorry. This isn't how I thought it would turn out."

She scoffs again, only this time, the heavy tears streaming down her face have her voice breaking into a million little pieces. "So what then? When the receptionist called and said that I was here, what were your intentions when you told her to send me down here? Were your intentions to fuck me again and hope that I'd never figure it out? To come by my parents' home and smile and laugh with me like you hadn't been inside of me? To drink with my brother like you hadn't betrayed his trust?"

I swallow hard over the lump forming in my throat, never having felt such raw hatred of myself in my life. She's right. She's supposed to be family. I've always sworn to protect her, and now, I'm the one she needs protection from.

Only it's so much worse than that because all I've been doing is thinking about what I wanted from her, but what about her? This is more than just sex for Aspen. She's been in love with me for years, and a betrayal like this isn't something she can just shake off. I'm breaking her fucking heart.

Aspen looks away, breaking the hold she has over me, and when the next words fall out of her mouth, I fucking crumble. "Get out," she begs.

"Aspen, please. Hear me out," I say, searching out her stare only to realize she can no longer look at me. "We can talk this through. Just give me a chance to explain."

"OUT! I don't want to see you."

The pieces of my soul shatter, and all I can do is hang my head as I turn and walk to the door, each step feeling so fucking wrong. Reaching for the door, I pull it open when her soft tone cuts through the heaviness. "Izaac," she says, her voice so fucking broken, it kills me. I turn back, catch her eyes, and wait for whatever she needs to say. "Since I was a little girl, I always thought there was nothing you could do or say that would make me not love you, even over these past few years when you've purposefully made it clear that nothing could ever happen between us. You were the sun in my sky, and I always thought that what I felt for you was impenetrable, but I was wrong because never in my whole life could I have thought you were capable of hurting me like this. Don't ever talk to me again, Izaac. I hate you."

I nod, and with that, I walk out of the private room, listening as she crumbles to the ground in agony. Her sobs fill the space behind me, and as I close the door between us, my whole fucking world burns to ashes at my feet.

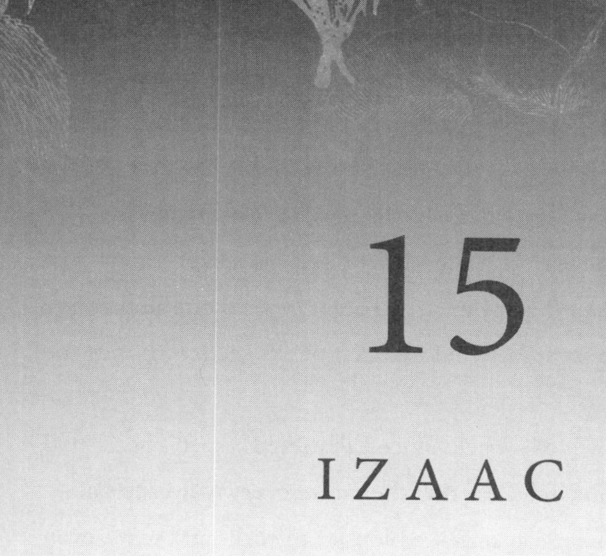

15

IZAAC

A smile stretches across my face as I walk through the construction zone otherwise known as Austin's restaurant. His renovations were finally approved, and the second he could, he put his team to work.

It's been a long fucking road getting to this point, and now that everything's starting to come together, I've never seen him so proud.

Right now, it looks like a fucking mess. They're still in the demolition stage, but by the end of the week, it'll start taking shape, and Austin will be right back on track for his grand opening in the fall.

He shows me around, pointing out the issues my architect was able to rectify, and as I take it all in, I do my best to appear excited. Don't get me wrong, I'm so fucking thrilled for him, but there's also a heaviness that has been weighing me down since the night Aspen told me she never wanted to speak to me again, and it's really starting to fuck with me. I can't concentrate, can barely work, and pretending as though her heartbreak doesn't mean anything to me is getting harder by the day.

I've never had to pretend to be happy for Austin before, I've always had his back and have always celebrated his achievements just as he's done for me, but today, I'm struggling. I'm just grateful that he's so caught up in his restaurant build that he doesn't seem to notice the way my smile falls flat.

It's been a little over two weeks since I shattered Aspen's heart, and she's made it crystal fucking clear that she meant every word she said—she never wants to see me again. She blocked my calls and texts, even on social media. I've tried knocking on her door and sitting outside her apartment for hours on end, just begging for the opportunity to talk to her, to try and earn her forgiveness, but it won't happen. I've fucked up the dynamics of our relationship, and it won't be long before Austin realizes something is up.

It's driving me insane.

It was never my intention to hurt her or betray her trust, but now that I have, the guilt is eating me alive.

I need to make this better, need to know that she forgives me, and if that means never getting to touch her again, then I'll find a way to deal with that.

All of this has me so fucked up. Hell, she's been right there all along, and now that she can't stand to look at me, I've never wanted to be in her life more. I've never realized just how much comfort there was in knowing she was there, even as nothing more than a friend or Austin's little sister, but now that she's gone, it's as though a big chunk of my soul has been torn away. Whether we were ever going to be something or not, I've always loved her. Like she said, she's family, and that means something to me.

If only I hadn't been so fucking blind to it before.

Plastering on a fake smile, I let Austin take me around the whole restaurant, pointing out where everything is going to go, despite having looked at the plans a million times before. He shows me exactly where his chefs will work, where his industrial fridge will be installed, and the exact path his runners will take to deliver food from the kitchen to his guests.

With every word that tumbles from his mouth, his pride shines even brighter, and by the time he starts talking about his menu, I almost forget how much of an asshole I am.

His phone rings, and after digging it out of his pocket, a wide grin stretches across his face. Austin throws himself to his feet, pressing accept on the call and holding out the screen as though it were a video call. "What's up, asshole?"

"Not much, Douchecanoe," I hear Aspen's tone fill the restaurant, and the very sound of it makes my back stiffen as my pulse races. There's no telling how this is going to go down. What if she's calling to tell Austin everything I've done? There's no stopping his fists when he's defending his little sister, and with me being right here in front of him, there isn't even a moment for him to try and calm down. "Are you at the restaurant? Mom said you were starting on the build this week. Can you show me?"

Oh, thank fuck.

I let out a shaky breath, narrowly escaping an early grave as Austin strides through his demolition site, stepping over old fallen bricks and trying to speak over the sound of the workmen tearing the place apart.

I listen to their whole conversation, and despite the smile she forces across her face, I can hear the devastation in her tone, and judging by the growing suspicion on Austin's face, he senses it too.

Once Austin's completed the full tour, he starts making his way back toward me when he suddenly turns the camera to show that I'm here, and her face instantly drops. "Look, Izaac's here," Austin says, clearly as a way to try and cheer her up—a tactic that's worked a million times before, only today, it's different. That tactic is never going to work again. "You wanna say hi?"

Aspen's face falls and something twists in my gut. "Nah, I'm good," she says, her dismissal making Austin blanch.

"You sure?" Austin asks. "Everything okay? You don't seem like yourself."

Austin sits down, and from this angle, I can see his screen and the lifeless face that stares back at him, but she can't see mine, though there's no denying the change in her tone since finding out I was here. "I'm good, just exhausted. I stayed up cramming for an exam all night."

"Nah," Austin says, shaking his head. "That's not it. Something's going on with you. You've been off for weeks now, and don't even pretend that I haven't realized you've been rejecting all my calls. Are you still pissed about the whole date thing? 'Cause that was two weeks ago, and you technically told him to fuck off before I even called. He hasn't . . . tried something with you, has he?"

Aspen rolls her eyes. "Do you even hear yourself? I'm fine. I'm just . . . tired."

I scoff. Despite not wanting the truth to come out, especially before I've had a chance to figure out what I'm supposed to say to him, that lie was more than obvious. A toddler could have picked up on it.

Austin's gaze flicks to me, his brows furrowed with concern, and I see the question in his stare, asking me if I have any ideas, and all I can do is shamefully shrug my shoulders. "You're not *fine,* Aspen," Austin says, turning his stare back to his little sister. "You know you can always talk to me, but I can see that whatever it is, you're not ready. Just know that I'm here when you are."

Aspen doesn't respond, just lets her gaze fall away, and it's clear to see the heartbreak across her face, the devastation in the way she holds her shoulders. She's falling to pieces and it has everything to do with me.

"I love you," he tells her.

"Yeah, love you, too," she mutters, her heart not in it.

"Listen, I have to stay here with the construction crew, but if you need company, just let me know. I can send Izaac around there for a movie night, or you can bombard him with awkward questions like you did when you were a kid. You used to love that shit."

Aspen scoffs. "Yeah, *used* to. Not anymore," she says. "But quit worrying about me. It's not necessary, and all you're doing is reminding me how much of a meddling asshat you can be. You're like Mom reborn. Mind ya business. I'm fine. Besides, I just wanna crash tonight."

"It's barely five in the afternoon."

"Yeah, and like I said, I was up all night cramming."

"Aspen—"

"I'm hanging up," she warns him.

"Don't you dare hang up on—"

The line goes dead and Austin lets out a heavy sigh, leaning back against his seat and tossing his phone onto the middle of the old table that's yet to be torn out. "Fucking hell. She's impossible."

I keep my mouth shut, really not knowing what the hell I'm supposed to say without making matters any worse.

"It's gotta be a guy," Austin suggests. "It's always a fucking guy. I mean, did you see the way she ignored you? She couldn't even give you a smile for fuck's sake. She always fucking smiles when she sees you."

"I don't know what to tell you, man. Maybe she's finally moved on."

Austin scoffs, shaking his head. "The fucking zombie apocalypse would come before we see the day that my sister finally moves on. And despite how much I fucking hate it, that crush of hers isn't going anywhere, but that doesn't mean there hasn't been some other asshole fucking with her."

Fuck.

I groan, knowing exactly what's about to come out of his mouth.

"Look, maybe you should head over there anyway, just suss it out. You've always had a way of making her talk. Maybe she'll open up to you."

Ha. If only he knew that opening up to me is how all this bullshit started in the first place. If he knew, sending me over there would be the last thing he'd ever do.

"I don't think that's such a good idea, man. She clearly doesn't want to see me. Why don't you head over there tomorrow instead?"

Austin shakes his head as a man from his construction crew calls out to him. He lets out a heavy sigh and gets to his feet, and as he walks away, he glances back over his shoulder. "You know how she gets when she sits and stews on shit. She needs to talk it out, and clearly talking to me ain't gonna happen. So you're up. Besides, I've got these guys here all week. I won't get a chance to get over there 'til the weekend, and I can't stand the thought of her being all broken up about something for that long. Just go figure it out, and if it's something that can be fixed, then fix it."

Shit.

Austin disappears into the back as I ball my hands into tight fists.

This isn't going to go down well. I'm the last person she wants to see right now, but there's no denying that the thought of her spending her night broken on her couch tears me apart.

All of this is my fault. I broke her, and it's my responsibility to put her back together. If there's even the slightest chance that she could forgive me and we could somehow move past this with minimum destruction, then I need to try.

And with that, I get up from the old table and storm right back out the door, determined to stand at her door for as long as it takes.

16

ASPEN

When you've been so deeply in love with someone for most of your life, it's statistically inevitable that at some point, that person will cause you pain. So naturally, over the past twelve years, I've cried many tears over Izaac Banks. Sometimes I cried over his actions or comments to push me away, and sometimes my tears were caused by the heartache of never being able to have what I've always wanted.

The past two weeks have been different than before. They're gut-wrenching.

I've never experienced a betrayal like it, and honestly, there are still so many pieces of the puzzle I don't understand. I have so many questions left unanswered, but all it comes down to is that when I walked into that dark room, he knew exactly who I was, and without saying a word, he touched my body. He put his fingers inside of me as his lips worked across my skin, and given the chance, he would have fucked me.

All I've done over the past two weeks is try to process everything, and I've come to the conclusion that the day of my mother's birthday lunch, when Izaac stood behind me in the pool, that was the moment he figured it out, and that was the moment he should have come clean. Sure, it would have been an awkward conversation, but neither of us knew, neither of us were at fault. It was a coincidence, nothing more and nothing less. We would have easily gotten past it, and at some point, maybe we would have even laughed about it.

But he made sure that could never happen.

He betrayed my trust. He knew I was walking in there to be with someone . . . anyone who wasn't him, and when he knowingly touched me, he stole that away from me. And now the one person I've always loved and wanted knows exactly how I taste. He knows how I sound when I come, how it feels when my walls stretch around him, and while that should be something that's celebrated, it leaves me feeling dirty.

Growing up, I always hoped that Izaac would be the man to take my virginity, and now . . . I guess the joke is on me. It's a cruel world we live in because I got exactly what I wanted, only it's nothing like I wanted at all.

I've pictured it a million times over the years, how I would give myself to him, how he would touch me, kiss me, and make me come alive. It would have been the perfect moment, but only after he accepted that I was the woman for him. It was supposed to be filled with magic and love. He was supposed to be my everything, and when I finally realized that was never going to happen, I gave myself to a complete stranger.

Only it wasn't, and now it's tainted by betrayal.

How could something I wanted so badly become something so horrible? Don't get me wrong, my first time was incredible. Sex with Izaac is clearly unbelievable, and he knows exactly how to give a woman exactly what she needs, and that piercing . . . my god! But if I knew I had the chance to be with him, to really give him my virginity, I would have done it differently, and I sure as hell wouldn't have done it in a dark club, believing he was anyone else.

I feel robbed. Betrayed. Defeated and broken.

My heart has never ached like this. All of me hurts.

How could he do this to me? How could he knowingly put his hands on me? What did he expect was going to come from this? That I would continue to visit him at Vixen and unknowingly become his dirty little secret?

The whole week following Mom's birthday, he flirted with me. He danced with me at Pulse, we took shots together, and then that night . . . I thought things were finally starting to change between us, that he'd finally realized I was no longer just Austin's little sister, that I was someone worth pursuing. Instead, he was just remembering how good it felt to be inside of me.

That call the night before, all the flirty texts, I thought they meant something, but now all of it's tainted. How am I supposed to get past that? Izaac Banks is far from the man I thought he was, and now I feel as though I'm grieving this idea I've always had of him.

I want to hate him. I want to scream at him and make him hurt the way that I do, but one thing is for sure, we can never go back. This changes everything, and sooner or later, Austin is going to notice that something is going on. When he finally puts the pieces together, his relationship with Izaac will forever be altered, and despite how badly I want to pulverize Izaac and make him pay for my pain and embarrassment, how could I possibly punish Austin like that?

A knock sounds at my door, and my head whips toward it.

I sure as fuck would remember if I buzzed someone into my building.

Getting up from the couch, I scold Nathan on level three for being such an asshole as I make my way to the door. I had high hopes for Nathan. He was supposed to be the good neighbor who never bothered me, but I'm starting to reconsider.

Already mentally preparing my speech to send Becs or Austin away, I reach for the lock before leaning into the door and quickly glancing through the peephole.

My body freezes, and I pull my hand away from the lock.

That motherfucker!

Izaac stands on the other side of my door, his hands gripping the frame on either side, his head hung low. He's been here a few times over the past two weeks, and each time, he's looked even worse. I hate that this is eating him up, but at the same time, that's not my problem.

He was the one who made the decision to keep me in the dark, and he was the one who decided to walk into that room, knowing damn well who stood before him.

My hands shake as tears fill my eyes. My chest aches worse every time I see him. Can I be in love with someone who would do that to me? He's not the man I thought he was.

"Open the door, Aspen," he rumbles out in the hallway. "I know you're there. I can hear you."

"You could be out in that hall in the middle of a psychotic break, and I still wouldn't open the door for you, Izaac," I say, turning around and flopping heavily against the door. "I've already told you, you're not welcome here. Not anymore."

"Let me in, Aspen. I just wanna talk."

"You're seriously fucked in the head if you think I'm about to let you in here. Just go."

"You don't think I'll wait you out?" he questions as I feel him fall against the door, probably mimicking my stance. "I've got all night."

I roll my eyes, scoffing with irritation. "You can't go two minutes without eating. You'll starve."

"Say what you want, but I anticipated this," he says, his voice no longer coming from above me, but below, having slid down the door until he's sitting against it. "I brought snacks."

Fucking asshole.

"And when you need to pee?"

Something bangs against the door. "What do you think this is for?"

"Ha," I say with a scoff. "Suit yourself."

Then just to make a point, I stride back across my apartment and drop down onto the couch, more than ready to spend every waking hour right here. If that asshole wants to sit at my door for the foreseeable future, then that's on his bad judgment. I have Grey's Anatomy to binge, and just because I'm a petty bitch, I'll turn the volume up just enough to drown out anything he might have to say, but not loud enough that he can actually enjoy the show. If he wants to sit there all night, then he can suffer while doing it.

Getting comfortable, I pull my blanket up over me and hit play, only I'm suddenly not able to concentrate like I was before, and what I would usually find the sweetest pleasure in has become background noise as all my attention remains focused on the closed door.

An hour turns into two, and when silent tears track down my face, I hit pause on my show before getting up and tiptoeing across my home. I see the slight shadow under my door, telling me that he's still here, and I have to give him credit, if roles were reversed, I would have taken off long ago. My bladder couldn't possibly handle a stakeout, and it'll be a cold day in hell before I pee into a bottle.

I stand by the door and lean against the drywall with a soft sigh. Despite how I feel about him right now, being close to him gives me comfort. I don't think I'll ever be able to forgive him. Then just as he has, I slide down until my ass hits the floor and we're sitting back-to-back, trapped in an awful silence with my front door between us.

Pulling my knees up to my chest, I wrap my arms around them and stare across my apartment, desperately wishing things could be different. Wishing he never had to hurt me like that. Wishing I never had to love him. Why couldn't this have been easy? Why did it have to be him in that room? I needed it to be anyone but him.

As if sensing my need for comfort, a block of chocolate slides under the door. "I can smell your perfume, Birdy. Do you have any idea what the scent does to me?"

He did not just call me that.

Anger blasts through my veins as I spring to my feet, and with the quickest flick of my wrist, I reach up and unlock the door before twisting the handle and letting his body weight do the rest. The door flings wide as Izaac crashes into my apartment, his back slamming against my floor as a loud *Oomph* tears from his chest.

"What the fu—"

"YOU DON'T GET TO CALL ME THAT!" I throw myself at him, my fists already swinging, and as my body crashes into his, he catches me with ease. He flips us until my back is against the creaky floorboards, and he hovers over me, his strong grip locked around my wrists, holding both hands captive above my head.

"You're an asshole," I grit, willing myself not to let him see me cry as he keeps me pinned.

"If I let you go, are you going to try to attack me again?"

God, why does he have to smell so good?

"Can't make any promises."

His gaze narrows, and he holds my stare for a moment longer, the tension radiating off both of us, but the longer he holds me hostage, the harder it becomes to remember why I want to hate him so much.

He keeps me pinned for a moment longer before finally getting up, and instead of being the perfect gentleman as usual, he just leaves me there, my legs and feet hanging outside of my apartment.

Izaac makes himself at home, striding through my little apartment and stopping in the kitchen, bracing his elbows against the counter and waiting for me to finally make a move.

Letting out a groan, I get back to my feet and kick my door closed, sensing his gaze locked on me, but what's new? I can always tell when his eyes are on me. "I suppose you're not going to leave now?"

"After I just waited two fucking hours to get through the door? Fuck no."

Rolling my eyes, I storm across my apartment and drop down onto the couch with a huff, pulling my blanket up over me and pretending the giant asshole isn't staring at me from my kitchen.

Quickly realizing that I'm not going to make this easy for him, he lets out a heavy sigh and strides toward me, cutting between the couch and the coffee table and dropping down onto it.

His knees almost brush against mine, and as my heart starts to race, I begin to fret.

I guess it's time to face the music.

"You ready to talk about it?"

I scoff. "Which of my actions possibly gave you the impression that I was ever planning on talking about it with you?"

He braces his elbows on his knees and leans forward, getting way too close for my liking. "So, you were just gonna hate me for the rest of your natural life?" he asks. "Or does this whole avoiding me bullshit have a shelf life?"

"You know, I haven't really thought about it, but when I told you that I never wanted to talk to you again, I kinda meant it, so let's just assume option one is the way to go."

"Tough luck. That shit doesn't work for me."

"Tough luck. You're not the one whose trust was betrayed. We're not playing a game here, Izaac. This is my life. These are real feelings and emotions you're playing with, and you don't get to decide how mine are going to heal. I don't think you're understanding just how bad you hurt me."

"That's just the thing, Aspen. I do. I know that I hurt you. I fucked up, but pretending that I don't exist and ignoring the issues isn't helping anyone. For Austin's sake and your parents', you need to be able to be in the same room as me."

I scoff, throwing myself to my feet and looking at him as though he's lost his mind. "You're fucking kidding me, right?" I say, feeling the tears prick my eyes as I pace in front of the coffee table, his heavy gaze locked on me. "Everything is always for their sake, but what about my sake, Izaac? You have known for years how I've felt about you. It's not a secret, and for as long as I can remember, I've gone out of my way to hide that, to cater to everyone else so things don't have to be awkward or weird. And you, you big fucking asshole, make a point to constantly remind me that nothing will ever happen. I get it, okay. You and me, it's nothing but a fantasy. But what I don't fucking get is why? After everything, after knowing exactly what this would mean for me, or how it would fuck with Austin, why you would even consider walking back into that room with me?"

The heaviest silence I've ever felt settles over my apartment like a storm cloud. I crash back onto the couch, my face buried in my hands, not trusting myself not to break.

"Believe me, Birdy, if I fucking knew, I would tell you."

Grabbing a cushion off the couch, I launch it at his stupidly perfect face. "I told you not to call me that," I say as he catches it and holds it to his chest. "And that's a bullshit excuse and you know it."

"I'm sorry, Aspen. I just . . . since that first night at Vixen, I haven't been able to get it out of my head, and I know that was your first time, and you don't really have anything to compare it to, but sex isn't just like that. It's never that fucking good, but with you . . . fuck, Aspen. Do you have any idea how rare it is to find someone so fucking compatible like that?"

"Wow," I say, getting up and walking into my kitchen, desperately needing something to distract me and keep me from breaking right down the center. "So you destroyed me because you like to get your dick wet. Just fucking great, Izaac."

"It's not like that and you know it," he insists, getting up and following me.

"Then what's it like? Because for me, I was going in there to forget about you, because the prospect of me and you ever being together was so fucking absurd to you that I'd finally given up. I was there to give myself to someone else, to finally rid myself of the fantasy that I could ever have what I've always wanted, and that's exactly what I thought I did. Do you have any idea what that feels like? I thought I finally had a chance to move past this and have a life, but noooo! Izaac fucking Banks strikes again."

"Surely you must know that if I had known that was you the first night at Vixen, I never would have done that."

I clench my jaw, glancing away. "Of course I know that," I say. "I'm not pissed about the first time. I mean, sure, I'm pissed that knowing it was you takes away from everything I was trying to achieve that night, but it was nothing more than a shitty coincidence. It's knowing that you stood behind me in my parents' pool and worked it out but decided that you should keep your mouth shut. It's knowing that when you were texting me after being at Pulse, it wasn't because you'd finally come around and thought that maybe I had something to offer you, it was because you were remembering how it felt to be inside of me, how it felt when I came around you. And it's knowing that when I went back, just as vulnerable as I was the first time, you still walked into that room, knowing exactly who I was, and took advantage. You had every chance to tell me that you were the guy in that room, and the fact that you hid it from me . . . fuck, Izaac, that hurts the most."

Devastation and guilt flash in his eyes, and despite the distance I've tried to keep between us, he walks right into me, pulling me into his warm arms and holding me against his chest. His hand comes up to the back of my head, his fingers threading into my hair. "You don't need to tell me what I did to you and how bad it hurt. Trust me, I know. I fucked up, and it makes me sick to my stomach. Nobody hates me more than I do right now," he tells me as the steady beat of his heart keeps me from falling apart.

"Ever since you were a kid, all I've ever wanted was to protect you from assholes like me, but the second I got a taste, I needed more.

And believe me, I know how fucked up all of this is. I've never invited someone to come back to Vixen before, but you? Fuck, Aspen. When I realized it was you . . . Nothing has ever fucked me up like that. You got in my head, and I didn't know what to do, and despite being Austin's little sister, I wanted to do it again." He pauses as if needing a moment to figure out how to word this without making me hate him more. "I told myself that I couldn't tell you because of how you viewed that first time, and I knew if you found out it was me, it would hurt and ruin that moment for you. But I still . . . fuck. I had you banned from Vixen so that you couldn't come back and that would be it. Your memories of that night would remain as you wanted, and it'd never be brought up again. But then you said how nothing could compare to how it was with me and started looking for random Tinder assholes to fuck, and I just . . . Something came over me, Aspen. I know it was a shitty lapse in judgment, and I should never have walked back into that room, but the second you showed up at Vixen, all sense of right and wrong flew out the fucking window."

"Izaac, I—"

"Tell me there's some way I can make it up to you. I hate that I've done this to you, Aspen. I need us to be okay."

I swallow hard, stepping out of his arms as a wave of nervousness flutters through me. God, I've got to be insane for suggesting this. It's bolder than I've ever been, but everything is already up in the air between us. Maybe this is my only chance.

Lifting my gaze, my expression sobers as my heart pounds out of control. "Teach me, Izaac."

He stares at me a moment, as if what I just asked him isn't registering and he needs to repeat it a few times in his head to truly understand. His brows slowly begin to furrow, and when a deep reluctance flashes in his dark eyes, the pending rejection cripples me. "Do you understand what you're asking me?"

I don't respond, just hold his gaze to let him see the seriousness in my eyes.

He shakes his head, inching back. "No. Despite everything I said, I can't. I won't do that to Austin."

I scoff, gaping at him incredulously. "You didn't seem to care what Austin thought when you walked back into that room, and you sure as fuck didn't spare his feelings when you stripped me out of my clothes or put your hands all over my body. What about when you flicked your tongue over my nipple and pushed those thick fingers inside of me? Were you thinking about him then? You had every intention of fucking me, Izaac, so why all of a sudden do you care what Austin thinks?"

"Aspen," he says, his voice dropping low in warning.

"No," I say with a disbelieving laugh. "So, it's okay for you to cross the line when it's something you want, but when it's the other way around, it's suddenly an appalling idea."

"Don't even start with that shit. You saw how fucking worked up I got over you. There's nothing appalling about it," he insists, stepping into me and taking my waist, his fingers digging in. "But you know just as well as I do that this is wrong. It's gonna get us in the kind of trouble we can't come back from. It's one thing fucking when you think we're strangers, but fucking when you know it's me . . ."

"Oh my God," I laugh, shoving his hands off my waist, "You're worried I'm going to fall for you even more than I already have."

Guilt flickers in his eyes, and he gives me a gentle stare. "Am I wrong?"

"Yeah," I scoff, having to pace the kitchen to keep myself grounded. "In what world do you think I could ever love you again after what you did to me? I've always valued you, Izaac, because I've always been able to trust that you would never hurt me, but you're not the man I thought you were, and I will never be able to trust you again. But there's one thing you're not wrong about—"

I pause and so does he, holding my stare as he slowly arches a brow, curiosity lingering in his dark eyes. "Dare I ask?"

I swallow hard, unsure why I should still feel nervous at this point. After all, the man has been deep inside of me, and after he so boldly admitted just how good it is with me, why can't I do the same? It's not like he doesn't already know. I've already told him, only I thought he was a completely different person then.

"It's why I came back to the club in the first place. With you, it just felt right. I never could have imagined that it could be that good, and I know that I don't exactly have anything to compare it to, but I can't imagine that anybody else could possibly be capable of setting my whole body on fire the way you did. And like you said, it's the first time you've ever been inclined to invite a woman to come back. We work together, Izaac. Our bodies are just . . . compatible. Now, I don't know if that would change now that I know it's you, but I know that what I experienced with you was incredible, and when something is that good, why deny yourself?"

Now he's the one pacing the kitchen and shaking his head. "I don't know, Aspen. I'm not denying how fucking good it was or the fact that I haven't been able to stop thinking about it since, but we're crossing too many fucking lines."

"Please, Izaac," I say, moving back into him and catching his arm to bring him to a stop in front of me. He meets my stare, and I hold it captive, knowing one wrong move and I could lose him forever. "I want to learn what my body is capable of, and I want you to be the one to teach me."

He groans, pushing my hands off his arm, a clear battle warring inside his mind. "This is fucking insane."

"And yet, you haven't told me no."

He shakes his head. "This is a fucking terrible idea. If I were to touch you again . . ."

He lets his words fade away, and as I watch him, it occurs to me that he wasn't worried about me falling deeper in love with him, which we both know I lied about when I told him I wouldn't. He's worried that he'll be the one falling for me.

"If you were to touch me again . . . what?" I prompt. "What are you scared of, Izaac? That you'll fall in love with me too?"

His Adam's apple bobs as he swallows hard, and I wait on bated breath for his response. "That's not something I'm concerned about," he tells me, something flashing in his eyes as he struggles to meet mine. "I've known you for twenty-two years, Aspen. If I haven't fallen in love with you yet, it's never gonna happen."

Well, fuck. That hurt.

I flinch away from him as though his words physically hurt me, but didn't they? I can practically feel the old scars opening all over again. "Wow. Nothing like a bit of honesty to finish off my Tuesday night," I mutter, watching as his shoulders sag, clearly not having meant to hurt me, but hell, he's on a roll. Why stop now? "Look, it's simple, if the answer is no, then it's no. I'm not going to hold that against you. I'll just find someone else. But if you don't mind, I'm done for tonight."

Humiliation pounds through my veins, and I turn away, desperately needing the time to nurse my bruised ego, but his hand closes around my elbow pulling me back to him. Desperation flashes in his eyes and I don't think he realizes just how tight he's holding on to me. "You wouldn't."

My brows furrow in confusion. "Why the hell wouldn't I?" I question. "I stupidly saved myself for you for so long, and you've made it clear, time and time again, that I will never be anything more to you than Austin's little sister. So why the hell shouldn't I go and fuck any man who looks my way? I'm twenty-two, Izaac, and if you don't want to teach me what my body is capable of, then someone else will."

"FUCK!"

He whips himself around, his hands at his temples, clearly needing a moment to find his composure, and judging by the way his shoulders rise and fall, he needs deep breaths just to keep control.

Is he . . . jealous of me being with another man? What in the ever-loving fuck?

When he turns back, his gaze is filled with a strange mix of fire and unease. "If, and it's a big if, I agreed to do this, it can't be here or at my place. Only at the club. Teacher. Student," he says, indicating to himself before pointing toward me. "That's it. Nothing more. No beds. No kissing. Just sex. It's strictly a professional relationship. Emotion is off the table. It doesn't even enter the fucking chat."

"That's all I'm asking for," I say, feeling a flutter of hope rising in my chest.

"Austin can never know."

I nod, not needing to voice my response. He knows we're on the same page regarding my brother. Having Austin know about this simply can't happen, even if this is as far as it ever goes.

"Fuck, Aspen," Izaac says, his hands balling into fists at his side as his control begins to slip. "I need to think about this."

"Okay. That's fair."

He clenches his jaw, striding toward my front door, only he pauses as he reaches for the handle. "You don't even look at another man until you have my answer. Is that understood?"

I nod, and with that, he disappears out my door, leaving me with a new hope and a heart that isn't quite so broken.

17

IZAAC

This is fucking insane.

When I fell through the door of her apartment, I was ready for anything she could have thrown at me. I was ready to get on my hands and knees and beg her forgiveness. But she blindsides me with a fucking curve ball.

Teach me.

FUCK!

Those words have circled my head for two long days, and even now, lying in bed on a lonely Thursday night, I can't stop thinking about it. No matter what I do, I'm fucked.

How could she ask this of me? But then, why the fuck haven't I told her no? Why didn't I refuse her the second she showed back up at Vixen? I should have walked away, not given her a chance to argue her point, yet here I am, still desperately trying to find the balls to turn her away.

Fucking hell. Look at me pretending I don't know why I haven't told her no. I know exactly why. It's because being inside of her is like waking up in heaven. Her body wrapped around mine was the sweetest rush of ecstasy, and when she came undone in my hands . . . I've never felt anything like it. I just hate that it has to be her. Why couldn't I find this physical compatibility with anyone else? Why does it have to be my best friend's little sister?

Getting involved with her any more than I already have is a mistake—a fucking colossal one—but what am I supposed to do?

Teach me.

God, I want this so badly. I want to have her in my private room at Vixen. I want to show her exactly what she can do and explore her every boundary. I want to know how quickly I can make her come, how hard, how intense, but I'm also dying to see just how long she can hold out. If she likes it rough or slow, what kinks she has, and just how loud she can scream.

But I can't have her fall in love with me . . . at least, any more than she already is. It's one thing when she thinks she's fucking a stranger, but to have her look right into my eyes as she comes, to have her holding on to me as I push inside of her . . . it's different. Aspen even wondered if I was at risk of falling for her, and I hate how blunt I was in my response. The way her face fell with agony . . . fuck. I'm such an asshole. She deserves so much better than the bullshit I could offer her, and the sooner she figures it out, the better.

I went to her apartment to try and make things better, but instead, I only reminded myself of why I'm not worthy of her love in the first place, not that I ever gave her a chance to offer it before.

I don't let women get close enough to love me, and hell, I sure as fuck have never loved one in return. What's the point? Not even my biological parents could love me. The woman who birthed me was supposed to love me without question, and she threw me away like I was nothing more than a rabid animal, and that shit left gaping scars—ones I've never been able to come to terms with—and because of that, I've learned that maybe some people simply aren't capable of falling in love or even accepting it when it hits you right in the face.

That's me. I'm broken.

Sure, I can fuck and show a woman a great time, but that's all I'm capable of offering. The second I get even a hint that someone is starting to feel something for me, I call it quits. Hell, I've never even kissed a woman. It's too fucking personal. Which is exactly why I have to keep Aspen at arm's length.

She insisted that she couldn't love me after what I did, and if she were anyone else, I'd believe her, but this is Aspen. She's been there through everything, seen me at my worst and no amount of bullshit has ever deterred her. On the other hand, I've never hurt her like this before, never betrayed her trust or taken advantage of her.

Fuck, that makes me sound like such an asshole, but I guess that's exactly what I am, and if I were to do this, all I'd be doing is proving it. I can't say yes without crossing Austin, and I can't say no without hurting her.

It's an impossible choice. Take a bite out of the forbidden fruit and sink into a world full of wicked promises or walk away while knowing she'll be giving everything she's got to someone else. All her firsts will belong to another man, and all those things I desperately want to explore with her will be someone else's discoveries.

Fuck, why does the idea of her with another man bother me so much?

I guess the question is, can I live with that? Can I face her while knowing some other man has been inside of her, that *I've* been inside of her but will never get that chance again?

If I'm completely honest with myself, I think I knew my answer the second she asked me to teach her, and I've been too fucking scared to admit how badly I want it, and too fucking ashamed at how quickly I'd stab Austin in the back for this.

What kind of friend does that make me?

Knowing I've dragged this on for long enough, I reach for my phone as something expands in my chest, and I hope like fuck it's not regret.

Opening a new text, I work my fingers across the keyboard, and with every next letter that appears on the screen, I feel the sharp sting of the knife as I stab my best friend right in the back.

Izaac - If I agree to this, you can't hold the dark room against me. This gives us a clean slate. I'll teach you exactly what your body is capable of, and in return, you forgive me.

I feel fucking sick, but it's not like the last few times I've texted her. Those were accompanied by the convenient excuse of being too drunk to think straight, but I don't have the same excuse tonight. This is nothing but cold, hard betrayal, just like the second night at Vixen.

Fuck, I really am an asshole.

The read receipt appears under my text almost immediately, and within seconds, a new text appears.

Aspen - That's all I'm asking for.

Izaac - It's just sex. Nothing more.

Aspen - I know.

Izaac - And Austin?

Aspen - He'll never know.

Fuck! What the hell am I doing? It's not too late to back out. Only, I don't want to.

Izaac - Be at Vixen on Sunday night. 10pm.

18

ASPEN

My hand tightens around the Vixen membership card that mysteriously showed up on my kitchen counter last night. It's clear that Izaac put it there, but the question is, why wasn't it slid under the door? How the hell did he get inside to put it on the counter? I know damn well I didn't leave my door unlocked, which could only mean that giant asshole has a key to my apartment. I suppose now that I've given him complete access to my body, he must believe he has access to my home too.

That raging asshole.

Though that also means the day he sat at my door, he did so with patience. He could have used that key and stormed in at any time, but he waited until I was ready. Surely that's got to mean something, right?

God, why do I have to love him so much? It would be so much easier if I could hate him and things like getting ready to leave for my dick appointment would feel a little more transactional. Instead, I'm wound up in a ball of nerves.

I have so many questions about how tonight's supposed to pan out. Am I allowed to touch him? He's already made it clear that kissing is off the table, but is that how he is with everyone he's with, or is that just a rule for me because kissing might make things a little too . . . personal? Though, I don't know what's more personal than when he pushes that ginormous pierced cock deep inside of me.

I'm so nervous. I told him I'd be fine, that knowing it was him wasn't going to affect me, and that I could keep myself from falling for him any more than I already had, but I'm almost positive that was a lie. I guess I won't really know until we're in that room and he puts his hands on my body. But knowing how good it is with him, how could I not have certain . . . feelings?

Are the lights going to be on or off? Will he meet me at the bar or am I expected to seek him out? Is he planning to fuck me and walk away, or will this be an all-night adventure? So many variables with so many unanswered questions, and every last one of them revolves around him.

I suppose I'd prefer this insane nervousness over the heartache and betrayal I've been dealing with the past few weeks. When his text came through, telling me he was in, it almost didn't seem real. I've wanted this for so long . . . Well, an alternate version of this. I would have preferred that when something happened between us, it was because he was so into me he couldn't keep his hands off me. That he was falling in love with me. But this is different. He doesn't love me, doesn't even see me as anything more than his best friend's little sister, and it makes me feel like such a joke.

Did he agree to this because he thought it was his only way to find redemption for what he did? Or was it because the idea of being with me again was too tempting that he was willing to risk everything?

Like I said, so many unanswered questions.

I stand in my bathroom mirror, my hands sweeping through my long hair as my gaze drops to the membership card that lies beside my makeup bag.

Member #02684

I've memorized it at this point.

I'm just about ready to leave when my phone rings, blaring through my bathroom, and my heart all but lurches out of my chest. I immediately assume it's Izaac calling to tell me this was a terrible mistake, but when I look down, I see that it's only Becs.

"Just checking in," she says, not wasting time with stupid greetings. "How're you doing?"

I roll my eyes. I never told her that Izaac was the guy at Vixen or anything that happened after that, and I sure as hell haven't told her that I'm meeting up with him tonight. I don't know why though. I usually tell her everything, but that doesn't mean she didn't notice things were off over the past few weeks, and when things are off, she's smart enough to connect it back to Izaac.

It's always about Izaac.

"I'm fine," I say with a groan. "Just like I was fine yesterday and the day before that, and the day before that."

"Alright, alright," she says. "Can't blame a girl for asking. You were practically comatose for two weeks straight. I was worried about you."

"I know," I say, leaning toward my bathroom mirror and applying just a little extra mascara. "I really do appreciate that you worry about me. It's nice knowing you care so much, but really, I'm all good now. I just had a rough patch."

"Were you ever planning to tell me about this rough patch?"

"There's nothing to tell."

Becs scoffs. "Right. It's Izaac, isn't it? Did he do something to hurt you? Because I swear, if he did, I will nut-punch him so hard, and then just for good measure, I'll nut-punch your brother too, because you know they're a package deal and all."

I laugh. "Nobody is getting nut punched. Though, to be fair, if anybody were going to do it, it'd be me. I've put in twenty-two years with those assholes. Surely I deserve some kind of long-service reward for my troubles."

"You know what? You're right. I'll organize something," she says. "We can invite them to your place and then drop the unsuspecting ass-faces right in the hallway."

"Sounds like a good plan," I laugh.

"Alright," Becs says. "If you're sure you're okay, then I'll leave you be. I need to crash. I've got a huge exam in the morning, and I can't fuck it up."

"Okay, get all the sleep you can."

"I plan on spending all night having sex dreams about your brother, so if you need me, no you don't," she laughs.

"Ugh," I groan. "You're disgusting."

"You know it. Love you, Whoreasaurus."

"Right back at ya, Tittymcgee."

Becs ends the call, and as I step back and survey myself in my tiny bathroom mirror, I smile. Don't get me wrong, I feel like a complete bitch for keeping her in the dark with all of this, but not even my shitty friend skills can put a damper on what I'm about to do.

Grabbing my membership card and my phone, I fly out of my bathroom and into my room, finding my favorite knee-high boots to match the little black dress I've chosen for tonight. You know, in case easy access is required. Then certain I have everything I need, I fly out the door, hoping like fuck I can somehow get a grip on these nerves.

By the time I arrive at Vixen and make my way down the stairs to meet Casey at reception, I can barely put one foot in front of the other. So much for taking control of myself. I feel like a bumbling idiot. There are still twenty minutes before I'm due to meet Izaac, but a part of me wonders if I should think of him as the faceless stranger.

Oh, God. Am I making a mistake here?

Reaching the bottom step, I find Casey, and as her gaze lifts to mine with a dazzling smile, I watch as uncertainty cuts across her face. Hell, she almost looks annoyed to see me. "Aspen," she says, her gaze narrowing. "How lovely to see you again."

Yeah, right.

I stride up to her, unsure what I'm supposed to do. Every time I've been here, there's been a completely different set of circumstances. I fish the membership card out of my handbag and hand it over. "I guess I'm supposed to show you this," I say, feeling just as awkward as I sound.

Her brows furrow. "Oh, I didn't realize you'd become a member."

"I, umm . . . yeah. Izaac organized it for me."

A deep suspicion flashes in her gaze as she copies the membership number into her computer and checks everything out, but the more she looks, the more irritated she seems to get. "Oh, it seems you have exclusive access to the VIP lounge," she murmurs before her narrowed gaze lifts to mine. "How do you know Mr. Banks exactly?"

Her question sets off alarm bells in my head, and I don't appreciate her tone, but not wanting to get on Casey's bad side, I simply smile. "Family friend," I offer, not wanting to give much more than that. "Known him all my life."

"He doesn't make exceptions like this," she says, slowly getting to her feet as she prepares the gold moth stamp for my inner wrist. "I've worked for him for over a year now, and he's never invited a woman to return, whether she's a family friend or not. Nor does he make allowances to bend the rules of our memberships. There's a strict process one must go through for the safety and health of our patrons, and it appears that Mr. Banks has accelerated that process and skipped you right ahead to a full-fledged membership."

Raising my chin, I sense a wave of jealousy radiating off her, and just like that, I can't help but wonder if maybe I'm talking to a kindred spirit—another woman who's been looked over by Izaac Banks. But either way, I don't like her line of questioning. "I suppose that's his business now, isn't it?"

Her gaze hardens before a fake smile stretches across her lips. "Of course. Forgive me. I didn't mean to pry. Just trying to wrap my head around it so I understand what to expect with your visits," she says before taking my wrist and pressing the stamp to my skin.

The moment she pulls away, she puts the stamper down and hands me my membership card, which I promptly shove back into my bag, hoping like fuck I haven't just gotten Izaac into a world of trouble. But then, Casey made a comment that's stuck with me. "You mentioned you've worked for Izaac for over a year now?" I ask as she leads me to the main entrance of the club.

"Mr. Banks," she says as if needing to put me in my place. "And yes, he's a wonderfully generous boss."

"So, Vixen is his? He owns this club, just like Pulse, Cherry, and Scandal."

"Yes, that is correct. However, Vixen is more of a . . . side project for him. The others are business, but Vixen . . . this is pleasure."

"I see," I say, a little hurt that Izaac had failed to mention that he owned a fourth club, though I suppose I can't blame him. That's not exactly an easy conversation to have.

Casey opens the main door and this time when she waves me through, I don't hesitate, suddenly unsure if she's someone I really want to be talking with. She sounds like someone permanently shoved a stick up her ass and that someone is probably Izaac.

I'm a little early, and so just like the last time I was here, I make my way down to the VIP lounge, flashing my special gold moth to the security guard who waits there. Then after making my way down the stairs and to the bar, I get comfortable, hoping that a stiff drink might help me relax.

The atmosphere is different from the crazy Friday nights that I've been here. The music is still electrifying, but everything seems more chill. The gathered members seem like they know each other well. They have their favorites, and they don't waste time seeking out anybody else. There's a familiarity about it, and that's somewhat soothing.

By the time the bartender arrives with my drink, a familiar face makes his way toward me, and I let out a sigh. With everything going on, I'd almost forgotten about this guy, but I've got to give it to him, he's persistent. Every single time I've been here, he's managed to sniff me out like some kind of bloodhound.

"Aspen, right?" he asks, taking the stool beside me at the bar.

I offer him a polite smile. "Yes, that's right," I say before an obvious cringe cuts across my face. "I'm so sorry, your name has slipped right out of my head."

He laughs and offers me his hand. "Ryatt," he chuckles. "But don't stress. People don't often come here to memorize names."

"No, they certainly don't."

Ryatt waves the bartender over and orders a drink for himself before offering one for me, but I shake my head. "I'm good, thanks," I say, holding up my still-full cocktail.

"So, I take it you're enjoying Vixen?" he asks. "It's not everyone's thing, but once you've accepted and embraced the lifestyle, there's no turning back."

"I see that," I murmur, letting my gaze shift around the VIP lounge to take in the familiar faces.

"What are you searching for, Aspen?" he asks, his hand falling to my arm. "I see you here, but never participating, and besides your first visit, you don't wear wristbands, so you've got me stumped. What are you hoping to get out of this?"

"I, uhh—"

A big hand weaves into the back of my hair, pulling my head aside as a set of lips crashes down on the sensitive skin of my neck, and just before I go to push the guy away, that familiar scent hits me, and I melt back into him.

Izaac's hand curls around my waist, holding me close, and just when I think I'm about to slip into a pleasure-filled coma, his lips fall away. "There's nothing here for you, Ryatt," Izaac says, a clear warning in his tone. "This one is taken."

"I think *this one,*" Ryatt snaps back, mimicking Izaac's deep tone, "can choose for herself."

My brow arches, the audacity of this man starting to get on my nerves as Izaac's hand shifts from my waist to the center of my back. "Come on."

I get up without question, willing to follow him blindly, when Ryatt reaches out and catches my elbow. "Woah, baby. Where are you going? We were only just starting to get to know each other."

I pull my arm free, not liking the feel of his touch against my skin, but Izaac quickly steps in. "She's not your *baby,* and I told you, this one is taken," he rumbles. "Don't make me repeat myself, Markin."

Ryatt's hands fly up in surrender. "Okay, hands off the merchandise. I get it. No hard feelings," he says. "If I knew you were hunting this sweet thing, I would have backed off earlier."

"Hunting?" Izaac scoffs in disgust as his hand shifts down to the curve of my back. "You see, it's phrases like that which leave me wondering if I'd sorely misjudged your character. The women in my club are not here to be hunted, and they're sure as fuck not merchandise either. Perhaps it's time for a review of your membership."

"No need to make any rash decisions," Ryatt says. "Just a little misunderstanding is all. Besides, you have no grounds to revoke my membership. I've done nothing wrong."

"It's my fucking club. I can revoke whatever the hell I want," he says, narrowing his gaze and holding Ryatt captive in his deadly stare.

It feels like long, painful seconds before Izaac finally turns toward me and presses against my lower back to get me moving, then once we're nearly at the door of the private room, he lowers his head, leaning into me. "I don't want you fucking with that asshole."

"Wasn't planning on it."

"I mean it, Aspen," he says, a hard bite in his tone. "He has a fetish for women who appear pure and innocent, and you've more than caught his attention. Every time you've been here, he's approached you, and it'll get to a point where he won't be so polite about it. You need to keep your wits about you while you're in here. Don't open yourself for conversation."

"I was just being polite—wait," I say, my brows furrowed as I step through the door of the private room. "How do you know he's approached me every time?"

"Surveillance footage," he tells me, pointing out the camera in the corner of the room. "After your first time here, Austin insisted that I delete any evidence of you being here. You caught Ryatt's eye the second you walked in."

"Oh, wonderful," I say as the door closes behind us. "We have a sex tape. Just what I always wanted."

Izaac rolls his eyes. "Correction. We *had* a sex tape. It's gone now. Nobody's going to see you like that."

"Damn," I say with a heavy sigh.

His brows furrow. "Shouldn't you be thrilled about that?"

I shrug my shoulders. "I mean, technically, yes. But that night was kinda . . . ya know. Would it have been absolutely terrible to watch it? Maybe not."

Izaac's gaze darkens, and he reaches for me, spinning me in his arms until my back is against his chest, just as he did the last time we were in here. His lips fall to my neck slowly working up until he reaches the sensitive skin just below my ear. "Would watching us like that have gotten you hot, Aspen?" he asks, his hands brushing across my waist and skimming over my hip, not stopping until he's reached the hem of my black dress at my inner thigh.

A shiver shoots right down my skin, and my chest heaves with anticipation. "Mm-hmm."

His lips continue moving across my skin, but I struggle to relax, all too aware that it's Izaac standing behind me.

God, this was so much easier when I thought I didn't know him.

"You're tense," Izaac murmurs, his fingers brushing across the soft skin of my thighs and sending a wave of goosebumps sailing across my skin. "You're nervous."

"Shouldn't I be?"

"It's not like we haven't already done this."

"Yeah, but I didn't know it was you."

"We can always stop before this gets too far."

A smirk settles across my face as my hand comes down over his on my thigh, my fingers threading through his as I push my ass back, feeling just how fucking rock hard he is for me. "You and I both know we're not stopping."

Izaac groans and grinds against my ass as he brings our joined hands higher up my thigh, making my core pulse with need. "What if I turned out the lights? Would that help? I need you to relax, otherwise, this isn't going to work."

I nod. "Maybe that's not such a bad idea."

Izaac's hands fall away, and he strides across the room. When he reaches the light switch, he turns and meets my gaze before slowly turning the dial and dropping the room into darkness, only he doesn't completely turn it off like I expected. Instead, he leaves the lights on their lowest setting, just enough for me to make out the striking lines of his strong body, and just like that, my nervousness fades into the abyss, leaving nothing but hungry anticipation.

19

ASPEN

Izaac stands before me, his dark gaze sailing over my body like a starved man about to devour his favorite meal. "What do you want to get out of this, Birdy?"

That word is like lightning straight to my core, and my knees tremble, watching as he slowly begins to circle me, moving behind me as his fingers brush across my skin, making me quiver. "I told you. I want you to teach me everything," I whisper, feeling my heart beat right out of my chest. "I want to know my limits, what I like and what I don't. I want to be pushed until I physically can't take it anymore, but more than that, I want you to make me feel like you did that first time."

He settles in behind me, taking my waist as his big body seems to crowd me, and when his lips come down on my neck, everything within me melts. "Oh, God," I breathe as my hand comes down over his, my nails digging into his warm skin.

I've always pictured his hands on my body, his mouth on my skin, and holy shit, it's so much better than I could have ever imagined. His every touch is like fire against my body, like electricity pulsing between us, and despite barely having started, I realize just how bad this idea was.

I'll never come back from this, but I'll be damned if I ask him to stop.

One hand slides up as the other goes down, and my body shudders, not knowing which touch to pay attention to, but either way, I'm lost in a world of bliss. His right hand reaches the base of my throat, and his long fingers close around it, not squeezing hard, but it's enough to make my heart race. His left hand dips down past my hip and to my core, slipping straight past the fabric of my dress. Izaac cups my pussy over my sheer thong, and I immediately grind down against him, knowing without a doubt he can feel just how desperate I am.

"We'll take it slow," he murmurs, the electrifying music daring to drown out the deep tones of his voice, but now that I know it belongs to him, the very sound of it seems to speak right to my soul.

His touch shifts to my shoulder, pushing down the thin strap of my dress as the heel of his palm presses against my clit, slowly circling, making my knees weak. If his strong arm wasn't braced across my body, I surely would have crumbled by now.

Moving the sheer fabric of my thong aside, Izaac drags his fingers through my wetness, a growl rumbling through his chest and vibrating against my back. "Is this all for me, Little Birdy?"

Oh, God. When he talks like that . . .

My eyes roll to the back of my head as I reach up behind me, my fingers weaving into his hair and holding on for dear life. As my head rolls to the side, his warm lips continue their sensual dance across my skin. "I've been wet for you for years, Izaac."

An appreciative grumble sounds in the back of his throat, and the animalistic tone of it makes my pussy clench just as he pushes two thick fingers deep inside of me. I groan, my breath shaky as I feel him inside me, curving his fingers against my walls.

"Holy shit," I murmur, my grip tightening in his hair as his hand dances across my chest and to my other shoulder, gently fingering the strap of my dress before pushing it off.

I feel his breath skate across my skin, and I want nothing more than to drown in him as he pushes his fingers in and out while driving me wild with the heel of his palm against my clit. It's already too much, and he's barely even started.

How am I supposed to survive this?

Every passing second only gets better. He wanted me relaxed, and I think it's safe to say he got exactly what he asked for, and me? I'm getting everything I asked for and more.

Holy fucking shit.

Those fingers!

"Izaac, I—"

His hand shifts to the back of my dress, and my words fall away, feeling a cool rush of air hit my skin as he slowly drags the zipper down my back. I release my tight grip in his hair, moving my hand to my chest just in time to catch my dress before it falls.

Then all too soon, he gently pulls his fingers out, leaving me empty as he backs up a step. "Let it fall, Aspen," he grumbles, the authority in his tone doing wicked things to me.

I'm all too aware that this is Izaac, and despite having paraded around in a bikini as often as humanly possible when he's around me, this is different. He's not just seeing my body, but he'll be taking the sweetest pleasure in it, and instead of looking away from the forbidden fruit like he always has, he'll indulge in it, lapping up everything I have to offer.

This is the point of no return. If I let my dress fall, there's no walking away. There's no changing my mind or taking it back. Once I bare myself to him, neither of us will be able to stop. As I glance back over my shoulder and take in the deep hunger in his dark eyes, I know I've been ruined for any man who dares to come after him.

Holding his stare over my shoulder, I watch with increasing desire as I finally release my hold on my dress, letting it fall to the floor. I stand before him in nothing but a sheer thong and my knee-high boots and as he takes me in, a deep growl of appreciation rumbles through his chest.

"Good girl," he praises. "Step out of it."

Doing as he asks, I take a slight step forward, stepping over the discarded black dress as my fingers brush across my chest, unable to keep my hands still. My nipples pebble at the touch, and I shudder, knowing this is only the beginning. From here on out, it's only going to get better.

His tongue darts out over his bottom lip. "Bend."

My brow arches as a wicked grin begins pulling at the corners of my mouth.

Well shit.

My heart pounds furiously as I begin bending myself in half, my ass high in the air with Izaac's greedy gaze locked between my thighs. Only he shakes his head. "Uh-uh," he rumbles, captivated by the sight. "Slower."

Yes, Daddy!

I slow my pace until I can't physically go any further, and in this position, I'm forced to keep my head down, unable to see him, but damn it, I sure as hell feel him, especially as he steps in behind me, his hand brushing across my ass and stopping right between my legs. "Now," he says, that deep tone holding every bit of authority. "Remove your boots."

The desire pools deep in my core and as I reach around to the back of my boots and find the small zip, Izaac moves the sheer fabric of my thong aside and thrusts his fingers deep inside my waiting cunt. I gasp, my walls contracting around his thick fingers. "Don't you fucking move, Birdy," he says, pressing his other hand to my lower back and keeping me still.

He rotates his fingers inside of me, and my walls tremble around him as my eyes flutter closed. It's so fucking good, even more so when he stretches another finger to my clit and rubs lazy circles. "Good girl," he says. "Boots. Off. Now."

Realizing the zipper hasn't moved an inch, I get to work, slowly drawing it all the way down until I can slip out of the knee-high boot before moving on to the other, and when they're finally gone, that thick tone sails through the room once again. "Take your ankles, Little Bird. Don't let go."

I swallow hard, and just as I curl my hands around my ankles, his fingers are replaced by something cool. My back stiffens, and as he pushes it inside me, I realize it's some kind of metal ball. I gasp as the heavy ball rests inside me, quickly followed by a second. They slowly move, massaging deep inside of me, and everything clenches. Don't get me wrong, I'm no stranger to sex toys, but this? Oh yeah, I'm definitely a stranger to this, but I plan to get well acquainted.

"That okay?" he asks.

All I can do is swallow hard and nod.

"Don't move, Birdy."

I feel as he shifts behind me, and before I even know what he's doing, he's on his knees, and just as his warm mouth closes over my clit, the balls begin vibrating inside of me. "Oh, holy fuck," I gasp, sucking in a deep breath, my knees buckling beneath me.

I feel Izaac's wicked grin against my core, but as my whole body begins to tremble, I can't even call him out on it. It's intense and so fucking good. And as those balls move inside of me, I swear I see stars.

My breath comes in uneven, deep pants, and as his tongue flicks over my clit, I feel that familiar tightening deep in my core. "Fuck, Izaac," I groan, my nails digging into my ankles as I squirm beneath his hold.

I can't take it. It's too much. Too intense, but damn it, I'm gonna see it through.

He works my clit better than I ever could with my fingers. Sucking, flicking, teasing until I'm practically riding his gorgeous face, all while the vibrating balls send me into a whole new dimension. "Oh, shit. I'm gonna—"

I can't get the words out before I explode, my orgasm booming through me like a fucking rocket, overwhelming my system and taking me higher than ever before. Whatever is controlling the vibration of the balls doesn't let up, nor does Izaac's tongue, and as my walls shatter around the balls, my orgasm intensifies.

My knees start to buckle, sheer will being the only thing keeping me up at this point, and as my orgasm pulses through my body, everything clenches. My walls begin to spasm, unable to handle the intensity for even a second longer, and as if sensing my limit, Izaac eases up and the vibration slowly fades, but he doesn't dare shut it off completely.

I collapse.

Izaac catches me before I hit the ground and gently lowers me until I'm sprawled on the cool floor, unable to catch my breath. "Holy fucking shit," I breathe. "I need to get me some of these balls."

Izaac grins. "On your knees, Aspen," he says, getting to his feet. "You think you're done just because you came? That was barely a warm-up."

Well, shit.

Unable to move, especially with the balls still inside of me, all I can do is sit up and lean back onto my hands, watching as he reaches over his shoulder and grips his shirt, pulling it over his head, and in the dim lighting, he looks like a fucking god—a Greek god just as he's always joked.

That dark gaze swings back toward me. "I thought I told you to get on your knees," he questions before holding up some kind of controller. He presses a button and the balls buzz to life with such intensity, it's as though Izaac had physically hotwired the fuckers and sent a million volts of electricity shooting through me.

"OH FUCK!" I gasp, my eyes widening with a strange mix of shock and pleasure.

"Don't make me ask again."

"Alright, alright," I say, scrambling to get to my knees while the balls circle each other, massaging my too-sensitive walls. The movement has my hips jolting, and I have to take slow, deep breaths to try and bring my body back down to earth. But as I see Izaac stride toward me with his hand at the button of his jeans, suddenly nothing else matters.

Am I about to do what I think I'm about to do? The very thing that I've dreamed about since the moment I learned what it was?

He slowly releases the button of his jeans, opening the top just enough to slip his hand inside. My mouth waters, following the movement as he fists that massive cock, slowly working up and down. "You're gonna take me in your mouth, Aspen. And you're not going to stop until I've emptied myself inside your sweet mouth. Is that understood?"

I swallow hard and nod, unable to find a single word worth saying out loud.

With that, Izaac pushes his jeans down over his hips and past his strong thighs before the rest of the denim drops to the ground. I don't even notice how he gets rid of them. My attention remains solely focused on the way he grips his thick cock, his big hand barely able to fit around himself as the shine of his piercing catches in the dim light.

I'd never thought I'd see him like this, let alone looking at me like that at the same time. It's the beginning of every sex dream I've ever had, and damn it, those dreams are going to be a tough act to follow, but judging by my first night in this very room, Izaac has absolutely nothing to worry about.

He strides toward me, and with every step, his stare seems to get darker. His fist slowly moves up and down his thick cock, and I start to panic about how the hell I'm supposed to take all of that in my mouth without literally dying. But hell, if anyone is up for the challenge, it's me.

Izaac moves right in front of me, and with his free hand, he grips the bottom of my chin, gently lifting as his gaze sails across my face. "So fucking beautiful," he murmurs, inhaling deeply. "You smell that, Birdy? That's the sweet scent of your arousal. You're dripping, aren't you?"

My tongue darts out across my bottom lip as I silently nod.

"Have you ever tasted yourself?"

I shake my head, my heart pounding a million miles an hour.

"It's okay. We'll fix that," he says. "But first, you're gonna taste me. Open wide, Birdy."

A wave of nervousness rockets through me, terrified that I won't be good enough. Don't get me wrong, I've done this plenty of times, and the guys I've been with have always seemed to appreciate my efforts, but I didn't care about them the way I care for Izaac. I want to please him. I want to be the best he's ever had, and anything else simply won't do.

After wetting my lips, I open my mouth, welcoming him in as my gaze remains locked on his. It's strangely intimate, and when his pierced tip finally brushes against my lips, I have to look away, unable to handle it.

Izaac steps in even closer as I close my mouth around his thick cock, immediately feeling his piercing at the back of my throat, but due to the sheer size of him, I wrap my fingers around his base, holding him still.

His hand circles around the back of my hair. He has control of my movements but allows me to continue as I please, getting a feel for how I move and groaning with appreciation. His hips jolt, and undeniable joy blasts through my chest at the sheer knowledge that he's enjoying himself.

Physically incapable of taking his whole length in my mouth, I add my other hand, working my fists up and down as my cheeks hollow out, sucking hard and circling his tip with my tongue, getting the most devilish satisfaction out of the feel of his piercing on my tongue.

"That's right, Birdy. Two hands," he grits through a clenched jaw. "Just like that."

I've never felt so damn good, and when Izaac clenches his jaw and trembles, I know without a doubt that nothing in this world would ever be better than this moment. Only, I've never been so wrong because when I pick up my pace and force his tip past my gag reflex, I'm rewarded by the sweetest vibration of the balls deep inside of me.

I gasp around his cock, my gaze shooting up to his in surprise, my hips jolting as I clench around the balls. "Don't even think about coming," he warns me. "This is my turn."

I grin, and considering the sheer size and weight of his thick cock, it's not even a little easy to do, but I'm down for the challenge. After all, this is supposed to be a teaching moment.

Keeping myself moving, I give it my all, and as his grip tightens in my hair and I taste the sweetest drop of pre-cum on his cock, I realize just how close to the edge he is, and I've never wanted anything more. I need to see him come undone, need to taste him in the back of my throat and swallow every last drop he has.

"Fuck, Aspen. You don't know how fucking much I've thought about your mouth on me."

Shock blasts through my system, and for a moment, I'm too fucking stunned to keep up my rhythm. Does he mean how much he's thought about my mouth over the past few weeks, or does he mean over the past few years? Because there's a significant difference between the two.

With his heated gaze locked on mine, that intensity returns tenfold, and as I go to drop my gaze, his hand returns to my chin. "Eyes up here, Birdy," he murmurs as the balls' vibration levels up.

I whimper, and my chest heaves, but as I continue holding his stare, the emotion wells up inside of me, and it's too fucking much.

I'm supposed to hate him, but seeing him so close to coming undone for me, I'm going to break. I'm going to fall for him all over again, and that's the last thing I want to come from this. Hell, it's the last thing he wants too.

Despite his demands, I look away, dropping my gaze just as a roaring "Fuck" fills the private room and his hips jolt forward, sailing even further down my throat. Izaac comes hard, shooting hot spurts of cum to the back of my throat, and without a single moment of hesitation, I swallow it down, claiming every last drop.

Only the moment is tainted by my fucked-up need to love him. Why did I have to go there? I ruined it for myself. It's only a little eye contact. Why am I making such a big deal about it? It's nothing. It's not like I've never looked the guy in the eyes before. Though, I suppose I've never done it while his cock was halfway down my esophagus. That shit tends to make a difference.

Izaac finishes, and when every last drop of him is gone, I pull back, releasing my hold from around his cock and lowering down on my knees as I try to catch my breath. My jaw aches from taking him like that, but it's a welcome ache, one I would take on every day if I could.

Izaac offers me his hand, and I gingerly take it before allowing him to pull me to my feet, and he stabilizes me with a hand at my waist. "You good?" he asks, just a hint of concern flashing in his dark eyes.

I cringe. "I've gotta lose the fucking balls."

His eyes widen just a fraction. "Oh shit. I got too caught up with how good it felt having your lips wrapped around my cock, I forgot to turn it off."

"No shit," I say, every little movement putting me on edge as he finally puts an end to the vibration, and then without warning, he steps even closer, pulling my body right against his. His fingers brush down my side, leaving a trail of goosebumps before reaching the apex of my thighs.

"Breathe in," he instructs. I do as I'm asked, and when he prompts me to breathe out again, he slowly pulls the balls free. The moment they are out, everything goes weak, and I crumble into his strong arms.

Izaac holds me up, his hand drawing soothing circles on my back. "Come on," he says, moving me through the room. "You're too worked up. You need to relax."

He leads me to the couch by the large ottoman I'd been on when I figured out his little secret, and as he sits down, he pulls me on top of him, my knees straddled on either side of his strong thighs. "You good, Aspen?" he asks again, and I can't help but wonder if he was able to sense the change in me earlier, but when he pulls me in and his warm mouth closes over my nipple, all train of thought falls from my mind.

"More than good," I moan, gripping his strong shoulder as I feel his hardness between my legs, but he doesn't make a move to plunge himself deep inside of me. Instead, he simply roams his hands over my body with feather-soft touches, and just as he said, it doesn't take long before I'm finally able to relax.

My hips begin to rock, grinding my core against his thick cock, as his lips move across my chest, teasing my pebbled nipples before trailing up to the sensitive skin below my ear. My body is on fire in all the right ways, and as my wetness becomes too evident to ignore, he locks his arm around my waist and gently lifts me.

Positioning himself beneath me, I feel his tip at my entrance, and then he slowly begins to lower me. I take him inch by inch, stretching wider than ever before. My walls tremble around his sheer size, and I don't dare move as I let my body adjust to his delicious intrusion.

His lips return to my neck, and as his tongue brushes over my skin, I relax around him. Finally, I start to rock my hips. I've never done this. The last time Izaac was inside of me, he took control. I was in his capable hands to do whatever he pleased, but this time, I'm taking the reins.

It takes me a second to get the feel of what I'm doing, but I quickly find my rhythm, and before I know it, my grip is tightening on his shoulder as I suck in a shallow gasp. "Oh, God," I breathe, my forehead falling against his as his fingers dig into my hips.

"Just like that. Take what you need."

His tone is so soothing, and I close my eyes, desperate to recapture the way it felt that first night.

Izaac reaches down between us, his thumb gently pressing to my clit and rubbing tight circles as I slowly begin to pick up my pace. My body quivers, the undeniable pleasure quickly taking over, and with each new thrust of my hips, I get closer to the edge.

"Izaac," I pant with desperation.

"Let it go, Birdy," he murmurs into my ear, his thumb circling my clit. "I'm right there with you."

Swallowing hard, I push myself harder. The idea of Izaac Banks being ready to come inside of me sends a wave of goosebumps across my skin. Only something holds me back. "I . . . I—"

With his free hand, Izaac reaches up and curls his hand around the side of my jaw, his thumb stretching to the bottom of my chin and gently lifting. "Look at me, Aspen. Open those beautiful eyes."

Fear pounds through my veins. I'm terrified of what happened earlier, so I shake my head, refusing to look at him. Izaac doesn't take no for an answer. "Now," he says in that authoritative tone that could bring me to my knees.

I can't resist a second longer and peel my eyes open to the dim room. My gaze immediately locks onto his, and I swear, he sees right through to my soul, reading every thought and desire that's ever pulsed through my body. "There you go, baby," he murmurs, holding me captive with that striking stare. "Now let go."

As if on cue, my body finally gives in, and my orgasm blasts through my body like a firework on the Fourth of July, decorating my vision with vibrant hues of black and gold. But as Izaac's fingers dig into my hips and he sucks in a sharp breath, my world comes back into focus.

I watch him closely, having sat in my bedroom for years on end, listening to how he sounded as he came and then having to sit opposite him at the breakfast table, pretending as though I didn't know what he'd done the night before, but this time, it's different.

This time I get to *see* it, experience it for myself, and to be the one who's making him come . . . Holy shit. On some level, I knew that was what was going to happen in here, but now that it's happening, I feel like a fucking goddess.

An intense thrill shoots through me. I become transfixed on his face, watching as the slightest crease appears between his brows and he sucks in a sharp breath.

Oh God. This is it.

My walls convulse around his sheer size and then finally, he empties himself inside of me, his body stiffening against mine and it's fucking everything I knew it would be and more. He's so fucking beautiful. Everything about him. As I bask in the afterglow and the knowledge that his cum is deep inside of me, all I can do is collapse against him, my forehead tipped against his as I struggle to catch my breath.

We remain in a comfortable silence, his big hand against my back until I finally find my composure. Then as if sensing my ability to think clearly, Izaac's hand drops to my thigh and gives a gentle squeeze. "Come on," he says. "That's enough for tonight. It's getting late."

His dismissal is like a bucket of ice water over my head, and as I remember where we are with all the hows and whys, I awkwardly pull myself away, feeling his warm cum dripping out of me.

Izaac gets up and moves across the room, returning only a moment later with a washcloth in his hand. He moves right into me, and as he goes to help clean me up, I pull back and take it from his hand.

"I can manage," I say, averting my gaze and hating this strange awkwardness that pulses in the air between us. This went from being such a real moment—two people on the same wavelength, sharing in the sweetest pleasure—to a meaningless business transaction. I feel dirty and used, but I was the one who wanted this. I set this in motion.

Izaac turns away to find his clothes, offering me just a moment of privacy, and I quickly clean myself up before scrambling for my dress. I don't know what happened to my thong or even remember when that was torn off my body, but I don't have it in me to search for it. Instead, I step into my dress and quickly pull it up just in time for Izaac to turn around, fully clothed.

"You good?" he asks for what must be the millionth time.

I give him a tight smile and turn around. "Would you mind zipping me back up?" I ask, my gaze focused a little too heavily on my discarded boots laying haphazardly on the ground beside me.

"Of course," he says, striding into me, but he makes it a point to keep a comfortable distance as he works the small zipper back up into place. I can't help but wonder if he's trying to reset the boundaries between us. He's being way too respectful considering the fact he just bent me over and put vibrating balls in my cooch, but shit, let's keep things professional. Why the hell not?

I suppose this is exactly what I asked for though. He said it was just sex, nothing more, and that's exactly what I agreed to. I just didn't realize it would make me feel so . . . ugly. Surely this means something to him. Don't get me wrong, I know he's never felt the way I do and never will, but I'm not some random stranger who wandered into his dark room, I'm me. His best friend's little sister. Surely that means *something.*

With my dress back in place, I grab my boots and lower myself into a chair, cringing at the dull ache deep in my core. I can only guess how that'll feel come morning, but it's a welcome ache that I'm sure I'll learn to love. After pulling my boots on and zipping them up, I get back to my feet and try to figure out what the hell I did with my handbag.

Finding it by the door with the almost full cocktail I'd ordered when I first got here, I stride across the room before forcing myself to stop. I look back at Izaac, that same awkwardness still lingering in the air. "I, ummm. I'm gonna get out of here."

He nods. "Did you want me to walk you out?" he asks, and I can't help but wonder if it's because he feels obliged to because I just had his dick in my mouth or because on some level, he still sees me as his best friend's little sister he swore to always look out for.

Either way, I don't like it.

"No, I'm good," I say. "I . . . uhh . . . don't exactly know what I'm supposed to say in this situation, so I'm just gonna . . . yeah."

I don't bother finishing whatever the fuck I was trying to say or even offer a goodbye before slipping out the door and bolting out of the private room like my ass is on fire. All that matters is getting as far away from Izaac Banks as possible and hoping like fuck that I didn't just royally fuck everything up.

20

IZAAC

I don't know how, but I'm still fucking baffled by what just went down. Somehow, I fucked up.

The door closes behind Aspen, and all I can do is stare after her. One minute we were on the couch, my cock still buried inside her warm cunt as she straddled me, and the next, we were tiptoeing around each other like fucking strangers. I don't know where the fuck we went wrong.

Physically being with her is incredible. The way we work together, the way she fits me, the way she gets off on my demanding nature. It's fucking perfect, so how the fuck did it go so wrong?

Maybe I pushed her too far, or maybe she decided it was too hard to take the emotion out of sex. I'm not going to pretend like I didn't notice the way she almost closed off moments before I came in her mouth. I saw the panic in her eyes, but she didn't give me the impression that she was willing to talk about it. Instead, she seemed intent on forgetting, which is part of the reason why I allowed us to continue. If I felt something was truly wrong, I would have cut it short and called it a night.

But the way she just ran out of here . . . I don't know. I've known Aspen all her life, and she's never once tried to get away from me like that, not even when I was entertaining other women. The mood shifted almost instantly, and what was supposed to be a post-sex fog turned into a chilling awkwardness.

I fucking hated it. Hell, even standing here still feels wrong.

She wasn't expecting me to cuddle, was she? Because I thought I made the limitations of this deal clear. She knew what she was getting into, and despite her feelings, she was more than happy to agree. I thought we were on the same page.

Maybe I misjudged her, or maybe she flat-out lied. She said there wouldn't be a problem. She was down with the conditions of our fucked-up little back-stabbing arrangement, but if she's not, if she can't handle this, then tonight is as far as it will go. The whole point of stabbing Austin in the back was to make things right with Aspen, and if this arrangement is only going to hurt her, then what's the fucking point?

Still staring after her, I will myself to forget it. If she wanted to talk it out, she would have stayed. Hell, knowing Aspen, she would have had it out here and now, not sparing anyone's feelings. She's feisty like that, especially with Austin. She doesn't like holding back, nor should she, but on the other hand, things are never that simple when it comes to the two of us. She spent two weeks ignoring me after she found out I was her faceless stranger, and now, I've just let her run out of here again.

Fuck. Am I about to have another two weeks of silence?

What if I hurt her? What if it was too much and her heart is breaking? What if I pushed her too far? I know we agreed that it was just sex, but when she was riding me, there's no denying that it felt different. That wasn't just sex, that was personal, and when I forced her gaze to mine . . . I've never come like that. I'm not going to lie, I struggled tonight. If she were any other woman, I wouldn't have had a problem, but with Aspen, it's a dangerous game, and we're toeing a line that either one of us could crash right over at any given time. She's already vulnerable when it comes to me, and if I'm not careful, I'll be the one who struggles to maintain the line between sex and emotion.

Shit.

Either way, something happened in here, and I'm not down with being in the dark. If I fucked up, I need to know so I can fix it.

I'm out the door before I even know what's happening. I race through my club, the VIP lounge still in full swing, but I barely notice, certain she's not lingering around. At least, she better not be, especially with the likes of Ryatt Markin here tonight, fucking *hunting* for women.

God, I can't stand that asshole. That fucker is getting way too bold with her.

Hitting the stairs, I fly up them two at a time before reaching the main floor and making my way to the entrance. Grabbing the handle, I yank it open before storming through to the reception area and scaring the shit out of Casey. She yelps, and I whip toward her, my gaze wide and frantic. "Did Aspen come through here?"

Her lips press into a hard line. "I really don't understand what you see in that girl," she muses, hurt flashing in her eyes that only serves to piss me off. "Did you honestly offer her a full membership? You know we have a waitlist, right? And don't even get me started on the membership fee. I know she didn't pay for it, which is totally unfair to our other members. Besides, she doesn't even fit with our current clientele, so what's your deal with her?"

"Since when did I give you the impression that you had a say or even a right to question my judgment on the way I run my business?" I ask, anger bubbling to the surface. "I asked you if Aspen came through here, and all I require from you is a simple yes or no answer."

Casey visibly swallows, her gaze dropping like the desperate sub that she is. "Yes, sir," she says, not daring to lift her gaze from her feet and making me regret for the millionth time ever touching her, but desperate men call for desperate measures. "You just missed her."

Casey's heavy into BDSM, and while I've dabbled here and there and enjoy being a dominant, she takes her role as a submissive way too fucking seriously. I prefer my women with a backbone. I like it when they argue back. Hell, I even like it when they want to challenge me and take control, and sooner or later, I know that Aspen will. She's still finding her feet, though.

Done with Casey's bullshit, I skip up the stairs, grabbing the railing and using it to propel me up them faster, and before I know it, I'm in the entrance hallway and barging through to the dark alley. I hurry out to the road and let out a heavy sigh of relief as I find Aspen's white Corvette.

She sits in the car, the engine running, and it's clear I have all of two seconds to catch her before she takes off.

I make every second count.

Hurrying around her car and putting myself in the street, I grab the handle of the driver's door and pull it open wide, watching as Aspen shrieks with fear, clearly assuming I'm some asshole on the street wanting to take advantage of a beautiful woman.

"Fuck, Izaac. What the hell do you think you're doing? You scared the shit out of me."

I clench my jaw, unsure why I suddenly feel so worked up. "What the fuck just happened back there?" I question. "One second we were good, and the next, shit got weird. Why'd you run like that? If I did something, you need to tell me. You can't just run away and leave me in the fucking dark."

She gapes at me as though I'm fucking clueless and should know better, and all it does is piss me off. She's fucking right, though, I *am* clueless, and I probably *should* know better.

Clearly seeing that I'm not interested in playing stupid games, she lets out a heavy sigh and cuts the engine, fixing me with a heavy stare. "You made me feel dirty."

My jaw practically dislodges from my face as it falls to the fucking ground. "The fuck? What are you talking about?" I demand, my mind racing through everything that just went down and coming up almost blank. "Was it the balls? I thought you were okay with that shit."

Aspen groans, rolling her eyes. "It's got nothing to do with the fucking balls."

"Then feel free to clue me in at any time."

The hardness in her eyes fades away before being left with a vulnerability that makes something ache in my chest. "You made it transactional, Izaac," she says, her shoulders sagging with the heaviness of what she's trying to say. "I know we agreed that it was just sex. I get that, I really do. But when you sent me on my way, you made me feel like I was some stranger off the street when, despite everything you say, you and I both know that it's more than that."

"It's not more than that," I argue, practically feeling my walls slamming into place. The drunk phone call and texts, the dirty talking. I know I was bold with her, but perhaps I've led her on, and that really wasn't my intention.

"But it is," she fires back at me. "No matter what you say, it'll always be more than that because, whether you like it or not, we have history. We've known each other all our lives, and while I agree that it's just sex, I won't agree to being treated like some second-class whore. What just happened in there was the equivalent of being kicked out after a one-night stand before you even got a chance to steal the guy's shirt. I mean, fuck, Izaac! I had your dick halfway down my esophagus! Don't you think that's at least deserving of being offered a drink after?"

I just stare at her, a slight smirk lifting the corner of my lips. "Are you saying you want to . . ." I swallow hard, "cuddle?"

Her face falls, staring at me as though she wasn't sure she was even speaking the same language. "When the hell did you hear me say that I wanted to cuddle? Fuck, Izaac. You know you're impossible, right?"

"I'm impossible? You're the one who ran away because you wanted to cuddle."

"For the last fucking time," she says, the frustration burning in her green eyes. "I DON'T WANT TO CUDDLE!"

"Shit, Aspen. Why don't you tell the whole fucking street our business?"

Aspen flies out of the driver's seat, her fingers jammed into my chest. "I swear to God, I'm going to reach down your throat and pull your testicles out through your mouth and strangle you with them," she grits through a clenched jaw. "Now leave me alone. I'm going home so I can make a little Izaac voodoo doll and drown it."

"No."

She gapes at me. "What do you mean *no?*"

"I mean that you've only been giving me bullshit answers because you're either embarrassed about something or too fucking scared to say what's really going on. So, cut the shit and tell me what's really going on."

Aspen clenches her jaw and fixes me with a hard stare, her hands propped on her hips as though trying to intimidate me into backing off, but she should know better than to try that shit on me.

"I'm waiting," I tell her. "I've got all fucking night."

Aspen groans. "Fine," she says. "We need to revisit the ground rules."

My face scrunches in confusion. "Why? What's wrong with our ground rules? We have them for a reason, and I don't know if you were in there, but they worked fucking well."

Her lips pull into a hard line, and she drops her gaze, studying my hands a little too closely. "You said you didn't want me falling in love with you. Is that still true?"

My brows furrow, unsure of what she's getting at. "Yes."

"Then we need to adjust the ground rules."

"What are you talking about, Aspen? Stop dancing around it and just say what you need to say."

She lets out a heavy breath, and I hate the flash of nervousness in her eyes. She should know not to be nervous around me, especially after what we just did. "When you're inside of me, no eye contact."

"What?" I scoff, having to keep myself from laughing at the absurdity of that request. "Why the fuck not?"

"Because when you're making me feel all these things, and it's so damn good, I'm already on edge. But then you go and look at me, and not just a quick glance, you force me to hold your stare, and it's too much. It's electrifying, and it makes something that's already there so much more intense. I don't know if it's because there's already something there for me, or if it's all just in my head, but when you look at me the way you do, especially when you're inside of me and you're just about to come, it makes me want something that you're not willing to give. But when I look away, that connection breaks, and it's fine, but I'm not going to lie, it leaves me feeling . . . shaky."

I watch her for a second, already shaking my head before I even know what's going to come out of my mouth. "No, fuck that," I say, not sure if I'm about to fuck everything up even more. All I know is that the idea of not having her eyes on me when I thrust deep inside of her doesn't sit well with me. "I don't know about you, but for me, when your eyes are on me, I fucking love it. I can read you so easily. You're an open book, Aspen. I see exactly how much you want it from the look in your eyes. It's not your body language that tells me if you want it faster or slower, or the sound of your desperate pants, it's those fucking eyes. There's gotta be a compromise here somewhere, because losing that eye contact, that's a hard pass for me."

"Have I told you you're impossible lately?"

"It's come up once or twice."

Aspen groans, and steps into me, dropping her forehead against my chest. "I hate this."

"We can always stop," I suggest, but the idea of never getting to sink inside of her ever again causes me physical pain.

"Not an option. You can't just get a girl hooked on something and tear it out from under her a second later. We both agreed to this, and now we're seeing it through. We already proved that we're shitty people by crossing that line. We might as well make it count."

"Fine," I say, finally wrapping my arms around her and pulling her in hard against my chest, the reminder of my back-stabbing crimes making me feel like a piece of shit. "We try this again and limit eye contact, only looking away when it's too much."

"And?" she prompts.

I roll my eyes, but truth be told, I kinda like catering to her needs.

"And I'll work on not being an asshole and kicking you out like a bad one-night stand. But I'm not cuddling."

"Get the cuddling out of your head. I never said anything about cuddling."

"Do we have a deal or not?"

"Yes," she groans. "We have a deal."

"About fucking time," I cheer, the sarcasm thick in my tone as I release my hold on her. "Now, I don't want you getting confused for a bad one-night stand or a stranger off the street, but this time, I really am kicking you out of here. It's almost two in the morning, and I've had to hear about your class schedule for the last four years. You've got a 9 a.m. lecture. You need to get home and get some sleep."

Aspen scoffs. "Well, maybe next time you shouldn't schedule your pussy appointment so late in the evening. It's called being considerate. You should try it sometime." She presses her lips into a tight line before her brows furrow. "Wait. Does this technically count as a booty call? It does, doesn't it? Holy shit. I feel so used."

"If anyone should feel used, it's me," I murmur. "Now get out of here before I have to physically drag your ass home."

Aspen rolls her eyes before stepping into me and pressing up onto her tippy toes. She drops a soft kiss to my cheek and the warmth of her lips leaves a weird tingle on my skin. "We're okay, Izaac," she whispers into the darkened street, barely lit by the occasional street light, but those three words do something to me I couldn't have possibly expected. They make me feel like the whole fucking world is in the palm of my hand as long as I have her right there with that dazzling smile locked on me.

Then with that, Aspen pulls away and offers me a small smile before finally ducking down into her Corvette, restarting the engine, and taking off, leaving me with only one more thing to do—watch and delete our latest sex tape.

I can't fucking wait.

21

ASPEN

Becs loops one arm through mine as we make our way across campus, my stomach desperate for a good meal. Apparently, spending your night being screwed within an inch of your life leaves a woman with quite the appetite. Though, does last night really count as being screwed? It was crazy and intense, but if we're being technical, it was more about that mouth action than a screw, but goddamn, those little metal vibrating balls! I wasn't kidding when I said I needed to get some of those.

As for what happened after the mouth action, I'm still not sure I want to classify that as a screw. It was too . . . personal. My body moving against his, his hot breath brushing over my skin, my nails digging into his shoulder. To call that a screw would be doing a disservice to myself

. . . and to Izaac. No, he doesn't screw. He fucks, and God is it good!

The only screwing that got done was out by my car once we were finished screaming at each other—more like when I was finished screaming at him—and he decided to veto the eye contact rule, but he'll come around. He has to. Unless he wants this to get even more complicated than it already is. I get that he likes seeing my expressions, and with anybody else, I'd be on board, but when Izaac looks at me like that while deep inside of me, I feel it in my chest. I feel the warmth spreading through my veins, the need pulsing through me, and I know without a doubt that I would never feel anything like this for another man.

Izaac is and will always be my forever, and the more we do this, the harder it'll become to pretend that part of me doesn't exist.

Becs drags me along, cutting across campus toward her favorite salad bar as she tells me all about the big business exam she just took, and judging by the relief in her eyes and the smile across her face, I can only assume she aced it. On the other hand, I've been stuck in lectures since nine in the morning, and after sleeping through my alarm and skipping breakfast, I'm officially starving. To be completely honest, I don't think the salad bar is going to cut it for me today. I'm going to need something big and juicy.

It's a short walk across campus, and before I know it, we're walking through the door of the number one lunch spot for college girls, and because all the girls like to come here, all the guys tend to follow too.

There's a long line, but considering it's the middle of the day, I'm not surprised. We talk shit as we slowly make our way to the front, and just as we go to step up to the counter to order, my phone rings in my hand.

Glancing down at the screen, I see Austin's name, and a pang of guilt flutters through my chest. I hate lying to him, but I'm at the point of no return. There's no taking it back now.

"What's up, Shitforbrains?"

"Not much, Crotchsniffer," he says. "Just reminding you that it's my birthday this weekend and you're required to show that unfortunate face of yours at Cherry on Saturday night."

"Ughhhh," I groan.

"Oh, is that your brother?" Becs asks, a wicked grin stretching across her face. "Can you let him know I got a new bedspread that I'd really love to show him sometime?"

I glare at my best friend. "Shut up and order your stupid salad," I tell her. "And while you're at it, order me a chicken caesar wrap with extra sauce, and don't forget my soda."

Becs rolls her eyes and gets busy ordering as Austin laughs in my ear. "Is that Becs?" he questions, clearly having heard exactly what she'd said. "You're bringing her to Cherry on Saturday night, right?"

"Not if you're planning on screwing her behind the bar," I say, knowing damn well Becs wouldn't miss it for the world.

"Chill out. I'm not gonna screw your friend behind the bar," Austin says, amusement thick in his tone as relief pounds through my veins. "I'll screw her in the middle of the packed dance floor while everyone continues having a great time around us, completely oblivious to the way she screams for more."

I gag, the thought of them together making me want to hurl. "I'm gonna kill you."

"Ahh, interesting," he says. "You don't like it now that the tables have turned, huh?"

Becs gives me a shove to get me moving, and I wander over to the side to where the other customers are waiting for their meals as another wave of guilt crashes through me. I suppose the tables really have been turned, the only difference is, I'm not just joking about screwing his best friend, I'm actually doing it.

"Have I told you lately that you're an asshole?" I question, feeling like a complete bitch.

"Uhhhh, you might have mentioned it here and there," he teases. I roll my eyes, and thankfully he changes the topic. "How're classes going? There's not long 'til graduation."

"Yeah, I—oh shit. Hold up, my lunch is ready," I say as Becs and I step forward to collect our meals off the counter. I squish my phone between my ear and shoulder, needing both hands to grab my wrap and soda before trying to balance it all in one hand. I grab the phone and try not to make an ass of myself in front of all these people. "What was I say—ohhhhh fuck!"

My soda and wrap go flying across the salad bar as some guy barrels into my chest, his drink instantly soaking me from head to toe. I screech, the chill from the icy liquid spilling right over the neckline of my shirt and down between my cleavage.

"Oh shit. I'm so sorry," the guy says, scrambling to get a better hold on his drink and put an end to my misery. He gets himself under control before finally lifting his head and hitting me with a beaming smile that could have the potential to blow me away if I weren't so cold and embarrassed.

"It's okay," I say, shaking the water off me. "It's just water. I'm fine."

"You're soaked and your lunch is spread from one end of the bar to the other. It's not okay," he says, his green eyes locking onto mine as he blindly reaches for the napkins on the counter. "Let me make it up to you."

Water drips profusely from my clothes as Becs steps closer, surveying the green-eyed dazzler. "Oooh, he's cute," Becs approves, not caring that the guy can very clearly hear her. "You know, apart from buying Aspen here a new lunch, you could always make it up to her by taking her out to dinner."

"Wait. What?" I rush out, my eyes widening in horror.

The guy arches his brows, clear interest flashing in his eyes as he looks back at me. "I uhhh . . . would love to take you out. That's if you're interested, of course."

"She's chronically single," Becs laughs as I mop up as much of the water as possible. "Of course she'd love to."

"The fuck?" Austin snaps in my ear, reminding me that he's still there. "Who's taking you out?"

"Shit," I grunt, trying to take the offered napkins while handing my phone to Becs. "Can you deal with Austin?"

She gingerly plucks my phone out of my hand and holds it to her ear. "Hey, Hot Stuff. What's going on?"

I roll my eyes as the guy finds my fallen soda and scoops it off the floor, practically offering it to me like he was about to propose. "I don't think I can salvage your lunch, but at least your drink survived."

I can't help but laugh as I take it from him, and not a moment later, he turns around to the staff behind the counter and re-orders my lunch. "That really wasn't necessary. You didn't need to replace my wrap. I could have done it."

"I wanted to," he says. "I wouldn't have been able to live with myself if I let a pretty woman buy her own lunch after I destroyed her first one. I'm Harrison, by the way."

"Aspen," I say.

A smile pulls at my lips, and I can't help but notice just how cute he really is, but the thought is cut short when I overhear Becs on the phone with my brother. "You should have seen it. This guy just shot his load all over your sister's tits, and now he's about to ask her out. It's like a Hallmark moment."

Becs meets my gaze as she listens to whatever Austin has to say about that, and as her grin widens, I can only imagine what he's saying.

Harrison inches toward me. "I mean, she's not wrong," he says. "I really would like to ask you out."

I worry my bottom lip, trying to figure out how to respond to that when Becs cuts through the awkward silence again. "Chill out, Austin. You'll definitely approve of this guy. He's a—wait." She leans toward us, her gaze landing on Harrison. "What do you do?"

"Pre-law," he confirms.

A grin tears across her face. "Hallelujah. There is a God," she cheers before getting back to her conversation with Austin. "He's a lawyer, just what you always pictured for her." There's a slight pause before she starts again. "Oh, stop. You're so dramatic. Learn to roll with the punches. Besides, isn't this what you wanted? If she falls in love with a cute lawyer, then she'll forget about He Who Shall Not Be Named, and she will have no ground to stand on when you accidentally fall into my bed."

I shake my head, my cheeks flaming with embarrassment. "I, ummm . . . I'm sorry you had to hear all of that," I tell Harrison. "But really, you don't need to feel obliged to ask me out. Just getting my lunch is more than enough."

Harrison nods. "I don't feel obliged," he says. "I was serious. I would love to take you out, but I can see we're not on the same page. So instead, can I give you my number, and when you inevitably change your mind, you can ask me out?"

"Oooh," Becs says to Austin. "He's cocky. I like that."

"Would you hang up the phone already?" I ask her.

She just grins, but I turn my attention back to Harrison and reluctantly agree. "Okay, fine. You can give me your number, but for the record, I won't be calling it."

"Uh-huh," he says in that same cocky tone, only now his eyes sparkle with amusement, and it makes something flutter deep in the pit of my stomach. Not in the way that Izaac always has, but there's definitely potential there.

Clearly seeing my phone is currently occupied, Harrison grabs one of the unused napkins and steals a pen off the counter before writing his number down and handing it to me. "Don't accidentally lose it," he says. "Otherwise, I'll be forced to knock on every single door around campus until I've found you."

I can't help but laugh as I take the napkin from him, and as if on cue, my new chicken caesar wrap shows up. He takes it from the poor woman who had to remake it before offering it to me. "Enjoy your lunch," he tells me with a wink, and with that, he strides out of the salad bar, his gaze sailing back to mine as he rounds the corner and makes his way out the door.

"Hoooooly shit," Becs says. "He was perfect. What the hell is wrong with you? You know he's going home to jerk off over you in the shower."

Becs flinches before cringing. "Shit, sorry," she laughs, clearly speaking to Austin. "Forgot you were there."

I roll my eyes and steal my phone back as we finally make our way out of the salad bar, and I'm not going to lie, I can't help but watch Harrison as he strides back toward campus. "Was your birthday the only reason you were calling?" I ask Austin, more than ready to give Becs a piece of my mind.

"Yep," he declares. "Unless you're ready to talk about whatever was stuck up your ass for the past few weeks, or are you over that?"

"I'm hanging up now."

"Don't you dare—"

I press the little red button before letting out a heavy sigh and sliding my phone into my back pocket. "Holy shit. He's impossible," I say, wondering just how quickly my shirt can dry in this blazing sun.

"He's impossible?" Becs laughs. "Have you looked in the mirror lately? You just had the perfect guy ask you out, and you turned him down. What the hell is wrong with you? I thought you were in your *who the fuck is Izaac* era?"

I cringe as we find a tree that offers just enough shade and drop our asses to the leaf-covered grass. "I mean, I might not quite be in my *who the fuck is Izaac* era anymore."

"What?" she grunts, her head snapping up as her honey-brown gaze zones in on mine. "What the hell are you talking about? The whole point of our night at Vixen was to fast-track your detox. What the fuck, Aspen?"

"Ahh shit," I mutter, feeling like a shitty friend for having kept this from her, but I know her too well, and if she thinks the only reason I didn't accept Harrison's date is because I can't get over Izaac, then she won't let up. Hell, I wouldn't put it past her to trick me into actually meeting up with him. "Promise you won't freak out?"

"Huh? What haven't you been telling me?"

"And you also have to promise never to even whisper a word of this to Austin because he will literally kill me."

"I swear to God, Aspen, if you don't hurry up and tell me whatever the hell is going on, I'm going to ram my fist up your vagina, yank out your ovaries, and drag you around campus by them."

The cringes come in hard and fast, and even though she never promised not to tell Austin, I don't need to worry about that. She'll keep this secret as long as she lives. "You know that night we went to Vixen?" I start. "And I slept with that guy in the dark room?"

"Yeahhhhhh," she says slowly.

"Sooooo . . ." I swallow hard, feeling my mouth go dry. "Turns out Izaac owns that club, and it wasn't a stranger in the dark room."

I watch her facial reactions as she starts piecing it together. First disbelief, then shock, and then— "HOLY FUCKING SHIT! YOU SLEPT WITH IZAAC?" Her eyes are wide as she continues to process, getting wider by the second. "YOU LOST YOUR FUCKING V-PLATES TO HIM? Oh my God. I need to lay down."

Becs collapses into the grass, her hand braced against her chest, and I remain quiet as I allow her a chance to process everything. It doesn't last long before she throws herself to her feet and starts pacing in front of me. "When did you find out?" she asks. "No. *How* did you find out?"

I cringe again, and honestly, if this were the Cringe Olympics, I would take the gold. "Umm . . . So, about that," I say.

"Spit it out."

"I kinda went back to Vixen the week after we went."

"YOU DID WHAT? WITHOUT ME?" she demands. "Who even are you right now?"

I fix Becs with a hard stare, my brow arching. "Can I talk without you freaking out?"

"Yeah, yeah," she mutters.

"Okay, so the week after we went, I was trying to move on. I really was," I tell her, knowing she's bound to comment on that. "That night at Vixen left me so . . . I was horny, okay? Really fucking horny. So, I downloaded Tinder and matched with this guy, and we were going to go out, but he showed up at my door and practically forced himself on me. He was only interested in fucking me, so I kicked him out, but—"

"Wait," she cuts in, holding up a finger when I go to call her out for it. "Have I taught you nothing? Since when do you tell strangers on the internet where you live? Are you insane?"

I roll my eyes and fix her with a hard stare. "Trust me. I learned that lesson already. Besides, Austin has already grilled me for that."

"And so he should."

"Do you want to hear what happened or not?" She makes a show of zipping her lips, and I take a deep breath to continue. "So, the night of the failed Tinder date, I was frustrated because the stranger from Vixen had opened me up to a whole new world, and despite my efforts, I couldn't scratch the itch he left behind. So without even thinking about it, I jumped in my car and took off."

"We are going to have words about this," she tells me.

"Believe me, I know," I tell her. "But anyway, you know how when you're there and the music is so loud you can barely hear anything? Well, when I was with him, his lips were right at my ear, so when he said something, I heard him clearly and recognized his voice immediately."

"Shit."

"Yeah. I mean, I probably would have been fine if it turned out that he didn't know it was me, and granted, he didn't . . . the first time. He figured it out at Mom's birthday lunch, right before we went out to Pulse, so by the time I showed up for the second time, he knew exactly who I was, and despite everything, he still touched me."

"Woah. That's kinda huge."

"No. Huge is the size of his cock," I say with a smirk. "Not to mention, it's pierced."

Her jaw almost hits the ground. "Bullshit. Izaac Banks is rocking the bling? Fucking hell, you lucky little whore. I've been dying to tick a cock piercing off my bucket list and have never been that lucky. How is it?"

My cheeks flush. Just the thought of how that piercing makes me feel causes a warm swelling deep in the pit of my stomach. "It's incredible. Izaac is . . . fuck, Becs. Everything with him is incredible."

She shakes her head as if needing a second to take it all in. "I'm assuming this is why you were a raging bitch for two weeks straight."

My lips twist into a cringe. "Guilty," I tell her. "It was one hell of a shock realizing it was him in that room, and so I screamed at him a little. I felt betrayed and dirty and like he'd taken something from me that I wasn't ready to give, you know? I was prepared to lose my virginity to a complete stranger and that's what I was content with, and finding out it was him who knew all these things about me . . . I don't know. I kinda spiraled for two weeks, and now that I've had a chance to reflect on it, I think what really gutted me was that even after being with me and how amazing it was, it didn't change a thing. He still didn't want me, and I had to swallow the pill that I'd never be enough for him. But anyways, he showed up at my door and refused to leave until we talked it out, and he wanted a way to make it up to me because he felt like shit, and before I could even think about what I was saying, I offered him an ultimatum."

Becs narrows her gaze. "Oh shit," she says, picking up her pacing again. "Please tell me you didn't say what I think you said."

I swallow hard. "I, uhhh . . . maybe suggested he could teach me the limits of my body behind Austin's back, orrrrrrr," I say, dragging it out. "I could find someone else who would."

Becs crumbles back to the grass. "Oh thank fuck," she says. "So it's over then?"

"Uhh no."

"WHAT?" she shrieks, her eyes widening like saucers. "Tell me that asshole didn't agree to that shit? Holy shit, Aspen. How could you be so stupid? It's one thing fucking him by accident, but knowingly going there with him is going to kill you. You're never going to be able to move past him now, and I'm sorry, but he's never going to want you the way you deserve. Are you really sure this is a good idea?"

"No," I admit, willing myself not to cry. "But whether I'm risking my heart or not, don't I deserve to have incredible sex? Nobody can make me feel the way he does, Becs. And what if this is my chance? What if he's suddenly seeing me as a grown woman instead of Austin's little sister?"

"I don't know," she says. "I think it's too risky, and you're opening yourself up to get hurt."

"Perhaps," I breathe, my shoulders slumping as I distantly notice that my shirt is nearly dry. "But he also told me that when he's inside of me, it's never been so good for him. We're compatible like that."

She presses her lips into a hard line, clearly seeing that she won't change my mind on this. "Okay," she finally says. "If you're sure you can handle it, then I'll support your decision to go down this road, but just know that if shit hits the fan, I'll be right here."

A smile pulls at my lips, and a huge weight lifts off my shoulders. "Oh, thank God," I breathe, crushing into her and wrapping my arms around her slim body.

"So, you two have really been . . .?"

"Yup," I say with a wide grin. "Last night."

"Oh my God, I feel scandalized. But also, you have to tell me every detail," she says, her tone shifting and putting me on edge. "First though, I think it's important to note that if you're screwing Izaac, your reasoning for why I can't screw your brother is kinda null and void now. You've got no ground to stand on."

My jaw drops, and I pull back, gaping at my best friend. "You wouldn't."

"Oh," she says, her gaze darkening, clearly thinking of what it'd be like to be with my brother. "I think you and I both know damn well that I would."

22

IZAAC

The strobe lights go off as I make my way through the dancefloor of Cherry, my gaze darting left and right as I seek out Austin. He's going to fucking kill me, and this time it's got nothing to do with the fact that I've buried my cock into his little sister three times this week already.

I'm late. Like really fucking late.

It's his twenty-ninth birthday, and just like every year, Austin goes hard for his birthday. Guys from high school and college are here, friends we've met from our days thinking we could make it as professional ice hockey players, and now, people Austin has met after college.

It's fucking insane. Even on a normal night at Cherry, the

atmosphere is never like this, but when Austin wants to party, the whole fucking world parties with him. He's just that kind of guy, and it's one of the many reasons why I've always valued him as my best friend.

If only he knew just how terribly I've been betraying him. Hell, if only he knew how fucking easy it was for me to do it in the first place. Every time I've seen Aspen since we agreed to do this, it's gotten easier to look the other way, to pretend that what we're doing is innocent and won't hurt anybody, but the truth is, when I see her, all of that bullshit seems to fade away.

Hell, it's even getting easier to pretend that she's not Austin's little sister at all.

Breaking through the edge of the dancefloor, I search through the crowd and finally find Austin sitting at a booth with a beer in his hand, laughing animatedly with a bunch of our old friends. I make my way toward him, having to stop a few times to say hi to people I haven't seen since Austin's last birthday.

Finally making it to Austin, he stands from the overcrowded booth and immediately pulls me into a tight hug, clapping his hand on my back. "Where the fuck have ya been, brother?" he asks, his tone suggesting he's already well and truly tipsy.

"Had delivery issues at Pulse," I explain, not bothering to get too deep into details when he finally pulls away. "Fucking bastards never showed up with my order, but who gives a shit? It's your birthday."

"Damn straight it is," he says, reaching toward the table and grabbing a beer. He hands it to me, and seeing the cap still on top, I take it without question. I trust these boys, but after being around the club life since I was old enough to pass with a fake ID, I've learned the dangers of accepting a drink you haven't personally witnessed being poured. Fuck, the number of ambulances I've had to call for women who've had pills slipped inside their drinks makes me fucking sick, but no matter what level of security I put at my doors, the drugs always find their way inside my club. It's inevitable.

Breaking the cap, I lift the rim to my lips and take a greedy sip. I don't make a habit of drinking in my own clubs. I like to keep it professional around my employees, but every now and then, nights like tonight happen, and if I'm going to drink, then I might as well do it somewhere I love. Though that rule of mine tends to be blurring a little, or perhaps it's just the presence of a particular woman who's so far under my skin, I can't fucking help to break every rule I've ever made.

Sitting down with the boys, we talk shit as I steadily make my way through my beer, not down with the idea of getting fucking wasted tonight. Alcohol and I don't really mix anymore. I always thought I could hold my liquor with the best of them, but now, every time I drink, I pull my fucking phone out and turn into a horny teenager, desperate for his best friend's little sister.

I've gotta keep my cool tonight, especially considering that she's here somewhere.

I don't search her out. I'm not looking to borrow trouble tonight, but I can sense her here, sense that dazzling green stare on me from somewhere across the club. I'm desperate to see her, desperate to put my hands on her and pull her against my body, which is exactly why I need to keep my distance tonight.

How the fuck am I supposed to hide this in front of Austin? My only plan is to get him as drunk as humanly possible. I love the guy, but he's fucking oblivious when he's drinking. More than down with my plan, I make my way over to the bar and talk with my bar manager, pointing out Austin and our group, and letting her know that anything they want, it's theirs tonight. Food, drinks, fucking personal dancers, my team is to make it happen. Then because I'm incapable of putting work aside for even a second, I check in with the day-to-day bullshit and make sure everything is running just as smoothly as I expect.

Making my way back to our booth, I glance up to find Aspen and Becs squished in between the group of guys, and it fucking grates on my nerves how they all look at her like a fucking meal, but what really gets me is how fucking gorgeous she looks in that metallic purple dress. It's tiny and barely held together by the thinnest strap. No wonder these motherfuckers can't keep their eyes off her. I can't blame them, neither can I.

This week has been fucking hard. I'm becoming addicted, and I don't think I'm strong enough to resist. If she were to call this whole thing off, the right thing to do would be to walk away without a backward glance, but to be completely honest, I think I would drop to my knees and beg her not to leave me.

When I'm not near her, I crave her.

When I'm not inside her, I need to be.

And when I come inside her, I wish for things neither of us are prepared for.

I'm fucking screwed.

I think I'm falling for my best friend's sister—the one thing I always swore I would never do.

Reaching the booth, I move in behind it, not wanting to risk getting too close to her, not with all of these eyes on us. Instead, I hover behind her, talking to a few of the guys lingering around, only keeping my eyes off her is almost an impossible task.

Aspen hasn't bothered to turn around, but I know she senses me here. It's in the way she laughs a little louder, how she rolls her neck, showing off that creamy skin I can't fucking resist, and how she fucking flirts with every guy who pays her the tiniest bit of attention.

Doesn't she know she's driving me insane? Ha. Of course she does. That's exactly why she's doing it. She knows things are shifting. She has to, but the more I deny it, the more I can pretend I'm not a complete piece of shit.

Austin leans around Aspen to shamelessly flirt with Becs, and I roll my eyes. It's almost fucking comical how desperately he wants to hook up with her best friend. Does he see how hypocritical it makes him? I know Aspen has more than pointed it out, but I'm almost positive Austin doesn't see it the way she does, and sure, maybe it is different. Aspen met Becs once they started college together, so when Austin first met her, she was already an adult. As for me and Aspen, she was just a child when she first looked at me as anything more than a friend, so I can understand Austin's reluctance about it. Hell, I fucking hated it back then. Sure, it was cute and I thought it would just fade away with time, but when I realized it was a permanent fixture, it shook me, and the way I interacted with her instantly changed.

How the fucking tables have turned. There's nothing I wouldn't do to be inside of her now. To fuck that smart mouth and spread those pretty thighs.

Fuck. I need to get a grip.

As Becs and Austin shamelessly flirt, Aspen groans and climbs over her friend, trying to get out of their little bubble before it turns into the most awkward threesome that ever existed. Only as she climbs over Becs and grips the table to pull her across, I catch sight of a gold shimmer across her wrist and blanch.

What the fuck is that gold moth doing on her wrist? Has she been at Vixen without me? Fuck. Casey and I are going to have to have words. She knows better than to allow Aspen through the door without letting me know about it first.

My heart pounds, a million different scenarios playing out in my head. Was she with someone else in there?

As she settles in on Becs' other side and happily sips her drink, I can't fucking take it any longer. I step in closer behind the booth and lower myself toward her, my face concealed from Austin by the back of Becs' head.

My hand instantly shoots over the top of the booth, clutching her wrist below the cover of the table. "What the fuck is this?" I murmur in her ear, watching the way goosebumps dance across her clammy skin, sweaty from hours of dancing with her best friend.

"Relax. Becs and I just went for a drink and to check out the . . .

scenery," she replies, keeping her tone low and private. "I wasn't with anyone if that's what you're asking."

I narrow my gaze, wishing I could see her face properly from here, but I have no reason to doubt her. "What's it to me if you were with anyone else?" I question, playing it off, but we both fucking know what I'm refusing to say out loud.

Aspen scoffs, trying to pull her wrist out of my grasp, but there's no way in hell I'm about to let her spend the next few hours wandering around my club with that stamp on her wrist and her brother barely a step away. As far as he knows, Aspen was banned from Vixen, and I don't intend to ruin his night by letting him know that I haven't exactly stuck to my word.

My thumb swipes at her wrist, smudging the gold stamp, and even long after it's gone, my thumb continues moving across her skin. "Did you see anything that caught your eye?" I ask, referring to her quick visit to Vixen.

"A few things," she murmurs, tilting her head toward me, her tone deepening with a hunger I'm now all too familiar with. "I wouldn't mind . . . stepping out of the dark room."

My brow arches, my thumb pausing on her wrist in surprise. "You wanna put on a show?"

"Maybe."

"If that's what you want, my sweet Birdy, then who am I to hold you back?"

Aspen groans, having to bite her bottom lip as her hand curls up to grip my arm, her nails digging into my flesh. "What did I tell you about calling me that outside the club?"

My head tilts closer to her, my mouth right by her ear, and to anyone looking, it would appear innocent, just two people trying to have a conversation over the sound of the music. "Try and fucking stop me," I say right into her ear, watching the way her pulse at the base of her throat picks up.

Fuck, I'd do anything to close my mouth over that right now.

Becs laughs, breaking me out of the spell Aspen holds over me, and I hastily pull away just as Becs grips Aspen's hand and gives her a shove toward the edge of the booth. "Come on, we're going dancing," Becs tells her. "I want to shake my ass for your brother."

"Fuck yeah. In that case, I'm coming," Austin declares.

"Oh, hell no," Aspen shrieks, leaning around Becs to glare at her brother. "We talked about this. You're not fucking Becs on the dancefloor."

Wait. What? Clearly I missed something.

"Is that a challenge, little sister?"

"Fuck, no," I say, more than happy to step in on this particular sibling rivalry. "No one is fucking anybody on my dancefloor. I don't want any of my cleaning crew having to scrape your cum off the fucking floor."

"Oh please," Becs says, her lips lifting into a wicked grin as the three of them finally barrel out of the booth. "I'd never be so reckless as to let it drip all over the floor. I plan on swallowing every last drop."

Aspen pretends to gag as Becs howls with laughter, and before I know it, the three of them are gone, taking a bunch of the rowdy assholes from college along with them, and it doesn't go unnoticed that all of their attention is on Aspen.

Dropping down into the booth, I become mesmerized by the way she moves, and when she watches me right back, the electricity pulsing between us is stronger than it's ever been. She puts on a show, just like she said she wanted, rolling her body and drawing me in with every move she makes. But I'm not the only one who notices her.

One of Austin's old college friends, Carter Starby, moves in behind her as she shakes her ass, and when his hand circles her waist and he pulls her in, I see red. Anger pulses through my veins. How dare he touch what's mine. I never fucking liked that asshole.

Aspen laughs it off, trying to push him away, but he doesn't take the hint and grinds against her ass. She shoves at him again, and he holds her tighter, his hands snaking up toward her full tits when she starts looking around, desperate for help. She searches for Austin, panic flashing in her eyes, but he's too fucking occupied with his tongue down Becs' throat. By the time that familiar gaze flicks to me, I'm already halfway across the club.

Relief shines in her eyes, and before the fucker can get his hands any higher, Aspen is behind me with my fist flying right into his fucking jaw. Carter stumbles back, too fucking shocked to know what hit him, and as he finally rights himself and tries to fight back, my security team intervenes, dragging his ass out of here. Austin doesn't even notice.

"Holy fuck," Aspen breathes, clinging on to my arm. "Are you okay?"

"Am I okay?" I scoff. Is this girl for real? She was the one getting felt up by some asshole who I'm sure would have assaulted her further if he had the chance. The fury of the whole situation burns through my veins, and instead of responding to her question, I press against her back. "Walk."

She doesn't hesitate to move her ass across the dancefloor and back toward our booth, only before she can step into it and take a seat, I keep her moving, directing her to the employee-only section of the club. We walk for what seems like forever, every step only working me up further. We weave through the maze of hallways until we finally reach my office, but before I get a chance to reach for the door, I fucking snap, grabbing her and shoving her up against the door of my office.

"Fucking hell, Birdy. Do you have any idea what you've been doing to me out there?"

"You think I don't?" she questions, pushing her ass back against me, feeling just how desperate I am for her. "I've been wet for you since the second you walked in."

I groan, finally bringing my lips down on her neck. I need to stop. I can't do this here, and with her . . . fuck. We have rules for a reason. This is only supposed to happen at Vixen, but the thought of Carter's hands on her body, of touching everything I want and crave. It drives me crazy.

"Aspen," I groan, desperation pounding through my veins. "Tell me to stop."

"I can't do that," she pants. "I need you inside me. I need you to fuck me."

Aspen reaches down, trying to bunch up her skirt, but with her body shoved so tight against the wall, she can barely move, but I'm not bound by those same restrictions, and within seconds, my hands are at my belt, hastily freeing myself from the confines of my pants.

Aspen reaches behind, gripping my cock in the palm of her hand and quickly working me, her thumb looping over my tip and lingering on my piercing, something I've noticed she tends to do quite a bit, but there's no objection here. I fucking love it.

She barely gets to work her hand all the way up and down before I have her purple metallic dress bunched up to her waist and her thong torn to shreds at our feet. She arches her back, pressing her ass back into me, and I groan as I take her hip, stilling her. Then guiding my tip to her entrance, I feel just how fucking wet she is, and without another second of warning, I slam deep inside of her.

She gasps, using her hands braced against the door for leverage to press back against me. "Holy fuck," she groans, her walls shuddering around me as they stretch and adjust to my sheer size.

She's so fucking warm inside, fitting me just right, and I grit my teeth as she clenches around me. "You like that, Birdy?"

"Oh, God. Yes. More," she cries out.

I give her what she needs while taking everything I've wanted since the last time I saw her, and fuck, it's everything I've needed and more. I pound into her, digging my fingers into her hip to hold her still as she squirms and jolts with pure satisfaction. "See how well you take me?" I demand, rolling my hips before slamming back inside of her, taking her deeper. "See what you do to me? This tight little cunt could bring me to my knees, Aspen."

I thrust again, both of us so worked up. "It's yours," she pants, trying to find purchase against the door. "All yours."

"That's right," I say, curling my hand around the front of her hip and diving between those creamy thighs, and as I pound into her, stretching the pretty pussy, I roll my fingers over her clit and watch how she nears her limits.

"Fuck, Izaac," she groans, trying to grind against my hand while also pressing back against my cock to take me deeper. I give her everything she wants as I feel that familiar tightening in my balls, but I hold off, needing to feel as she comes undone around me.

I roll over her clit again before gently pinching it. "Come on, Birdy. I know you're right there with me. Let me feel you come on my cock. Squeeze me."

Aspen's walls tighten around me, and I groan, the sensation setting me on fire. Nothing will ever compare to being inside her. "I . . . I'm so fucking close," she pants.

I feel her body trembling, but despite how close she is, she needs something more, and without hesitation, I reach around her and grip the door handle before shoving it open. The door opens with a bang, slamming against the drywall. I shuffle us inside before kicking the door closed behind me, and the second I get her near my desk, I bend her over it, not giving a shit about the paperwork that scatters across the small office.

Taking both of her hips, I fuck her hard and fast, gritting my teeth until finally, she cries out, her sweet little cunt shattering like glass as she reaches her climax. She comes hard, crying out with desperation as her hand finds mine on her hip and squeezes hard.

I come with her, shooting hot spurts of cum deep inside her as her body turns into a spasming mess. "Holy fuck," she groans, her walls convulsing as her high continues to climb.

I don't stop thrusting until she comes back down, her body relaxing heavily against my desk, and I brace my hands on either side of her, needing just a moment to catch my breath. "Fuck, Birdy," I breathe, leaning down to her and pressing a kiss to her shoulder before finally inching away and falling out of the warmth of her sweet cunt.

All too aware of just how reckless this was, I hastily fix myself up, tucking my cock back inside my pants and doing up my belt before focusing my attention on Aspen. She crosses her arms under her face, using them as cushioning against the hard desk as she simply watches me. I step back into her, taking the skirt of her dress and pulling it down to cover her perfect ass. "I feel you dripping out of me," she murmurs, still caught up in the post-orgasm bliss.

I take a second, her words making my cock spring back to life, and I do what I can to find just a little bit of control. But damn, now that I know my cum is spreading between her pretty thighs, it's almost impossible to think of anything else.

"We shouldn't have done that," I say, looking around the office for something that could help clean her up. "Anyone could have walked in. My staff. Your brother."

"I know. Isn't it exciting?" she says. "We should do it again."

"As much as I love being buried inside of you, we're not risking that again. Becs will come looking for you soon."

Aspen straightens herself up, and when she looks at me, there's a deep disappointment shining in her beautiful green eyes, and fuck, it kills me. Since we started doing this, I've never told her no. Well, at least not when she was asking me for more.

"Right. Got it," she says. "How fucking stupid could I be? You were just looking for a quick fuck, and I was just the desperate whore you knew you could get it from. Thanks a lot."

My brows furrow, but before I get a chance to even question her, she's out the door, kicking it shut behind her with a heavy thump.

Fuck. What the hell just happened?

Needing answers, I follow her out of the office, but as I walk back through the same maze of hallways and back out to the club, I find no sign of her. "Hey," Austin says, stepping into me as he gazes out at the crowded dance floor. "Have you seen Aspen? I can't find her."

Panic soars through my chest, and I shake my head, hoping like fuck he's not able to get a good read on me right now. "I umm . . . I think she said something about going to pee," I tell him, watching as he physically relaxes.

He leans over and whispers something to Becs, his hand dangerously low on her back. Her phone is in her hand, the screen lit up, and as she glances down and looks over a text, her body stiffens. Then in an instant, her gaze snaps up and meets mine, and the chill within them sends a wave of unease blasting through me.

She knows.

Then without another word to Austin, she steps around him and walks away, her shoulder ramming into my arm as she passes.

23

ASPEN

Hangovers suck, but hangovers that include an accidental screw in a back hallway suck even more. Don't get me wrong, it was a lot of fun—until it wasn't. When Izaac stormed through the club and took me down into the employee section, I honestly thought I was about to receive the lecture of a lifetime, but when he put his hands on me and shoved me against the door, I knew exactly what he needed because it was everything I was needing too.

He broke all the rules. No sex outside of Vixen.

I mean, surely he knew I was willing to break them, but him? I didn't expect it, and it wasn't until we were in his office that it really occurred to me what was happening. Izaac Banks broke the fucking rules.

He complicated things.

But that's nothing compared to the realization that it meant nothing to him, not like what it meant to me. I thought maybe this was a huge step in the right direction. He said things he's never said before, admitted how I could bring him to his knees, and the moment he was done and that coldness crept back into his gaze, I realized how fucking stupid I'd been to believe him.

It was nothing but desperate sex for him, and he was willing to say whatever he had to say to get it. Joke's on me.

He played against my feelings, and it fucking sucks. Hell, I think I would have preferred he took some other woman back there and saved me all of this heartache.

For the past few weeks, I've felt the shift between us, but since we started this teaching experiment a little over a week ago, I've seen him more than I ever did. I've been with him four times this week, each session becoming more intense as we learn the limits of each other's bodies. But last night, that was different.

Each time we've been together, it's only gotten better, and I foolishly convinced myself that this was heading in the right direction, that if we just kept going at it, he'd eventually fall in love with me, but Becs was right. He's never going to want me. But I should have known better anyway. When this first started, Izaac warned me point-blank that he was never going to feel for me what I've always felt for him.

Maybe Becs was right. Maybe I need to walk away before he truly breaks me and I end up at the point of no return.

What the hell am I supposed to do?

I trudge through my small apartment, my head pounding as I search for Aspirin and a glass of water. Hell, I could use a massage and a spa day too, but something tells me that's not in the cards for me today. Instead, I settle for UberEats and a day of tormenting myself.

After finding the Aspirin, I crash on my couch, and as I reach for my throw blanket, my phone rings from somewhere in my bedroom. Groaning, I get up and make my way into my room and find my phone on my bedside table, still plugged into the charging cable.

Walking around the side of my bed, I step up to my bedside table and gaze down at my phone, my heart sinking when I find Izaac's name across the screen.

The call rings out, and the moment the sound fades from my room, I let out a shaky breath. Talking to him is only going to make matters worse. I need a day or two to nurse my wounds before facing that, but what it comes down to is that this thing with Izaac . . . I need to end it. Only I'm not sure I have the strength to physically say the words.

Grabbing the phone, I turn on my heel and stalk back to the couch, but before I crash down against the soft cushion, my phone rings again. Against my better judgment, I let out a heavy groan and accept the call. "Is there something you need from me?"

"You told Becs?" Izaac demands, disbelief thick in his tone.

"Are you kidding me right now?" I ask, my eyes widening at the audacity of this man. "That's really what you want to talk about? Get fucked, Izaac."

Rage fills my veins, and before he gets a single word out, I end the call, tossing my phone down on the couch as I press my hands to my temples and try not to scream.

I've said it before, and I'm sure I'll say it a million times more; Izaac Banks is impossible. Hell, if I knew being the woman he currently takes pleasure in would drive me insane, perhaps I would have reconsidered my lifetime crush on the asshole.

The phone rings again, and I clench my jaw, knowing I should ignore it, but there's too much fight left in my veins. If he wants to have it out, then I'm all for it. Scooping the phone up, I hit accept and press it to my ear, only before I can even think of a slew of insults to throw at him, he beats me to it. "Did you just hang up on me?"

"Of course I did," I throw back at him. "You're an asshole, and I'll happily do it again."

"Just . . . fuck! Don't hang up, okay? I just . . . I don't understand what the fuck is going on with you. One minute you were into it and the next you flew out the fucking door. Again. I thought we talked about this. If you have something to say, then fucking say it."

"Ha," I scoff. "Right back at ya."

"What the fuck is that supposed to mean?"

Is he serious right now? Can he honestly not see what's going on between us, can't even pull his head out of his ass long enough to see how things are starting to shift, that he's falling for me just as much as I've fallen for him? But hell, if he wants to ignore it, then so be it. "You know what? If you haven't figured it out by now, then who the hell am I to try and help you along?"

The need to hang up on the bastard pounds through my veins, but

I try to keep what composure I can as I listen to his frustrated groan. "Last night," he starts, a clear cringe in his tone. "It wasn't just some quick fuck. It was—"

He cuts himself off, and it only frustrates me more. "It was what? It meant more than that?"

"No," he says, not bothering to sugarcoat his rejection.

"Ahh, so it was just a quick fuck then. Thanks a lot. You really know how to make a woman feel valued."

"Fuck, Aspen. I—"

"Do me a favor," I say, my voice shaking as I feel a thick lump appear in the back of my throat, tears threatening to spill over my eyes. "The next time you're looking for some whore to sink your dick into, leave me out of it. I'm not down with being used as some wet hole for you to fuck."

"That's not what it was," he insists.

"Then go ahead and enlighten me," I tell him. "The floor is all yours. What was it?"

Izaac falls silent, and I shake my head, disappointment swelling in my chest.

"Why am I not surprised?" I scoff, never having felt so small and irrelevant in my life. "You've tiptoed around it all week, and every time you touch me, I can feel that it means something to you, but you're too fucking scared to admit it. You're a coward, Izaac."

Not prepared to allow him to break me further, I end the call and crash down onto the couch, my face buried in my hands as the tears fall. I sit there for twenty minutes, my world crumbling out from beneath me as I curl up with my blanket, desperately wishing things could be different. Wishing he could just love me the way I've always needed him to.

The phone rings again, and as I look toward it, my heart sinks.

I know I shouldn't answer. I should let it ring out and cut this off before he's able to hurt me further, but I'm a sucker for punishment, and where Izaac is involved, I'll always come running.

Answering the call, I simply lift it to my ear, not willing to keep fighting with him. He's silent too, neither of us knowing what to say or where to go from here, but I'm done wondering, done waiting around for something that'll never happen.

"Are you ever going to love me, Izaac?" I murmur, the tears starting all over again.

The silence is heavy, and I know exactly what he's going to say before the word is forced from his lips. "No, Aspen. I can't. I won't."

I nod, the weight of his words pulverizing my heart into a million fractured pieces. "Okay," I say with a shaky breath, the tears rolling down my cheeks. "Don't call me again."

And with that, I hang up one final time before finally allowing myself to truly crumble. Pulling my blanket back over me, I curl up on the couch and sob against the armrest. I never should have gone into this arrangement with hopes that Izaac would fall for me. It was stupid.

But I was so close.

I had everything I ever wanted within reach, and yet no matter how much I put myself out there, I'll never be enough for him. I will never have his heart, his affection, his unconditional love.

It's time to move on, time to find someone capable of loving me the way I need, and despite how hard it's going to be for me to let go, I need to try. Besides, there could be someone out there for me and he's just been waiting all this time, only I've been too blinded by a stupid childhood crush to see it.

My gaze settles on a napkin left discarded on my coffee table, and I can't help but reach for it, finding Harrison's number scrawled across it, the napkin torn in places where he was too heavy with the pen. My heart doesn't race, and it sure as hell doesn't feel like this is about to be some monumental, earth-shattering moment in my life, but I owe it to myself to try.

Then after entering his number into my phone, I shoot off a quick text.

Aspen - Hey, is this Harrison? It's Aspen. You blew your load all over me at the salad bar.

His response comes almost instantly.

Harrison - How could I possibly forget? I've been thinking about that load ever since I shot it all over your tits.

A laugh bubbles up my throat, and I find myself smiling. I like a man who's able to take a joke and run with it without taking things too far. He clearly has a good sense of humor, but he proved at the salad bar that he's also kind and thoughtful. He doesn't hesitate to fix something when he fucks up, and he's straightforward about what he wants.

He's exactly what I need, only despite the cocky grin and cheeky words, he didn't make my heart race, not the way Izaac always has.

Aspen - I know I'm a few days late, but would it be completely left field if I accepted your proposal and allowed you to take me out?

Harrison - I knew you'd come running back! It's my cocky boyish charm, isn't it? You couldn't resist.

Aspen - Could you put your cocky boyish charm away for just one second and answer the question?

Harrison - I'd fucking love to take you out.

A smile lingers on my lips, and I do what I can to wipe the tears away. This could be a new beginning for me, something to look forward to, and if it doesn't work out, then it doesn't matter because there are always other fish in the sea. Though, there are also blood-hungry sharks in the sea, but I don't think any kind of shark could take a bigger bite out of me than Izaac already has.

My phone buzzes again, and I glance down, expecting to find another text from Harrison, outlining whatever he might have in mind for our date, but instead, I find Izaac's name across the screen.

Ahhhh shit. What could he possibly want now? Did he not think he hurt me enough already?

I should delete it.

Only morbid curiosity gets the best of me, and despite knowing better, I open his text.

Izaac - Vixen. 8pm. Tomorrow night. I'm going to fuck that smart mouth, and only when you're begging for more, I'm going to fuck the attitude out of you.

I stare at his words, realizing he thinks he can fix this with sex. But there's no fixing this. How can he possibly think I'd be willing to meet him after hearing those words come out of his mouth? He's never going to love me. I'll never be what he wants. I'm nothing but a good time.

I'm done.

This has to end.

I won't be going back to Vixen, and I sure as hell won't be allowing Izaac to use my body. I was kidding myself when I asked for this, and just as Becs predicted, I was the one who got hurt. It's time to offer my heart the respect it's always craved.

From here on out, Izaac Banks is dead to me.

24

IZAAC

My jaw clenches as I glance down at my watch. 8:30 p.m.

Aspen is chronically late. It's a sickness. But when she's meeting me, she's always been on time. Even early on occasions, but tonight feels different. I hurt her yesterday. I had no fucking choice. She was asking for something I can't give, no matter how I feel about it.

I had to lie. I had to tell her I'd never love her, but I think I already do.

I'm not capable of giving her what she needs. Not worthy of it. I don't even know how to love someone, and I'm sure as hell not going to use her to experiment with that. She deserves so much better. All I'm going to do is hurt her, so it was best I shut her down before I let it get too far.

She hurts now, but in time, she'll move on, despite how much the thought of that tears at something deep in my chest.

I didn't expect her to challenge me on it last night. I figured after what went down at Cherry, we'd fight it out. When I called her yesterday, I knew she'd let loose. I expected her to scream, to come up with every insult under the sun and launch it directly at me, but I wasn't expecting her to call me out on my shit. I wasn't expecting her to challenge me.

She asked me if it meant more, if I was ever going to love her, and for her to ask me that means she already knows the truth. She can feel the shift in our relationship just as I can, and she's right, I'm a fucking coward for not being able to admit it.

I thought maybe tonight, we could talk it out face-to-face. After we fucked all the pent-up anger out of our systems, we could sit at the Vixen bar down in the VIP lounge, or perhaps find a booth that offers a little more privacy and fucking talk for the first time . . . ever. Put everything out on the table and reestablish the lines that have become so blurred that I don't even see them anymore.

But something tells me she's not just late—she's not coming.

The ice clinks in my glass as I lift it to my lips, drinking what's left in the bottom.

Why do I feel so fucking worked up at the thought of Aspen blowing me off? That's not how this was supposed to go. She would come, we'd fuck, and I'd get her out of my system . . . for the next few days, at least. But the desperation I feel for her always comes back, and each time it does, it's more intense and so much harder to ignore. That much was proven at Cherry when I broke all my fucking rules and took her outside my office.

I've made a point not to break the rules. We put them in place for a reason and now everything is fucked up, and because of that, I'm standing alone at a bar, being stood up by the woman I always swore I'd never want.

What the fuck is wrong with me?

Hell, since Cherry, I haven't even taken a moment to consider Austin's feelings because suddenly what he wants doesn't matter to me anymore. On some level at least. He'll always be my best friend, and I'll always value his opinion, but she's what matters now. She's my priority, and right now, she's hurting so fucking bad that she couldn't even show up to call me a fucking asshole.

Shit.

I need to get over there.

I need to make this right, but I don't know how to do that, especially considering I can't give her the one thing she wants. How am I supposed to fix this?

Pulling my phone out of my pocket, I bring up her name before hitting call and holding the phone to my ear, then as it rings, I make my way out of the club. There's no answer, but I'm not surprised. After she asked me not to call her yesterday, of course I tried, but every single call got denied. She didn't even respond to my text.

Shit. What if something is wrong? What if I've pushed her too far, hurt her too much? What if she's lying on her bathroom floor unable to breathe?

Picking up my pace, I fly past Casey, ignoring whatever bullshit comes out of her mouth as I try Aspen's phone again.

No answer.

Fuck.

Getting out to the street, I barrel into my Escalade and hit the gas, flying toward Aspen's apartment. It's only a short ten-minute drive, but I do it in six, speeding right through the red lights and flying way above the speed limit.

My front tire runs up over the curb as I come to a screeching halt outside her apartment, and within seconds, I'm out of my car and storming through the entrance to the complex. My heart races with every step I take, forcing myself faster, convinced something terrible has happened.

I don't know what I'm about to walk into, but I prepare myself for the worst, knowing that whatever it is, it's on me.

Reaching her apartment, I shove my spare key into the lock, the very one both Austin and I had made in case of emergencies, and without a second of hesitation, I throw the door open. Rushing inside, my gaze shoots from left to right, desperately seeking her out.

"ASPEN?" I call, racing toward her bedroom.

"WHAT IN THE EVER-LOVING FUCK DO YOU THINK YOU'RE DOING?"

I pause, twisting around toward the sound of her voice, and find Aspen standing in the doorway of her small bathroom with a vile of mascara in her hand and a glare bigger than Texas across her face. "I thought—"

"Whatever the fuck you thought, you're wrong," she says, clearly not impressed with my intrusion.

"Where the fuck have you been? You were supposed to meet me at eight."

Aspen scoffs and turns away, walking back into her bathroom and getting to work on her makeup, though she doesn't need it. She's fucking flawless. "I wasn't supposed to do shit," she tells me. "Besides, I'm going out. I've got a date."

Over my dead body.

25

ASPEN

I'm gonna kill him. It's the only logical thing to do.

What the hell does he think he's doing storming in here like that anyway? I swear, the audacity of this man infuriates me like never before, but I do what I can to keep my composure. After all, Becs and I are going out tonight. Not that Izaac needs to know that. I might have fudged the details about my plans, but if I mean so little to him, then why should my plans matter?

I continue getting ready for my night, more than pleased with the look on his face.

"The fuck did you just say?" Izaac demands, hovering in the bathroom doorway as I put a little blush on my cheeks.

"You heard me loud and clear, Izaac. I'm going out on a date. You know, it's one of those things people do when they like each other. The guy asks the girl out and then she gets all flustered and says, *Of course, I'll go out with you,* and then he takes her out for a night to remember, and it's absolutely magical."

He gives me a blank stare. "I know what a fucking date is, Aspen."

"Oh. Could have fooled me," I mutter, turning back to my mirror while searching out my favorite lip gloss. "I thought your idea of treating a woman well was fucking her like a whore in dark hallways and making her feel like a fucking idiot for wanting you so bad."

Finished with my makeup, I stride out of the bathroom, forcing him out of my way before I hook around to my bedroom and search through my closet for something to wear. If I were just meeting Becs, I would usually wear jeans, boots, and some kind of top that showed off just a little bit of cleavage, but now that this asshole thinks I'm going out on a date, I have no choice but to dress the part.

Izaac goes to follow me into my bedroom, but I hold up my hand, stopping him by the door. "Careful," I say as I turn back toward my closet. "There's a bed in here. I wouldn't want you to accidentally break your rules and fall into my bed."

"Fucking hell," he mutters. "Can we just talk about this?"

"Oh, sure. Let's chat," I say, pulling out two little black dresses, one much more revealing than the other. I hold them up toward Izaac. "Which one?"

His brows furrow. "What?"

"For my date tonight. Which dress should I wear?"

He groans and rolls his eyes before pointing to the more modest dress of the two. "That one," he mutters, clearly not thrilled about having any part in helping me dress for another man. I mean, don't get me wrong, Harrison and I do have a date planned, but it's not until Friday night, so until then, I will take every pleasure in torturing Izaac with it.

"Good choice," I say, tossing the modest dress over my shoulder and holding on to the skanky one. Becs would be so proud.

Izaac rolls his eyes and turns away before striding toward my coffee table and dropping his ass onto it as I strip down to my bra and thong. He watches me through the open doorway, and I do what I can to put a little extra effort into dressing, taking my time as I pull the soft fabric up my body. "You wanted to talk?" I question, raising my voice just a bit so he can still hear. "I have to leave in ten, so you're gonna have to make it fast."

He clenches his jaw. "This isn't the kind of conversation you can just throw around in ten minutes," he says, watching as I pull my bra off from beneath my unzipped dress. "I thought we could have a drink at Vixen and clear the air. I don't like how things went down over the weekend."

"Oh, yeah. Look, today just isn't a great day," I say, walking out of my room when I realize how much fun I could have with this. If he wants to deprive me of the love I know he has to give, then I'll deprive him of what he wants—sex.

"I just—"

"Would you mind zipping me up?" I ask, walking right between his open knees and making a show of pulling my long hair over my bare shoulder before sitting down on his lap. I glance over my shoulder, meeting his heavy stare. "Please."

He holds my gaze for a moment before finally letting out a breath and turning his attention to my back. He takes hold of the little zipper and slowly drags it all the way to the top before letting his fingers dance across my skin.

His touch sends a wave of goosebumps rising over my body, and I hastily stand before making my way back to my room. "Thanks."

He clears his throat and tries to get back on track, but I still have no idea what it is he came here to say, and honestly, I don't think he knows either. "What's going on here, Aspen?" he questions as I find a pair of heels to go with my dress and make my way back out to the living room. "Are we going to keep doing this or are you out? I know what I said yesterday wasn't what you wanted to hear, but I think if we can reestablish where the lines need to be drawn that we—"

I walk back into him, and without warning, I put my heeled foot right in the center of his chest. "Would you mind?" I murmur, indicating toward the long straps of my heels that need to be wound around my ankle and up my calf.

His words fall away as his gaze settles on my leg, and when he lifts his hands and brushes them across my skin, a shiver sails right down my spine. He takes the long laces and starts working them around my legs, strapping me in, but when he's done and the perfect knot is tied at the back, he doesn't let go. His hands work higher up my leg, right to my upper thigh before leaning in and dropping a kiss to my knee.

I pull back and switch legs, and as he wraps the lace around my leg, his dark gaze lifts to mine. "I know what you're doing, Aspen."

"Do you?"

He doesn't respond, just keeps holding my gaze as he ties the little knot in the back, and it's like a spell has been cast over me. The tension between us is sky-high, and if he were to brush those skilled fingers over my skin one more time, I'd surely break and ride him right there on my coffee table.

Pulling my leg away, it's like a wave of cold water washes over me, and the spell breaks, then as I find my bag and stride to my door, Izaac stands. "We agreed that you wouldn't be with anyone while we were doing this," he says, his voice thick with concern.

I reach for the door, slowly opening it, and at this point, I don't know if I'm walking out and leaving him here or if I'm trying to kick him out. "Well, lucky for you, you're off the hook," I tell him as he walks toward me, pain radiating through my chest. "I'm calling it quits. I'm not down with being a punching bag to you. I have real feelings, Izaac, and you've made it crystal clear that you're never going to want any more than that, so what's the point in going back for more? All you're doing is hurting me and lying to yourself in the process, and I don't want any part in that. I asked you to teach me the limits of my body and you've done that, so congratulations. You've got your *get out of jail free* card and now you can walk away with a clear conscience. We can pretend nothing ever happened."

He shakes his head. "And if I'm not ready to walk away?"

I shrug my shoulders. "That's not my problem," I tell him. "I can't keep sleeping with you knowing it's only sex to you when it's so much more to me. We set the ground rules for how this was going to work, and those rules don't work for me anymore. So unless you're ready to say what we both know you're refusing to admit, then I'm out. I'm not interested in letting you hurt me over and over again. I deserve better. I deserve someone who's going to love me the way I need. You said you can't give that to me, so if you'll excuse me, that's exactly what I'm going to find."

I go to step around him when he catches my elbow and pulls me back to him, his hands at my waist. "Don't, Aspen. Don't go out with this guy."

"Why?"

"Because I'm not done with you, and I'm not ready to watch you fall into the arms of some other man."

"Then kiss me."

His brows furrow, and he pulls back just an inch, his grip tightening on my waist. "What?"

"Break all the rules and kiss me," I beg him. "Prove to me that there's a reason why I should endure this when you're not willing to give me what I want."

He shakes his head, fear flashing in his eyes. "You told me that you could handle it. You said this wasn't going to happen. I'm not the one fucking things up here. This is all you."

"Perhaps that's true," I say, my gaze falling away, all too aware of what I said. "But you're the one who broke the rules when you threw me against that door at Cherry. Don't you remember what you said to me? How you growled in my ear with desperation? Gritted your teeth and said *see what you do to me?* How you told me my sweet little cunt could bring you to your knees. That shit means something, and you know it."

"Aspen, I—"

I scoff, seeing the rejection in his eyes, and pulling myself out of his arms before fixing him with a hard, broken stare. "I might not have been strong enough to not get emotionally attached, but you can't be the only one who gets to choose which rules to follow or break."

He just stares at me, seeing there's no point in arguing, and fearing this is the last time I might ever see him, I step right back into his arms and push up onto my tippy toes. I press my lips to his, just how I've always wanted to, and when I pull away, I hold his dark stare, noticing how rigid he's become. "If you don't want me, then let me go," I tell him before pulling free of his strong grasp. "Lock up when you let yourself out. I have somewhere to be."

And with that, I stride out of my apartment, leaving behind Izaac Banks and any hope for a future between us.

26

ASPEN

Walking into Joe's Bar, I spot Becs sitting in a small booth, and the moment her gaze lifts to mine, she offers me a small smile. The moment she sees the look on my face, her smile fades. I make my way toward her and drop down into the booth. "I need a drink."

"Oh shit, what happened?" she asks as I make myself comfortable and steal the glass right out of her hand. I hold the rim to my lips and drink it all before finally putting it down. When I glance up, I find her concerned gaze fixed on me.

"Izaac is what happened," I tell her and she indicates to the bartender to get us two more of whatever she was just drinking. "He's such an asshole. I mean, the audacity of that man blows my mind. He deserves a fucking award for being the most delusional human being on the planet."

She cringes. "What did he do this time?"

"I told him it was over, that there would be no more visits to Vixen unless he was able to break his own goddamn rules and admit he feels something for me, and if he couldn't do that, then I was walking because I deserve better—"

"Damn straight, you do," she cuts in.

"But then that freaking douche canoe had the nerve to tell me not to go out with Harrison tonight because he's not done with me yet. Like what the hell is that? He only just told me on the phone yesterday that he could never love me."

"Wait. What? You were supposed to go out with Harrison tonight?" she asks. "But like . . . You're kidding right, he didn't actually say that. Like you're paraphrasing, right? Because if he did, that shit is harsh."

"Oh, he definitely said that. I asked him point-blank. Will you ever love me, and he straight up said no. But I gotta give him credit. At least he was honest and didn't laugh at me for being so fucking blind."

"Come on, you know he'd never laugh at you about that," she tells me. "Despite this strange little thing you've got going on, he's always cared about you."

"Yeah," I scoff. "As Austin's little sister."

She cringes. She knows it's true but thankfully switches gears. "So, what were you talking about with Harrison? Are you supposed to be out with him tonight?"

"No, but for what it's worth, I ended up texting him yesterday, and we're going out later in the week," I explain. "But when Izaac came barging through my apartment after I bailed on his planned fuck-fest, I may or may not have suggested my date with Harrison was tonight and that I was blowing him off for another guy."

"Holy shit," Becs laughs. "I can only imagine how he took that."

"He wasn't exactly thrilled about it," I offer. "But getting ready for my hot date while he was in my apartment trying to convince me that we should just pretend all the bullshit from the weekend never happened was actually pretty entertaining."

"I see," she says as our drinks are delivered to our table. "You clearly put in all the work. You look like a snack! I bet he was salivating the whole time."

I can't help but laugh as I scoop up my glass. "Not going to lie, I definitely played it to my advantage."

"So what's going to happen now?"

I shrug my shoulders as I sip on my drink. "Honestly, I have no idea. I told him if he isn't able to break the rules and admit what's happening here, then I'm not interested in being his punching bag. I told him to let me go."

"Do you think he will?"

"That's the part I'm not sure about."

"I think you're doing the right thing pulling away from him," she tells me. "I know you were hoping for a different outcome, and I was really rooting for you. I want you to have everything you've ever wanted, but not at the cost of your heart. If doing this with him is going to keep hurting you, then I think you need to take a step back and reevaluate what the right thing for you is going to be."

I nod. "I know you're right, but I really don't want to admit it."

"I know you don't. It's hard to let go of something you've wanted for so long."

I feel my eyes start to sting with the threat of tears, and I blink them away, taking a long sip of my cocktail to try and mask the emotions welling up in my chest. I always knew there would come a time when I would have to force myself to let go of Izaac, I just never expected it would hurt this bad. Hell, after the past few weeks, I started to wonder if I'd have to let go of him at all. I thought something was starting here. I thought I finally had my chance.

"Okay," I tell her. "I need you to talk about something else, otherwise I'm going to start sobbing, and once I start, I don't think I'm going to be able to stop."

"Alright. Well . . . ummm," she pauses, a cringe stretching across her face as she lifts her glass to her lips and takes a hefty drink. "I kinda did something stupid, and I don't want you to hate me, but like . . . ahhh shit."

"Oh my god," I groan in disgust. "You slept with my brother."

"Guilty," she says. "But in my defense, it didn't happen on the dancefloor at Cherry. You kinda disappeared after you and Izaac had office door sex, and so it was just me and Austin for ages with all of his friends, and when he got sick of batting them away, he asked if I wanted to go, and I was having such a good time with him that the thought of him leaving without me just kinda . . . sucked. And then one thing led to ano—"

"Woah. Okay. I don't need the details of how you and my brother had sloppy drunk sex."

"I'm sorry," she says, burying her face in her hands. "You've been so adamant that you didn't want us to do that, and the second I have a few drinks in me, I turned into a horny beast and couldn't take my hands off him."

"You don't have anything to be sorry for," I tell her. "I'm the last person who should be passing judgment, especially considering I've been preoccupied by Izaac's dick for the past few weeks. But after seeing you two at Cherry the other night, I knew it was going to happen sooner or later. He couldn't keep his hands off you."

"No, he couldn't," she says, her cheeks flushing.

"I guess we should celebrate," I tell her, raising my glass. "Welcome to the family."

Becs stares at me, her face falling. "Huh? What are you talking about? We're not dating. It was just one night. That's it. I don't intend on doing it again."

"Oh, I know," I say, a grin stretching across my face. "But give it time. It's inevitable. You'll soon realize how amazing he is, and you won't be able to resist falling in love with him. Besides, if Austin was willing to risk the *don't touch my best friend* rule that he's lived by for the last twelve years in order to have just a taste of you, then he's already falling for you."

Horror crosses her features, truly thinking about what I just said. "Oh, fuck."

"Yep."

"Am I going to marry your brother?"

I nod. "I think so."

"Holy fucking shit. I need shots."

"Yep."

Realizing waiting for the bartender to come to us is only going to slow us down, we get up from the booth and make our way over to the bar, more than aware that tonight is about to get a little messy. We get comfortable, and as soon as the bartender comes over to us, Becs takes the lead. "Tequila. And keep it coming."

God, she's a woman after my own heart. No wonder I like to keep her around.

Our first round of shots is placed in front of us, and we pounce on them like rabid animals as Becs whines about Austin being out of state to meet with some highly sought-after interior designer. I order another round.

This is going to be a long night.

Over the space of the next few hours, we go from graceful, self-respecting patrons of the bar, to being kicked out for public drunkenness.

There's no other way to put it. I'm a mess, but Becs on the other hand, she's about ready to fall off her feet.

We stand in front of the bar, and I help Becs into her Uber, wishing we could go together, but from this particular bar, we live in separate directions, and we've learned long ago that it's just easier to catch separate rides.

Her Uber takes off, and I stand out front for a few minutes, waiting for my ride to show up, and as the cool air whips through the night, it helps sober me up . . . a bit. A few minutes turn into ten when frustration takes over, and I open my app to see what the hell happened to my driver before realizing I never actually booked my ride.

What a fucking idiot.

I laugh to myself as I fall back against the side of the building, using it as a crutch to keep me upright, and while I mentally try to convince myself that texting Izaac about how much of an asshole he is probably isn't a great idea, I start booking my Uber.

My stupid drunk fingers move across my screen, making an array of typos, and by the time I see my option laid out before me, my face scrunches. I don't exactly like what I'm seeing. The closest Uber is ten minutes away. I could almost walk home in that time. What's the point in even waiting? Sure, it's a bit chilly tonight, but who doesn't love a good stroll? Besides, after all the Izaac bullshit, I could use the walk to clear my head.

I turn in the direction of home, putting one foot in front of the other, and with nothing but time and silence to keep me company, I can't help but question every moronic thing I've done over the past few weeks. Why did I have to kiss him like that? I mean, it's not like it was some big show-stopping moment. It was barely a brush of my lips across his, but the way his body went rigid like that . . . that was weird. He almost looked . . . fearful.

But why would he react like that? We've already done so much worse, and it's not as though he wasn't begging me to change my mind. I thought he wanted the physical connection, just not the emotional one.

I try to think over the times I saw him with other women over the years, filtering through every single one of them until I realize that I never once saw him kissing them. Don't get me wrong, his lips roamed far and wide over their bodies, but never on their lips. That's a little weird for a man who has never been afraid of public displays of affection.

Does he have some weird repulsion to kissing? Is that why he didn't kiss me in my apartment tonight? I could have sworn he looked as though he wanted to, but maybe I was imagining that.

God, I can only imagine what it'd be like to truly be kissed by Izaac Banks. I feel as though he's the kind to start slow and cautious, but then he'd take control. He'd dominate the kiss until I was trembling.

I wonder if a woman can come from just a kiss.

I need to Google that at some point. Actually, why not now? After all, there's no time like the present, and it's not as though I have anything else to do right now.

Holding up my phone, I lean toward the little microphone as the streets become less business-focused and more residential. "Hey, Siri. Can a woman orgasm through kissing?"

Bringing my phone closer to my ear, I press the volume button at the side and listen closely, determined to hear exactly what my favorite little robot mastermind has to say about this. "I don't have an answer for that."

Huh. Well, that's shit.

I let out a sigh and pull up Google instead.

Hmmm . . . interesting.

Apparently it's possible, not likely, but still possible, and that's always a bonus in my book.

Perhaps this needs to go on my sexual experience bucket list. Besides, if any man would be capable of getting me there with nothing more than a kiss, surely it would be Izaac. He's so damn good at everything. Makes a woman wonder just *how* he became so good at it.

I bet it was that girl who always came around during his college years. She was a bit of a skank, but I could tell that she had a wild side. I always hated her, but I suppose now I owe her a thanks.

My mind takes me on a wild journey, going over everything Izaac has said to me over the past few weeks when I hear the soft sound of someone on the pathway behind me.

My heart lurches in my chest as I immediately think the worst, and I find myself holding my breath. I pick up my pace before finally finding the courage to look back. There's a man in a black hoodie, maybe twenty or so steps behind me, and I instantly berate myself for only now being more aware of my surroundings. Hell, even for being stupid enough not to have waited for my Uber.

Then just to be sure that I'm not overthinking this, I cross the road and turn down the closest street, even though it'll add time to my walk.

I wait, my gaze focused hard over my shoulder as I keep up my pace, trying to put distance between us, but the hooded guy appears around the corner.

Well, fuck. I'm being followed.

It's past midnight, so I can assume that he could be leaving a friend's place and innocently trying to make his way back home just as

I am, but am I really that naive to believe that?

Not even a little bit.

This guy wants something from me, and I can only assume it's the one thing mothers warn their little girls about, the one thing that plays on a woman's mind every time she walks to her car by herself, the one reason why you're always told to go with a trusted adult when entering a public restroom.

Fear laces every cell of my body as my hand viciously begins to shake.

Why did I choose to walk home alone?

How could I be so stupid?

Then without even a second of hesitation, I take off at a sprint, my heart pounding faster than my strappy heels against the concrete pavement.

27

IZAAC

Kicking my feet up on the end of my desk, I stare at my home computer screen as Austin holds up the plans, showing me the shit he discussed with the interior designer he met today. It's almost one in the morning, but I don't mind. I've been a night owl since the moment I first opened Cherry.

"I think she's in," he tells me, bracing his elbows against the small table in his hotel room and leaning toward his laptop. "I showed her the blueprints and the vibe I'm going for and she said she was interested in flying in and checking out the restaurant. Said it could be a great addition to her portfolio."

"No shit. That's great news."

"Yeah. Don't get me wrong, the hype already circling the restaurant is going to ensure a successful launch, plus we're already booked out for the first six months. But with her name attached to it, there's no telling how fucking great this could be."

"With or without her, this restaurant is going to be fucking incredible."

His eyes light up like Christmas morning, and I can't help but smile, so fucking proud of him. This has been his dream for so damn long, and now that the end is finally in sight, he can barely contain his excitement. "Thanks, man. You know I couldn't have done any of it without you."

"Don't give me all that sentimental crap. I have literally done nothing but stand on the sidelines and watch the magic happen. This is all you."

Austin rolls his eyes as I lean back in my desk chair and prop my hands behind my head. "How do you feel after last night?" I ask. "You seemed pretty fucking smitten with Becs."

"How would you fucking know? You were barely there for a minute."

I scoff. "I was there long enough to know you were doing something you shouldn't have been doing."

Fuck. I'm such a hypocrite.

Austin drags his hand down his face, a seriousness coming over him. "I don't know what to tell you, man. There's something about that girl. She's so fucking fiery. Whatever bullshit came out of my mouth, she was so quick to counter. It was refreshing. Plus, she's fucking gorgeous. I just . . . I wanna get to know her."

I let out a heavy sigh. "You took her home, didn't you?"

He grins. "Can you blame me? She's got me ready to risk it all."

My brow arches. "Even Aspen's wrath?"

"Even that."

I gape at my best friend. He's never thought about a woman long enough to consider anything. Hell, he likely doesn't remember the names of half the women he's been with. "Shit. What does Becs think about that?"

The smirk that stretches across Austin's face is the same one he had right before we ended up in cuffs in the back of a police cruiser. "She's not exactly on the same page, but don't worry. I'll wear her down. Give me six months," he says. "She'll be living with me and have my ring on her finger, mark my fucking words."

"Fucking hell," I mutter under my breath. "You talk a lot of shit, but you've never said anything like that about a woman. Are you really sure about this? You barely know her."

"I know her enough to know that she's worth taking the risk. Plus, Aspen fucking adores her, and she's always been a good judge of character. At least, mostly. I've kinda been questioning it since that whole Tinder date thing. But what I'm trying to say is, if Aspen loves her, then there's a good reason for that."

"What do you think Aspen is going to say about all of this?"

He shakes his head. "I think she'll come around to the idea. It might take a little while, but—" he cuts himself off as his phone rings, and a smirk lifts the corners of his lips. "Speak of the fucking devil."

He holds up his phone, flipping it around to show me Aspen's name across the screen before laughing to himself. He hits accept and holds it to his ear. "Do you have any fucking idea what time—" his words fall short, his face falling with horror. "Wait. Slow down. What's wrong?"

My heart races as my feet fall from my desk, more than ready to break into a fucking sprint to get to my girl, but I wait on eggshells, desperate to know what the fuck is going on.

Austin's gaze flashes to mine through the screen, his face turning white. "Fuck, Aspen. I'm out of town," he rushes out, a clear panic in his tone as he throws himself to his feet. "I can't—where are you?"

Aspen responds, and his stare shoots to mine again, my keys already in my hand, waiting for the fucking signal. "What's going on?" I demand.

Austin listens to whatever his sister is saying, his horror and fear increasing tenfold. "Izaac's gonna come and find you, okay? Stay hidden. Don't fucking move."

"What. The fuck. Is. Happening?" I growl, now on my feet, itching to fucking run.

"Someone's following her. She's hiding in the hedges outside some house, but she doesn't know where she is."

"I'm on my way."

I fly out the door, not bothering to disconnect the Zoom call as I hear Austin trying to soothe my girl in the background. "He's on his way," he tells her. "He'll call you from the car, but don't hang up my call until his is coming through. You understand me, Aspen? It's gonna be okay. He's coming for you. Izaac's not going to let anything happen to you."

I barely catch the end of his sentence when I storm through my front door, not wasting a fucking second to lock up behind me. If someone wants to ransack my home and steal every fucking possession I have, then let 'em at it. I don't fucking care. All that matters is getting to Aspen and making sure she's okay.

Fuck. If anything happens to her . . .

Reaching my Escalade, I quickly unlock it before yanking the door open with such force, I almost pull the whole fucking door right off its hinges, then before I even get the chance to blink, I'm in the driver's seat and flying down my long driveway.

I can only assume Aspen is somewhere near her college campus, so I take a right and head that way as I bring up her name on my phone and hit call. It connects through my Bluetooth system, and before the first ring has even ended, her voice fills my speakers.

"Izaac?" she whispers, her voice shaking and so full of fear, it cripples me.

"I'm on my way, baby. I'm not going to let anything happen to you," I promise her. "Where are you?"

"I . . . I don't know," she says in that same shaky tone, clearly on the verge of tears. Her voice is so quiet, I have to strain to hear, but I listen to every fucking word, desperately wishing I could take her far away. "I was walking home from a bar when I saw some asshole following me, so I turned down some random road and started running. I'm hiding in some bushes outside someone's house, but he knows I'm here somewhere. He's looking for me, Izaac. It's only a matter of time."

"Okay, can you pin your location?"

"I—" there's a slight pause, and when her voice comes again, the raw panic almost guts me. "I don't know how. I've never done it before."

"It's alright. Just hang in there, Birdy. I'll find you," I soothe, trying to keep her calm. "Where were you walking from?"

Terror pounds in my chest, each vicious beat of my heart threatening to take me down at just the thought of what could happen to her, and I try to push my Escalade faster, never having felt this kind of raw desperation in my life.

"J . . . J . . . Joe's Bar," she stumbles out. "It's close to campus."

I nod, knowing it well. Austin and I used to spend way too many late nights there during our college years, and from her apartment complex, it would have been a short walk. Though I don't know why the fuck she would have been walking at this time of night. She knows better than to put herself at risk like that, but it's not something we need to discuss right now. All that matters is getting to her before he does. "Okay. Good. What else can you give me?"

"Umm . . . I think I turned down the first street after reaching the residential area. I just . . . I don't know how far down I am or—"

I hear the panic enter her tone, and I quickly work to try and calm her, needing her to think straight in case she needs to act. "That's okay. Tell me what you see. What kind of bushes are you in?"

"There's . . ." she pauses, hopefully trying to take it in and find some kind of landmarks that will help me find her. "There's a house across the street. Its windows are boarded up, and the grass is overgrown. It's the only lamppost on the street that's not working."

"And you're directly opposite it?"

"Yes," she says. "In the bushes behind a white picket fence."

"That's good, Birdy. Can you tell me how close he is?" I ask. "Do you have time to get to the door of the house and knock?"

There's silence for a minute. "I . . . I'm not sure," she tells me. "I don't think anyone is here. There's no car in the driveway, and the mailbox looks like it hasn't been checked in a while. I don't know if I can risk getting to the door and waiting for someone to answer it without him finding me."

"Then stay put. Don't try to move," I tell her. "You're safer where you are. Do you have your handbag? Is there anything sharp you could use as a weapon?"

"Ummm . . ." I hear as she starts scrambling, the task seeming to give her something to concentrate on, putting a little more confidence into her tone. "A pen or umm . . . my keys."

"Perfect, baby. I want you to put your bag down and hold on to that pen. Until I get there, that's your lifeline, and if that guy finds you, you're going to use it. Do you understand me? You do whatever you have to do to get away. Plunge it into his throat. His eye. Anywhere that's going to drop him."

The shakiness returns to her voice. "I'm not sure I can do that."

"You can and you will," I tell her. "Now, what about those heels? Are you still wearing them?"

"Yes."

"Take them off. I know it feels wrong, but if you need to run, I want you to be sure in your footing. You can't risk tumbling. Take them off and keep them hidden in the bushes with you."

The line goes quiet, and I can only assume that she's taking her heels off.

"I—" she sucks in a terror-filled breath.

"What's wrong, baby? Are you okay?"

She remains silent.

"Is he there?"

An almost inaudible squeak falls from her lips, and I grip the steering wheel tighter, my knuckles turning white as I fly closer toward the college. "You're going to be okay," I promise her. "Don't make a sound. Just listen to my voice. I'm nearly there."

She sniffles in response, and a piece of my soul disintegrates into ash. "Shhh, baby. Put your thumb on the end of the pen so it doesn't slide through your fingers if you need to use it. Hold it tight."

She whimpers, and I realize I have to say something to keep her grounded and keep her from freaking out. She needs to be calm and in control in case it comes down to fighting for her life. "I'm sorry I hurt you, Aspen. That's the last thing I ever wanted to do, but there's just something about you that drives me insane. We're like fire and ice, Birdy. The second you look at me, my hackles are up, and I'm just waiting for the day that you realize I could never be enough for you." I swallow hard, never realizing how vulnerable I would feel after admitting this. "You were right yesterday. I am a fucking coward, and when I sank into you at Cherry, it was so much more than just a quick fuck."

She sucks in a breath, and I cringe, needing her to keep as quiet as possible. "You don't know how fucking badly I wish I could give you everything you've always wanted. I hate hurting you and constantly pulling away. You're so fucking beautiful, Aspen. Even before any of this started, I've always thought that, and I've always wanted so much for you. I want to protect you and see you get the whole fucking world, and if I'm completely honest, I think that's part of the reason I fight with you so much. I need you to see that I'm not good enough, and when we're screaming at each other, it keeps me from saying something I know I shouldn't. It keeps me from admitting just how fucking badly I want you."

"Izaac."

Her tone is barely a whisper, just a single confirmation that she truly hears me.

"I'm almost there, baby. Just hang in there."

"Where are you, Pretty Girl?" I hear a voice say. "Come out, come out, wherever you are. I know you're in here. I just want to play for a minute."

FUCK!

I hear as she takes a shaky breath, and I have to silence myself as I speed around the corner, almost losing control of the fucking car. Two more fucking streets and I'll be there.

She's going to be okay. She's got the pen, and she's ready to strike. She's a fighter. She's not going to let anything happen.

"You know, when I'm with you . . . I don't know how to describe it, Birdy," I tell her, swallowing over the lump of fear in the back of my throat as her whimpers start gaining traction and getting louder, threatening to give her away. "I know it started as just sex, but I think you know it's so much more than that. When I touch you . . . fuck. I've never felt anything like it, Aspen. There's something about you that has me on my fucking knees. You've got me hooked, and I'm not even close to being ready for you to walk away from me. How fucking selfish is that?"

I fly past Joe's Bar, taking the most natural route toward Aspen's apartment complex, and the second I hit the residential area, I turn down the first street, just as she told me she did. I fall silent, my eyes so fucking wide as I start searching for the house with the boarded-up windows, but I see him instead.

The asshole puts on a show, glancing back at my car before continuing to innocently make his way down the street as though he was just out for a midnight stroll instead of trying to rape my fucking girl on the side of the street. Then as I barrel toward him, pushing my Escalade to its fucking limits, I see the bush behind the white picket fence—the very bush my innocent Little Birdy is taking shelter in—and I realize just how fucking close he was to finding her.

Rage overpowers me, pulsing through my veins and infecting me with a vicious venom, and just as I pass him, I skid to a stop, my front tire hitting the curb and blocking his path, then before he even gets a chance to run, I throw myself out of the car, my fist already flying.

I crash into him, instantly cracking my knuckles across his jaw and hearing the sickening sound of bone crunching. My momentum sends us both flying to the ground, and I come down over him, my fist swinging again.

Blood spurts across the pavement, but I don't stop until the fucker is out cold, and even then, I barely manage to pull myself away. "Izaac?" I hear on a shaky breath, the terror-filled sound the only thing that's able to pull me to my feet.

My gaze shoots out toward the thick bush behind me when I find her standing there, her body scratched up from the thick branches within the bush, and I fucking run.

Step after step, I pound against the pavement until I'm standing right before her. She reaches for me, throwing her arms around my neck as she whimpers, and I lock my arms around her back, dragging her right over the picket fence and into the safety of my arms.

She crumbles, heavy sobs tearing from the back of her throat as I hold on to her. "You're okay, baby. I've got you," I murmur into her ear, my hand making soothing circles on her back, but truth be told, I think I'm just as scared as she is. The fear of not getting to her in time. The fear of losing her, of letting something happen to her and not being there to save her. Of failing her.

I hold on to her like I would never let go until her tears finally begin to dry. She peers around me, taking in the lifeless body on the ground. "Is he . . . dead?"

I shake my head. "As much as I wish he were, he's just out cold."

She visibly swallows, refusing to let go of me, and honestly, I don't think I could fathom the thought of releasing her right now.

"The ball's in your court, Aspen. What do you want to do? Call the police and have him arrested, or get out of here?"

She shakes her head. "I want you to take me home, but I wouldn't be able to live with myself if he got away and hurt someone else."

"Okay," I say. "I'll take care of it."

Taking her back to my car, she scrambles for the passenger seat before brushing her hand over the lock and buckling in as I grab my phone that's still connected to Aspen's and turn back to the asshole on the street. Ending the call with Aspen, I call the police, and as I wait for them to arrive, I put the asshole up against the lamppost, and using his hoodie, I tie him up, making sure he can't escape if he were to become conscious.

I launch myself over the white picket fence and scrounge through the thick bush for Aspen's shoes and handbag, and then as we wait, I make my way around to the passenger's side of my Escalade. The second she opens the door for me, she falls right back into my arms.

I hold her tight as I give Austin a quick call, letting him know that Aspen is safe and unharmed. He asks to talk to her for a minute, and by the time she's convinced him not to get on a flight to come back home, the cops are screeching down the road.

We both give a quick statement with a promise to keep our phones on if they need to get in contact with us. As they cart the asshole into the back of an ambulance, I help Aspen back into the passenger side of my car and hit the gas.

Only as I take a right toward her apartment complex, she shakes her head. "I really don't want to be alone tonight," she tells me. "Would it be too much to ask if I crashed at your place?"

"Anything you want, Birdy," I say, taking her hand and holding it as though it were my only lifeline.

28

ASPEN

As Izaac sails down the road toward his place, he clutches my hand so tight I start to lose feeling in my fingers, but I don't dare let go of him. How could I?

He saved my life tonight.

If he wasn't there, keeping me calm, I would have crumbled. I don't think he'll ever know just what he did for me, but I will always be grateful for it.

Anything could have happened. Rape. Violence. Death.

I didn't look into that asshole's eyes, but I could feel how much danger I was in. When I started to run, I could barely breathe. I've never been that scared in my life.

I heard his every step from where I hid in the bushes, slinking toward me, trying to coax me out. My palms were clammy, my knees were shaking so much I could have sworn I was making the leaves rustle around me. I would have been found for sure.

In my fear, it didn't even register to me that Austin was out of town. Deep down, I knew. Becs and I had talked about it before we left the bar, but in that moment of fear, I couldn't think straight.

But Izaac.

This incredible man saved my life.

He didn't hesitate to come for me, talking me through my fear by having to face some of his own. I don't even know if what he was saying was the truth, but it's what I needed at that moment.

He kept me calm. He forced me to let go of the fear and put everything in perspective. He gave me a fighting chance if I were to be found, and he talked me through exactly what I needed to do if the worst were to happen.

Like I said, he saved my life tonight, and I will always love him for that.

We're halfway back to his place when his thumb brushes across the top of my hand, and I glance up to find his dark gaze locked on mine. "You okay?"

I shrug my shoulders, still feeling shaky. "I, ummm . . . maybe. I guess. I'm not really sure."

"I know you don't want to hear this, but what the fuck were you doing, Aspen?" he questions, keeping his tone neutral so I know he's not trying to pick a fight, simply wondering exactly the same thing that's been circling my head since the moment I flew into those bushes. "You know the risks of walking home alone. Austin and I have practically drilled it into you for years. If you were stuck, you could have called me. You know you can always fucking call me, no matter what's going on between us. I would have come."

"I know," I say, glancing away, unable to bear the look in his eyes. "I fucked up. I know that. But I was drinking, and I wasn't thinking straight. The Uber wasn't going to come for a while, and I figured I could get home quicker if I walked. I know it was stupid. I just . . . I wasn't thinking."

He presses his lips into a hard line and focuses his attention on the road, still refusing to release my hand. "What about your date?" he asks. "He couldn't drive you home?"

Guilt soars through my chest, and I drop my gaze to my lap. "There was no date," I admit. "I was meeting up with Becs. I just . . . I said it because I was being a petty bitch, and I wanted to hurt you because . . . Well—"

"Because I hurt you," he finishes for me.

I let out a heavy breath and nod, so fucking ashamed of myself. What kind of person purposely hurts the man they love? An hour ago, I thought I was so clever for fooling him into thinking I was going out on a date with Harrison, but now, it just feels spiteful.

"Did you mean what you said before?" I ask, risking a timid glance over, not wanting to linger on my pettiness. "On the phone?"

His lips press into a hard line as a strange tension fills the air. I'm sure he's sick of me pushing him on this, but after everything that was just said, how could he expect me not to?

Izaac clears his throat and releases my hand before his gaze flicks toward his dashboard. "Are you going to be okay if I stop for gas?"

Disappointment fires through my chest, and it becomes clear that everything he just said was for the purpose of keeping me calm. He didn't mean a damn word. "Oh, umm . . . yeah," I say as a single tear rolls down my cheek.

I keep my gaze locked out the window, refusing to allow him to see me cry, and just as the tear falls from my cheek and hits my collarbone, Izaac pulls off the side of the road and into the gas station.

There's one other car parked at the pump, but seeing that it's a woman who's clearly just trying to go about her business, I let out a breath. I don't think I can handle any more trouble for one night.

Izaac brings his car to a stop on the other side of the pump next to the woman before discreetly putting my window down just an inch, and despite the emotional whiplash he's been giving me, I appreciate the thought.

He gets out and I track him like a hawk as he makes his way around to my side of the car, and even though he's no longer sitting right beside me, I still feel safer than I've ever been. He pays for his gas before taking the pump and inserting it into the tank, and as I watch him through the side mirror, he leans back on the back door and props his foot against the side step.

He reaches out, his fingers casually looped over my open window, and as he waits for the tank to fill, I can't help but notice the woman on the other side. Her gaze flicks between the pump she's using and Izaac, eating him up in a way I wished I could always do so publicly.

"Wow. I like your car," she tells him in a blatant attempt to open a flirty conversation.

My gaze narrows, and I immediately look at the woman like some kind of predatory competition. How dare she flirt with him. He's mine . . . at least . . . kinda. Okay, maybe not at all, but I like to think I have some kind of stake over him, and after the night I've had, I doubt he'd argue with me. Though, this is Izaac Banks we're talking about, and arguing is his favorite thing to do.

I shift my stare back to the side mirror, watching how he responds, and a wicked grin stretches across my face as he simply smiles and nods. "Thanks."

After knowing him for so long, it's clear he was just being polite in the hope she'll get the idea and be on her way, but judging by the way her eyes light up, she thinks she just found her future baby daddy. But like hell I'm about to let that happen, especially right in front of my eyes.

She puts her pump away before stepping around to our side, leaning up against the pump as though she has all night to sit and talk. But if you ask me, she's just asking for trouble, and not the good kind.

"My ahh . . . brother was looking to buy one," she says. "How do you like it?"

Ahh, clever woman. Asking him questions that drag him away from yes and no answers and force a sentence out of his mouth. I see this isn't her first rodeo.

"Yeah, it's good. Fucking great actually," he says, his face lighting up. "If he's gonna buy it, make sure he gets all the inclusions. He won't regret it."

Great. Assface over here fell for the oldest trick in the book. I wonder if he realizes she just made the brother up. Probably not. He likes to see the best in people and wouldn't dream that a woman would lie just to get in his pants.

"Oh, I'm sure the top-of-the-line model with all the inclusions is his current wet dream," she laughs, before stepping closer and offering him her hand. "I'm Star, by the way."

Star? What kind of pornstar name is that?

Izaac smiles politely, and it guts me. He hasn't smiled like that at me in ages. All I get now are awkward cringes and bedroom eyes. Though don't get me wrong, I have no aversion to those bedroom eyes. They're downright the sexiest thing I've ever seen. But sometimes, it'd be nice just to see him . . . smile.

He takes her hand. "Izaac."

"Nice to meet you, Izaac," she says, batting her stupid false lashes. "You're out quite late for a Monday night. Usually, the streets are dead when I'm making my way home."

"What can I say? I'm a night owl."

Gag.

Is he . . . flirting with her?

"Oh yeah? Me too. Though I wish I wasn't. These night shifts are killing me," she says.

"Yeah, I get that," he says as the tank finally fills. "I own a few nightclubs in the city, so nights have become my days."

Is he seriously interacting with her? Where are the curt nods and cutting her short? Where's all the bullshit he so comfortably gives me?

She creeps forward again, her eyes widening as she sucks in an exaggerated gasp. "Holy shit! A nightclub owner? That's insane," she laughs. "I'm not going to lie, I'm impressed. That's got to be literally the coolest job on the planet."

He grins, eating this shit up. "It's definitely got its perks."

Okay. Surely he's just fucking with me. Is this payback for letting him think I was going out on a date tonight? Because judging by how he reacted when I told him I was meeting up with a Tinder date and then how jealous he got over the idea of me going out tonight, I can only imagine how he spent the last few hours.

"Would I be too forward in asking if I could check them out sometime?"

My hand snaps up to his, clutching his fingers with raw desperation as they grip the top of the open window. His gaze flicks back, colliding with mine through the dark window tint for the slightest moment, but that mere second is more than enough to know that despite this woman's blatant attempts to flirt with him, he's here with me, and nothing is going to change that.

Stepping closer toward the passenger door, his hand slips further inside the window and he adjusts his hold on my hand so that his fingers lace through mine, and my heart starts to race.

It's everything.

I've held his hand plenty of times in the dark room, and for the whole car ride here, but this is different. In the dark room, it's about a physical connection, about sex, and before pulling into the gas station, it was about comfort, about making sure I knew I was safe. But this is the first time he's intentionally held my hand just because he wanted to, because the thought of pulling away is harder than giving in to what he really wants. He's not out there stressing over what Austin might think or how this is so fucking wrong, he's doing it because deep down, even though he might not realize it, I think he might love me too.

Izaac squeezes my hand, his thumb brushing across my knuckles, and as he focuses his attention on Star, he gives her yet another polite smile. "Of course. There's always room for more customers at my clubs. Look up Scandal. It's my newest one. Bring your friends and have a great night out," he tells her. "But if you wouldn't mind, my girl has had a bit of a wild night, and I need to get her home."

"Your girl?" she gapes with horror as her gaze shifts to his arm and follows it down to his hand that's shoved through the small gap above the window. It takes a moment, but her stare finally meets mine through the dark window tint, and seeing how unimpressed I look, she quickly inches back from Izaac. "Oh, shit. I'm so sorry. I didn't realize."

"It's fine," he says. "Happens to the best of us."

Star offers him a tight smile before scurrying away like a mouse that's just been caught red-handed, and honestly, I wasn't sure the human species was capable of moving that fast.

Once she's flown out of the gas station, Izaac releases my hand and puts the gas pump away before finally making his way back around the car and into the driver's seat. He turns on the engine and slowly drives out to the main road, the two of us now sitting in uncomfortable silence, his hand kept way over on his side.

I let out a heavy sigh. This constant tension between us is becoming a pain in my ass.

The silence is unbearable, but luckily for me, I'm not the one to break. "What the hell was that back there?" he asks, a few streets away from his place.

I fix my stare out the window. "What was what? I don't know what you're talking about."

"Bullshit. You grabbed my hand because you were jealous."

I scoff, my head whipping toward him as my eyes widen like saucers. "Me? Jealous? Yeah fucking right," I laugh. "I hate to break it to you and bruise that precious ego of yours, but I've had to watch you fawn over random women for years. If I were the type to get jealous, I would have gone insane years ago."

He smirks, reaching for my hand, and naturally, I lift it right into his, letting him lace his fingers through mine again. "Whatever. You were jealous."

Fucking asshole.

I roll my eyes and let out a frustrated sigh. "Like you're one to talk. If the shoe was on the other foot and I was the one out there flirting with Star, you wouldn't have been able to handle it."

"You and Star?" he questions. "Don't get me wrong, I don't like to share, but that would have been hot."

"Ugh," I groan. "Need I remind you of how you acted when I had that Tinder date? You called Austin and sabotaged it. Not to mention, I saw the jealousy in your eyes when you thought I was leaving for a hot date tonight."

Izaac scoffs. "That wasn't jealousy. I was just trying to control my raging erection after you tried to seduce me."

"Tried?" I question. "There was no *trying* about it. I succeeded."

Izaac falls silent, and when he discreetly pulls his hand out of mine, acting as though he needs it to drive, I watch as he rebuilds the walls around him. Apparently, my hero for the night has disappeared, leaving me with the usual broody asshole who does anything in his power to pick a fight.

Disappointment spreads through my chest like a disease, and it becomes all too clear that this is a pattern for him. He starts thinking something could happen, starts believing that everything is going to be okay, but then he gets inside that idiotic head of his and shuts down like an old computer malfunctioning with a virus.

He's *my* virus.

Realizing it's pointless trying to fight this and knowing we will only end up going in circles, I let my hand settle back into my lap and sit in the tension-filled silence until we finally pull into his long driveway.

My lips press into a hard line. I haven't been here in ages, and now that he's closed himself off to me, I'm starting to regret the decision to come here. Over the past few years, I've purposefully gone out of my way to avoid his home, because every time I'm here, I picture how it could be or what my life might look like if we were ever to be together. The kitchen I'd cook for him in. The shower we'd share as we told our war stories from the day. The bedroom we'd make love in. The nursery where we'd raise a child.

Shit.

This is exactly why I shouldn't be here. I get carried away, and now I've backed myself into a corner. Is it too late to tell him to turn around and take me home? It's after two in the morning. He wouldn't mind. He'd do it without question, but I've already stolen too much of his night. Not to mention, if he were to drive me back to my apartment, it'd be almost three before he finally got home and got to sleep. Don't get me wrong, I'm pissed with him right now, but I'm not a completely careless bitch.

I can handle one night. I think.

All I need to do is find the spare room, lock the door behind me, and go to bed. Hell, I can even pretend I'm on a tropical island instead of in the home I've spent the past few years dreaming of sharing with him.

What could possibly go wrong?

29

IZAAC

Aspen storms inside my home, and I watch after her, my brows furrowed. She's had one hell of a night. The last thing she needs is to have it out with me again. Yet as she finds the spare room and shoves the door open, I find myself following her in. "What the fuck is wrong with you now?" I demand, instantly regretting both my choice of words and my tone.

She whips around, her eyes wide. "Are you fucking kidding me? Holy shit, Izaac. You must be fucking blind to your own bullshit," she says. "Where do I even start? You come to my rescue. You panic when I'm in trouble. You get jealous when I consider being with other men. Any of that ring a bell for you?"

She gives me an expectant stare, and when I don't respond, she continues.

"Have it your way," she snaps. "When you're inside of me, you insist on holding my stare. When I need comfort, you hold my hand like you'd never let it go. When you think you're about to lose me, you sit at my fucking door for hours until I give you the time of day to try and make it right. And yet you have the audacity to insist that I don't mean anything to you."

"Birdy—"

"No. No more Birdy. No more anything," she tells me. "When I was in those bushes, I was terrified, and the only thing that gave me focus was the words you whispered to me, and then you had the fucking balls to shut down when I asked you if you meant it."

She shakes her head, and I don't respond, sensing that she's not even close to being done. "I'm sick of this shit, Izaac. I'm sick of watching you start to open up only to put your walls back in place and act like I don't mean a damn thing. It's fucking bullshit," she says, stopping to meet my stare, her green eyes filling with tears that shred me to pieces. "It hurts, and I'm over it. So if you fucking want me, just say it and I'm yours. I love you, Izaac. I fucking love you, but you're killing me."

"Aspen, I—"

"No," she demands, shoving her hand against my chest, fury brimming in her wet eyes. "Stop. I don't want to hear any more of your fucking excuses. Just tell me you love me. We both know it. I can feel it every time you touch me, every fucking time you look at me, so just admit it. Put me out of my misery and tell me I'm yours."

My chest constricts. I thought we'd been through this. I thought she knew where I stood. "Don't do this, Aspen," I grit through a clenched jaw, able to see how the rest of the night will go if she keeps pushing, and trust me, it would be even uglier than our last argument.

Anger flashes in those beautiful green eyes and she lifts her chin, fixing me with a defiant stare that could terrify the dead. "You. Love. Me."

My heart pounds a million miles an hour, maybe even faster than when I was flying toward her in my car and listening to her terror-filled whimpers through my speakers.

Why is she doing this? Why is she trying to make this harder? Does she get off on the pain? Does she like it when I'm left with no fucking choice but to hurt her? I can't fucking do this.

Holding her stare, I tear my own fucking heart right out of my chest as I blatantly lie. "I don't."

"You're a terrible liar."

I step away from her, needing space between us. "Why the fuck do you keep pushing this, Aspen? I've already told you I can never love you. I can't allow myself to want you like that. I don't want to hurt you."

She shakes her head. "For someone who claims he doesn't want to hurt me, it seems to be the only thing you're capable of."

"That's a low fucking blow, and you know it," I tell her. "You're forcing me to do this. You're practically standing before me and demanding I draw some kind of line between us. Do you really think that's what I want?"

"No, I know exactly what you want, but you're too goddamn scared to do anything about it."

I scoff. "This is getting us nowhere. Just go to bed, Aspen. You've had a big night."

I go to turn on my heel, more than ready to pretend this shit never happened, when she steps around me and shoves the door closed. "You're not going anywhere," she says. "I get that you're not willing to fight for this, but I am, and I'm not going to stop until you finally admit what we've both known since the moment you touched me."

Anger fires through me, pulsing through my veins like a fucking tsunami, and I clench my hands into fists, unable to control the recklessness pounding within me. "You're a fucking child, Aspen."

She laughs, looking at me with such disdain it fucking breaks me. "Oh, real nice. I'm the fucking child? I'm the one fighting for something real while you're the one backing away, too fucking scared of his own damn shadow to even understand what he's feeling," she seethes, pushing into me, her hand hard against my chest.

"Don't fucking push me on this," I spit, feeling my patience slipping out of my grasp.

"Do I feel like a child when you fuck me, Izaac?" she pushes, stepping into me and forcing me to back up. "Do I feel like a child when you bend me over a fucking table and slide that big cock deep inside of me? When my body gets you so fucking worked up and you grip my hips and come hard inside of me, are you thinking I'm a child then?"

I clench my jaw, slipping faster than ever before. "That's not what

I meant, and you know it."

"Then be fucking real with me and stop throwing excuses around to try and deter me. I'm not walking away from this."

The last of my control slips, and I grab her, throwing her up against the fucking door and forcing a loud gasp from deep in her chest. "You want the fucking truth?" I roar, my fingers gripping her so damn tight. "I want you more than anything I've ever wanted in my goddamn life, and it fucking kills me that I can't be what you need. The mere thought of anyone else putting their hands on you drives me insane. And when I told you I'd never love you, it's not because I don't want to, because believe me, I fucking want to. I want it so fucking bad it aches. I can't love you because I'm not capable of it. I don't know how."

My breath comes in sharp, ragged pants as I come back to earth, realizing what the fuck I just said, exposing my deepest insecurity and revealing my vulnerabilities, but I watch as the fight visibly leaves her.

Aspen lifts her hand to my cheek, her green eyes softening as my grip loosens on her body. "You big asshole," she breathes. "Of course you're capable of it. You've been doing it since the day I met you. You show love in the way you've always protected me, ever since I was a little girl, in how you look for me in every room, in how you always want the best for me."

I shake my head. "That's different. That's just . . . growing up together."

"Perhaps. But this here, you coming to get me tonight and going to extremes just to make sure I am okay. You put your own hang-ups on hold just to help me through that, and when you finally grabbed me and pulled me into your arms like you'd never let me go, that is love," she explains. "This crazy need to have each other like at Cherry, the need to always be in the same room, the need to fight for something because nothing else has ever felt so real. I don't know why or how you ever allowed yourself to believe that you weren't capable of it, but you are. You are, and you do know how. You do it every fucking day."

"Aspen."

She shakes her head, her fingers brushing across my jaw and dropping to my shirt before bunching into the material. "You love me."

"I—"

She smiles wide, and it's the most beautiful thing I've ever seen, fucking crippling me with the way her eyes shine within the darkened room. "You, Izaac Banks, are in love with me."

My chest heaves with terror-filled breath, the truth lingering right there between us, and whether I have the balls to admit that she's right or not, it makes no difference.

Aspen breathes just as heavily as I do, and when she falls back against the door and lifts her chin, I see determination in her eyes. She pulls against her hold on my shirt, forcing me in. "Kiss me."

My eyes widen as something grips hold of my heart, squeezing too fucking tight I could burst. "What?"

"You heard me," she relentlessly insists, pulling against my shirt as my hands turn into fists. Does she know what she's asking of me? It's practically the first rule in the Aspen and Izaac guidelines. No kissing. I don't fucking kiss anyone, but those lips . . . they're so fucking full. I'd give anything to taste them. It's the only part of her I've never claimed. "Kiss me."

My hands shake, and when I don't make a move, I see the frustration begin creeping into her eyes again. If I do this, there's no going back. I'll never be able to separate myself from her again or survive without her. But I stand by what I've always said. I'll never be enough for her. She's too fucking good, and I'm a broken piece of shit who'll never be able to completely open up and give her what she needs.

It shouldn't be this hard. She shouldn't be forced to fight with the man she loves just to get any type of affection. It should be easy.

I shake my head, the deepest regret booming through my chest as everything I've ever wanted stands right before me, begging for me to take it. "I can't."

I go to pull away but she tightens her grip on my shirt, pulling me back to her, and the way she looks at me, the way she holds me captive can't be ignored. "Break the fucking rules and kiss me, Izaac."

Every last shred of control shatters into a million broken pieces, and I launch myself toward her. My hand grips the back of her neck, and as my other snakes around her back and pulls her in, I crush my lips to hers, kissing her deeply. Aspen gasps into my mouth as though not having expected me to break, but she quickly relaxes into my arms, her body molding against mine as though it were always supposed to be right there.

Her full lips move against mine, and I fucking die.

How could I have not been kissing her since the moment this started? Every nerve in my body is on edge, desperately craving more, and I greedily take everything she's giving, my tongue working into her mouth and warring with hers.

She tastes like fucking heaven, like a fallen angel gifted right into my arms, and I was right. How could I ever let her go now?

I'm in love with this woman, and I've been so fucking blind.

Aspen has been right here this whole time, daring me to love her back, begging me to give in to what she already knew was right there. She could have walked away at any time, could have given up on me a million times over, but she stayed and fought for what she believed in.

A fierce desperation booms through me, and I scoop her up into my arms, her legs locking around my waist as I yank the door open and stride down to my bedroom. She groans into my mouth, and before I'm even a few steps down the hall, I reach for the small zipper at the back of her dress—the same fucking dress she tortured me with earlier this evening.

Aspen scrambles for the back of my shirt, pulling it up between our bodies and forcing me to break our kiss, and the second the shirt is gone, I waste no time unzipping her dress and letting it fall down to her waist.

I push through to my bedroom, my cock already painfully hard and desperate to be inside of her. Then striding to the foot of my bed, I take hold of her and throw her down.

She crashes against the mattress, barely catching herself on her elbows as she stares back at me, her gaze filled with the deepest lust that it's almost impossible to keep away. "Holy fuck," she breathes, her eyes sailing over my face and down to my bare chest.

I reach for the front of my pants, unbuckling my belt as the raw need for her almost brings me to my fucking knees. "Dress, Aspen. Off. Now."

She doesn't waste a single moment, gripping the black fabric at her waist and wriggling out of it, taking that sheer black thong right along with it. She tosses them aside, and as her elbow settles back into place, her brows furrow, and she looks around.

"Wait," she rushes out as if only just realizing she's on my bed. "Your bed. I thought . . . We can't—"

My pants fall to the ground, and I step out of them as I fist my straining cock and kneel against the end of my bed. "We're breaking all the fucking rules now."

By the time she lets out a shaky breath, my hand is locked around her ankle, dragging her down the bed toward me until her beautiful thighs are spread on either side of mine. I come down over her, the movement forcing her thighs further apart. She hooks her leg over my hip, opening herself up to me as the scent of her arousal lingers in the air. A wicked grin stretches across my lips as I lean back into her and kiss her again, knowing without even touching her just how fucking ready she is for me.

My cock rests heavily against her stomach, and she closes her hand around me, the soft touch making me shudder. "Baby," I breathe against her lips, my hand roaming down the length of her body and to her thigh.

"Oh, God," she sighs. "I could get used to you calling me that."

My lips move down to the side of her neck, and her body arches off the mattress, her full tits pressed against my chest. "I'll never get used to this."

She tightens her grip on my cock. "Don't make me wait," she pants as her thumb swipes across my tip and over the piercing. "I need you inside me."

With both of us right on the edge, I can't wait a second longer as I reach down between us and take hold of my cock. I adjust myself over her, lining up with her entrance, and as I press against her, pushing inside, she gasps, her whole body trembling around me. "More," she breathes.

I push slowly, taking her inch by inch as my hand grips hers, our fingers lacing together. She squeezes it tight, and I claim another inch. "Izaac," she groans, but whatever else she has to say is swallowed when my lips come back to hers.

Not stopping until I bottom out inside of her, I groan into her mouth, the sound vibrating through my chest. I hook my arm beneath her knee, pulling it high, and when she gasps, I finally start to move.

I take it slow, never having felt anything quite so emotionally raw as our bodies become so entwined it's impossible to tell where mine ends and hers begins. Her arm slips beneath mine, and she curls it back around to clutch my shoulder, holding it so damn tight it's as though she fears I'll wake up from this fever dream and walk away, but I can't possibly walk away now.

This woman right here, the only woman I've ever taken to my bed, is mine, and I don't plan on giving her up.

I take deep, precise thrusts, each movement made with the intent to further her pleasure, and fuck, I've never wanted someone to come more. I want her to feel everything I can give to her. I want her to scream my name and know that it was me who made her come alive. I want to ruin her for any other man so when she finally realizes that I'm not enough, she'll still come right back into my arms.

I want it all.

Our bodies grow sweaty, our kisses messy and desperate, but I've never felt anything so fucking good. This isn't the same as when I've been with her in the dark room or at Cherry, and it sure as fuck has never been like this with anyone else. This is personal, this is an emotional connection and not just about getting off. It's the same as when I held her hand at the gas station—it means so much more, and now that I know just how fucking incredible it can get, how could I ever want anything less?

"Fuck, Little Birdy," I groan against her skin as I thrust into her sweet cunt. "You're ruining me."

She smiles as her body begins to tremble, her eyes hooded as they lock onto mine. "That's all I ever wanted."

Fucking hell.

Her walls stretch with each thrust, and as my balls tighten, she clenches around me. "Oh, God, Izaac," she pants, her nails digging into my shoulder. "I'm gonna come."

"Let me feel you," I murmur into her ear, my lips nipping at her earlobe before dropping to the sensitive skin below her ear. "Come for me, baby. Squeeze that perfect little cunt around me."

Aspen sucks in a gasp, and as I drive into her again and again, her walls contract around me, and she throws her head back against the mattress. "Oh, fuck," she groans as she turns into a quivering mess, her hips jolting with pleasure, but I don't dare stop as she rides out her high on my cock.

As her walls convulse around me, and those beautiful hips jolt and take me on a wild fucking ride, I can't hold off a second longer. She claws my back, her high intensifying, and I come with her, shooting hot spurts of cum deep inside of her.

My grip tightens on her body, and she crushes her lips back to mine, her fingers weaving into the back of my hair until we're both a fucking mess on the mattress.

As we come down from our high, her body relaxes around me, and I scoop my arm around her back, scooting up the bed and rolling until she's hovering over me. She instantly lays her head against my chest, and her hand rests right over my beating heart. "That was—"

"Intense," I finish for her.

I feel her smile against my chest as my hand lingers on the sweet curve of her bare ass. I can't help but gently squeeze it as she groans and lifts her head off my chest before climbing up my body and straddling my waist. She gazes down at me as I claim her thighs, and I can't help but notice the small flash of regret in her eyes. "I suppose I should probably go to the spare room."

I simply stare at her. "Baby, you're not going anywhere. You're sleeping here with me," I tell her. "But I hope you don't think you're finished for the night because I can feel my cum leaking out of you, and now that you're straddled over me, I can't wait to watch you ride me."

A grin pulls at her lips. "Oh yeah?"

I nod. "Take the fucking reins, Birdy. Show me what a good little whore you are and ride me."

Her gaze darkens, and as she adjusts herself over me, I find I can't take my eyes off her. "Have it your way. But just so you know, if I'm the one running the show, then you'll come when I say you come, and not a second before. Got it?"

Well fuck.

I take her hips and grind against her sweet pussy. "Give me your worst."

30

ASPEN

As I walk through the front door of my parents' home, my arms threaten to fall off from the heavy bags of groceries hanging from them. I don't know why I suggested that I could cook for everyone. I can't even cook. But when Austin called to say he had exciting news about the restaurant, the words just seemed to stumble right out of my mouth.

Either way, I'm in charge of our meal today, and I'm taking my job very seriously. Even if they don't like it, they better put fucking smiles on their faces and tell me how damn good it is.

Not having enough hands to close the door behind me, I have no choice but to give it a shove with my ass, and the second the thud of the door echoes through the house, I almost crumble. "Hellllllpppppp,"

I groan, barely able to put one foot in front of the other.

A laugh cuts through the foyer, and my gaze snaps up to find Izaac leaning against the railing of the stairs. "You couldn't have gone for a second trip?"

My gaze shoots left and right in a panic, my heart racing. "What the hell are you doing here?" I say under my breath as he pushes off the railing and strides toward me. He gingerly takes the bags out of my hands, leaving me with nothing but the bottle of wine, and I hold on to it tightly, realizing just how much I might need it.

"You think Austin was going to have some big announcement and not invite me?"

Shit. He has a good point.

He leans in and presses a kiss to my cheek, just as he would have always done in this situation, only this time, he lets his lips linger, and my heart begins to race. It's only been a few days since that unfortunate walk home from Joe's Bar, the gas station, the kiss of all kisses, and of course, his bed.

If I had it my way, I never would have left the safety of that bed. The warmth. The happiness. The six incredible orgasms I had between that life-changing kiss and the moment I was forced to roll out of bed and get my ass back to my apartment for my midday lecture. We only came up for air long enough for Izaac to oversee me officially cancelling my dat with Harrison, and then we were right back in each other's arms.

Hearing footsteps in the hallway, Izaac pulls away from me and makes his way deeper into my family home, hopefully toward the kitchen with all of my groceries, and as I watch him go, I start to really panic. How the hell am I supposed to hide this from my family? It's one thing sneaking around with Izaac when we both have our own homes, but to be in the same room, surrounded by my family? Shit. I don't know if I'm capable of keeping the love-struck joy off my face.

"Ugh," Austin says, striding past Izaac as he makes his way toward me. "Who invited you?"

"You did, asshole," I say as he rolls his eyes and awkwardly pulls me into the first, and hopefully last, weird side hug. Only he makes it worse when he drops a kiss to my cheek.

"You know I love you, right?"

I shove him away from me, gaping at him. He must be sick. Maybe he caught something while he was out of town. "What the hell has gotten into you?" I say, wiping his kiss off my face as though it could somehow poison me.

"Can't a brother just show a little affection toward his baby sister?"

"No," I scoff. "You're being weird. You'd sooner fart on me than show me affection. What's going on?" I suck in a gasp, my eyes widening in horror. "Oh shit. Are you dying? Can you leave me the restaurant in your will?"

Austin rolls his eyes and lets out a heavy sigh, and when I smirk and go to find the rest of my family, he pauses in the foyer and pulls me back, wrapping me into a proper hug, the bottle of wine squished between us. "I'm really glad you're okay," he murmurs. "I feel like shit that I wasn't there for you on Monday night. I don't know what I would have done if Izaac hadn't found you in time. I'm so sorry, Aspen. It's always been my job to protect you, and I let you down."

I pull back out of his arms and offer him a real smile, not one of the usual sneers we're so comfortable throwing at one another. "You didn't let me down, Austin. It was a shitty situation, and you handled it perfectly. You weren't close enough to get to me on time, so you made sure someone else was, someone who would protect me just as fiercely as you would. And he did. He stayed on the phone with me the whole time and kept me calm. He even had me make a weapon out of a pen and then beat the shit out of that asshole. You did everything right, and I'm so thankful that you were there to answer the call when I needed you."

"Ugh," he says, his face twisting with disgust. "Don't go and get all sentimental on me. I don't like it."

"You started it."

"Yeah," he scoffs. "Remind me to never do that again."

I roll my eyes, and we finally walk out of the foyer and leave the sappy shit behind. As we make our way past the living room and into the kitchen, I find Mom already going through my bags with Dad at her side, trying to put it all back in. "Hey. Hands off. It's my show today," I say to Mom, stepping into her other side only to get an equally as big hug from her, maybe even bigger than Austin's had been.

"Oh, my sweet girl," she says, refusing to let go. "I'm so sorry you went through all of that. You must have been so scared."

A wave of emotion crashes through me, and I hold on to her tighter, momentarily unable to get the words past the lump forming in my throat. Even though it's been a few days and I've spoken to her at length on the phone, there's still just something about being wrapped in my mother's arms that offers me the type of security I could never get from anywhere else, not even with Izaac.

Her hand roams up and down my back, and as I finally start to find a little composure, I lift my gaze. Finding Izaac's stare on me, the memories of that night bring up a lot of emotion in both of us. He holds my stare for just a moment before reluctantly looking away, because had he not, I surely would have given it away.

Dad leans in and wraps his arms around Mom and me before pressing a kiss to my temple. "Are you really okay, sweetheart?" he asks. "And don't even think about lying to your old man."

"Really," I say, wriggling free of their death grip. "I'm okay. I was a little shaken, and it definitely wasn't a great situation to be in, but I'm fine. The ambulance took him away with a police escort and both Izaac and I made our statements. So if it's okay with you, I would very much appreciate it if you could all get your asses out of my kitchen so I can cook us all an incredible lunch."

Mom rolls her eyes as Dad mutters under his breath, and I let out a sigh of relief as they finally make their way out toward the living room. Only Izaac remains right where he is. "Ahhhh. Isn't anybody else the least bit concerned?" he asks, making Mom, Dad, and Austin all stop and look back. "Aspen can't cook for shit, and I don't know about you guys, but I have a busy week coming up. I can't risk the food poisoning."

My jaw practically falls to the floor. He did not just say that.

"I'll have you know—" I start to argue when Austin cuts in. "Yeah, not gonna lie. I'm worried about that too. I'm interviewing potential staff this week, and it's not gonna be a great look if I keep running back and forth from the toilet."

The boys snicker as though it's the funniest thing in the world, and I stride over to Izaac and grab his arm before shoving him right out of the kitchen and into my moronic brother. "Get your asses out of here. The only reason either of you would spend the next week shitting yourselves is because you finally realized how far up each other's asses you are and it turns into a bloody competition of who can claw their way out faster."

Austin simply stares at me. "How dare you speak of my ass like that."

"For what it's worth. My money's on asshole number 2," I say, indicating toward Izaac. "Don't get me wrong, he definitely seems like an ass man, but when it comes to yours, even the women are running in the opposite direction."

"There goes my appetite," Dad mutters before walking away with Mom.

Izaac smirks, meeting my stare. "Thank you. I appreciate your vote of confidence," he says. "And because you brought it up, I am indeed an ass man."

Austin gapes at his best friend before whacking him up the side of the head. "Don't say shit like that to my little sister. What the fuck, man?"

I can barely contain my laughter. If only he knew what else he liked to say to me. Hell, if only he knew the kinds of things he's *done* to me, all the different positions he's bent me into, and the way he's shoved that big, delicious co—

Izaac's laughter cuts off my train of thought, and I quickly turn back toward my bags before the blush gets a chance to sneak into my cheeks. "Alright, both of you get out. I've got magic to make."

Austin scoffs. "I've got pizza waiting for when you fuck it up."

"And I've got a girthy twelve-inch pink dildo that I'll ram right up your ass," I throw back at him. "After all, it must be lonely for Izaac up there. I'm sure he could use the company."

Izaac visibly swallows, his face twisting. "I suddenly feel very uncomfortable."

"Me too," Austin mutters. "Should I be clenching my asshole like this?"

I grin wide, and with that, the boys stride out of the kitchen, muttering to each other, and I can only assume that muttering has a lot to do with shit-talking me, but it's fine. It wouldn't be a family lunch without the three of us getting under each other's skin.

Finally free to get to work, I start unloading all the bags before making my world-class famous spaghetti and meatballs, because let's face it, it's the only thing I'm a little competent in making. Actually, come to think of it, I really don't know how I've survived all of college living alone.

Austin, Izaac, and Dad make their way out back and stand on the deck, looking out over the view with beers in their hands. They're just in front of the kitchen window, and I can't help but notice the way Izaac discreetly watches me. Every step I take, his dark gaze tracks, only looking away when Austin holds his attention.

My heart races, and I absolutely love it. This right here could be our forever, and I've never wanted anything more.

The food is almost done, and I'm pretty confident that I'm not going to poison everybody, but hell, if I did, I'd definitely choose Austin to be the lucky winner to reap the rewards of that particular gift. I start digging out all the plates and cutlery before dashing over to the walk-in pantry to find Mom's fancy saltshaker. If Austin wants to hit us with some kind of announcement, then surely we can use the fancy saltshakers.

Stepping into the pantry, my gaze shifts over the shelves while cursing Mom for always reorganizing her kitchen. I swear, ever since Austin and I moved out, she has occupied her time by doing ridiculous things like flipping her house around. She must get a sick satisfaction out of the way Dad can never find anything and always asks her for help. I guess it's kind of sweet.

Finding the saltshaker on one of the top shelves, I push up onto my tippy toes and reach for it just as the walk-in pantry plunges into darkness. I gasp as a big body presses into me and a set of warm hands falls to my waist. I'm whipped around, and before a smile can even stretch across my lips, Izaac's lips are on mine.

He kisses me deeply, and I melt into him, every nerve in my body on edge until I remember where the hell we are and shove him off me. "What the hell do you think you're doing?" I whisper-yell. "You're gonna get us caught."

He goes to step into me again, and I shove my hand against his strong chest and have to force myself not to spread my fingers and feel the tight ridges of his pecs beneath his shirt. I mean, would it really hurt if I just felt them for a second?

Shit.

"Slow your roll, Cowboy. We're not doing this here."

"Come on," he groans. "I bet I could make you come before anyone even realizes we're gone. It'll be the perfect appetizer to whatever the fuck you're trying to make in here."

"First off, my spaghetti and meatballs are going to be amazing. And second, I'm not doubting that you can get me off that quickly. In fact, we both know damn well how fast you can make me come, but it's not happening in my mother's pantry," I tell him. "And while we're on the topic of inappropriate things that Izaac Banks likes to do, can you at least attempt to not make it so obvious?"

"That's all part of the fun, Birdy. Doesn't it get you hot knowing we could be sprung at any moment?" he questions. "Besides, Austin's too preoccupied sexting Becs to even take notice of what we're doing."

My jaw drops. "He's doing what?"

The pantry door swings open, and my mother stands before us, her knowing gaze locked on the way his hands grip my waist and how our bodies seem fused together.

My eyes widen in horror as silence stretches between the three of us, and when her gaze lifts to mine, the silence begins to cripple me. "Mom, I—"

"Oh, this is going to be fun," she says, a wicked grin stretching across her face.

Izaac's hands fall from my waist, but they don't go far as his fingers trail down my arm, brushing past my wrist before gripping my hand. "Angie, I can explain," Izaac starts, ready for the fallout.

"No need to explain, love. I've hoped for this for a long time."

"Really?" I breathe.

A softness flutters through her eyes as she looks at me fondly. "Of course, honey. I've always known just how much he meant to you, and for a while, I worried it might never happen, so seeing that something is finally beginning to blossom between the two of you warms my heart like you'll never know. I could never have asked for a better match for my little girl. However," she says, her gaze darkening as it flickers toward Izaac. "This is my pantry and was not intended for your unsanitary fondling. If you wish to do unsavory things to my daughter, perhaps do it in your own pantry."

Oh shit.

Izaac clears his throat, and I laugh, never having seen him so awkward in the million years that I've known him. "I, uhhh . . . I'll just see myself out."

"See that you do," Mom says.

Izaac cringes and takes a step to move past Mom in the doorway when she stops him with a hand on his wide chest. His gaze locks onto hers and the tightness in her eyes tells me exactly what's about to come out of her mouth. "He's going to kill you."

Izaac nods. "I know."

"Don't keep him in the dark for long," she warns. "The longer you wait, the harder it will be for him to move past it."

"Any advice for how I'm supposed to break the news?"

Mom scoffs and indicates toward her beloved pantry. "Not like this."

Izaac nods again, quickly turning into a bobblehead. "Noted."

And with that, he walks away, leaving me to deal with my mother, only instead of getting scolded for getting caught with my fingers in the cookie jar, she steps right into me, wrapping me in her warm arms. "I'm so happy for you, love."

"Thanks, but don't get ahead of yourself," I warn her, pulling back as we hover in the kitchen. "It's only new. Like, super new. Who knows how it's going to turn out?"

"You forget, Aspen. I've known that boy nearly his whole life. I've had to put Band-Aids on his wounds and watch from the audience as he received awards at school. I'm as much of a mother to Izaac as his own mother is, and so I know his heart just as I know yours or Austin's. He's a good boy, and he loves your brother fiercely. He wouldn't risk anything with you unless he planned to make it count."

I cringe. "And if I kinda forced him into it?"

"I stand by what I said. He's strong and knows how to say no, so whatever you forced him to do, he wouldn't have done it unless he saw it going somewhere. But with the good comes the bad, and he bears a lot of scars from before his adoption, so when you need to be, be patient, and when you need to push, you push."

I step into her again, pulling her into another hug. "Thanks, Mom."

"Awwww gross," Austin's voice booms through the kitchen. "What's that smell?"

My face falls, horror blasting through me.

The meatballs.

"SHIT!"

I race out of the walk-in pantry and find Austin hovered over my meatballs, looking at them in horror. I shove him out of the way, and when I peer into the pot, devastation burns through me.

"Ahh, fuck," I say, just as the sound of the doorbell fills my childhood home.

"Perfect timing," Austin says. "That'll be our pizza."

I gape at him. "You assumed I'd screw it up?"

"No," he laughs as Izaac strides in, his face scrunched at the smell of the burned meatballs. "I fucking hoped for it."

31

ASPEN

Austin sits across from me at the dining table, the sparkle in his eyes brighter than ever before as he scoops up his first slice of pizza and fixes me with a smug grin. "Great lunch, little sister," he chides. "This is my favorite." He takes a hefty bite and exaggerates a moan, rolling his eyes at the guilty pleasure. "Mmmmmm. Delicious."

I pick up a single slice of garlic bread and toss it across the table, smacking him directly in the center of his big-ass forehead, only it falls right onto his plate and he happily scoops it up, places it on top of his pizza slice, and eats the stupid pizza like a goddamn sandwich. "I hate you. You know that, right?"

His grin just widens. "I know. Isn't it marvelous?"

Fucking brothers. Why did my mother insist on providing me with one? Though, I suppose, I was the little sister he was provided with. If I were the older sibling, I'd be sure to hold that power with great respect and use it to my absolute advantage.

Mom sits by Austin as Dad takes up the head of the table, leaving Izaac with nowhere to sit but right next to me. I swallow hard. Any other day, it would be fine, but the way he so boldly locked us in Mom's pantry and hasn't stopped looking at me since are the perfect ingredients for disaster.

Everyone digs into lunch, scooping up slice after slice, and I'm not going to lie, despite the frustration I feel for my burned meatballs, this pizza is incredible. Austin always splurges when he's treating his family, and I love that about him. Christmas and birthday presents are always over the top, and there's no denying the thought he puts into every single one of them.

After finishing off my second slice, I reach for my drink and take a needy sip when Izaac leans forward, taking another slice and placing it onto my plate. My brows furrow, and I meet his eye, loving how he so casually looks out for me. It wasn't forced or done out of being polite, he just did it because it's what felt right to him, but it seems I wasn't the only one to notice.

"The fuck?" Austin grunts. "What was that? She can get her own pizza."

Izaac rolls his eyes and fixes Austin with a stare. "It's called being polite. You should try it sometime."

Austin scoffs. Every last person at the table knows just how polite my brother is. He was always known as the golden boy. Great at sports, an amazing friend, perfect grades, and always the first to open a door for someone. The whole fucking town knows it. The only person who doesn't reap the rewards of his perfectness is me, but I wouldn't have it any other way. I love that he lets his guard down with me and can be an ass because, when it comes down to it, that's just his way of telling me he loves me. When it really counts, he pushes the bullshit aside and is real with me, and even though those moments are rare, that's what makes them special.

Seeing Austin has nothing to say, Izaac's lips kick up into a wicked smirk, and as his elbow accidentally knocks his now-useless cutlery off the table, I lean back in my seat and try not to focus on the incredible man beside me or the way he made love to me on Monday night.

Nothing will ever compare to that moment. It's forever ingrained in my memory, etched into my brain like a timeless carving.

Dad clears his throat and glances toward Austin as Izaac leans down between us to find his fallen cutlery. "What's this big announcement you've dragged everyone here for?" he asks, crossing his arms over his big chest and waiting expectantly just as the slightest brush trails up my calf. "Is this about your trip out of town?"

Oh no.

Izaac's fingers roam higher to my knee as he straightens in his seat, no one any wiser that his hand isn't anywhere near where it's supposed to be. I shoot a warning glare his way, but he just casually reaches for the pizza on his plate and takes a bite, waiting for Austin to say whatever he brought us all here to say.

His fingers roam higher to my inner thigh, and I curse myself, knowing exactly what he intends to do, but it's not as though I can really say anything about it right now. All I can do is curse myself for wearing a dress today.

"No, actually," Austin says as I reach for my glass of wine and take a hefty sip, only as Izaac's fingers slip beneath the hem of my dress and find the apex of my thighs, I suck in a gasp and promptly choke on my wine.

All eyes fall to me, Izaac's included. "You good?" he asks with false concern.

"Mmm-hmm," I say, setting my glass back down. "Went down the wrong way."

Knowing this game is far too dangerous, I cross my legs, blocking any access to the promised land, and Izaac immediately settles his hand on my knee, giving it a tight squeeze before pushing it away and spreading my thighs beneath the table.

I swallow hard, keeping my gaze locked on Austin as he talks. "My meeting with the interior designer went great," he says as Izaac's hand dives for my pussy, rubbing me over my sheer thong. My hips jolt, and when his fingers work their way beneath the fabric and directly to my clit, my hands begin to tremble. "She confirmed during the week that she'll take on the job and will be coming out once the renovations start wrapping to get a better idea of what we're working with, and while that's great news and could do incredible things come launch, that's not the announcement I brought you all here for."

With my trembling hands becoming too obvious on the table, I drop one to my lap as the other clutches Izaac's wrist, holding him so fucking tight I'm sure I'm cutting off his circulation, but good God, I'm going to explode if he doesn't ease up.

His fingers are like magic, knowing exactly how to touch me, and he's using every little thing he's learned about me over the past few weeks and putting it to the test. After all, he dared to tease me how quickly he could get me off in the pantry, and now, he's standing by his word.

"Ahh shit," Izaac says. "Is this the big announcement where you tell us you've fallen madly in love with Becs despite barely knowing her?"

I clench my jaw, trying to find anything to focus on which isn't the overwhelming pleasure rocking through my core. "You and I are gonna have words about that, by the way," I warn him, making a show of reaching for my wine as though my hips aren't violently jolting beneath the table. "Don't act like I don't know how much you've been texting her."

Izaac's fingers plunge deep inside my pussy and my walls clench around him in surprise, and I suck in a sharp breath before trying to play it off, but luckily all eyes are on Austin.

"There's nothing going on between me and Becs," he says as Izaac curls his fingers and begins massaging deep within me, right over my fucking G-spot, making my thighs shake with desperation, my chest heaving with heavy breaths. "We're just texting. It's nothing."

"Uh-huh," Izaac grins.

Austin rolls his eyes. "Can I tell you assholes my big announcement, or what?"

"Language," Mom scolds as Izaac's thumb rolls over my clit, sending me into a world of pure ecstasy. It's too much. I'm going to come at my fucking childhood dining table.

Holy fucking shit.

My fingers clench tighter around his wrists, but he's relentless and pushes me harder, his fingers scissoring deep inside of me and making me bite down on my lip to suppress a moan. I grab my wine again, mostly so I can lift it to my face and hide the shaky breaths tearing from deep in my chest, but I don't hesitate to take another desperate sip.

"Okay, so," Austin starts, his gaze shifting nervously toward me as my walls clench around his best friend's fingers, so close to the fucking edge. I can't hold on to it any longer. I can't hold back. "I've been playing with the name for the restaurant, and I'd like to call it Aspen's."

"Holy fucking shit," I gasp as I come harder than I've ever come in my life, my gaze awkwardly locked on my brother's as my walls rapidly convulse around Izaac's fingers, but damn him, he doesn't even try to stop.

I shatter like fucking glass. My whole body trembling.

Tell me I didn't just come at my childhood dining table surrounded by my family.

Fuck me.

"Yeah?" Austin asks, watching me too fucking closely, probably able to see my flaming cheeks and the look of utter shock on my face. This is not fucking happening. "I wasn't sure if you'd be down with it, but what do you think?"

Mom gets teary-eyed as Dad chuffs with pride, but all I can do is stare at him, momentarily paralyzed by the way Izaac's thumb lazily continues rolling over my clit as I come down from the greatest high known to man. But when he finally pulls his fingers free and fixes my thong back into place like the gentleman that he is, I try to focus on what the hell is being said.

"I . . . I love it, but are you sure?" I ask him. "This is your dream. You're the one putting in all the work. You should name it after yourself."

"You're my little sister, Aspen. Literally, everything I have ever done since the moment you were born was to show you that you could do anything or be anyone you ever wanted to be. If you weren't around, I never would have pushed so hard to make it happen," he tells me. "Despite how we tease each other, you've always been my greatest supporter and my best friend. So yeah, I'm sure. I'd like to name it Aspen's."

My eyes grow watery as I get up from the table and rush around to my brother's side, taking my glass of wine with me and making sure my dress is pulled down properly before pulling him into a tight hug. "I love you too," I tell him. "Thank you so much."

My knees are still shaky as I meet Izaac's eye across the room and watch as he picks a tiny bit of pizza crust off his plate and pops it into his mouth. Only he doesn't stop there, holding my gaze as he makes a show of sucking his fingers clean. "Mmmm, that was fucking delicious," he says right as I take a sip of wine.

"Couldn't agree more," my father says, leaning back and rubbing his full stomach.

Holy fucking shit.

My wine spurts from my fucking nose, redecorating Mom's good dining table, and I hastily grab a bunch of napkins and start mopping up my mess as Izaac laughs to himself.

"Jesus Christ," Austin mutters in annoyance, his white shirt now stained with wine as he tries to shake it off his arms, splattering wine across the whole damn room. "Learn how to swallow."

Izaac chokes on a laugh, his wicked gaze meeting mine. "Oh, she's got no problem there," he says under his breath.

Fucking hell. He did not just say that.

"Do you have any mock-ups for the front of the restaurant?" I rush out, desperately trying to change the topic from my ability to swallow before Austin or my parents have a chance to process what was said.

"Yeah, actually. I do," Austin says as I hastily hurry back to my seat, more than happy to move this right along. "I've got a bunch made up that I want to show you. I think you'll really like them, but I want your honest input. If your name is going up on the wall, I want it to be just right."

"Do you have them here?" I ask. "I'd be happy to take a look after lunch."

"Would I risk dropping a bomb like that and not bring them along? Fuck, Aspen. Do you even know me at all?"

I roll my eyes and refill my wine, not stopping until it's almost flowing over the rim. "Good point," I mutter, and with that, we get stuck right back into our lunch. Mom and Dad bombard us all with questions about life, hitting Izaac with all the ins and outs of his club shit while sucker punching me with all the college bullshit.

An hour later, the dining table is clear and the mess from my failed spaghetti and meatballs has been cleaned up, but damn, my arm is sore from having to scrub the bottom of the meatball pot.

With plenty of sun left in the afternoon sky, I trudge down to my room, hoping I remembered to leave a cute bikini here the last time I dropped by. I close the door behind me before scrounging through my old closet and finding a small red triangle bikini. It's old and will barely cover me, but it'll get the job done. Besides, the only person who's going to look is Izaac, and there's nothing there he hasn't already spent long hours drowning in.

Peeling my dress off, I toss it onto my bed before reaching behind me to unclip my bra, and just as the purple lace falls to the ground, my bedroom door opens and I grin wide as Izaac discreetly steps in, his heated gaze roaming over my bare chest. "You mind, perve?" I tease. "I'm trying to get dressed here."

"By all means," he says, stepping into me and hooking his thumbs into the waistband of my thong. "Let me help."

I shove him off me, trying to keep my tone low. "I think you've done more than enough."

Izaac laughs and grips my chin, lifting it until my eyes lock onto his. "And I'll do it a million times over," he murmurs, his tone so damn low that my pussy aches for him all over again. "I'll never tire of your sweet little cunt."

I swallow hard. "You're playing a risky game today."

"I know," he admits with a heavy sigh before reaching for my bikini top. He pulls it around me before tying it in a perfect knot in the center of my back and taking the second set of strings to wrap around my neck, only he uses it to his advantage as he pulls me in against him.

Once the bikini top is firmly in place, he brushes my hair back over my shoulder before skimming his fingers down my arms as though mesmerized by the feel of my skin beneath his. "I'm not going to lie, Birdy. That speech he gave at the table about why he's naming his restaurant after you made me feel like a piece of shit."

"I know," I murmur, dropping my head against his chest. "Do you think we're doing the right thing?"

"Fuck no," he scoffs. "Your mom was right though. The longer we keep him in the dark, the worse it's going to be, but I don't know if I can tell him. How the fuck am I supposed to explain this without gutting him? He'll never trust you again, and me . . . He'll fucking despise me."

Guilt radiates through my chest, making it harder to breathe, and he pulls me in tighter, and despite everything that's gone down today, I sense that same rejection within him. "Just say it," I sigh, feeling the hurt well up in my chest.

"Don't get me wrong, Aspen. I want this. Since the second I touched you, I've wanted it, but I think we need to cool it, just until I can sort this out with your brother. It fucking kills me to not have his approval, and before, when it was just sex, I was mostly okay with it. But now that it's more than that . . . it matters."

My hand scoops beneath his arm and around his back, clutching onto him as though he might disappear at any moment. "He's never going to approve of this," I say, my heart shattering within my chest. "Don't walk away from me."

"I'm not walking away," he promises, his lips brushing across mine. "I just—"

My door flies open and my head whips up, finding Austin standing before me with his laptop in his hand. He comes to a screeching halt, his brows furrowed as he takes in the sight before him—me half naked in his best friend's arms, and despite the heavy conversation, from the way Izaac holds me, anyone would think he was just about ready to throw me down and have his wicked way with me.

"WHAT THE FUCK?" Austin roars, throwing his laptop aside as the deepest betrayal flashes in his eyes. Rage overcomes him, and as he bounds toward us, I distantly notice how his laptop shatters, then before Izaac even gets a chance to step away and explain what the fuck is going down here, Austin rears back, his fist flying toward his jaw.

Izaac quickly dodges the punch, but Austin's momentum propels him forward, and in the blink of an eye, his strong fist slams across my cheek. I crumble, flying back against my bed and dropping to the ground as pain booms across my face, throbbing in agony. I whimper, clutching my face as Izaac launches for me. "Fuck, Birdy. Are you okay?" he rushes out, his eyes wide as I hear my parents somewhere down the hall racing toward the loud commotion. He reaches for my hand, gently lifting it off my throbbing cheek, and whatever he sees has his gaze darkening with fury.

Tears spring from my eyes as Austin moves in, horrified as he looks over Izaac's shoulder. "Fuck. Aspen," he grits. "I'm sorry, I—"

Izaac whips around, every bit of that fury locked onto my brother, and he snaps, springing toward him. His fist strikes out like a fucking python, clocking Austin in the jaw. "You fucking punched your sister, asshole!" Izaac roars, shoving him against the drywall as my old photo frames fall to the ground, but Austin snaps back, and they quickly start trading blows until it turns into a fucking brawl on my bedroom floor.

Blood splatters across the carpet, but it's impossible to tell who it's coming from. This isn't how this was supposed to go down. I knew Austin would be angry, but I thought we'd be able to talk it out. Not this.

Realizing they're not planning on stopping anytime soon, I peel myself off the ground and hobble toward them, pain throbbing in my cheek. They're not fucking teenagers anymore. They're almost thirty. They can't be doing this shit.

Moving closer to them, I try to grab Izaac to separate them, but it's no use, not even when Dad rushes in behind me, shoves me out of the way, and grabs Austin. Mom cries, rushing to my side and looking over my face as Dad roars. "What the fuck is going on in here?"

The sound of his demand seems to sober everybody as the boys finally fall apart, both of them heaving for air, and as for the blood splattered on the ground, now that they're broken apart, it clearly belongs to both of them.

Horror pulses through me, and I go to move toward Izaac, but his haunted stare leaves me rooted in the spot. "Somebody better start talking," Dad demands.

"He's fucking her," Austin spits as he gets to his feet, wiping the back of his arm across his blood-soaked face. He glares at Izaac, watching his every last move as he grips his ribs and gets to his feet, the look in his eye confirming exactly what he just said.

"It's not like that," Izaac insists as Dad sucks in a shocked gasp, but Izaac doesn't take his eyes off Austin's. "Just give me a chance to—"

"How long?" Austin grits through his clenched jaw. "How fucking long have you been going behind my back and taking advantage of my sister?"

"That's not—" I rush in.

"HOW FUCKING LONG?"

"Austin," Mom says, trying to calm the situation as tears stream down my face, feeling my whole world burning to ashes at my feet.

Izaac takes a hesitant step toward him, the guilt so obvious on his face. "Since your mom's birthday," he admits, not wanting to sugarcoat anything and giving it to him straight. "A little over a month."

Austin's gaze swings to me, and the look he gives me almost drops me to my knees. The betrayal in his eyes is like nothing I've ever experienced before, the hurt, the guilt, the heartbreak. "Austin," I breathe. "I—"

He looks back at Izaac, shaking his head. "Nearly twenty-five fucking years, and the only thing I've ever asked of you was to never touch her," he says, the heaviness in his tone breaking me. "You're fucking dead to me."

And with that, Austin turns on his heel and stalks out of my childhood room, leaving me a fucking mess as I fall into my mother's arms.

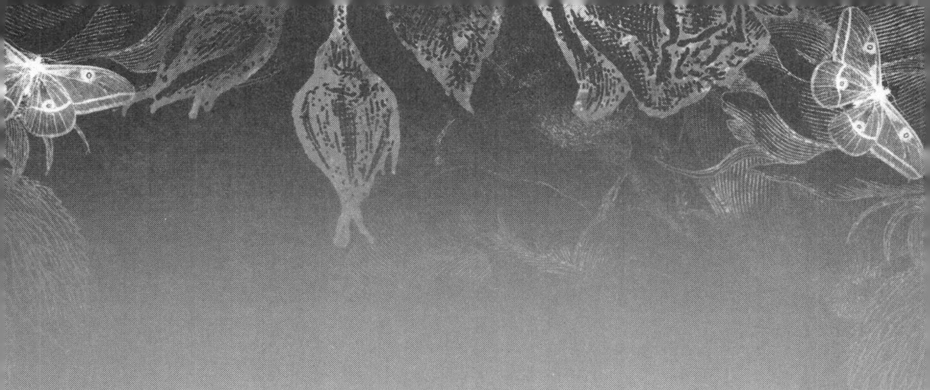

32

ASPEN

My brother has always been my greatest supporter, my best friend, and the biggest pain in my ass, and now, he feels like nothing more than a cold stranger.

I'm out of options.

The day he stormed out of my childhood bedroom, I ran after him. I tried talking to him, gripping on to his arm and begging him to hear me out like a child, but he shook me off, got into his car, and drove away. I've tried calling. Texting. Hitting him up on social media, until he finally got sick of it and blocked me. It's been almost two weeks of radio silence, and not just from him. Izaac has been just as cold. Refusing to see me until he's mended things with Austin, and sure, that's commendable, but what about me? What about the way I hurt? Does that not matter to either of them?

God, I've never felt more alone than I have over the past two weeks. They're assholes. I know Izaac never officially admitted that he was in love with me, but I know he is. So how can he just shut me out like that?

Fuck, it hurts, but that's always been his specialty.

Pulling up outside Austin's door, I prepare myself for a world of hurt. If he's not taking my calls and refuses to hear me out, then he leaves me no choice. I need to make this right.

My brother is one of my favorite people in the world, and while I hate that my betrayal is eating him up, he surely must have seen it coming or at least considered it as a possibility over the years.

I've been in love with Izaac for so damn long, how could he not have seen it coming? And I don't just mean a stupid little crush. No, this is the whole shebang. The soul-shattering, breath-taking, all-or-nothing type of love that forever alters the way you view life. It brings your priorities into perspective, and now that I know what it's like to have just a glimpse of that overwhelming happiness, I'm not about to let it slip through my fingers. And if that means Austin will need to suffer, then so be it. If he loves and values me in the way he says he does, then he'd want this for me. He'd want me to experience the greatest love this world can offer.

Letting out a heavy sigh, I get out of my car and stare up at Austin's home. It's not quite as extravagant as Izaac's place, but it's definitely nothing to turn your nose up at either. Austin has worked his ass off since finishing college and has proudly given himself everything he's ever wanted while fighting Mom and Dad tooth and nail, refusing their constant need to offer him the world. He set out for independence, and that's exactly what he's built for himself.

I make my way toward the door of a house that's always felt like home for me, despite the rare occasions I've actually stayed here. Nerves settle in the pit of my stomach, and before I get a chance to chicken out, I lift my fist and rap against the hardwood door.

I wait a minute, and as it quickly turns into two, I grit my teeth.

That asshole is ignoring me.

His car is parked in the driveway, and judging from the way his stupid doorbell camera lights up, he knows it's me standing out here.

I knock on the door again, this time taking a page out of Izaac's book. "I'm not going anywhere until you hear me out," I call through the door. "I love you, Austin, and whether you want to hear that or not, I don't care. You're my big brother, and I'm not just going to let you shut me out. You're too important to me, so if you want me to get lost, you're gonna have to answer the door and hear me out first."

I'm not going to lie, I really didn't think this through before I jumped in my car and drove over here. Hell, I didn't even know if he was going to be home. I took a shot in the dark, and thankfully, I was right. Though, had he not been here, that wouldn't have stopped me from searching every other place he's ever been, starting with the restaurant.

I get no response and let out a heavy sigh, wondering just how hard it would be to scale the side of the house and break through one of the upstairs windows. I'm not stupid enough to bother wasting time with the downstairs windows. He locks them up like Fort Knox, but upstairs, he's a little more relaxed.

It's not going to be easy, but I think I could pull some epic Black Widow moves and get my ass inside.

Stepping back, I lift my gaze to the top story of Austin's home, scanning over all of the windows. When Izaac had to wait at my door, he had the patience of a saint, but I don't possess that quality. If I can just find something to climb up on, then I can—

The familiar sound of the door unlocking from inside cuts through my break-in plan, and my back stiffens. Holy shit. I didn't expect him to actually come to the door, let alone think about what's supposed to happen once I actually get to talk to him. I was just going to wing it, but perhaps I need some kind of game plan. Though, I suppose it's a little too late for that now.

The door swings open, and I go to step forward, only I pause, finding Becs standing before me.

"What . . ." My brows furrow, a deep confusion fogging my brain. Surely she would have told me if something more happened between them, right? Even if Austin was speaking to me, he would have kept this from me, but I never thought she would. "What are you doing here?"

"Don't worry. I wasn't trying to get in your brother's pants again," she says before I get a chance to overthink it too much. "It just hurts me seeing how broken and sad you've been over the last two weeks, and I thought maybe if I could be a voice of reason, I could get through to him and help close that gap between you."

"And?" I say, a little too hopeful.

She cringes, and all that hope plummets to the ground, exploding into a million fiery pieces. "I don't think he's ready to even think about it, let alone begin to accept it," she says before stepping into me and wrapping me in a warm hug. "I have to go, but I'm going to accidentally leave the door open, and if you decide to go in there and try your luck, then that's your prerogative, but just so you know, I don't think it's going to be pretty."

"Thanks," I say with a heavy sigh as she pulls away.

"Call me if you need to have another wine night. We can get drunk and talk shit about these damn boys," she says, and with that, she steps off Austin's porch, leaving the door open just as she said.

I stare down the open door, nerves bubbling deep in my stomach.

Well, here goes nothing.

Stepping over the threshold, I welcome myself into Austin's home and silently pad through the house until I find him sitting in his living room, his foot propped up against the coffee table and looking sorry for himself. Then hearing me as I walk into the room, he lets out a frustrated sigh and gets to his feet. "I told you, I didn't want to—"

Austin cuts himself off as his gaze finally snaps up, realizing it's me and not Becs walking back in. "The fuck do you think you're doing?" he snaps, storming around the couch and fixing a heated glare on me. "I thought I made it pretty fucking clear that I didn't want to see you."

"Yeah, well, you punched me right in the middle of my face, so the least you can do is stop being such an asshole and give me at least two minutes of your time," I throw back at him, closing the distance between us.

His gaze flickers to the yellowing bruise across my cheek, and the flicker of guilt in his eyes tells me that I might still have a chance to make this okay. Only, it's gone just as quickly as it came. "I don't owe you shit," he tells me. "I'm sorry I clocked you in the face, but it doesn't change anything. You're fucking my best friend. You betrayed my trust and went behind my back."

"I'm sorry," I tell him. "It just . . . kinda happened. I didn't mean—"

"What?" He scoffs. "You didn't mean to spread your legs and invite him in? The fuck is wrong with you, Aspen? Do you hear yourself? Look at it from my perspective. You've practically thrown yourself at him your whole fucking life, and now that you're not a kid anymore, you figured you'd wave your ass in his face and wait for him to take the fucking bait."

"That's not—"

"Don't even try to justify it. He's taking advantage of you, Aspen. How could you be so fucking stupid not to see that? He's getting laid while you're living it up, thinking that after all this time he's finally going to love you? Reality check. He's not," Austin roars, every word stabbing me right through the heart and rendering me speechless. "This is Izaac Banks we're talking about. How fucking long have you known him? Have you ever seen him care about a woman? Fuck no. He's not capable, which is why I never wanted you anywhere near the bastard in the first place."

"That's not fair. I've loved him all my life."

"I don't give a shit, Aspen, because what it comes down to is that he's never going to love you in return. What aren't you understanding? He's not capable of it. He doesn't know how to love a woman, and you're sure as hell not going to be the one to make him see the light. So congratulations. All you've done is destroy a lifelong friendship because you couldn't keep your fucking legs closed."

My hand snaps out, rocking across his face and leaving my palm stinging. "You have no idea what you're talking about."

"Don't I?" he scoffs, clenching his jaw. "Then enlighten me. If he really fucking loves you, then where is he? Because I sure as fuck don't see him here breaking down my door in order to fight for you."

Horror blasts through me, and I stumble back a step, truly hearing what he's saying. Izaac hasn't tried to fight for me. "No," I say, shaking my head. "He loves me. I know what I felt."

"Right," Austin grunts, looking at me as though I were nothing but a piece of filth beneath his shoe. "You've had some fucked-up infatuation with him for twelve years, but you don't really know him, not like I do, and you, you don't mean shit to him. You're an easy fuck, just like every other woman who's ever thrown themselves at him. It's embarrassing. So, here's what's going to happen. You're going to end whatever the fuck you're doing with him, and you're never going to see him again. After that, then maybe we'll talk. Until then, get the fuck out. I've got nothing to say to you."

I crumble, dropping to the ground as every part of me shatters, blackening the already broken fragments of my soul. Tears spring from my eyes, rolling down my cheeks as a heavy lump forms in the center of my throat, making it almost impossible to breathe.

How could he be so cruel?

I'm an embarrassment. He's never going to love me. He's not here fighting for me.

Austin is right.

And I'm nothing more than a fool. All I've done is set myself up to be pushed away. I knew that was a possibility, *but I felt it.* That connection between us was real. I couldn't have imagined it. And when he kissed me in his spare room and took me to his bed . . . That meant something. I know it did.

But if Izaac truly felt something real for me, then surely he would have been here, doing everything he could to try and make this right, to fight for Austin's approval. So where the hell is he?

Devastation grips hold of me until I'm nothing but a crumbled mess on Austin's floor, and then without even a glance back, my brother walks away, leaving me to wallow in my self-pity and heartbreak.

Almost twenty minutes go by before I find the strength to finally pull myself to my feet. I haven't heard from or seen Austin since the second he walked away, all I know is that he's right. I have to end it with Izaac. I've imagined it all inside my head.

He hasn't tried to fight for me.

Izaac warned me right from the beginning that he was never going to love me, and maybe he feels something, but he said so himself, he doesn't know how to love, and I was the foolish, lovestruck idiot who was too blind to actually hear what he was saying.

Every part of me aches as I turn on my heel and trudge back

toward the front door, each step heavier than the last, knowing what I have to do. Me and Izaac—we're done. We were done the second Austin found me in his best friend's arms. We were done before it even started.

I forced this relationship onto him. Sure, it started as a complete coincidence, but the day he stormed into my apartment and demanded I forgive him for what happened during my second visit to Vixen, I should have turned him away. I never should have demanded he teach me. We could have called it quits, and sooner or later, everything would have gone back to normal.

But now . . . everything is ruined.

Austin is never going to see me as his innocent little sister ever again. He's never going to love me like he used to, and as for their friendship, I don't know if there's any saving it now.

With a heavy heart, I walk back out to my car, and as I drive away from the home I'm no longer welcome in, I drive on autopilot, not knowing where I'm going, all that matters is that it's away from Austin.

I thought his love for me would be enough to pull us through. I thought he'd still hold on to me and tell me that everything was going to be okay. I knew he was angry, but this . . . I've never felt so broken.

I drive for hours, sailing down the highway and back until my tank is almost empty, ignoring the calls and texts from Mom and Becs. They're probably only making sure I'm still alive, but am I? What am I supposed to say after that? I sure as hell don't feel alive.

It's after ten when I finally pull to a stop. My eyes are swollen and sore from hours of crying, and my chest . . . just feels empty, but as I gaze out the window to Izaac's home, the emptiness turns into a great chasm of heartache.

Getting out of my car, I find myself standing there for a few moments, leaning against the closed driver's door and just staring at his home. It's hard to convince myself that all the dreams I ever had about building a life with Izaac never mattered in the first place. Then before I can find the courage to walk up to the door and bring an end to everything I ever wanted, the door opens and Izaac appears, looking just as broken as I feel.

There's a grim expression across his face, and when he steps over the threshold and makes his way toward me, I prepare for the worst.

This is it. He's calling it quits just as he should have done from the beginning.

It's a good thing. At least he'll be the one to do it so I won't have to be the one to tear my own heart to pieces. It's better this way, and one day, maybe years from now, I'll be able to come to peace with it all, but damn, it's going to hurt for a long time.

I can barely meet his eyes as he moves in before me, and just when I expect him to say the words that will tear me to shreds, he takes another step and pulls me into his arms. His body folds against mine, and he holds me there, his hand on the back of my head as my face squishes against his strong chest, hearing nothing but the sound of his beating heart. "I don't want to lose you, Birdy."

My gaze lifts to meet his, unsure where he's going with this.

"I said from the very start that I didn't want to hurt you," he tells me, his other hand clutching my waist. "And now I have no fucking choice."

"Izaac," I breathe, my hand on his chest fisting into the material, not ready to hear the words come out of his mouth.

"I'm sorry, Aspen. I should never have allowed it to get this far. I've always known how you felt about me, and despite how you said that it wouldn't change anything, I knew it would. I allowed it to continue, knowing that you would get more attached."

"Don't," I say, my voice wavering. "Don't start acting as though you never felt it. I know you did."

"I'm not trying to say that I didn't. I think we're at a point now where I can no longer deny it. What I feel for you, Aspen . . . it fucking kills me that this can't just be easy. I can't just sweep you away and call you mine. Austin's been my best friend for twenty-five years, and despite how I feel about it and how I know it's going to tear you apart, I stand by what I said at your parents' house. I can't do this with you, not until Austin is okay with it."

Tears roll down my cheeks, and he hastily wipes them away. "He's never going to be okay with it," I tell him.

Izaac nods and understanding dawns in my chest. "I know."

"So, this is it?" I cry, pushing out of his arms. "We just go on pretending that we never happened."

"We have to."

I turn around, unable to even look at him without crumbling. He's discarding what little is left of my heart as though I never mattered. He moves in behind me, his arms locking around my waist as we stand in a broken silence, neither of us willing to walk away.

"Austin thinks I whored myself out to you, and that you took advantage of me," I murmur. "He said as long as I was still seeing you, he was done with me."

"Fuck," Izaac breathes, turning me in his arms. He takes my chin and lifts it until my red-rimmed eyes are locked on his. "Do you think I took advantage of you?"

I shake my head. "Austin said—"

"I don't give a shit what Austin said," he tells me. "I want to know what you think."

Unable to hold his dark stare without crumbling, I drop my gaze back to his shirt as my hand slips beneath the material, skimming across his abs and up to his chest to feel the warmth beneath my palm. "I think I was the one who took advantage of you," I tell him. "You came to me asking for a way that I could forgive you, and I backed you into a corner that I knew you couldn't get out of. I forced this on you and fought with you every time you tried to pull away. You told me from the start you could never love me the way I wanted you to, and I didn't listen."

"I don't want you walking away from this thinking that," he murmurs. "I sure as fuck don't see it that way, and if at any point I wanted to say no, I would have. I was selfish. I had a taste of you and I wanted more in every sense of the word."

"And now you don't?"

"It's not that I don't. It's that *I won't,*" he tells me. "Us together, we can't make this work without tearing your family to shreds, and I won't do that to them, and I won't do it to you. You deserve someone who can love you the way you need. Someone you can walk through the door with who's not going to send your family into turmoil. Or hell, someone you don't need to lie about just to be with him. It'll fucking kill me, but I want all of that for you. Falling in love with someone shouldn't be so damn hard, Birdy. You shouldn't have to fight so much just to have someone tell you they love you." He takes a heavy breath, needing to step away. My hand falls from his chest, and when he meets my stare, his gaze is haunted. "I'm too fucking broken. I have issues, Aspen. Deep-rooted issues that are never going to go away, and yeah, when I'm with you, I get to pretend that they don't exist, but they do. So go, Aspen. Go fall in love with someone who isn't me. Go have your happy ending, build the big fucking house with the picket fence, and have all the children who look nothing like me."

Every word that comes out of his mouth is torture, but we've never spoken about houses with picket fences or children, and I can't help but wonder if this is the dream he wanted for us—the dream he so foolishly believed could come true.

"Please don't do this," I whisper. "I know you love me, Izaac. I feel it every time you touch me. *You're in love with me.* Don't push me away."

"I have to."

I find myself backing up until my ass hits the edge of my car. "You're wrong," I breathe, whimpering as my whole world burns to ashes. "You're not broken, and no matter how hard you push me away, it'll always be you. There is no happy ending for me without you."

He shakes his head, devastation in his eyes. "Just go, Aspen. We're done."

And with tears streaming down my face, I turn and walk away.

33

ASPEN

Becs stares at me, a cringe pulling at her lips as she takes the small shot of tequila and lifts it to her lips. "So, uhh," she says, pausing to deal with the burn that sails down her throat before sucking the lemon and licking the salt off the back of her hand. "Your brother just texted. Apparently, he's headed to Vixen tonight to go for round two with Izaac."

Well, shit.

"Good luck to them," I say, reaching across the bar and grabbing my shot. "I hope they're happy together."

As I take my shot, Becs laughs. "Doubt it. I don't see a reconciliation in their future. At least not anytime soon," she offers. "Austin has been working out in his garage and beating the shit out of his punching bag, so I'm pretty sure he's only going to get another crack at Izaac's ribs."

"If only he had someone who cared enough to warn him," I say, watching as the bartender refills our shots and getting giddy as we each pour the salt onto the backs of our hands.

"That's the spirit," Becs says before pausing and letting out a heavy sigh. "I mean, the two of them going at it would be kinda hot though."

"Hot isn't the word I'd use for it," I say, thoroughly disgusted by the thought of Becs getting off to my brother and Izaac getting all hot and sweaty in a brawl. "But I'm not gonna lie, I wouldn't mind being a fly on the wall for that one."

Her eyes light up as she grabs the two shots and hands me one. "Then let's go," she says, getting overly excited. "I haven't been in ages. I miss Vixen. We could get a little freaky and then hide behind the bar while the guys have it out. Really, it's a win-win situation."

I gingerly take the shot from her outstretched hand as I feel the tequila rushing to my head. "I mean, he did tell me to go find Mr. Forever. Who's to say that my dream man isn't waiting for me at Vixen's VIP bar right now?"

Becs grins, already scooping her bag off the bar and getting to her feet. She takes the shot and makes a face as it burns on the way down. She slams the little shot glass down. "Oh, hell yeah. That was good," she says before a wide grin tears across her face. "You know, that Izaac of yours is a very jealous creature. There's no telling what he might do if he were to see you having a little fun with your future Mr. Forever."

I grin right back. If Izaac wants me to be with someone else, then why the hell shouldn't I? It's not like I'm even close to getting physical with another man, nor do I want to, but I'm not ready to give up on Izaac yet. Seeing me opening my options to other men might just be the kick up the ass he needs.

Becs is right, Izaac is a jealous creature. Just the thought of me going out on a Tinder date was enough to risk him going to Austin for help. Not to mention, my non-date with Harrison drove him insane. He's not going to give me the time of day if I were to just walk through the door of Vixen, but if I were to draw him out by playing on his weaknesses, then I might just get my chance to reel him back in.

"This is a terrible idea," I tell her as I slide off the barstool with absolutely no intention of backing out. Now that the little seed has been planted and the thought of just laying my eyes on him is within my grasp, there's no stopping me now.

"I know. Isn't it exciting?" she laughs, looping her arm through mine. "Besides, what's the worst that could happen? If someone approaches you and you're not feeling it, say no thanks, and we keep drinking at the bar. And if someone does approach you and it makes you feel all tingly down in your girl bits, then see where it goes. But preferably in private. Can you imagine what your brother would do if he walked in to see you getting it on with some strange guy? He's already on edge."

"Holy shit," I grunt, able to picture the way he'd go off so easily, but honestly, after the cruel words he threw my way, he deserves to suffer. I'll just have to find another way to make it happen. I'm down with making Izaac watch me with another man, but having Austin see that shit? Hell no. There are some lines not even I would cross. "This is going to be a disaster."

Becs grins. "Hell yeah, it is."

We both laugh as we stumble out of the bar and to the road.

Becs works on getting us an Uber, and I drop down onto the curb to wait. I've more than learned my lesson about walking anywhere after spending the night drinking. "I hope you don't think you're going to swoop in and make Austin your special little guy after he goes for round two with Izaac."

"Why the hell not?" she asks, a smirk playing on her lips as she drops down beside me. "He's going to need someone to help calm him down. Besides, if he gets wind that you're there, shit is going to hit the fan, and I can't have you sulking for another week because your big brother was mean."

I roll my eyes. "He was more than just mean."

"I know," she says with a heavy sigh. "And while I'm definitely not excusing anything he said to you, he was also just saying that in the heat of the moment. He was pissed off and spiraling. He'll eventually come around, and when he does, I'm sure he'll be on his knees begging for forgiveness. He just needs some time to get there. Besides, he's naming his restaurant after you. That's gotta count for something. You don't do that shit unless you really love someone, and he really loves you. He's just hurting."

"You seem to know a lot about how he's feeling," I mutter.

"Because I might have accidentally on purpose ended up at his place on Wednesday night."

My jaw drops, and I gape at my best friend. "You did what?"

"I know. I'm sorry," she says with a heavy sigh. "But there's just something about him. I keep trying to pull away, but then my phone dings with some cheesy text from him, and this stupid grin stretches across my face, and before I know it, I'm giggling like a damn schoolgirl. I don't know what's wrong with me, Aspen. I've never liked someone like this, and I'm really trying not to because I don't want to hurt you and because I just . . . I don't like guys like this. What the hell is going on with me? I don't ever go back for seconds, and I know you said it's inevitable, that I wouldn't be able to resist, but I thought you were just exaggerating. Now the whole *welcome to the family* bullshit you said is playing in my head, and honestly, I'm kinda freaking out. Make it stop. I'm not a *fall for someone* kinda girl, especially assholes who make my best friend cry."

A smile pulls at my lips. "I really wasn't kidding when I said it was inevitable. Austin is a huge pain in my ass, and I've never wanted to hate on him so much in my life, but he's also my brother, and deep down, I know you're right. He just needs time to come around, and when everything goes back to normal, I'll want nothing more than for him to be happy. If you're the person who can do that for him, then I don't want you to pull away from it. Besides, I know it's scary, but don't you owe it to yourself to at least try?"

"Can't I try after you guys have made up?"

"I don't think it works like that," I tell her as the Uber pulls up. "Live in the here and now, Becs. Give in to all the gooey goodness, but I swear to the Hemsworth Gods, if I accidentally walk in on you two, you're both dead to me."

Becs laughs as she pulls me up from the curb. "Cross my heart and hope to die."

I roll my eyes, and after the Uber arrives, it's only a few minutes until we pull up outside of Vixen. Becs can hardly sit still, and honestly, neither can I, but my gut tells me it's for very different reasons. Nerves creep through my body. This really was a stupid idea.

It's not as though Izaac is going to set eyes on me and immediately declare his undying love. I'm going to have to work for that.

Becs grabs my hand and all but hauls me down the alley toward Vixen. "Oh, God, I always get such a thrill coming down here," she says. "But before we cause havoc, we drink."

"Music to my ears."

Reaching the door, we make our way inside, and within minutes, I'm rolling my eyes at Casey's sneer. As we walk through the door with our pretty gold stamps on our wrists, Becs spares me a curious glance. "What the hell was that about?" she questions, referring to the clear animosity between me and Casey.

"Honestly, I'm not really sure," I tell her. "But my guess is that she's just as crazy about Izaac as I am, and in that case, you'd think she'd be a little nicer to me considering we're stuck in the same lonely boat, both of us mindlessly drifting out to sea without a single destination in sight."

"She sounds like a bitch."

"Oh, she is."

Making our way through the club, we detour straight to the VIP entrance, and after flashing our gold moth stamps to the security guard at the top of the stairs, he waves us through.

The familiar electrifying buzz of the music pulses through my veins, and despite the heartbreak I feel and this insane longing I have for Izaac, I can't deny how proud I am of everything he's achieved here. Hell, with all of his clubs. He's built all of this from the ground up, and I don't see an end in sight. He's going to keep going until he's conquered every state in the country. Shit, I wouldn't be surprised if he wanted to take this internationally.

"Holy shit," Becs says as we hit the bottom step and walk into the VIP lounge. "I swear, it gets better every time I come in here."

"Were you actually planning on taking part tonight?" I ask, glancing down at the green band around her wrist, letting the world know she's down to put on a show in the middle of the club with multiple partners. "Maybe a repeat of your first night here?"

"Honestly, I don't really know," she says, pulling at the wristband that's identical to the one on my wrist. "I think I just asked for it because that's what I did last time, but I think I might just sit and watch."

"Woah," I say, gaping at her as we make our way to the bar. "What the hell happened to my best friend?"

Becs rolls her eyes, and we take our seats before quickly ordering our drinks, and just as usual, two perfectly made Cosmos show up before us. With our drinks in hand, we spin around on the barstools, and as we gaze out at the intriguing sights around us, I feel a familiar stare from across the club. My skin immediately dances with goosebumps.

Shivers sail down my spine, and I glance over my shoulder, finding Izaac standing with one of his security guards, listening to whatever he says, but he's keeping every bit of his attention on me.

He doesn't make a move to come to me, but the questions flicker in his dark eyes. What am I doing here? Am I just having a drink with a friend or have I come to play? Am I here for him? Or am I here for something different—*someone* different?

When he finishes his conversation, he strides around the club, his dark stare locked on mine, and I can't help but drop my gaze, taking him in. He's so fucking mouthwatering. It's barely been a week since we . . . since *he* called it quits. A week since I've heard that raspy, deep tone. A week since I've felt his hands on my body, and I've never been so desperate.

I need him.

But I came here to show him what he lost, and I'm not the kind to back out so quickly.

"I hoped I'd see you again," a deep tone rumbles through the VIP lounge, forcing me to lift my greedy eyes off Izaac and to the man standing behind Becs at the bar. For a moment, I assume it's Ryatt Markin, keeping up his trend of stalking me the second I walk into the club, but I find a different face, one Becs has been very up close and personal with.

"Hey," she says to the man who happily enticed her into the best group project she's ever been a part of. "I didn't expect to see you here."

"Same could be said for you," he murmurs as his dark gaze lifts to mine, his eyes hooded and filled with a deep interest before dropping back to Becs. "I was starting to wonder if maybe we'd scared you off."

"Not at all," she says, her cheeks flushing. "It was . . . ummm . . . definitely a night to remember."

"Are you interested in a repeat performance?" he murmurs, his fingers brushing over her skin.

"I . . . uhh. Don't get me wrong, I really want to. That night was . . . wow. I've never experienced anything like it, but I'm waiting for someone, and I was hoping that maybe when he got here . . ."

The man laughs. "Say no more," he chides. "I know that look. You've found someone special."

Becs blanches. "Woah. Let's not be hasty. Don't you go scaring a girl by throwing around big accusations like that," she says, greedily taking another long sip of her Cosmo as I laugh at her pain, desperately ignoring the heavy gaze coming from across the club. It's strange he hasn't disappeared into his office like he usually does when he's not ready to play.

"And what about you?" the man asks, his gaze on mine as he steps around Becs and offers me his hand, his dazzling eyes locked on mine. "Caesar."

I take his hand, my cheeks flushing under his heavy stare. "I'm Aspen."

"Beautiful name for a beautiful girl."

Goddamn. My stupid cheeks. I feel the burning, but I also feel Izaac's stare like two lasers penetrating the back of my head. "Thank you."

His gaze drops to the green wristband. "You wear green," he states.

"I do," I say with a nod, lifting my Cosmo to my lips. "I've never done this before."

Caesar nods. "We'll take it slow," he says, offering me his hand again. "Would you like to go somewhere a little more private?"

My gaze flicks toward Izaac, and I watch as he slowly shakes his head. Honestly, I don't even know if he realizes he's doing it, but his disapproval has me getting to my feet and placing my hand in his.

Caesar leads me across the VIP lounge toward a small seating area, and the nerves begin settling inside of me. It's a little cramped over here and won't allow for too many people, nothing like the wide-open space he was in with Becs last time. There were at least four guys with her that night, but this space will allow for three at most. Though so far, he hasn't made a move to welcome anyone to the party.

He takes the glass out of my hand before placing it down on the small table in front of us. I expect him to ask me to sit down, to ease me into it, but instead, he moves in behind me, adjusting my body just enough to put me directly in Izaac's eye line.

Caesar's hands fall to my waist, his lips skirting over my neck. "Mmmm, beautiful Aspen. You smell divine," he murmurs as his hand lowers down my thigh and brushes across my bare skin. I suck in a breath, melting back into him, unable to keep from picturing Izaac's hands on my body, his lips on my neck.

His fingers find the spaghetti strap of my dress, and he slowly rolls it down my shoulder before his lips roam along the exposed skin. My knees shake, and as his hand clutches my waist, I feel another body step into my side.

I gasp, but before I can process, his hands are on me, grazing over my sensitive skin. There's no denying how good it feels, but when my gaze shifts back to Izaac, I can't help but feel this is wrong. So damn wrong.

Anger flashes in Izaac's stare, his hands clenched at his side, and it's clear that whatever bullshit I'm trying to prove, it's working. He tracks their every movement, watching as their hands lay claim to what's already his, as their lips dance across the skin he's so familiar with.

Damn it feels so good, but they're not him.

Izaac's gaze moves back up to mine, and the hurt I see there reflects the agony that's stared back at me through the mirror all week, and a part of me wants to keep going, wants to see how far I can push this, but the other part—the rational part—knows that I need to stop. This isn't what I want, and all I'm doing is hurting him and myself.

Caesar's hand slips down over my hip, trailing lower until it brushes over my thigh again, only this time he doesn't follow the same trail back up, he lingers, his fingers pushing closer toward my core, and the second they brush across my pussy and my hips jolt in response, Izaac turns and walks away.

Agony tears through me, and without his eyes on me, the spell is broken, and all I feel is dirty. "Stop," I say, my body tensing up. "Stop, please."

The two men immediately pull back, their hands flying away from my body as though I'd physically hurt them, and I whip around, my eyes already starting to fill with tears. I need to make this right. How on earth could I have thought this was a good idea? Izaac would never sink to this level to try to make me hurt this way.

"Woah, pretty girl, is everything okay?" Caesar asks. "We didn't hurt you?"

"No, not at all," I tell them, letting them see the regret in my eyes. "I'm sorry. I'm just . . . I'm a mess. I had no business coming here tonight."

"Say no more," the other guy says before they both nod and walk away.

What the hell was I doing?

I need to get out of here. Only, how can I leave things like that with Izaac? I need to see him.

Not willing to risk picking up my drink after it was put down by some man I've never formally met before, I leave it behind and cut through the VIP lounge. My hands shake as I try to blink back the tears. God, he's never going to speak to me again.

Knowing he's got to be around here somewhere, I consider going back to the bar and asking them if they could get him for me, but there's only one place I know he'll come for me, one place we can truly be alone and talk through everything—the dark room.

Bypassing the bar and Becs, I make my way to the familiar room and step inside before dimming the lights just the way I like it. They're low enough that I can still see but dark enough to have settled my nerves. I don't get those kinds of nerves with him anymore unless butterflies count, but it feels right to take us back to basics.

Making my way into the center of the room, I prepare to wait. He's not going to scramble after me like a love-sick fool. He's going to make me suffer, and he'll leave me here just long enough for me to wonder if he's coming at all, but in the end, he'll come because he can't stand the idea of hurting me even though I was the cold-hearted bitch who set out to cause him pain.

What can I say? Izaac Banks is a better person than I am. He always has been.

The seconds quickly turn into long, drawn-out minutes, and before I know it, at least thirty minutes have passed when I finally hear the door close behind me. The relief overwhelms me, and I close my eyes as I let out a heavy sigh. "I'm sorry," I whimper, certain he can't hear me over the loud music in the club, but I know he senses it. He always does.

Izaac doesn't respond, but when I feel the slight touch at my waist and the soft breath at my shoulder, I sag against him. His arm curls tighter around me, holding me against him, only as his cologne hits my nose, my body stiffens.

This isn't Izaac.

"My sweet angel. So pure and innocent. I knew you'd wait for me."

My eyes widen in horror, and I whip around, pulling out of the man's hold. "Oh, no, no, no," I rush out, finding Ryatt Markin behind me. "I'm so sorry. I was waiting for Izaac."

"You left the door open," he purrs, stepping toward me and tracking my every movement as I back up. "Surely you know the rules of the private rooms by now."

I shake my head, confusion flooding through me. I mean, yeah. I know the rules. If I leave the door open, anyone is welcome to walk in, but I said no. Shouldn't he immediately back off like Caesar and his friend did? Am I getting something wrong here? Am I fair game? This doesn't feel right. I don't like it.

"No, I . . . I'm sorry. I wasn't thinking," I tell him, trying to step around him to make a break for the door. After all, this is the one man Izaac warned me about. "Let me get out of your way so you can get on with your night."

"Come on, now. Don't be like that," he says, his gaze sailing up and down my body with a sick hunger, side-stepping to block my escape. "Don't you think Banks has already had his fair share of you? I'm not going to lie, he's been keeping you locked away in this room, keeping you away from everyone else, and it's got me thinking that there must be something real special about you, something he doesn't want to share. And I get it, you sure are a sight to look at, but you'd be more beautiful without that dress."

He goes to reach for me and my eyes widen. "No. Don't touch me," I growl, my whole body on alert as my heart starts to viciously pound in my chest. "I'm not interested. Now get out of my way. I'm leaving."

"You see, that's just the thing, baby. You're not going anywhere," he says, his tone dropping. "Now that I've walked in here, Banks is going to revoke my membership, and I'm not risking being kicked out without taking a bite of his little slice of heaven first."

"You've got another thing coming if you think you're putting a single hand on me."

Ryatt laughs. "We'll see about that," he says, and not a moment later, he launches toward me, the loud music drowning out my screams..

34

IZAAC

What the fuck am I doing?

Aspen is out in my club, about to let Caesar Eros and Dustin Jacobs fuck her, and all I did was walk away. Where's my fucking backbone? She doesn't want this. I saw it in her eyes, begging me to put a stop to it, needing me to come and take what's always been mine, but instead, I walked away, just like I should have done the second I realized she was the innocent woman who wandered into my dark room.

Don't get me wrong. I'm fucking livid, seeing those assholes put their hands on her welled up something in me that I've never felt before. Yet, here I am, sitting in my office instead of knocking out those fuckers and pulling her into my arms.

Only, I don't think I'm jealous.

This rage within me stems from somewhere else. When it comes to Aspen, what she's doing out there isn't about the emotional connection that she shares with me. It's not even about sex. It's about trying to make me hurt like I hurt her. It's about forcing me to break, forcing me to understand these feelings that have run rampant through me since the second I touched her. But fuck, doesn't she know I already understand what this is? I know I never said it out loud, but I knew it the second I kissed her.

There's no denying it now, I'm in love with her, and right now, the woman I love is about to have two men eight inches inside of her.

Just fucking great.

I had to walk away. I'm at my breaking point.

When she wanted to go out with that asshole from Tinder and the dude she met on campus . . . Now that was jealousy in its rawest form. She wanted to go out with them to make some kind of connection, and while I'll never claim to own her body, I won't hesitate to claim that everything on the inside belongs to me. It always has, and the thought of her giving that to anybody else eats at me.

I want her. But tonight, what she's doing with Caesar and Dustin, that's her decision, and after I walked away and told her to find some other man to love, I don't have a single right to stop her. Anything she does here is on her, and whatever fallout might come from it is also hers to deal with.

Fuck. That makes me feel like a dick because there's no chance in hell that she won't regret this. She's going to spend the next few weeks drowning herself in tequila and hating herself for going through with it. Hell, then she'll hate me for letting it happen, but how am I supposed to step in now? I swore that it was over, swore I'd walk away until I had Austin's blessing, but we all know that's never going to happen.

But shit, if Austin knew I allowed this to happen in my club and I didn't put a stop to it . . . fuck. There goes any chance in hell of rebuilding our friendship. He'll never trust me again, nor should he.

That's my girl out there.

I let her go and nothing has ever hurt me more.

I've spent the last three weeks trying to make things right with Austin, trying to explain myself and fight for everything I had with Aspen. I've camped out at his restaurant until he's had police forcibly send me away. I've broken into his home. Stepped in front of his goddamn car, but he refuses to hear me. Refuses to give me a chance, but if he knew how I felt, knew just how much I love her, maybe he'll hear me out. Perhaps he might even consider looking past all the bullshit to see that maybe I could be good for her.

Who am I fucking kidding?

What's the point? After the way I broke her, there's no going back. I can't fix this now. I always knew I'd never be good enough for her, and with every move I've made, I've only proved that further. Perhaps she truly is better off with someone else.

Fucking hell.

My hand grips the edge of my desk and I force myself to try and calm down, only as the seconds turn into minutes, I find myself flying out of my chair. I need a fucking drink.

Storming back out to the main floor of the VIP lounge, my gaze immediately scans the club, searching every crevice and corner for her and when there's no sign of her, my stomach sinks. Where the hell have they taken her?

Finding Becs still sitting at the bar, her gaze locked on the drink in her hand as opposed to the fucking orgy happening ten feet away from her, I make my way toward her as a strange uneasiness grows in my gut. "Hey," I say, moving in beside her, certain that she's about to tell me to get fucked. That's when I notice both Caesar and Dustin across the club, entertaining some blonde.

Becs glances up at me, her brows arched in confusion as I pause and scan the room again. "Where's Aspen? I thought she was fucking those two assholes."

"What do you mean?" Becs questions. "She couldn't take it. She made them stop, and then I watched her walk away. I figured she was with you. She's been gone for a while."

Fear pounds through my chest. "What?"

"Hey," a familiar and very pissed-off tone cuts through our conversation. "We need to talk."

Fucking hell. Austin's timing has never been great. "Not now," I throw at him through a clenched jaw, my gaze shooting right back to Becs. "Where?"

"The fuck?" Austin grunts, reaching for me. His hand fists into the back of my shirt, and he pulls me back a step before shoving me against the bar. His stare fills with fury, and his fist comes hurtling toward my jaw.

I dodge, barely evading needing a jaw reconstruction before grabbing his fist and pulling him into me. "I said not now," I seethe, letting him hear the absolute fear in my tone before violently shoving him away and grabbing Becs. I pull her to her feet and her eyes widen, fear evident in her eyes. "WHERE THE FUCK IS SHE?"

"Woah," Austin says, finally realizing he's not the only bastard in the room, and seeing the woman beside me isn't some random Vixen member, but the woman who has been keeping his bed warm. "Get your fucking hands off her."

He barrels into me, gripping my arm and yanking me off her before turning toward her, his gaze roaming up and down her body as though I might have hurt her. "Are you okay?" he rushes out, panic flashing in his green eyes—eyes so fucking similar to Aspen's. "Wait. What are you doing here?"

Unease flashes in her eyes. "I, uhhh . . . hi," she says sheepishly, only pissing me off. Is this woman kidding me? Does she not understand that Aspen is here somewhere and nobody knows where the fuck she went or who she's with? Fucking hell.

"Enough of that shit," I say, trying to shove Austin out of the way to get to Becs again, but Austin whirls on me.

"What the fuck is your problem?" he spits. "First, you put your fucking hands on my sister, and now you're grabbing Becs? What the fuck has gotten into you?"

"I don't have fucking time for your bullshit, Austin," I roar, getting in his face. "You want to hate me, then fucking hate me. We can have it out later, but right now, I don't give a shit because every fucking second you waste trying to get in my face and remind me what a fucking bastard I am is one more fucking second that Aspen is left fending for herself, so either get over your bullshit and help me look for her or fuck off."

His eyes widen in horror. "Aspen?" he demands. "What the fuck is she doing here? I thought she was banned."

"Really? You want to get into that right now? Just fucking great. Well you sit here and talk to your fucking girlfriend about that. Hell, maybe order yourself a fucking drink. In the meantime, I'm going to go find your sister and make sure she's not doing something she'll fucking regret, or worse."

"You're fucking kidding me," he scoffs. "Let her go. If she wants to act like a fucking whore, that's her business."

My fist swings faster than I can even understand what I'm doing, and before I know it, I clock him in the face, my fist crashing into his nose, blood spurting across my bar. "That's your goddamn sister you're talking about," I spit. "Have some fucking respect."

"IZAAC!" Becs shrieks, following Austin down to the ground and gripping his shoulder in horror. Her gaze snaps up to me. "What the fuck is your problem? If you were so damn worried about her, then you never should have let her go in the first place. If she's not with you right now, it's because she doesn't want to be. You don't fucking deserve her after the shit you've put her through."

Every single word she says is true, but that doesn't mean that I'm about to walk away and let her do something stupid. If I find her and she's content with what she's doing, then I'll walk away, but if she's in trouble and I didn't do something to help her, I'll never fucking forgive myself.

Becs flies back to her feet, leaning over the bar and yelling toward my bar staff. "Can I get some ice please?"

As she straightens up, I take hold of her wrist and fix her with a hard stare, letting her have the full force of my rage. "Either tell me where the fuck she went or get out of my goddamn club."

Her eyes widen as Austin pushes up to his elbows, muttering something about his nose being broken, but I don't fucking care. In any other situation, I'd probably be down there beside him, my nose in worse condition. I've always had his back, and he's always had mine, but not now. Not when it comes to Aspen.

Becs visibly swallows and the fight leaves her. She points down the hallway toward the row of private rooms, and just like that, I know exactly where she went, and there's only one reason why she'd go down there.

I take off at a sprint before Becs even gets a chance to argue and come to the door of our room barely a second later. The door is locked and my rage turns into blind fury. My doors don't have locks so someone must have shoved something against the handle. Doors don't get locked in my club. It's not exactly a written rule, but it's a common practice that's known to my members. In case of emergencies or if someone wants to make a quick getaway, they should be able to do that.

Bringing my foot up, I slam my boot against the door, not giving a shit if I splinter the wood. I'll replace it, but what I can't replace is Aspen, and as the door barges open and slams against the internal drywall of the dark room, I find her, blood smeared across her face and fear in her eyes.

Ryatt Markin stands before her, and I take a second, trying to figure out what the fuck is going on, but finding her dress torn with red marks across her skin and a blood-soaked pen in her hand, I understand exactly what just went down.

Aspen whimpers, finding me at the door and realizing nothing is going to happen to her now, she falls to her knees, barely able to catch herself as violent sobs break free from her chest.

My stare lands on Markin.

He's just as beat up, only unlike Aspen, he's been stabbed with that damn pen, just the way I taught her to. He clutches his neck, blood pooling over his hand as he quickly drains of color. He's going to die here tonight and Vixen will turn into a crime scene. Hell, it'll probably be shut down, but I'm okay with that as long as my girl is alright.

But it'll be a cold day in hell that I let this asshole go out without fearing my wrath first.

Striding toward him, I grab him by the blood-soaked throat and watch as his eyes widen in fear, and then as he bleeds out, I lay into him, my fists pounding one after another until he's no longer able to hold his weight and drops to the ground.

"FUCK!" I distantly hear Austin roar from somewhere behind me before Becs cries out. "Holy shit. Aspen."

I feel Austin at my back, his strong grip clutching at my arm and trying to pull me away. "Stop. He's fucking dead," he grits, desperately trying to pull me away, but I can't stop. This motherfucker just tried to rape my girl. "Stop, Izaac."

I pull against his hold, but the bastard is relentless, and when Aspen rushes in, putting herself right in front of me, gripping my face, and forcing me to meet her haunted green stare, I finally begin to calm. "It's okay," she breathes, tears streaking down her face. "I'm okay."

The fight leaves me, and I throw myself at her, wrapping her in my arms and holding her against my chest. "I'm so fucking sorry," I murmur into her hair as she breaks, her heavy sobs vibrating against my chest. "You're okay, Birdy. It's over. I've got you."

I say it over and over until I finally start to believe the words, and I realize that I will never let her go, never force her to walk away ever again. Aspen Ryder is mine and I'll forever be hers.

"Fucking hell," Becs says. "What are we supposed to do?"

I shake my head. I've been trained for this shit, had to deal with it a handful of times, but right now, all that matters is Aspen, and seeing that I can't handle this, Austin quickly takes over, glancing at Becs, whose mascara is now smudged down her cheeks. "Call the police and let them know what happened and that a man is dead, then let the bar staff know there's been an incident and the club needs to be vacated immediately," he tells her.

She quickly nods and goes to make her way out of the room, but not before sparing one more glance toward Aspen, a deep guilt in her eyes. "Anything else?" she asks Austin.

He shakes his head. "Just stay at the bar after that. You don't need to see any more of this."

She nods again before finally making her way out of the room that once held so many fucking incredible memories for me and Aspen, but now it's tainted by what happened here tonight. "There's security footage, so anything that went down in here is on record," Austin says, starting to pace. "She won't get in trouble for this."

"I should have seen this coming," I mutter, holding on to her even tighter as she falls apart in my arms. "The bastard has been infatuated with her every time she walked through the fucking door."

Austin curses under his breath, shaking his head. "Can you just . . . can you take her home without fucking that up?"

"Me? I'm the one fucking everything up?" I demand. "The only thing I fucked up was walking away from her because of your fragile ego. So yeah, I'm gonna take her home, but I'm taking her to my place, which is where she's going to be indefinitely because one more fucking day away from her isn't going to cut it for me. So when you man-the-fuck-up and realize just how much your bullshit is hurting the people around you and come begging for forgiveness, that's where you'll find her."

"You're fucking kidding me, right?"

"Fucking hell, Austin. Do I sound like I'm kidding?" I spit at him, scooping her into my arms and holding her to my chest. "Get it through your fucking head. I am in love with your sister, and yeah, she deserves a shitload better than any life I could ever provide her, but for some fucked-up reason, she chose me, and now that I have her, I'm not giving her up. I'm done pushing her away just to make things right with you because you've made it damn clear you're never going to come around to it, but this shit right here puts it all in perspective. Aspen nearly got raped waiting for me in that damn room, and she had to fight off her attacker alone because I was too fucking worried about what you think. But look at you, Austin. You're so fucking angry with us that you can't even look at her or find the decency to ask if she's okay. You might despise me and be pissed with her, but she's still your sister, and she needs you."

His mouth opens, and I see the fight flare in his eyes, but he quickly shuts his mouth again, realizing now is not the time to get into it. I'm sure we'll still have it out, and when we do, it's not going to be pretty, but right now, all that matters is getting her home.

And with that, I step around Austin and walk out of the dark room, leaving this fresh hell behind.

35

IZAAC

Pulling up at the top of my circle driveway, I cut the engine and hurry around to the passenger side before opening the door and reaching for Aspen. She didn't say a word the whole way home, just sat there silently crying as I held her hand, feeling completely helpless.

I didn't know how to help her or what to say to make it better, but I don't think anything I could have done would have helped.

Tonight she killed a man in order to save herself, and no matter what, I will stand by her. Whatever she needs from me is hers.

"Come on," I murmur, scooping her into my arms, just as I'd done in the dark room. "Let me get you cleaned up."

She nods against my chest, and it's the first real response I've gotten from her. Without skipping a beat, I make my way inside my home and walk straight into the bathroom. I keep her turned away from the mirror as I peel her out of her blood-soaked dress and help her out of her heels.

I toss the dress into the bathtub, certain that at some point, the cops are going to be knocking on my door and demanding they take Aspen down to the station for questioning, and when they do, they're going to want to enter her dress into evidence. But as for the blood on her face and under her nails, I'll be washing it away. I don't want her to have to live with the evidence on her body for a second longer than necessary. Besides, as Austin said, every room at Vixen has surveillance. The cops will have everything they need to close this case. The only gray area is the solid beating Ryatt took from me right as he took his final breath, but considering the circumstances, I'm sure that will get looked over. But if it doesn't, then I'll gladly accept any consequence that's thrown my way.

Reaching into the shower, I turn on the taps, and when the water is warm enough, I lead Aspen in, only she clutches on to me, refusing to let go. Quickly tearing my clothes off, I step into the shower with her. "Everything's going to be okay," I tell her as I lather soap between my hands to clean the blood off her.

She snuggles into my chest as the water runs red at our feet, her arms so tight around my ribs I can barely take a full breath. "I thought . . . He wanted to . . ."

"It's okay," I murmur, my hand brushing over the back of her head, trying to keep her calm. "I know what he wanted, but you fought back. You didn't let him touch you. You did everything you were supposed to do."

"I didn't know what to do," she cries. "All I could remember was what you said about the pen and holding my thumb on the end so it wouldn't slip through my fingers, but I didn't want to do it. I didn't mean to kill him. I just wanted to get away. I . . . I couldn't, but then he grabbed me and threw me down, and I hit my head. The next thing I knew, he had his hand under my dress, and I tried to scream. I screamed for you, but the music was too loud. Nobody could hear me, and I realized I was on my own. I had to fight him off, otherwise, he was going to—"

She pauses for a second, not ready to say what we both know was going to happen, not ready to face the harsh reality of everything that happened tonight, but I'm not here to force that on her. All I want is for her to be okay.

"I had to do it," she whispers, heavy sobs tearing from the back of her throat.

"You did," I tell her with pride as a pang of horrendous guilt cuts through my chest, realizing I was sitting at my desk, doing nothing but sulking while all of this was going down. "You did what you had to do, and even though you were terrified, you fought. You didn't let him win, Aspen. You were a rockstar, and I fucking love you for how brave you were."

"You told Austin that you're in love with me."

"Yeah," I murmur, wiping blood from her face. "I did."

"You never told me."

"I didn't need to," I tell her. "You knew. It's just like you said, you could feel it in the way I looked at you, and when I touched you, there wasn't a bit of doubt. You've known all along. It was just a matter of me understanding what it was, but if that's what you want, I'll tell you every day of the rest of our lives."

"I thought you'd given up on us," she tells me, breaking me all over again. "You told me to leave and fall in love with somebody else, and then Austin told me that you didn't even try to fight for us. I thought you were done."

I close my eyes and let out a sigh. Of course Austin said that. "Birdy, I've been so far up Austin's ass these past few weeks, demanding he hear me out, that I practically know how many times he shakes his dick after he takes a piss," I tell her. "I've been arrested twice for trespassing, and nearly run over by your asshole brother, but sure, if that's his version of me not trying, then I haven't been trying."

At that, she lifts her head off my chest, her eyes searching mine. "You've been fighting for us?"

"Every fucking day, Aspen, and trust me, it hasn't been pretty. Your brother can be a real asshole when he wants to be."

"Tell me about it," she mutters under her breath, somewhat sounding like herself, and making me wonder if talk of our relationship is helping to take her mind off everything that just went down.

Wanting to keep her calm, I tip her head back and run the water through her long strands of chestnut hair before lathering shampoo through it. I'm sure I'm not doing a very good job, but it's better than the alternative of having blood matted in it.

"I'm not walking away this time," I tell her, keeping the topic on us. "I fucked up, Aspen, and I understand if you want to keep that distance between us. I don't deserve another chance after how much I've hurt you, but I'm done waiting for Austin to come around. He made it clear tonight that he can't get past his anger. At least, not yet anyway. And I'm done hurting the woman I love to cater to his emotions. I want to be with you, Aspen. I want to start a life with you. I want to build a home and have a bunch of kids with your beautiful green eyes."

"And if I'm locked in a prison cell?"

"It's not going to come down to that," I tell her. "You're going to be okay."

As if finding a little shred of strength, Aspen begins rinsing the shampoo out of her hair. She closes her eyes, and it's clear that she's deep in thought, but there's no telling where her head has gone. Though it doesn't go unnoticed that she hasn't exactly responded to me saying I want to be with her, but now isn't the time to push it.

We finish in the shower, and I reach for a towel before wrapping her up and leading her back to my room. I find a shirt for her to wear, and soon enough, she's curled in my arms with her head resting against my chest. "I killed a man, Izaac."

I nod. "You did, but I don't want you to linger on it. It was an act of survival. It was self-defense. You did nothing wrong," I explain. "I know it feels impossible, but I want you to get some sleep. You're in shock. Sooner or later, the police are going to knock on the door, and they're going to want to take you in for questioning, and when that happens, it'll be good to go in with a clear head."

"And if I don't have a clear head?"

"Then it's okay because Vixen has surveillance cameras." Aspen nods against my chest, and as she lets out a shaky breath, I feel the hot tears fall from her eyes and pool on my chest. "Everything's going to be alright, Birdy. I'm going to be right here. I'll take care of you."

Aspen doesn't respond as she lays in my arms and tries to sleep. It takes almost an hour for her to stop trembling, and when I'm sure she's finally asleep, I lean toward her, press a kiss to her forehead, and slip out from beneath her.

I fix the blanket around her shoulders and hope like fuck that she doesn't wake while I'm gone, but I have to get back down to Vixen and figure out what's going to happen from here. And despite knowing how badly Austin wants to kick my ass right now, it's not fair for all of this bullshit to fall on his shoulders. It's my club. I should be the one down there answering questions and consoling my staff.

After sparing another glance at Aspen and making sure she's all good, I pull on a shirt and a pair of sweatpants and take off again. My phone has been ringing non-stop for over an hour, but I've kept it on silent, determined to settle Aspen first.

The drive back to Vixen takes no time at all, and as I pull down the road, I find the street lit with red and blue lights. There are cops everywhere, police cruisers, ambulances, and a good section of the road is marked off with police tape.

Taking a quick look around, I find the guy who looks like he's in charge and make my way toward him while distantly noticing Austin sitting in the back of an ambulance, reluctantly getting his broken nose looked at.

"Sir, you can't be here," an officer says as I stride toward his superior, watching the cops flood in and out of my club.

The cop's whiny tone gets the sergeant's attention, and he whips around, ready to fend me off, but seeing the determination in my eyes, he pauses and waits for whatever I've come to say.

"My name is Izaac Banks," I say, having no doubt that Austin has already given him my information. Hell, he probably belongs to one of the many missed calls on my phone. "I'm the owner of Vixen, and I'm happy to give you any information or answer any questions you might have. I just have one condition to my cooperation."

He arches a brow. "Let's hear it," he says, his tone telling me I have wriggle room and that I'm not about to be dragged away in cuffs for beating the shit out of an almost dead man, assuming he's already seen the footage and knows what happened.

"You leave Aspen alone for the night. I've taken her back to my house to get some sleep. She's shaken, scared, and has every intention of cooperating. She will be happy to answer any question you throw at her. However, after everything she's been through tonight, I just ask that you give her a few hours to rest and come to terms with everything that's gone down tonight."

"Son, you understand I have a dead body and a lot of unanswered questions."

"I do. However, I also know that every square inch of my club is monitored by surveillance, and every question you could possibly have can be answered by watching the footage."

He presses his lips into a hardline. "So it seems," he says. "However, I will be running my investigation as I see fit, and until my officers get a chance to completely go through that footage and rule out any wrongdoing, Ms. Ryder will require extensive questioning."

"I understand that, and I am happy to take your officers to my place to get her. I just ask that she be allowed a few hours of rest is all. Your officers are welcome to camp outside my home if they want. In the meantime, is there anything you can tell me in regard to my club? I have a lot of employees who would no doubt be wondering if they have a job right now, and quite frankly, I'm wondering the same thing."

The sergeant talks to me for a while, explaining how these things usually work, and twenty minutes later, after an officer has confirmed that Aspen did indeed act in self-defense and that they won't be pressing charges, I finally get to walk away with a promise to bring her down to the precinct to make a statement first thing in the morning.

I find Austin leaning against his car, halfway down the road, his gaze locked on the sight before him, watching as Ryatt's body is wheeled out on a gurney, locked inside a body bag. The sergeant didn't give much information in regard to how soon the cops will clear out of my club or when I'll be able to reopen for business, but I can safely assume it could be a while. After all, I'm going to need to do a complete renovation on that particular room.

"She's in the clear," I tell him, settling in at his side and leaning against the hood of his car, leaving just enough space between us in case he decides to start throwing punches again.

He nods, his gaze dropping to the asphalt, and the guilt radiating off him nearly drops me to my knees. "She almost got raped tonight, and I was too busy hating her to even ask if she was okay."

My lips press into a hard line, and I nod, not knowing how he expects me to respond.

"She's my fucking sister. *My baby sister,*" he says. "If something had happened, or if I'd lost her. Fuck. You don't know the cruel things I said to her when she came to me, begging me to hear her out. I practically called her a desperate whore who couldn't keep her legs crossed and then kicked her out, and when she broke down and cried on my living room floor, I ignored her as though she didn't matter."

"She knows that's not what you think," I tell him. "She's just waiting for you to come around and talk it out."

"You don't fucking get it," he says. "She walked into the room and was attacked, and while she would have been fucking terrified, in that moment, she thought that she couldn't rely on me. That I wouldn't have her fucking back, and she would have been right. If she had called me needing help, I would have let the call go to voicemail. Fuck, it wouldn't have even rung because I fucking blocked her. It's bad enough that I was out of town when that asshole tried to follow her home, and now this? I keep letting her down."

"Then get your head out of your fucking ass and make it up to her," I snap. "Do you have any idea how much she's hurting because of the bullshit you've been throwing at her? It's killing her, and you're too caught up in your own feelings to even see what you're doing to her."

"Stop talking about my sister like you fucking know her. You don't."

"I do."

"Oh, that's right. Because you think you're suddenly in love with her? She let you fuck her a few times and now you're declaring your undying love?"

I grab him by the scruff of his shirt and pull him in. "You might be my best friend, but talk about her like that again, and I won't hesitate to drop you," I tell him before releasing my hold on his shirt and shoving him away. "This isn't something that's going to go away. I want to be with her. I want to start a life with her, and fuck, maybe even one day, if she'll have me, make her my wife. This isn't just some stupid phase, Austin. When are you going to see that? Do you really think I would put twenty-five years of friendship on the line if this didn't mean anything?"

Austin clenches his jaw. "What kind of life do you think you're going to give her?" he questions, not impressed. "You're not right for her. You own nightclubs and want to expand across the country. What's that supposed to mean for Aspen? Is she supposed to spend her life following you across the world, watching you chase your dreams while she sits back twiddling her fucking thumbs? Fuck no."

"Honestly, I don't know, but what I do know is that she deserves the right to decide that for herself rather than having you decide it for her. You've clearly shown that you don't actually give a shit about what she wants. These past three weeks have more than proven that."

"So what? I'm just supposed to accept that you're together now?"

"Yeah," I scoff. "That's exactly what you're supposed to do.

Because while I can handle you pulling away and treating me like shit, she can't. You are the fucking sun in her sky and these past few weeks you've forced her to live in absolute darkness. She needs you now more than ever, so get the fuck over it. Swallow your pride and be there for her."

Having said what I needed to say, I go to walk away when he calls out behind me. "And you?"

I stop and turn back, too fucking tired for this. "Honestly, I don't give a shit anymore. You might despise me for going behind your back to be with her, and up until two hours ago, I would have done anything to earn your forgiveness, but now I'm wondering if that was for her sake or yours," I tell him. "I betrayed your trust in the worst way, and I've spent the past two months hurting her over and over again because of the crippling guilt I felt for what I'd done. But you're supposed to be her greatest supporter. You're supposed to want the world for her and help her achieve everything she's ever dreamed of, and seeing the way you've treated her over these past few weeks . . . I don't know, man. You're not who I thought you were. So yeah, I'm sorry I betrayed your trust and went behind your back, but I'm not sorry that I fell in love with your sister and found something so fucking real that it hurts just to be away from her. If you can come to terms with that and learn how to be in her life without tearing her down, then great. If not, then I'm done. I'm going to be with her with or without your approval, and I really fucking hope that you can get on the right side of this because it's not going away. I love you like a brother, Austin, and it would mean the world to both of us if we didn't have to keep this from you."

"So, that's it, huh? You're just throwing away twenty-five years of friendship?"

"Nah, man. You are," I tell him. "You're choosing to believe that I'm not good enough for her, that I'm too fucking broken to offer her anything real without even trying to dig a little deeper and see what's right in front of your eyes, and because of that, you're punishing all of us."

"You're really that in love with her?"

I nod. "Yeah, man. I am."

He lets out a heavy breath, nodding. Not because he agrees, but because he's trying to hear what I'm saying, and with that, I finally turn and walk away, hoping like fuck he's able to make the right decision and return to Aspen as the loveable brother she's always idolized and adored.

36

ASPEN

It's after midday by the time Izaac and I walk out of the police station, and I'm not going to lie, today hasn't exactly been the best day for me. From the second I woke up, Izaac had me down at the police station answering questions, forcing me to relive it all, and just when I thought it couldn't get any worse, the detectives had me watch the surveillance footage from the dark room, and it sent me into a blind panic. I spent an hour trying to calm down, and the second I was able to, they hit me with the rest of their questions.

I don't regret it though—the questions, not the pen-stabbing. That's going to take me a while to come to terms with, and something tells me that I'll be spending long hours with a therapist trying to work through it, but I'm glad it's over. The police asked me what they needed to know, and with the footage they were provided, it was easily marked as self-defense. They still need to do an autopsy and tick all of their boxes, but they've told me I'm off the hook. That didn't stop them from giving me the don't leave town speech.

As for Izaac, considering the circumstances, his part in it was shrugged off, but he didn't seem concerned. If they wanted to hit him with battery charges, he was willing to accept them.

Izaac pulls up outside my apartment, and I press my lips into a tight line, glancing up into those dark eyes. "Are you really sure this is a good idea?" I ask. "I get that you're all about not holding back and wanting to make this happen, but you realize by kidnapping me and taking me home to your place, you're essentially forcing me to move in with you, right?"

He gives me a blank stare.

"We fight, Izaac. All the time," I point out, just in case he hadn't figured it out yet. "Me moving in with you while this is still so new . . . it'll be a disaster. Not to mention, you've never lived in such close quarters with a woman . . . like, ever. And your mom doesn't count."

"Aspen—"

"Do you know how gross we are?" I ask. "Our hair comes out in the shower and clogs the drain, and when it gets tangled in my fingers, I make little swirlies with it on the shower screen."

"Would you shut the fuck up about your shower swirlies and get your ass up to your apartment and start packing?" he demands. "I'm not changing my mind. I want you with me. Besides, in case you haven't noticed, trouble seems to follow you everywhere you go, and it would be a shitload easier keeping you out of it if you came home to me every night."

I scoff, gaping at him. "Oh, I see. This is all because you think I need a full-time babysitter."

"I swear to God, Aspen. Either walk your ass upstairs and start packing your things, or I'll—"

"You'll what?"

"You're infuriating, Aspen Ryder."

"Right back at ya, Izaac Banks."

"Get your ass out of my car."

A stupid grin tears across my face, and I roll my eyes before grabbing my bag and reaching for the door handle. By the time I get out and am standing in front of his Escalade, he's right there with me, his hand pressed to my lower back as he leads me toward the main entrance of the apartment complex.

It's a quick walk up to my apartment, and the second we get inside, Izaac storms right into my bedroom closet, grabbing handfuls of clothes and tossing them onto my bed, and all I can do is watch.

This really is going to be a disaster. But I can't wait.

Living with Izaac has been something I've dreamed about for years, but it was always so unachievable, and honestly, I don't even really understand how we got here. It's all happening so quickly, but I'm here for the ride. If he's ready to finally see what's been in front of his face all this time, then who the hell am I to keep him from that?

I lean against the doorframe of my bedroom, a slow smile spreading across my face.

Izaac Banks is in love with me.

God, I've known it for weeks, but it's so surreal.

As if realizing he's emptying my closet all alone, he looks back at me, watching the way I stare at him, and I see the need to tell me off flashing in his eyes, only it's gone a moment later. He steps away from the closet, his gaze locked on me, and as he stalks toward me, a thrill pulses through my veins.

Izaac moves right in front of me, lifting his hand and brushing his fingers down the side of my face, his gaze darkening as he holds my stare. His fingers trail down to my chin before lifting, and not a moment later, his lips are on mine. He kisses me deeply, his hand falling to my waist and pulling me in tighter against him.

Our kiss is brief and lasts only a moment, but God, it's everything. He pulls back just an inch before dropping his forehead against mine. "Do you have any fucking idea what you're doing to me?"

A smile pulls at my lips, and just as I go to melt back into him, a knock sounds at my door. My brows furrow, and I hold Izaac's stare. "You expecting anyone?" he asks.

I shake my head. "No. It's probably just Becs coming to check on me after everything that went down last night."

He nods and pushes away from me before striding to the door, not bothering to look through the peephole before grabbing the handle and pulling it open.

"Oh great. You're here," Austin's voice rings through my small apartment.

Unease pounds through my veins as I keep my distance. I know

Austin was at Vixen last night, but I was in too much shock to even remember if he said anything or not. All I know is that the last time I spoke to him, he left me sobbing on the floor of his living room with my heart in pieces, and I'm not going to lie, I'm not exactly looking for a repeat performance.

Izaac moves out of the way as Austin strides into my home, his cautious gaze coming to mine. "What are you doing here?" I ask, barely able to hold his stare as Izaac closes the door behind him and lingers in my living room.

"I came to talk," he mutters, looking just as uncomfortable as I feel.

I bite the inside of my cheek, already feeling myself beginning to break. I don't know if I can do this right now. The nasty words he said are still too fresh in my mind. Every part of me hurts every time I think about how our relationship has fallen apart over the past few weeks. I don't know if I can take any more of it.

Austin slowly creeps toward me, and I shake my head. "I don't have anything to say to you."

"I know," he says, nodding his head. "After the way I've treated you, I didn't expect you to say anything, but there's a lot I need to say to you."

I hold his stare, waiting for him to get on with it when he awkwardly shifts his gaze to Izaac and arches a brow. "You mind?" he asks, very unsubtly requesting he get lost.

Izaac just grins and flops down on my couch, his arms spread out as though he's as comfortable as ever. "Not at all," he says, nodding toward me. "Go right ahead."

Austin shoots a glare at his best friend. "Really? You're gonna be like that?"

"Someone's gotta make sure you keep your bullshit to yourself," Izaac throws back at him.

Austin rolls his eyes and lets out a heavy sigh, knowing Izaac well enough to know there's no point arguing this. If he says he's staying, then he's staying. End of story.

I keep my arms crossed over my chest, terrified of how this is going to go down, and when Austin moves right into me and pulls me into a tight hug, it's the last thing I expect. I pause for a moment, needing a second to process what's happening before I shove him off me, only he's holding too tight and clearly doesn't plan to let go any time soon. "You know I love you, right?" he murmurs, the words like a knife right through my chest.

"You don't treat the people you love like that, Austin."

"I know. I'm sorry," he says. "I really fucked up."

"Ya think?" I grunt, blatantly refusing to hug him back.

Letting out a sigh, he finally releases me and takes a hesitant step back, his green eyes locked on mine, and the sincerity within them has me wanting to crumble. "You're my little sister, and all I've ever wanted was to look out for you and make sure you had the best of everything. The best schools, the best friends, the best opportunities, but when it came to Izaac . . . I was selfish. I wasn't thinking about what you wanted, and I couldn't see anything past my own hurt. I fucked up, Aspen. I said things to you that I'll never be able to make up for, and the way I acted . . . I should have been there for you and given you a chance to explain what was going on. Instead, I was blinded by rage."

I clench my jaw, feeling the tears begin to well in my eyes when I raise my chin and decide to give it to him straight. "Do you know why I was at Vixen last night?"

A hardness creeps into his face, but he remains silent, waiting for me to continue. "Because you lied and told me that Izaac didn't fight for me. I was there trying to prove something to myself, and don't get me wrong, I'm not trying to say that you're at fault for what happened in that dark room. I was the one who made the decision to go there and behave the way I did. I walked into that room and put myself in a vulnerable position, and that will always be on me, but you're the one who put it in my head. You planted the seeds that told me that I wasn't enough, and because of that, I needed to see what he would do."

"You have no fucking idea how sick it makes me knowing what I said to you," Austin tells me.

"You practically called me a whore," I remind him, just in case he might have forgotten. "You were acting as though I laid out naked for him and waved my ass in his face until he broke, and that's not even a little bit close to what went down. It was—"

"Woah," he says, cutting me off. "Spare me the details. It's bad enough knowing it happened, let alone having a visual of it in my head."

I cringe. "Sorry," I say. "But just know that neither of us purposefully set out to hurt you. It just . . . happened."

Austin holds up his hand, the conversation wavering too close to sex for him to be able to continue down that path. "Just . . . stop," he begs. "I can't hear about how you two just happened. Maybe one day I'll be able to stomach the idea of it, but not yet."

"Noted," I say with a nod.

Austin holds my gaze for a moment, heaviness lingering between us. "Look, about what I said at my place," he starts, resignation thick in his tone. "Surely you know that I don't think that at all. I know I'm overprotective and tend to lose my shit whenever I hear that you're dating someone, but surely you know that I don't really think that. There's just something about the idea of you and Izaac together that makes my skin crawl, and after this insane crush you've had on him all your life, it was just the easiest way to strike back."

I nod and step toward him. "You know him, Austin. You know he's a good man with morals and a kind heart. I know you've always wanted someone for me who would protect me in the same way that you do, but open your eyes. He's always been that guy," I murmur, sparing a glance toward the incredible man in question and melting at the way he stares back at me, a softness in his eyes that I've always loved. "When I was hiding in the bushes and you were out of town, he didn't hesitate to come for me, and it's been that way since we were kids. Why wouldn't you want that for me?"

Austin presses his hands to his temples and starts to pace across my small living room. "Of course I want that for you," he finally says. "It's just . . . it's a hard pill to swallow."

"I know."

He pauses, looking back at me with that same hurt in his eyes.

"You're really moving in with him?"

I shrug my shoulders, knowing this is moving fast, even by normal relationship standards. "Apparently, I'm a hazard to myself and need constant babysitting to be safe."

Austin rolls his eyes. "Well, I could have told you that."

I press my lips into a tight line. "You're still mad."

"I'm going to be mad for a while," he admits. "It'll take a minute for me to get used to this, and I can't guarantee that every time I see the two of you together, it's not going to make me want to knock the bastard out, but you're my sister, and despite everything I've said and the way I've acted, you're my favorite person in the world, and if this is what truly makes you happy, then I want that for you."

I feel the first ray of hope blossoming in my chest, quickly spreading through my body and wiping out the darkness as though it were never there. "Really?" I ask, distantly aware of the way Izaac gets to his feet.

"Yeah, really," Austin confirms. "Just don't go flaunting it in front of me, and we'll be good."

I throw myself at my brother, my arms locking so damn tight around him. I'm almost positive I'm strangling him, but instead of complaining or pushing me away like he usually does, he wraps me in his arms and holds on just as tight. "You forgive me?" he murmurs in my ear.

"Depends. Are you going to stand here and pretend like I'm the only one who's been going behind the other's back and falling in love with their best friend?"

Austin stiffens and pulls back, his eyes wide with alarm. "You, uhhh . . . know about all of that, huh?"

"Of course, I do. You're hardly discreet, and Becs has a big mouth. She tells me everything."

"Shit," he grunts as Izaac moves in at my side, and I don't miss the way Austin tracks his every step, but thankfully Izaac is smart enough to keep his hands off me. "Are you okay with it? You don't hate me?"

"There's a lot of things I want to hate you for right now, but that's not one of them. You're perfect together, and if anyone is going to drive you insane and make you suffer for the bullshit you've thrown at us, it's Becs."

Austin grips the back of his neck and rolls his eyes. "Yeah, she kinda has been."

Pride booms in my chest. I knew Becs would have my back with this.

I grin wide, but it quickly fades away when I look between the boys. "And as for you two?" I ask, nerves slicing through my veins like a million tiny razors. "Are things going to be okay here?"

"He's said what he needed to say," Austin informs me, sparing a cautious glance at Izaac. "And despite everything, he's still my best friend. Assuming he's down to forgive me too."

Izaac scoffs. "Depends. Are you going to help me move all her shit into my place? I can't do it on my own."

"Uhhh . . . and what do you think I am?" I ask, offended by the idea that I won't be very much help.

"A hindrance," Izaac teases before focusing on the asshole before him. "What do you say? I don't plan on walking away from her, and I'd really fucking like it if I didn't have to walk away from you."

Austin groans and looks around at the piles of my shit scattered from one end of my apartment to the next. "We can't just call a moving company and go and get a beer instead?"

"Nope."

"Then fine," he says with a heavy sigh. "But do me a favor and keep your hands off her until I'm out of sight. I'm not even close to being ready to see that shit again."

A wide smile pulls at my lips, and while everything is still strained between us, I know everything is going to be okay, especially when I go to throw myself at him again and he quickly evades my affection. "Ughhh, get away," he grunts, my playful, pain-in-the-ass brother is back from the dead. "There's no telling where those hands have been."

I can't help but laugh as Austin rolls his eyes, and not a moment later, he has his car keys in his hand. "I'll go find boxes and tape," he says, turning on his heel, clearly not thrilled about being roped into helping us. "And when I get back, I swear to God, if I can smell sex in the air, we're really going to have problems."

Austin disappears out the door, and I burst into laughter just as Izaac grabs me and pulls me against his chest, his strong arms so perfectly wrapped around me. "I love you so fucking much," he says and every syllable out of his mouth does things to me I never knew were possible.

His lips drop to mine, and he kisses me deeply. "Say it again," I murmur against his warm lips, knowing with every fiber of my soul that I will never get used to how good it sounds to hear those words on his lips.

"I'm in love with you, Aspen," he tells me, pulling back just an inch to meet my stare. "I'm done pulling away and denying what was right here all along. You're mine and I'm yours, and I'm ready to start building a life with you. I've already wasted so much time."

"You really mean it?" I ask. "We're doing this?"

"Fuck yeah, we are," he tells me, grabbing my ass and hoisting me into his arms. "Now, shut up and kiss me before I'm forced to throw you down on that coffee table and fuck you until you scream."

My brow arches as I hold his stare, my core already throbbing. "Don't threaten me with a good time, Banks," I warn him, already getting wet at just the thought of what he could do to me. "Not unless you can back it up."

He stares right back at me, a wicked grin stretching across his perfect lips as he turns and walks through the threshold of my bedroom. "Oh, I can more than back it up."

"Prove it," I challenge, the giddiness rocking through me as his hands tighten on my ass. "But you should know, I don't plan on changing my mind until I've been thoroughly fucked, and something tells me that could take hours."

"Your brother will be back in twenty minutes tops," he warns me.

I grin wide, desperate to feel the way he so easily sets my body on fire. "Then you better lock the door because I don't intend on making this a quick game, and I can guarantee that he's not going to like what he hears when he walks back into my apartment."

"You're fucking trouble, Birdy."

I hear the soft click of the bedroom door locking, and when Izaac's heated gaze returns to mine, the air between us becomes electrified. He kisses me deeply, and not a moment later, he throws me down on my bed before shrugging out of his shirt. As my greedy gaze takes in his sculpted body, he comes down on top of me, more than ready to spend every minute of the rest of our lives giving me everything he's got.

EPILOGUE

ASPEN

THREE MONTHS LATER

Walking through the door of Aspen's, a wide smile breaks across my face. It's Austin's opening night and every seat is filled. There's a line waiting out the door, despite the restaurant having been booked out months in advance. There's media out front interviewing the people waiting in line and getting shots of the celebrities and socialites who managed to somehow score a booking.

Izaac's hand hovers on my lower back, leading me through the restaurant and toward our table where my parents are already seated, and they quickly stand, welcoming us in. I walk around to Mom and she pulls me in for a quick hug, dropping a kiss on my cheek. "How are you doing, sweetheart?"

"Perfect," I say, having graduated college a few weeks ago and now enjoying every minute of life with Izaac, despite how he forces me out the door every day to go to work. Don't get me wrong, I'm working for one of the best PR companies in the state, and every second of it has been incredible, but leaving our bed every day is the hardest thing I've ever done.

"Oh good," Mom says before I lean toward Dad and give him a quick hug. He presses a swift kiss to my forehead, and after greeting Izaac, we all sit down. I see Austin rushing around the restaurant, visiting tables, and making sure everything is running smoothly for opening night. He stops by to say hi, gives me a kiss on the cheek, and calls me a loser before side-eyeing Izaac. It's taken a while, and despite his ability to keep his mouth shut and be happy for me, the relationship between the boys has remained strained. But Austin is trying, and that's all I can ask for.

He scurries away, making sure to get his best waitress to stop by our table and give us the kind of service that's reserved for royalty. She takes our orders, and as we wait for our meals, I sip on a glass of wine with Izaac's hand resting on my thigh.

"How's work going?" my father asks Izaac, knowing how talking about his clubs always gets him excited. "Keeping busy?"

"Always keeping busy," Izaac says, his gaze flicking toward me. "But there have been some new developments."

My brows furrow, trying to figure out what the hell he's talking about. I don't think any of his clubs were going through any renovations at the moment, apart from the dark room at Vixen, which he decided to tear out completely to add more floor space for the VIPs, not that he's been giving me many details about it. He makes a point not to bring it up unless I specifically ask, which I don't.

Izaac keeps watching me as if trying to decipher my reaction, but all I can do is stare back in confusion. "What are you talking about?"

Izaac grins, and when he looks at me like this, it's like everyone else fades into the background. "I, uhh . . . might have bought another club."

My jaw drops, and I gape at him. "You did what?"

"Yeah, I closed on it last week."

"Holy shit," I breathe, throwing my arm around him and awkwardly hugging him from my seat at the table. "That's amazing."

"Oh, congratulations, honey," Mom coos before calling over the waitress and ordering another bottle of wine. "We have to celebrate!"

"Woah. Celebrate? Who the fuck is celebrating?" Austin demands, skidding to a stop behind us as he does another lap of the main floor. His eyes are wide in horror as he looks between me and Izaac, and after dropping his gaze to my right hand and seeing the diamond ring resting on my finger, his hand comes down on Izaac's shoulder, and he leans in so as to not cause a scene. "You proposed to my fucking sister without even talking to me about it first?"

Izaac's hands fly up in innocence. "Wrong fucking hand, bro."

"Oh, umm . . ." Austin clears his throat before straightening up and offering me an awkward smile. "My bad. What are we celebrating?"

"Izaac just purchased another club," Mom supplies.

"No shit," he says. "Where?"

Izaac launches into his rundown of the new club, giving us all his incredible plans as our meals are delivered. He gives us everything we need to know. Location, size, capacity, and even goes into his vision for the layout, though it's hard to imagine without getting to look at it, but he promises we can swing by tomorrow and he'll show me everything.

Austin congratulates him and quickly excuses himself when he hears a little commotion coming from the kitchen, and the second he's gone, Izaac turns back to me with a lazy, knowing grin. "I'm thinking of calling it Little Birdy."

I gape at him, my heart racing. "What?"

"Well, I can't have all of my clubs named after you and not this one."

My face scrunches with confusion. "What are you talking about? They're not named after me."

He stares back at me, his brow arching before giving me a smug grin. "Aren't they?"

I shake my head. Maybe all of this mind-blowing sex is damaging his brain cells. "How?"

"Cherry," he says. "You were nineteen when that club opened, and as much as I want to say it's because you were in your red lipstick phase, it's not." He gives me a hard stare, willing me to understand where he's coming from to keep from having to say it in front of my parents, and I suck in a gasp. This is about my virginity. But how could it be? Why would he name his club after that, especially back then? Unless he's always wanted me, always wanted to be the one to take my virginity.

Holy fucking shit.

I search his stare. "But that was long before—"

"Mm-hmm," he says as if reading where my mind is going. "Even then I think I loved you. I just didn't realize it until you forced me to."

Everything softens within me, and when he squeezes my thigh, I try to remember that my parents are sitting right across from me. "Pulse?" I ask.

He shrugs his shoulders, his gaze resting on mine. "You were twenty. And that was the first time I noticed just how fast mine was every time you'd walk into a room."

My cheeks flush, and I gape at him. Surely he's making this all up. "And Scandal?"

"Isn't it obvious? You and me together . . ."

"Would be the biggest scandal that's ever rocked our families," I finish for him.

Izaac nods, lifting his hand from my thigh to my cheek, and the second his fingers brush across my skin, I lean into his touch. He holds my stare, as if finishing our conversation in silent messages, willing me to understand why he would call his final club Vixen, and honestly, I think I can work that one out too. "You're insane," I tell him, unable to keep the smile off my face.

He shrugs again as if to say, *I'm only human. What did you expect?* And I lean in before pressing a kiss to his lips.

"Enough of that shit," Austin mutters, walking by us again and smacking Izaac up the back of his head. "Hands off my baby sister."

I can't help but laugh as I pull back, and not wanting to upset him on his big night, I focus on the delicious meal in front of me as everyone falls into conversation.

An hour later, I'm standing with Izaac in front of the restaurant, saying a quick goodbye to Austin and congratulating him on such a successful night. Every guest has walked away with a smile on their face, and I've never been so proud. I overheard an influencer going live and showing the world how incredible this new restaurant was. She was raving about the place, and I'm not going to lie, there might have been a tear or two in the very corner of my eye.

Austin disappears again, and as Izaac leads me back to his Escalade, I can't help but overhear Mom talking to Dad a little further down the road. "Shirly was telling me about this new club in the area called Vixen. She said it was easily the best night of her life. I think we should go some time."

My stomach drops and Izaac gapes at me. "They're gonna need a permanent ban," I tell him. "There is no way I'm walking into that club ever again if I'm at risk of seeing my parents getting it on."

"Come on," Izaac teases. "They're still young. It's healthy."

"They can be healthy all they want, but not at Vixen. I mean, shit, Izaac. What if they're not the boring missionary type. You don't know what they're into. What if you walk onto the main floor to see my father on his knees with a ball gag in his mouth?"

Izaac's face falls, and I laugh at how the color drains from his face. "Okay. Yeah. Good point. Consider them officially banned."

"Thank you," I say, reaching for the front of his shirt and pulling him in. "You know who isn't banned though?"

He arches his brow. "You wanna go?"

I bite down on my bottom lip, holding his hooded gaze as I slowly nod. I haven't stepped foot inside Vixen since that night and have been too nervous to even consider it, but I think I'm finally ready. "I do," I tell him. "But I don't want you taking me in one of your private rooms."

He watches me carefully. "I'm not sharing you."

"I don't want you to."

He leans on the car, pressing against me as he winds that big hand around the base of my throat and forces my chin up. "Then what do you want, Birdy?"

A grin stretches across my face as I trail my fingers down his chest, not stopping until I'm palming his erection through the front of his pants. "I want to put on a show, but only for you, and you won't be touching me until you're on your knees begging to taste me."

He groans. "Baby, don't do that to me. You know I can't resist touching you."

I shake my head. "If you want to play, then we play by my rules," I tell him, my lips grazing over his in the sweetest tease. "You've already taught me everything I need to know about my body and my limits, but now it's my turn to teach you a little something about yours."

Izaac swipes his thumb across my bottom lip. "Okay, Birdy. Have it your way. But just remember, you asked for this, and when it comes to fucking, your self-control is nowhere near as good as mine," he tells me. "You're gonna break long before I do, and when it comes down to it, you'll be the one on your knees begging."

"You really think you're that good?" I murmur, clutching the front of his shirt and refusing to let go.

"Care to make it interesting?"

My brow arches with the thrill of excitement pulsing through my body, already on the edge. "A bet?"

He nods. "What do you want, Birdy?"

I press my lips together, thinking it over and wondering just how far I can push my luck. "Hmmm okay," I finally say, more than ready to make it interesting. "If I win and you break first, we get a puppy."

"A puppy?" he asks. "Since when have you wanted a puppy?"

"Since now," I tell him, smug as ever while also knowing that he gets me anything I ask for simply because that's his favorite thing to do. "Besides, they're cute. It can be the start of our family, and you're gonna need something to cuddle when you inevitably lose."

Izaac laughs. "Okay. Have it your way. You win, we get a puppy."

"And not that it's going to happen, but if by sheer luck you don't break? Then what do you get?"

"If I win …" he says, his tone dropping low as he leans back into me, taking me by the back of my neck and holding my stare hostage. Electricity buzzes in the air around us, and I suck in a breath at the way he holds my stare, my hand gripping his shirt and refusing to let go. "If I win, Birdy, I make you my wife."

Well, shit.

A smile pulls at my lips, and I tilt my chin just a little bit higher, closing the gap between our lips and kissing him deeply. He quickly takes control, his tongue sweeping into my mouth and taking my breath away. When he finally pulls back, he holds my stare. "What's it going to be? Do we have a deal?"

I've never been one to cheat, never thrown a game, or given less than everything I've got, but for the first time in my life, I've never wanted to lose so badly.

A wicked grin cuts across my face, and I kiss him one more time. "Game on, Izaac Banks. Game on."

Thanks for reading

If you enjoyed reading this book as much as I enjoyed writing it, please consider leaving an Amazon review to let me know.

For more information on Haunted Love
find me on Facebook –

www.facebook.com/sheridansbookishbabes

Stalk me

Join me online with the rest of the stalkers!!
I swear, I don't bite. Not unless you say please!

Facebook Reader Group
www.facebook.com/SheridansBookishBabes

Facebook Page
www.facebook.com/sheridan.anne.author1

Instagram
www.instagram.com/Sheridan.Anne.Author

TikTok
www.tiktok.com/@Sheridan.Anne.Author

Subscribe to my Newsletter
https://landing.mailerlite.com/webforms/landing/a8q0y0

More by Sheridan Anne

www.amazon.com/Sheridan-Anne/e/B079TLXN6K

DARK CONTEMPORARY ROMANCE - M/F

Broken Hill High | Haven Falls | Broken Hill Boys

Aston Creek High | Rejects Paradise | Bradford Bastard

Pretty Monster (Standalone) | Haunted Love (Standalone)

DARK CONTEMPORARY ROMANCE - REVERSE HAREM

Boys of Winter | Depraved Sinners | Empire

NEW ADULT SPORTS ROMANCE

Kings of Denver | Denver Royalty | Rebels Advocate

CONTEMPORARY ROMANCE (standalones)

Play With Fire | Until Autumn (Happily Eva Alpha World)

The Naughty List

PARANORMAL ROMANCE

Slayer Academy [Pen name - Cassidy Summers]